PENGUIN BOOKS

RASHOMON GATE

I. J. Parker, winner of a Shamus Award for the short story "Akitada's First Case," is the author of *The Dragon Scroll*, *Rashomon Gate*, and *The Hell Screen* and lives in Virginia Beach, Virginia.

RASHOMON GATE

I. J. PARKER

PENGUIN BOOKS

PENGUIN BOOKS

Published by the Penguin Group

Penguin Group (USA) Inc., 375 Hudson Street, New York, New York 10014, U.S.A.
Penguin Group (Canada), 90 Eglinton Avenue East, Suite 700, Toronto, Ontario,
Canada M4P 2Y3 (a division of Pearson Penguin Canada Inc.)
Penguin Books Ltd, 80 Strand, London WC2R 0RL, England
Penguin Ireland, 25 St. Stephen's Green, Dublin 2, Ireland (a division of Penguin Books Ltd)
Penguin Group (Australia), 250 Camberwell Road, Camberwell, Victoria 3124, Australia
(a division of Pearson Australia Group Pty Ltd)
Penguin Books India Pvt Ltd, 11 Community Centre, Panchsheel Park,
New Delhi – 110 017, India
Penguin Group (NZ), 67 Apollo Drive, Rosedale, North Shore 0632, New Zealand
(a division of Pearson New Zealand Ltd)
Penguin Books (South Africa) (Pty) Ltd, 24 Sturdee Avenue, Rosebank,
Johannesburg 2196, South Africa

Penguin Books Ltd, Registered Offices: 80 Strand, London WC2R 0RL, England

First published in the United States of America by Minotaur,
an imprint of St. Martin's Press 2002

3 5 7 9 10 8 6 4

Copyright © by I. J. Parker, 2002
All rights reserved

THE LIBRARY OF CONGRESS HAS CATALOGUED THE HARDCOVER
EDITION AS FOLLOWS:
Parker, I. J. (Ingrid J.)
Rashomon gate : a mystery of ancient Japan / I. J. Parker.—1st ed.
p. cm.
ISBN 0-312-28798-4 (hc.)
ISBN 978-0-14-303560-2 (pbk.)
1. Japan—History—Heian period, 794-1185—Fiction.   2. Kyoto (Japan)—
Fiction.   3. Nobility—Fiction.   I. Title.
PS3616.A745 R37 2002
813'.6—dc21   2002017136

Printed in the United States of America

Except in the United States of America, this book is sold subject to the condition
that it shall not, by way of trade or otherwise, be lent, resold, hired out, or otherwise
circulated without the publisher's prior consent in any form of binding or cover other
than that in which it is published and without a similar condition including
this condition being imposed on the subsequent purchaser.

The scanning, uploading, and distribution of this book via the Internet or via any
other means without the permission of the publisher is illegal and punishable by law.
Please purchase only authorized electronic editions and do not participate in or encourage
electronic piracy of copyrighted materials. Your support of the author's rights is appreciated.

For Tony

ACKNOWLEDGMENTS

Several wonderful people have helped Akitada into the world. My most profound thanks go to my friends and fellow writers Jacqueline Falkenhan, John Rosenman, Richard Rowand, and Bob Stein, who have read and sometimes reread the draft, making suggestions and giving me moral support when I needed it. Their kindness and expertise were equally inspiring. I am also indebted to Yumiko Enyo for her help with matters pertaining to Japanese customs. Finally, I must thank two consummate professionals: my agent, Jean Naggar, and my editor, Hope Dellon.

LIST OF ILLUSTRATIONS

CHARACTERS

JAPANESE FAMILY NAMES PRECEDE GIVEN NAMES.

MAIN CHARACTERS

Sugawara Akitada	Clerk in the Ministry of Justice
Seimei	Family retainer of the Sugawaras and Akitada's secretary
Tora	A former highwayman, now Akitada's servant

CHARACTERS CONNECTED WITH THE CASES

Hirata	Professor of law
Tamako	His daughter
Oe	Professor of Chinese literature
Ono	Assistant to Oe
Takahashi	Professor of mathematics
Tanabe	Professor of Confucian studies
Nishioka	Assistant to Tanabe
Fujiwara	Professor of history
Sato	Professor of music
Sesshin	Buddhist monk; president of the university

Ishikawa	Graduate student
Lord Minamoto	Student
Nagai	Student
Okura	A former student

Others

Lord Sakanoue	Lord Minamoto's guardian
Kobe	Captain of the Metropolitan Police
Omaki	A musician in the Willow Quarter
Mrs. Hishiya	Her stepmother
Auntie	The manageress of the Willow wine house
Madame Sasaki	A talented performer
Kurata	A merchant and customer of the Willow
Hitomaro	An unemployed swordsman
Genba	A former wrestler
Lords Yanagida, Abe, Ono and Shinoda	Prince Yoakira's friends
Kinsue	Prince Yoakira's servant
Umakai	A beggar

PREFACE

Rashomon Gate is the story of Sugawara Akitada, a fictional minor official in the Japanese government during the eleventh century. At this time he is almost thirty years old and, to the regret of his mother, neither married nor successful in his career in the Ministry of Justice. On the other hand, he has a knack and manifest penchant for solving crimes, a trait which has gained him the friendship of men of high and low degree.

While the characters and events are imaginary, certain historical facts about the capital city of Heian Kyo (modern Kyoto), the university system, law enforcement, and the customs and tastes of the eleventh century have been carefully incorporated into this tale, which involves Akitada in the solution of a series of puzzles during the courtship of a reluctant bride.

The story of the disappearing corpse was suggested by two tales (numbers 15/20 and 27/9) in the late-eleventh-century collection *Konjaku Monogatari*.

The maps of Heian Kyo and of the university are based on historical sources, and the other illustrations are intended to resemble Japanese woodcuts. A historical endnote gives additional information about pertinent aspects of life at the time.

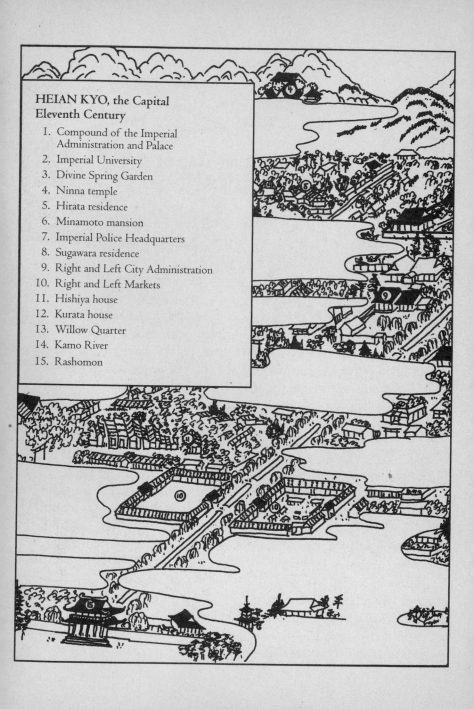

HEIAN KYO, the Capital
Eleventh Century

1. Compound of the Imperial
   Administration and Palace
2. Imperial University
3. Divine Spring Garden
4. Ninna temple
5. Hirata residence
6. Minamoto mansion
7. Imperial Police Headquarters
8. Sugawara residence
9. Right and Left City Administration
10. Right and Left Markets
11. Hishiya house
12. Kurata house
13. Willow Quarter
14. Kamo River
15. Rashomon

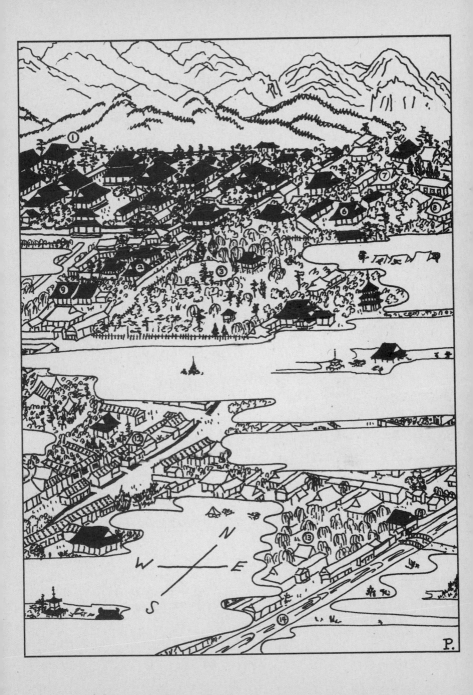

PROLOGUE

RASHOMON

The corpse was headless. It lay huddled in a dark corner where only the faint light of the moon filtering through the wooden shutters picked out the paleness of naked skin from the prevailing gloom.

A dark shadow moved in the gray light, and an ancient voice rasped, "Look around for the head!"

"What for?" growled another voice. A second shadow joined the first. "It's no use to anybody but the rats." The speaker cackled suddenly. "Or hungry ghosts. For playing kickball."

"Fool!" The first shadowy creature turned and, for a moment, the moonlight caught a wild mane of tangled white hair. It was a woman, crouching demonlike over the body, her claws quickly tucking some white, soft fabric inside her ragged robe, "I want the hair."

"Are you blind? That's a man!" protested her male companion. "There's not going to be enough hair on it to get a good grip." He leaned to peer at the body. "Besides, he's an old one."

"He's been well-fed." She tweaked the corpse's belly and slapped his buttocks. "Feel his skin! Soft as silk, eh?"

"So? Much good that's gonna do him. Poor beggar's dead."

"Beggar?" the woman shrieked with derision. "Touch his feet! You think that one walked? Not likely. Rode in coaches and palanquins, I bet. Now go find that head! He'll have long hair all twisted up neatly on top. That's worth ten coppers at least. The *good people* don't cut it off like you 'n' me. Their women have hair so long they can walk on it. I wish we'd get one o' them!"

The man snickered. "Me, too. I'd know what I'd do to her!" he said and smacked his lips suggestively.

The old woman gave him a kick.

"Ouch!" He cursed, then backhanded her viciously. In a moment they were fighting like a pair of hungry alley cats. He gave up first and retreated a few steps.

She rearranged her robe, making sure she still had her booty, then snapped, "We gotta get out o' here before the patrol comes. Go look for that head! It's gotta be somewheres. Maybe it rolled behind that bunch o' rags back there."

"Them's not rags!" muttered the old man, poking the bundle with his foot. "It's another one."

"What? Let's see!" She scurried over, peered and straightened up disappointedly. "Just an old crone. Nothing worth taking on *her*. Starved to death from the looks o' her, *and* cut her own hair off long ago. Where's that head?"

"I tell you, it's not here," whined the man, poking around in all the corners.

"Well," she said in a tone of outrage, "I don't know what the place is coming to. Now they're not even in one piece. You suppose the patrol will call the police?"

"Naw," said her companion. "Too much trouble for the lazy bastards. You done?"

"Guess so." She looked about. "Two tonight?"

"Yeah. You get anything?"

"A loincloth and socks," she muttered, secretly touching the fine silk of the dead man's undergown which nestled between her sagging breasts. "Bet some bastard made off with the head and the rest o' his clothes. Let's go!" She shuffled towards the doorway.

"Wonder who the old guy was," he said as he followed her down the stairs.

"What do you care?" she snapped. On the ground floor, she peered cautiously into the street from behind one of the huge pillars. "When that one was alive he'd not waste a thought on you 'n' me! Well, now he's dead and his socks'll pay for our supper and that loincloth'll buy some cheap wine. It all comes out even in the end."

ONE

THE WISTERIA ARBOR

*A*kitada straightened up and stretched his tall, lanky frame wearily. He had spent the best part of this beautiful spring day bent over dusty dossiers in his office in the Ministry of Justice. With a sigh he rinsed out his brush and reached for his seal.

Across the room, his secretary Seimei rose to his feet. "Shall I bring the case of the Ise shrine versus Lord Tomo next?" he asked eagerly.

Seimei was over sixty and deceptively frail-looking with his nearly white hair and a thin mustache and goatee. Akitada marvelled, not for the first time, that his old friend seemed to be positively thriving on this tedious work. Seimei was the only one left of the family retainers of the Sugawara family. He had risen in the household, by his own effort and Akitada's father's encouragement, to become steward and clerk. When his master had died, leaving behind a sadly diminished estate, a widow, two daughters and a minor son, Seimei had looked after all of them devotedly until Akitada had finished his education and gained his first government position. Recently, after Akitada's promotion to senior judicial clerk in the ministry, his young master had chosen him as his personal secretary.

"Must you?" Akitada sighed. "I have been cooped up with these documents for upward of too long and don't think I can bear another minute of it."

"The path of duty is near, but man seeks it in what is remote," Seimei remarked primly. He was much given to sententious sayings. "Even the ocean has grown a drop at a time. As Master Kung says, serving His Majesty must be your first duty." But seeing Akitada's drawn face, he relented. "A brief rest is what you need. I shall brew some tea."

They had acquired the taste for tea only recently and the herb was prohibitively expensive, but Akitada found it more refreshing than wine and Seimei swore by its medicinal properties.

When the older man returned with two cups and a steaming pot, Akitada was pacing the floor. Outside a bird was singing. "I wonder," Akitada said, listening wistfully, "if we could not find the time to ride out into the mountains." He accepted a cup of tea and drank thirstily. "I thought we might visit the Ninna temple."

"Ah! A strange story, that one," Seimei said with a nod. "It's been several weeks now, and people haven't stopped talking about it yet. I am told the emperor himself went to visit the place and inscribed a plaque with his august sentiments. It is said that Prince Yoakira was instantly transported into Buddhahood through the fervency of his prayers. Now people are streaming to the temple praying for miracles."

"And of course the temple has benefited from their contributions," Akitada remarked dryly.

Seimei gave his master a sharp look. "Of course," he said. "But there is also some talk about demons devouring his body. They say he had many warnings from the soothsayers lately."

"Miracles! Demons! Ridiculous. There should have been a thorough investigation."

"There was. The prince arrived with a small party of friends and retainers, and entered the shrine alone by its only door; he chanted for an hour while his companions sat outside, waiting and watching the door. When he finished his devotions but did not come out, his closest friends went in together. They found nothing but his robe. The monks were called, and later the police and the imperial guards. All of them searched the temple and its surroundings for days without finding a trace of the prince. Finally the monks petitioned that the emperor acknowledge a miracle, and so he did."

"Nevertheless I don't believe it!" Akitada pulled his earlobe, frowning. "There must be an explanation. I wonder if . . ."

Suddenly a shouting match erupted outside the ministry.

"That sounds like Tora!" Akitada was at the door to the veranda in a few strides, Seimei right behind him.

In the courtyard two men were facing each other threateningly. One was small, still in his twenties, with a weak face not markedly improved by a mustache, and dressed in the shimmering silk and the formal lacquered headgear of a court official. The other was not much older, tall and muscular, handsome, but dressed in a plain cotton shirt and trousers.

The courtier was advancing, his wooden baton raised to strike, when the other said in a dangerously low voice, "If you touch me with that toothpick, puppy, I'll shove it down your throat and stop that nasty mouth of yours for good!"

The official paused uncertainly. Flushed, he sputtered with rage, "You . . . you . . . would not dare!"

The tall man bared a handsome set of teeth and took a step toward him. The courtier retreated several feet and looked about for help. His eyes fell on Akitada and Seimei who had stepped up to the balustrade of the veranda.

"What is the matter, Tora?" Akitada asked the former highwayman who was now his houseman.

The tall young man turned. "Oh, there you are." He waved to them with a grin. "We sort of collided at the corner, me being in a hurry, and him not looking where he was going. I said I was sorry, but the pretty boy threw a temper tantrum, called me names, and wanted to hit me with his toy."

"Is that uncouth savage your servant?" the stranger demanded in a voice trembling with fury.

"Yes. Were you injured in the encounter?"

"It is a miracle I was not. I demand that you punish this person immediately and forbid him to enter the imperial enclosure in the future. He is clearly unable to recognize his betters."

"Did he not apologize?" Akitada asked.

"What does that signify? If you do not do as I ask, I shall have to call the guard from the gate."

"Perhaps we should discuss the matter further. By the way, my name is Sugawara Akitada. May I know yours?"

The little man drew himself up importantly and recited, "Okura Yoshifuro. Secretary in the Bureau of Ranks, Ministry of Ceremonial. Junior seventh rank, lower grade. I am on my way to speak to the minister and have no time to waste with minor officials."

Akitada raised his heavy brows. His normally pleasant, narrow, aristocratic face assumed a haughty expression. "In that case you may wish to discuss the matter with Counsellor Fujiwara Motosuke, a member of the council of state. He is by way of being a special friend to Tora and myself and will vouch for us."

The color receded from the other man's face. "Naturally I would not dream of troubling a man of the counsellor's standing," he said quickly. "Perhaps I have been rather hasty. The young man has apologized, as you rightly reminded me. It behooves people of rank to be understanding of the feelings of the common man. Did you say your name is Sugawara? A pleasure to make your acquaintance, sir. Hope to meet again." With a polite bow, he turned and rushed off so quickly that his lacquered headgear slipped over one ear.

Tora opened his mouth to shout with laughter, but Akitada cleared his throat warningly and waved him inside.

"Well, I guess you showed him who's in charge!" grinned Tora as soon as the door closed behind them.

"What possessed you to pick a fight with an official?" Seimei cried. "You will surely cause your master trouble!"

Tora bristled. "Maybe you think I should've let him hit me?" he demanded.

"Yes." Seimei wagged his finger at him. "You should indeed. How can you give yourself such airs? Remember that it is always the biggest dew drop that falls first from the leaf."

"What was so urgent?" Akitada interrupted.

"Oh." Tora pulled a folded paper from his shirt and handed it over. "There's this letter from Professor Hirata. A boy brought it to your house just when the carpenters got there to start work on the south veranda. They look like a proper bunch of louts, so I need to get back."

Akitada unfolded the letter. "Well, you can go back now," he said when he had read it. "Heaven forbid the louts should do violence to my mother's favorite veranda. But this time walk!"

When Tora had gone, he said to Seimei, "I am invited to dinner. I know I should have visited them before, but . . ." He let his voice trail off uncertainly. As usual, his conscience smote him.

"A very kind gentleman, the professor," Seimei nodded. "I well remember the time when you went to live with him. How is the young lady? She must be quite grown up."

"Yes." Akitada pondered. "Tamako must be about twenty-two by now. I have not seen her since my father died and I moved back into our home." Akitada's mother disapproved strongly of any ties with the Hiratas, but he could not honestly blame his reluctance to see Tamako on Lady Sugawara's snobbery. Too much time had passed, and he was afraid that they would not have anything to say to each other any longer. He said, "The professor writes that he needs my advice. He sounds worried. I hope nothing is wrong." Sighing, he said, "Well, Seimei, old friend, back to work!"

Two hours later Akitada carefully dried the ink on the last sheet of commentary on the legal intricacies of the case and remarked, "Apart from the exalted status of the litigants, this is a simple suit. May I take it that we have whittled down the backlog of cases under review?"

"Yes. There are only another twenty dossiers, all of them minor matters."

"In that case, Seimei, we are entitled to make an early evening of it. Let us go home!"

◆

The sun was already slanting across the green-glazed roofs of the
government buildings, when Akitada, on his way to the Hiratas,
walked along Nijo Avenue, past the red pillars of the gate leading
into the Imperial City. He squinted into the bright light, dodging
the steady stream of clerks and scribes flowing through the gate
on the way to their homes in the city.

From this gate, called *Suzakumon, Suzaku* Avenue stretched
south to *Rashomon*, the great two-storied southern gate of the
capital city. Along its entire length, Suzaku Avenue, more than two
hundred feet wide and bisected by a wide canal, was lined with
willow trees. A multitude of people, native and foreign, of high
and low degree, pedestrians, ox carts and horsemen moved along
this main thoroughfare all day long. Akitada thought it the most
beautiful street in the world.

To the west, ahead of him, the pale greens of many trees in their
spring foliage screened one of the residential quarters. From this
vantage point the area looked like a vast beautiful park, but Akitada knew better. The northwestern quadrant of the city had, like
its eastern counterpart, been planned for the palaces, mansions
and villas of the "good people," the great noble families, the high-
ranking court officials, and members of the imperial clan, while
the southern two thirds of the city were occupied by the common
people, and by the markets and amusement quarters. For no apparent reason, people had begun to abandon the western city and
crowded into the eastern half or moved to the countryside.

Their palaces and villas had burned down or fallen into decay.
Many of the humbler homes had been abandoned to squatters and
cutthroats. Only the trees and shrubs had thrived, and a last few respectable families, like the Hiratas, lived quiet, isolated lives there.

As Akitada passed down street after street, some of them bisected by canals and crossed by simple wooden bridges, he saw
that several more homes had become empty since he had last
walked this way. He wondered how safe Tamako was when her father was teaching at the university.

To his relief, the Hirata villa appeared unchanged. Its wall had been kept in good repair, and the same gigantic willows flanked its wooden gate. The scent of wisteria blew over the wall on a soft breeze. With a sense of homecoming Akitada raised his eyes to the elegantly brushed inscription over the gate: "Willow Hermitage."

A white-haired servant, bent with age, opened the gate and greeted him with a wide, toothless smile. "Master Akitada! Welcome! Come in! Come in!"

"Saburo! It is good to see you again. How is your health these days?"

"Well, there's a pain in my back and my knees are stiff. And my hearing's going, too." The old man touched each defective part in turn and then broke again into his big grin. "But it will have to get much worse than this before I'm ready to go. No man could ask for a better life than mine. And now here you are, come back a famous man!"

"Hardly famous, Saburo, but I thank you for the welcome. How is the professor?"

"Pretty well. He's waiting in his study for you, Master Akitada. But the young lady asked to speak to you first. She's in the garden."

As he made his way along the moss-covered stepping stones, Akitada basked in the warmth of the old servant's welcome. To be called "Master Akitada" again, just as if he were the son of the family, brought back the happy year he had spent here as a youngster.

When he rounded the corner of the house and saw a slender young woman among the flowering shrubs, he called out cheerfully, "Good evening to you, little sister!"

Tamako turned and looked at him wide-eyed. For a moment an expression of sadness passed over her pretty face, but then she smiled charmingly and ran towards him, hands outstretched in greeting.

"Dear friend! Welcome home! You make us very happy. And you look so distinguished and very handsome in that fine robe." She stopped before him, her hands in his, and smiled up at him.

Akitada was lost in surprise. She had become quite lovely, with that slender face and neck and an elegant figure.

"How is it that you are not married yet?" he blurted out.

She released his hands and looked away. "Perhaps the right person has not asked yet," she said lightly. "But then I hear you, too, are still single." Smiling up at him again, she added, "Shall we walk to the arbor? I have a particular favor to ask of you before you see Father. And then I must go see about dinner and change into a more proper gown."

He saw, as he walked with her, that she wore a plain blue cotton robe with a white-patterned cotton sash about her small waist. It seemed impossible to improve on the picture she made and he told her so.

She turned her head slightly and thanked him with a blush and a smile. "Here we are," she said, pointing to a wooden platform under a trellis covered with flowering wisteria. The purple blooms hung in thick clusters suspended from a leafy roof.

Akitada looked around him. Everywhere plants seemed to be in flower or bud. The air was heavy with their mingled fragrances and the humming of bees. When they sat down on two mats which had been spread on the platform, he was enveloped by the sweet scent of the wisteria blossoms and felt that he had walked into another, more perfect world, one which was far more intensely alive with colors, scents and the sounds of birds and bees than any existence on this earth had any right to be.

"Something is terribly wrong with Father," said Tamako, breaking into his fancy.

"What?"

She took his exclamation literally. "I do not know. He won't tell me. About two weeks ago he came back late from the university. He went directly to his study and spent a whole night pacing. The next morning he looked pale and drawn and he hardly ate anything. He left for work without any kind of explanation, and has done the same every day since then. Whenever I try to question him, he either maintains that nothing is wrong, or he snaps at me to mind my own business. You know this is not like him in the least." She looked at Akitada beseechingly.

"What do you want me to do?"

"I have been hoping that he invited you to dinner to confide in you. If he does, perhaps you can tell me what has happened. The uncertainty is very upsetting."

She looked pale and tense, but Akitada shook his head doubtfully. "If he has refused to tell you, he will hardly speak to me, and even if he did, he may ask that I keep his confidence."

"Oh," she cried, jumping up in frustration, "men are impossible! Well, if he does not speak, you must find out somehow, and if he swears you to secrecy, you must find a way! If you are my friend, that is!"

Alarmed, Akitada rose also. He took her hands in his and looked down at her lovely, intense face. "You must be patient, little sister!" he said earnestly. "Of course I shall do my best to help your father."

Their eyes met, and he felt as if he were drowning in her gaze. Then she looked away, blushing rosily, and withdrew her hands. "Yes, of course. Forgive me. I know I can trust you. But now I must see about our dinner, and Father expects you." She made him a formal bow and walked away quickly.

Akitada stood and watched her graceful figure disappear around a bend in the path. He felt perplexed and troubled by the encounter. Slowly he walked towards the house.

The professor received him warmly in his study, a separate pavilion which was lined with books and looked out on a stand of bamboo, an arrangement of picturesque rocks and patterned gravel outside a small veranda. This room, where Akitada had worked on lessons with the professor, was as familiar to Akitada as any room in his own home. But the kindly man who had been a second father to him had changed shockingly. He looked prematurely old.

"My dear boy," Hirata began as soon as they had exchanged greetings and seated themselves, "forgive me for summoning you so abruptly when you must be very busy with official duties."

"I was very glad you invited me. This has always been a happy place for me and I have missed Tamako. She looks all grown-up and quite lovely."

"Ah, yes. I see she has already spoken to you." Hirata sighed, and Akitada thought again how tired he looked. The professor had always been tall and gaunt, with prominent facial bones made more severe by a long nose and goatee, but today there seemed more gray than black in his hair and beard, and deep lines ran from his nose to the corners of his thin lips. He said, "I am afraid I have been very unkind to the poor child, but I could not bring myself to burden her with the matter. Well, it seems it is beyond me to solve it, so I have presumed on our friendship to ask your advice."

"You honor me with your confidence, sir."

"Here is what happened. You may remember that one evening every month we gather for devotions in the Temple of Confucius? All the faculty wear formal dress on the occasion. Since we spend the day lecturing and teaching, we leave our formal gowns and headdresses on pegs in the anteroom of the hall in the morning and change into them just before the ceremony. Do you know the room I mean?"

Akitada nodded.

"I was in a hurry that evening, having been kept by a student, and simply tossed on my gown and hat and found my place in the hall. About halfway through the service I became aware of a rustling in my sleeve. I found a note tucked into the lining. Because it was too dark to read it there, I took it home with me."

Hirata got up and walked to one of the shelves. From a lacquer box he extracted a slip of paper and brought it to Akitada, his hand shaking a little.

Akitada unfolded the crumpled paper. The note was brief, on ordinary paper, and the handwriting was good but unremarkable. It read: "While men like you enjoy life, others do not have enough to fill their bellies. If you wish to keep your culpability a secret, pay your debts! I suggest an initial sum of 1000 cash."

Akitada looked up and said, "I gather one of your colleagues is being blackmailed."

"Thank you for that, my boy." Hirata smiled a little tremulously. "Yes. It is the only conclusion I could arrive at. I am afraid someone on the faculty has committed a serious . . . wrong, and another is extorting money in exchange for his silence. Apart from the shocking fact that two of my colleagues appear to be signally lacking in the very morals they are expected to inculcate into our students, it would be a disaster if the matter became public. The university is already in danger."

"You surprise me."

Hirata shifted uncomfortably. "Yes. We have been losing students to the private colleges, and our funds have been cut severely. A scandal could mean the closing of the university." He looked down at his clenched hands and sighed deeply. "I have spent every minute since the incident trying to think what to do. Now I have to pin my hopes on you. You are clever at solving puzzles. If you could identify the blackmailer and his victim, I might be able to deal with them in such a way that the university's reputation won't suffer."

"You may overestimate my poor abilities." Akitada spread the note out on the floor between them. "You did not recognize the handwriting?"

Hirata shook his head.

"No. I suppose not. It is not particularly distinguished. Yet the note is hardly an illiterate effort. 'Culpability' is a rather learned word. Could a student have written it?"

"I cannot say. Students never go into the anteroom. And it is true that the writing looks ordinary, but some of my colleagues are hardly great calligraphers. Besides, handwriting can be disguised."

"Yes. Hmm. One thousand cash is an impressive sum to the average person, and this is to be only the first payment. Whatever malfeasance is involved must be serious to be worth that price to the guilty man. What could be so damaging to one of your colleagues, and who could pay that much?"

The professor made a face. "I cannot imagine. It is certainly more than I can raise easily."

"What have you done so far?"

"Very little. I could hardly ask any of them if they have laid themselves open to blackmail." He passed a hand over his lined face. "It is terrible. I found myself looking at all of them with suspicious eyes and dreading every workday. Then, just when I was becoming completely distracted, I thought of you. I have known these men too long to see them with unbiased eyes. You, as an outsider, may have a clearer vision."

"But I can hardly start hanging about the university asking aimless questions."

"No, no! But there is a way. Of course you may not be able to take off the time, but we have an opening for an assistant professor of law. The incumbent, poor fellow, died three months ago, and the position has not been filled. The best part is that you would be my associate and we could meet on a regular basis without arousing suspicion. Could you take a short leave of absence and become a visiting lecturer? You would be paid, of course."

The image of his office at the ministry with its stack of bone-dry dossiers, and of the sour face of his superior, Minister Soga, flashed before Akitada's inward eye. Here was escape from the hateful archives, and an escape which promised the added incentive of a tantalizing puzzle. "Yes," he said, "provided the minister approves it."

Hirata's tired face lit up. "I think I can almost guarantee it. Oh, my dear boy, I cannot tell you how relieved I am. I was at my wits' end. If we can stop the blackmail, the university may limp along for another few generations."

Akitada gave his old friend and mentor a searching look. "You know," he said hesitantly, "that I cannot agree to suppress evidence of a crime."

Hirata looked startled. "Oh, surely . . . yes, I see what you mean. No, of course not. You are quite right. That is awkward. Still, it is better to take action to stop it. You must do as you see fit. I certainly don't know what is going on."

A brief silence fell. Akitada wondered if the professor had perhaps agreed too quickly. And had there not been the slightest emphasis on the word "know"? Finally Akitada said with a slight chuckle, "Well, I shall certainly do my best, but I am afraid that I shall be a very poor teacher. You must send me only your dullest students or our scheme will quickly come to ruin."

Hirata cheered up. "Not at all, dear boy!" he cried heartily. "You were my best student and have since acquired more practical knowledge of official duties than I have ever possessed."

There was a soft scratching at the sliding door to the corridor.

"Father?" Tamako's soft voice was a welcome interruption. "Your dinner is ready. Will you come to the main hall?"

"Of course. Right away. We are quite finished reminiscing," Hirata called. They heard her footsteps receding.

"May I inform your daughter of this matter, sir, or will you?" Akitada inquired.

Hirata paused in the process of rising and straightening his robe. "Why? I would rather not involve her," he said doubtfully.

"She is so concerned about you that the truth will be a great relief to her," Akitada persisted.

They walked out into the corridor together. "You have always been very fond of my child, haven't you?" Hirata asked inconsequentially.

"Yes. Of course."

"Very well. We shall tell her together over dinner."

TWO

THE IMPERIAL UNIVERSITY

A week later Akitada entered, as one of its teachers, the grounds of the august university in which he had received his own education.

The imperial university, or *daigaku*, covered four city blocks just south of the greater imperial palace, or *daidairi*. Its main gate was on Mibu Road and directly across from the *Shinsenen*, the Divine Spring Garden, a large park where the emperor and his nobles often held summer parties.

On this sunny morning of the Blossoming Month, Akitada stood just inside this gate, looking at the familiar walls and gates, the tiled roofs of lecture halls, libraries and dormitories lying peacefully under a placid sky and swaying pine trees, and was seized by a familiar panic. Like an adult son who will never quite lose a feeling of inadequacy around a parent, Akitada was once again in the grip of that atmosphere of stem authority and intellectual superiority which had awed him as a youngster.

He forced down the lump of adolescent panic and took in subtle signs of neglect. Weeds were growing against walls which needed patching where pieces of whitewashed mud had fallen off, revealing the timbers, rubble, and woven branches which sup-

The IMPERIAL UNIVERSITY

1. Main Gate—leading to Divine Spring Garden

2. Temple of Confucius and Confucian studies

3. Department of Buddhist studies

4. Fine Arts faculty

5. Suzaku Avenue Gate

6. Student dormitories and kitchens

7. Department of Chinese classics

8. Department of mathematics

9. Law faculty

10. Shrine and store houses

11. University administration

12. Staff kitchens

ported them; the dirt road was pitted and marred by puddles; and from the curved roofs of the halls and gates large sections of tile were missing.

A group of chattering students, nine or ten young men, all in their late teens and wearing the mandatory dark cotton robes, passed him, falling abruptly silent as they approached. Giving him nervous looks, they turned into the courtyard of the administration hall and took off running.

Not everything had changed, Akitada thought with a smile. The students were still up to their usual pranks.

He could not blame them. It promised to be a beautiful day, much better spent on a lark than in a musty classroom. The sky was pale blue silk and the dark green pines and pale-leafed willows rose against it like delicate embroidery. In the courtyard nearest him, a cuckoo suddenly burst into its characteristic *ho-to-to.*

Akitada had come early, because he wanted some time to look around and perhaps meet some of his new colleagues. Walking through the small gate into the courtyard of the Temple of Confucius, Akitada decided it was appropriate for him to pay his respects to the patron saint of education. Besides, it was here that Professor Hirata had discovered the blackmail note.

Coming into the temple hall from the sunlight, Akitada was surprised by its gloom, but his eyes soon adjusted and he could make out the life-sized wooden statues. The great master Confucius occupied the center of a dais, with his fellow sages lined up on either side. Akitada bowed deeply before "Master Kung," as Seimei called him, and asked for inspiration in his new duties.

His teaching assignment, though a mere cover for snooping, was taking on daunting proportions. Akitada did not think that he could fool bright youngsters with a less than professional effort. He had considered backing out, but in the balance the dusty archives at the ministry held more terror than the probing questions of students.

Somewhere a door closed. He looked around but saw no one. The statue of the sage looked at him through heavy-lidded eyes, his hand stroking a long beard. One needed age to become wise.

Who was he to pass himself off as a teacher? Such fraud was no part of the Confucian philosophy.

He reminded himself of the ministerial archives. To his surprise there had not been the slightest problem getting a temporary leave from his duties at the ministry. His Excellency, the Minister of Justice, had stared at him coldly and informed him that his presence was needed more urgently at the university than in his present sphere. Soga had somehow managed to convey that they could manage without Akitada on a permanent basis.

Sighing deeply, Akitada bowed to the master again, apologetically, and then walked through the hall to the small anteroom under the eaves. Here were the pegs where the professors had hung their formal robes for the rites. A door connected the room to the temple hall, and another door opposite led to the outside. Akitada opened the latter and looked out into the main courtyard. Shrubbery surrounding a stand of pines hid this entrance from general view. Anyone could have entered or left without being seen.

He turned and was staring at the row of pegs on the wall, when a slight cough startled him.

The door to the temple hall had opened a crack, and through it a long-faced man was watching him from under bushy eyebrows.

"Ah! A visitor!" he cried, stepping fully into the anteroom. "May I offer my humble services in showing the honorable gentleman around?" Middle-aged and gawky, he bowed rather more deeply than Akitada's sober gown and casual headdress required. He wore a wrinkled and disordered robe of poorly dyed cotton, and thick hair escaped in all directions from his topknot. Akitada took him for a servant.

"Nishioka is the name," the odd man said genially. "Master of Confucian classics. You see, you are in good hands. May I ask the gentleman's honored name?" He peered inquisitively at Akitada. His broad nose twitched with curiosity.

Perhaps the man's appearance was due to a scholarly disregard for aesthetics, but given his shaggy brows and lantern jaw, he was certainly one of the least impressive intellectuals Akitada had ever met. Still, he returned the bow, saying, "I am Sugawara and a colleague of yours for the next few weeks, though I am to teach law. Are you assistant to Professor Tanabe?"

The other smiled broadly. "Delighted! Absolutely delighted! Yes, indeed! I have that honor and pleasure. A great scholar and a constant inspiration to me! He is perhaps a friend of yours?"

"A former teacher rather. A tough one."

"Ah! I see! Well, yes. Some of the students seem to feel that he is demanding. So you are to teach law. Do you know Hirata?"

"Yes. He *is* a friend, in addition to being a former teacher."

"No doubt he appointed you for that reason?"

Akitada stiffened. "I beg your pardon?" The question sounded impertinent, suggested favoritism.

Nishioka's face lengthened comically. "I see that I have offended. Perhaps I did not phrase my question properly. I merely meant that you must have been an outstanding student."

"I see. Thank you. As you see, I am becoming reacquainted with the places where I spent my youth. Do you get many visitors here?"

"Oh, no. That is why I came to ask your business. I try to keep myself informed about the comings and goings. I wish I had more time to chat, but Professor Tanabe is preparing his lecture, and I must help him. If I may, I shall pay you a visit in the law school soon. You will want to know all about the teaching staff and the students." He bowed deeply and disappeared as suddenly as he had come.

Akitada left also, reflecting that Nishioka seemed to keep himself well informed and would be a useful source of gossip.

Unable to shake his reluctance to begin his duties, he peered into courtyards as he passed, remembering his student days. The small Buddhist temple looked abandoned, but from the courtyard next to it came the sound of lute music. This was the domain of the arts faculty, comprised of the teachers of music, painting and calligraphy. Akitada had spent happy hours here as a student. Though he lacked musical skills himself, he loved all sorts of instrumental music, especially flutes. Besides, he had found the resident musicians and painters a cheerfully informal lot who were always happy to include lonely students in their celebrations.

Someone, a virtuoso, was plucking the lute strings in the

building on the left. Akitada's heart started beating faster and he followed the sound. But when he turned a corner, the music stopped. He caught a glimpse of a small, plain corner room where two people, a man in his late thirties and a very pretty, heavily made-up young woman, sat side by side, completely engrossed in each other. Both held lutes, but the man put his down to embrace the girl, who giggled.

After a moment's hesitation, Akitada went to the veranda steps and climbed up. He walked noisily and cleared his throat. Inside he heard the man curse softly and call out, "Who is it?"

Akitada stepped up to the open door, bowing slightly. The girl was now sitting demurely a few feet away from the man.

"Who the devil are you?" growled the musician. Like Nishioka, he was far from handsome, having a low, sloping brow and big fleshy lips, but his eyes were large and rather beautiful.

Akitada was embarrassed. "I beg your pardon for the intrusion. My name is Sugawara and I am to fill in for Professor Hirata's assistant. The lute music was so beautiful that I could not resist finding the player and expressing my admiration."

The man grimaced. "Well, you've found him," he said ungraciously, then turned to the woman and said, "Run along now and practice!"

The young woman scrambled up, took her lute, bowed, and tripped out. She was both heavier and clumsier than Akitada had expected. Her rough cotton gown placed her among the lower classes, but she had tied a very handsome sash of red-and gold-figured brocade around her waist.

"I'm Sato," the musician now said, "and, as you saw, I earn a bit on the side by giving lessons to that stupid girl. It's against the rules, of course, so you had better not mention it. Have a seat." He gestured to the mat and reached for the wine jug and two dirty cups, which were standing next to him. "The wine is very good and fresh. She brought it. Gets it from the place where she entertains." He poured and offered Akitada a cup.

Akitada saw the greasy smudges of lip rouge on its rim and

said, "Oh, thank you, but it is too early in the day for me. Besides I shall need all my wits about me if I am to lecture."

"Nonsense!" growled the other. "Wine improves the performance, but suit yourself." He emptied Akitada's cup. "I am quite drunk already and start my flute class shortly. Towards evening I sober up enough to visit my favorite wine shop where my friends and I make real music. You can come if you like. It's the Willow, next to the river by the Sixth Street bridge."

The Kamo River near the Sixth Street bridge was lined with the restaurants, brothels and houses of assignation of the capital's pleasure quarter. Akitada said politely, "Thank you. I look forward to hearing you play the flute some day, but now I must go to my own class." He rose and bowed. The other waved while emptying another cup of wine.

When Akitada emerged into the street again, he caught a furtive movement across the way. Someone had been standing under the gate which led to the student dormitories. He had ducked away as soon as Akitada had come out. For a moment Akitada was tempted to investigate, but he reminded himself that youngsters delighted in playing tricks on their elders. He turned down a side street which led to the "three faculties," a series of courtyards housing the schools of Chinese classics, mathematics, and law respectively.

Here he encountered the first sign of academic activity. A senior student, to judge by his age and his dark uniform, came from a side gate leading to the Chinese classics department. He was looking through a thick stack of papers he carried and gave Akitada a brief incurious glance as he passed. Akitada thought him extraordinarily handsome except for a frown of discontent.

Suddenly nervous about being late, Akitada called after him, "Good morning! Can you tell me, have classes already started?"

The young man paused, looked at Akitada over his shoulder, snapped, "No," and continued on his way.

Such rudeness from a student was so unexpected that Akitada stared after him. What could possibly have happened to cause that young man to behave in such a manner? Since there was no one else around, he decided that it must still be quite early. Perhaps he should investigate further.

The school of Chinese classics was the most prestigious in the university. Its professors held the highest rank, and its graduates were the most likely to win first place honors and advance rapidly in the government.

The large main hall, customarily used for lectures, was connected to smaller flanking halls by covered galleries. There was no one about in the gravelled courtyard or in the galleries. After a moment's indecision, Akitada climbed the steps to the central hall and entered. The vast dim space lay silent, and the classrooms were empty. Once he thought he heard a step in the main hall, but when he went back he found nobody. He began to wonder where all the people were. In his day, the place would have been bustling even at this early hour.

Then the handsome student suddenly walked into the hall. He stared at Akitada, muttered, "Forgot something," and headed for one of the classrooms.

"Just a moment, young man," Akitada snapped.

The student turned around. "Yes?"

"What is going on here? Where are the professors?"

"Oh, if you want the great man, he's in the library, along with his personal sycophant," the young man said curtly and jerked his head towards the western wing, before walking away.

Shaking his head, Akitada walked along the covered gallery. He was by now intensely curious about this student's teachers. In the library, he found two men seated side by side, bent over a yellowing scroll. The older man, tall and with a fine head of white hair, wore a splendid brocade robe. At the sound of the door he looked up angrily.

"Yes, what do you want?" he barked when he saw Akitada. His face was smooth-shaven and still handsome, but his flashing black eyes fixed Akitada disdainfully. "I am very busy and cannot be troubled with trivial matters."

Feeling himself flush, Akitada apologized and introduced

himself. The elegant gentleman thawed a little, gave his name as Oe, and introduced his companion as his assistant Ono.

Ono was in his early thirties, small, slender and weak-chinned, a defect which he had sought to disguise by wearing a mustache and a small chin beard.

"Get some tea, Ono!" Oe commanded, and the younger man jumped up, bowed deeply and scurried out. "Can't abide the fellow," Oe said, without lowering his voice. "No sense of dignity at all and he looks like a squirrel. Acts like one, too. But he's useful. Wouldn't have anyone who wasn't. Sugawara, did you say? Good family that, but sadly come down in the world. Sit down! You were a student here before my time?"

Akitada nodded.

"Hmm, law is not a field that appeals to many, but Hirata's a sound man, I hear. Mind you, he's nearly incompetent when it comes to self-advancement. Many a time I have offered to introduce him to the right people, and he turned me down. I have friends in the highest ranks, you know, the very highest . . ."

At this moment Ono entered with a tray holding a teapot and bowls, and his superior interrupted himself to reprimand him for his slowness, his clumsiness, and his choice of tea bowls. "You would think you would know by now that I drink only from the imported porcelain cups," he snapped.

"How stupid of me," Ono said immediately, bowing deeply several times. "Shall I go get them now?"

"No, no! We will make do this time. Did you steep the tea properly?"

"I think so." Ono turned to Akitada. "The professor has extremely refined tastes, unlike anyone else in this university. I often tell him that he is wasted on the yokels from the provinces who attend his classes."

Far from being flattered by this speech, Oe snapped, "Don't be an idiot, man! I have plenty of students from the best families. There is Prince Yoakira's grandson, Lord Minamoto, and a nephew of the prime minister, both of them with imperial blood in their veins. How dare you say I teach yokels?"

Akitada, trying to divert Oe's wrath from the hapless Ono, said quickly, "Just now I met a very superior looking young man in the main hall. An older student. Very tall and handsome."

"Older?" Oe frowned at Ono.

"It must have been Ishikawa, sir. He came early to pick up the essays."

"Ishikawa? He's a nobody. Graduate student. Clever, but comes from a poor family and stays here on scholarship. Mind you, he makes himself useful by reading papers for me. I am pressed for time, you know. The Kamo festival is coming up, and I am arranging a poetry match between the university faculty and the nobles. We were just reviewing the account of such a contest on the occasion of Emperor Mou Tsung's river party. Very appropriate, as we are to meet in the lake pavilion of the Spring Garden. No doubt you will be invited. Do you compose?"

"I am afraid my poor talents are solely in the area of prose," Akitada said awkwardly. "A memorial on encouraging farming by easing the rice tax, and a report on Buddhist practices in the provinces."

"Hmm. I can't abide the Buddhists. The Chinese knew how to deal with them. Kicked all the monks out of the temples and melted down the gold buddhas for the imperial treasury. Recite some lines from the thing on farmers!"

Akitada confessed that he could not remember enough to oblige.

"That should tell you something. If it were good, you'd remember. I myself composed a memorial several years ago. It went like this."

Oe recited in a deep, resonant voice. Akitada began to understand the man's reputation. The syllables and lines rolled from his tongue like music.

Ono sat enthralled. When Oe finally stopped, his assistant reached into his sleeve for a tissue to dry his moist eyes. "Beautiful!" he sighed. "Nothing better has ever been written. Not even Po Chu has your way with assonance and the balanced line."

"You can take the tea things back," said Oe sourly. "I must return to my work, Sugawara, but I expect to see you around."

Akitada removed himself from the presence of the great Oe. He took a shortcut to the school of law by walking through the courtyard of the mathematics department. A stranger blocked his way.

"Who are you?" he demanded in an irate tone.

Akitada explained and discovered that the irascible person was the incumbent in mathematics. Professor Takahashi was a lean man, in his fifties, with thinning hair and the wrinkled face and neck of an ill-tempered turtle. He peered at Akitada for several moments before acknowledging his status as a colleague.

"I cannot imagine what possesses them to use temporary people," he said nastily. "Our reputation is bad enough as it is. However, I dare say this is better than letting Hirata struggle on alone. He is getting past it. Have you met any of the others?"

Akitada mentioned his morning's encounters.

"Nishioka is an intellectual zero. He has his nose in everybody's business instead of doing his duties, and Sato is a drunk with the libido of a badger," Takahashi informed him. "Oe, of course, is our great man! Fortune smiles on him. Those empty-headed court nobles are impressed by all that passion and thunder. And fame fills the pockets nicely. The man has even acquired a summer villa on Lake Biwa. Next he will, no doubt, be appointed to the Council of State."

For a moment Akitada was bereft of words. Takahashi seemed to have few qualms about blackening his colleagues' reputations. What a change from the kindly man who had held this position before! Akitada said, "I see there have been many changes here since my time. Apparently few of my former professors are still teaching. Besides Professor Hirata there seems to be only Professor Tanabe left, and he was busy preparing his lecture when I arrived."

"More likely taking a nap," snorted Takahashi. "He's senile, I'm afraid. But see for yourself."

"How are the students?"

"Blockheads, most of them. What can you expect? Their parents are either doting courtiers who have nothing but pleasure on their minds and don't want the young monsters troubled with work, or they are officials in the provinces where schools are conducted by illiterates."

"Surely you exaggerate," Akitada protested. "Professor Oe spoke very highly of some of his aristocratic pupils, and I understand he uses one of the graduate students to read his papers."

"Oh? I did not know that such a thing is permissible. Since the definition of professional ethics has apparently been modified, perhaps we can all turn over our responsibilities to students and enjoy ourselves in our summer homes. Which graduate student is it?"

"I am afraid I cannot tell you." Akitada had had enough of Takahashi's slanderous comments on everything and everyone, but he could not afford to alienate him. Therefore he said politely, "It has been an honor to meet you, sir, but I am expected in my own department. I think classes are about to start."

"More's the pity! Another day of one's life wasted! But don't let me stifle your enthusiasm. A temporary assignment is, after all, not a life sentence!"

Akitada fled. Outside he gulped fresh air and let the morning breeze cool his temper. When he crossed the street to enter the courtyard of the law school, he thought he saw Nishioka walking away, but the fuzzy topknot could have been anyone's.

Hirata was in an empty classroom arranging seating mats and checking the supply of ink stones, brushes and water containers at every student's place. When he saw Akitada, his face lit up and he asked him about his morning.

Akitada sighed. "I have met several of your colleagues. The experience has been depressing."

Hirata laughed. "Let me guess! Takahashi was one of them?"

"Yes. And an inquisitive fellow called Nishioka, a tipsy lute player with his arms around a prostitute, and a self-proclaimed poet laureate who heaps abuse on his admiring assistant. Oh, and there was also a very rude student who apparently despises them both."

Hirata chuckled. "Ah, yes. You have been busy! The student must have been Ishikawa. He is expected to take first place in the next examinations and is a bit too sure of himself. I fear his arrogance will stand in his way in the future." Hirata's smile faded. "In this world, talent and ability will not suffice if a young man from a poor background does not also have humility and grace."

"What has happened to this place? Nothing seems the same. There are signs of neglect everywhere. The students are arrogant, and the professors malign each other. Surely things were not this way in my day?"

Hirata paused in his arrangements and looked at him. "I'm afraid the times do not favor us." Then he smiled again. "But come! It isn't so bad. You will like your students, and may come to appreciate some of your colleagues, too."

"Professor Oe claims that the grandson of the late, sainted Prince Yoakira is a student here."

"Oh, yes. Poor boy. He attends your class."

For a moment, Akitada was intrigued but, being pressed for time, he returned to his primary purpose. "I looked at the anteroom of the Temple of Confucius. It seems readily accessible from outside. Do you remember who attended the rites with you?"

Hirata was hanging a large diagram of government organizations on a standing screen. "Oe and Ono were there. They never miss. Takahashi must have been there, but I don't recall seeing him. Nishioka and Tanabe, of course. Fujiwara and Sato I'm not certain about. Fujiwara can be unreliable about such duties, though he is an absolute genius. He drinks, I'm afraid, and Sato is his boon companion. Actually, I think you will like them both when you know them a little better. We also invite our top students, though they don't always accept. Much too tedious for them, I'm afraid. But Ishikawa was there that night, I believe."

"I was surprised to find Sato entertaining women in his rooms. He claimed he was giving a lesson, but it looked like they were practicing something other than the lute."

Hirata raised his brows. "My dear boy," he chided, "you sound like a prude. We have known about Sato's private lessons for some time. They are, of course, theoretically against the rules, but performers and entertainers from the pleasure quarter are eager to learn Sato's technique and the special arrangements he is famous for, and he needs the money. His salary seems to run through his fingers like water and he is always in debt. You must make allowance for the artistic temperament."

"His behavior certainly makes him a target for our blackmailer."

Hirata stopped smiling. "He could never pay such a sum. At least, I would not think so. I hope it isn't Sato. He is a genius and has a large family to support."

"That makes it worse. Anyway, so far he is the only one of your colleagues who is clearly involved in an illegality or immorality. There is another point which has occurred to me. What did your robe look like? Was there another one very similar to yours?"

"Of course! I should have thought of that. It was green silk, with a small white pattern of cherry blossoms. But I don't believe anyone else could have had the same design."

"In the dark a very small pattern might not have shown up. Did anyone else wear green?"

"Tanabe, Fujiwara and Takahashi."

Akitada looked startled. "So many?"

"We are all the same rank. Green is our rank color."

"But not Oe's?"

"Oh no! The head of the Chinese literature department outranks us all by one degree. Oe always wears blue."

"I see. And the others all hold lesser ranks?"

"Yes. Well, it is shameful to admit it, but of my three colleagues in green, I should prefer it to be Takahashi. It would serve him right."

They were interrupted by the clatter of many steps on the wooden stairs and boards of the veranda. Young voices were shouting and laughing.

"Here come your pupils," remarked Hirata with a smile.

"Mine?" Akitada felt a sudden panic. "I thought you were preparing for your own class."

"Oh, no. But don't worry! They are only raw youngsters who need to learn the workings of our government, department by department, before they can study the laws which govern each and by which each governs. You used to know this so well you could have recited it in your sleep."

The door burst open and groups of fresh-faced boys, ranging in age from twelve to eighteen, bowed their way in, found their seats, and knelt, ramrod straight in their neat dark cotton robes. To Akitada's surprise, the last person to enter was easily in his fifties. He too wore a student's robe, bowed, and found his seat. Akitada looked at Hirata.

"That is Mr. Ushimatsu," Hirata whispered. "He has taken a long time to get admitted and will take even longer to pass the first of our examinations, but he tries so very hard that I have become quite fond of him." Taking Akitada by the arm, Hirata stepped forward and bowed to the class. Akitada quickly followed suit, and the students solemnly bowed back.

"This is your new instructor, Master Sugawara," Hirata announced. "He comes to us from the Ministry of Justice and has recently served as *kageyushi*. You may ask him anything." Having made this generous promise, Hirata bowed to Akitada and the class and left the room.

Silence fell. Akitada sat down behind his desk and looked at his students, who stared back at him without blinking. They seemed ordinary enough youngsters—all but Mr. Ushimatsu, who was regarding him with open-mouthed expectancy. One boy, younger and frailer than the rest, sat apart a little. He was a handsome lad but had dark rings under his eyes and delicate features. He alone was completely detached, as if he cared nothing about the class or the new teacher. Akitada gave him an encouraging smile which was not returned. The boy merely looked away.

"Excuse me, sir!" It was Mr. Ushimatsu who had spoken up. "What's a kageyushi do, sir?" he asked.

One of the other boys snorted. "Stupid! A kageyushi's an investigator of outgoing officials."

Far from being offended, Mr. Ushimatsu bowed to the boy and said humbly, "Thank you. It is kind of you to instruct me."

Embarrassed Akitada told the class, "I was sent to Kazusa

province when the provincial governor was being recalled. Our government makes certain that every official's records are in order before a new appointee takes over. Perhaps some day you, too, will be called on to check records or govern a province. That is why you must study hard now to be prepared."

Another boy asked, "Was it very hard work, sir?"

Akitada hesitated. "Not so very hard. I had help from some good people, but . . ." All eyes hung on his lips. "Well, there were some evil people there who, out of greed, plotted and committed murder, which made the assignment unusually diffi—" He broke off.

The frail boy had jumped up. He looked perfectly white and his fists were clenched. "May I please be excused, sir?" he gasped, then dashed out the door without waiting for an answer, slamming it behind him.

Akitada looked after him in surprise. "What is that boy's name?" he asked.

"That's Lord Minamoto," volunteered one of the boys immediately.

His neighbor added with bitter satisfaction, "He thinks he's better than the rest of us and can do what he wants."

THREE

RABBIT

*E*arly the following morning, Akitada met with Seimei and Tora. His mother was still blissfully unaware of his new occupation, and Akitada hoped to escape before she could send for him.

They were in Akitada's room, which looked out on the sadly overgrown garden. In the distance Lady Sugawara's veranda struck a jarring note with its pale new wood next to the dark, weathered walls of the ancient Sugawara mansion.

"My mother has grown quite fond of you, I think," Akitada told Tora. "Offering to repair her veranda was a master stroke."

Tora smirked. There had at first been a certain stiffness between the old lady and the former robber. "I am to see to the garden next," he stated proudly.

"Well," Akitada said, "that's why I wanted to talk to you. The garden will have to wait. I have an assignment for you. I am working on a case at the university and shall need you both." He explained about the misdirected blackmail note.

Tora clapped his hands. "Great!" he cried. "I like investigating. Just turn me loose and I'll find out what's going on at that school."

Seimei sniffed. "You had better watch your step! They are not your ramshackle friends from the city. Professors are learned noblemen, and the students young gentlemen. They have been studying the precepts of Master Kung and have immersed themselves in the wisdom of the five sages." He turned to his master. "Perhaps I had better take off a few days also, sir. That way I can make sure this young hothead does not get into trouble."

Akitada smiled. "No, my friend. I shall need you in the government offices. Professors are officials of rank, and that means the Bureau of Education will have files on them." He picked up a sheet of paper and handed it to Seimei. "See what you can find about these people in the archives and by talking to the clerks. Especially any recent changes in their financial standing."

"What do you want me to do?" Tora asked eagerly.

"You may present yourself at the university as my servant. Mingle with the staff, servants, students, groundskeepers and so forth. Pick up any gossip about the professors and students that might tell us what is behind the blackmail."

Tora nodded and rubbed his hands. "I may need some money, sir."

"Don't give him a red copper, sir!" cried Seimei. "He will spend it buying wine for every low class person he encounters."

Tora protested, "Haven't you always told me that walls have ears and bottles have mouths? I thought I'd be the wall and listen to the wine talking."

"Make sure the wall is sound or our plan will collapse," Akitada said dryly, as he counted the copper coins on a string before handing it to Tora.

Tora grinned and tucked the coppers in his sash. He headed towards the door, with Seimei following more slowly, when Akitada remembered something else. "Seimei," he called, "while you are checking the names on the list, try to find out how the late Prince Yoakira left his estate and who will benefit from his death."

Seimei turned. "Oh, sir! You must stop this nonsense about the prince's death. It's not reasonable and . . . not really your affair. Besides it is most unwise. Think of the people involved! If word gets out about what you suspect, they will destroy you." He flushed. "I beg your pardon for speaking bluntly."

Tora's eyes were bright with curiosity. "What are you talking about?"

Seimei muttered, "The master thinks the prince was murdered."

"Truly?" Tora sounded thrilled. "That's a lot better than demons devouring him. You wouldn't believe the stories people are telling about that. Horrible!" He shuddered.

Akitada smiled. Tora was notoriously nervous about supernatural events. "They can't be any more ridiculous than the pious tale of a miraculous transfiguration," he said dryly, adding, "By the way, don't mention any of this to my mother or sisters. Perhaps you had better take care of your household duties before leaving, Tora."

◆

Tora made short shrift of his chores by relegating most of them to the kitchen help and sauntered into the university shortly after the start of classes. From many halls came the sounds of young voices reciting answers or the dry tones of professors lecturing. The streets, courtyards, and most other buildings were silent and empty.

Tora saw few promising sources of information until he strolled into the courtyard of the administration hall. Here he came face to face with one of the clerks, a short, middle-aged man, dressed shabbily in an old gray robe and faded black cap, who carried a wine jar and was accompanied by a gangly youth in a dirty student's robe who was gingerly balancing a stack of three steaming bowls. When the clerk saw Tora, he stopped in his tracks, a guilty look on his face. The gangly youngster stumbled and almost dropped his food.

Tora noted with interest the clerk's florid complexion and decided to try his luck. "Having a second breakfast?" he remarked with a grin. "Lucky fellow! Getting paid a good salary for doing nothing and fed well on top of that! I see you have a good appetite when the food is free."

The man bristled. "It's not free! And what's it to you?" he blustered, but he cast an uneasy eye on Tora's neat blue robe and small black cap.

Tora drew himself up. "Nothing whatsoever, my man. I want to ask directions and, since there doesn't seem to be anybody else about, you'll do. I'm the new Professor Sugawara's assistant. Can you direct me to his office?"

"Oh! I do beg your pardon, sir." The clerk bowed deeply, a sudden movement which brought his hip in collision with the gaping youth and upset the stack of bowls, one of which tumbled to the ground, spilling a savory-smelling stew of vegetables. The clerk immediately turned and cuffed the youngster's ear. The unfortunate lad blinked and almost dropped the other two bowls, but Tora caught them in time, handing them to the clerk, while the young man crouched, cleaning up the spilled food.

"Oh, dear!" cried the clerk. "Thank you kindly. I cannot imagine why I pay this clumsy oaf for his services. My soft heart always gets me in trouble. Well, sir, you go out that gate," he pointed, "then turn right and cross the next street, and you will find the law school in the last courtyard to the south. And please forgive my rudeness. I should have recognized a learned gentleman immediately. The name is Nakatoshi, administrative clerk, at your service." He bowed again.

"Not at all, my dear fellow," smiled Tora, basking in his new role. "My name is Kinto. As you see, I am earning my daily bowl of rice just like you, and if it comes to that, I am sure you people have your own skills, or you wouldn't be in charge of a bunch of learned professors." He slapped the man's shoulder and laughed at this witticism.

Clutching the teetering bowls and the wine jar tightly to his chest, the clerk smiled thinly. "You are very understanding, sir. Great care is required to keep track of everybody here. We have almost four hundred students; hard work for only three clerks. My colleagues and I find that by mid-morning a bit of sustenance does wonders for the concentration. Thank heaven, the staff kitchen is next door and not at all bad."

Tora, who had sniffed the aroma of the stew appreciatively, said, "It smells delicious! Positively gives a man an appetite. Please don't let me keep you from enjoying your snack."

"Thank you." The clerk hesitated, then said, "Perhaps you might like to join us and sample the food? The cooking in the staff kitchen is vastly superior to that done for the students."

"A pleasure, my dear Nakatoshi, on condition that you allow me to replace the spilled portion and pay for my share." Tora clinked the string of coppers in his sleeve.

Nakatoshi expressed himself deeply honored, reluctantly accepted the money from Tora, and dispatched the youngster for more food. Leading the way into the hall, he took Tora to a dusty cubicle where two elderly clerks shuffled about among tall shelves filled with papers and boxes. Both were pale, bent, and nearsighted from their work, but cheered up at the unexpected company. Nakatoshi introduced Tora, who immediately engaged his hosts in conversation about the terrible working conditions at the university and the general poverty of its staff.

When the student returned with the rest of the food, Nakatoshi told him severely, "It's a good thing you did not spill anything else. I would have taken it out of your wages if this gentleman had not made it good."

"Thank you for your kindness," the student told Tora politely.

Tora thought that, on closer inspection, there was something very much like a rabbit about his protruding front teeth and the long ears, but his voice was pleasant and his speech courteous.

"You can go sweep the hall for the rest of the hour," Nakatoshi ordered, and the youth nodded and left.

"I hear that the grandson of Prince Yoakira is a student," Tora remarked after a few bites.

Nakatoshi looked uneasy. "Well," he said, "we are not really supposed to talk about it, but seeing that you are going to be a member of the university, I suppose it's all right. Yes, the boy was left here the very evening after the miracle. His fees were paid by his uncle, Lord Sakanoue, a very grand person, far above people like you and me. I had the honor of making the arrangements and took the young lord to his quarters. He looked very pale and was trembling. I was worried that he might be suffering from some illness and started to ask him questions, but he got quite haughty and told me to mind my own business. That's the nobility for you! Already the great lord, and no more than ten years old!"

"A child of such august rank in a place like this!" muttered one of the old men through a mouthful of rice. "It's no wonder he looked ill when he saw the dormitories. I expect they send his food in from the outside, or he would be dead by now."

Tora chewed a bit of bean curd and smacked his lips. "This is very tasty. I'm glad I ran into you fellows. Are things really so bad for the students?"

The three clerks exchanged glances and grunted. "They treat animals better than they do students here," muttered Nakatoshi. "Of course that means we get some cheap help." He jerked his head towards the hall, where they could hear the sounds of energetic sweeping.

The other old man suddenly joined the conversation. "How can they house and feed them better on what the government allows us? I can remember when the university got twice as much every year, plus extra gifts from grateful parents. Nowadays we all starve, students, staff and faculty alike."

Tora regarded the empty bowls and reached for the wine flask. There were only a few drops left. "Allow me to pay for another round of wine!" he offered.

This was gratefully accepted, and Nakatoshi shouted the order to the student in the hall.

When they were well into the second pitcher, Tora considered the time ripe to probe some more. "Isn't it a bit strange," he asked, "that the son of a great family like the prince's should live here where conditions are so bad?"

"Hah!" cried one of the old men. "The very thing I said when I heard."

The other one nodded. "All the other children of the high nobles are day students and come only for their classes. The dormitories are for the sons of provincial families."

"Well," said Tora, "I have a friend who keeps preaching to me what a fine thing getting an education is, but from what you fellows tell me, it seems even ordinary clerks and humble assistants like me are better off than the students. At least we can buy decent food and wine."

"Speak for yourself!" Nakatoshi, his face positively glowing, gave his two colleagues a wink. "Perhaps your professor pays you well for your services, but let me tell you, we could not manage a simple meal like this without other sources of income." He chuckled.

One of the old men looked up and cleared his throat warningly, but the wine had loosened Nakatoshi's tongue and he boasted, "Our work is not without its fringe benefits." Leaning a little closer to Tora, he said, "For example, we are in the unique position of being able to advise those who would like to put some money on the outcome of academic competitions."

"Nakatoshi!" said the old man sharply.

"You don't mean you make book on the examinations!" Tora exclaimed, putting an arm around Nakatoshi's shoulders.

Nakatoshi giggled. "Not the term I would use, my friend, my very good friend," he babbled, "but similar. Say, would you like to see some odds for the upcoming poetry contest? Maybe wager a little? It's between Oe and Fujiwara on our team, and Okura and Asano for the government. What do you say?"

Tora grinned broadly. "This is my lucky day, and you're a man after my own heart!" he cried. "I can tell I shall like it here. Tell me more!"

But the old man who had grumbled all along now snapped, "Better watch your tongue, Nakatoshi! You remember what happened last spring."

"Nothing happened, you old fool!" Nakatoshi muttered.

"Who's an old fool?" The old man glared. "You nearly got killed when you sold the name of the favorite in the examinations for two strings of coppers a piece, and then another fellow won."

"That wasn't my fault," cried Nakatoshi. "We went over the

grades of all the candidates carefully, and there was only one possibility. But then they picked a fellow who never got above a 'satisfactory' on anything except calligraphy! It was a fluke, I tell you. Anyway, that can't happen again now that we handle the bets ourselves."

Tora laughed and patted Nakatoshi's shoulder. "Mistakes happen in the best business. As for me, I look forward to placing a small wager with you as soon as I check out who's who."

They parted on friendly terms. On his way out, Tora walked past the poor student, who was just putting away his broom. For a moment he considered leaving him a few coppers as a tip, but then he remembered that, for all his politeness, the youngster had not addressed him as "sir," and went in search of a new quarry. Eventually he strayed into the large enclosure which contained the student dormitories. At this hour these were empty except for a couple of slovenly women with brooms and pails. Tora ignored them and crossed an open area dotted with pine trees and small shrubs, heading towards the service buildings. The largest of these was the kitchen: empty, filthy and filled with the rancid stench of moldy grain and rotting fish.

The cook and his helpers were taking their ease under a large paulownia tree behind the building. They were seated in a circle around a cracked bowl, pitching coppers towards it. A set of dice made the rounds and small heaps of copper coins lay before each man. There were four rough-looking adults and a handful of scruffy youngsters. When they saw Tora, they snatched up the money and jumped up.

"Don't disturb yourselves on my account," grinned Tora. "I'd be the last man to begrudge a working man his well-earned rest. For that matter, I like a good game myself."

The cook, recognizable by his girth and the many food stains on his clothes, was a cross-eyed brute who pursed his thick lips and looked Tora up and down suspiciously. The others settled back down and waited. Tora hitched up his gown, saying, "Better not get this new outfit dirty. My master'll have it out of my wages," and sat down cross-legged amongst them. "What're the rules?"

"You in service then?" asked the fat cook.

Tora nodded and began to count his coppers into neat little piles. The others watched avidly.

"Do a bit of gambling, do you?" the cook wanted to know.

"Not for a while. I was a soldier once and a buddy showed me how to roll the dice, but it was against the rules then."

The cook grunted and flopped down with the dull thud of a sack of rice. "Glad to have you," he growled. "Here, you can check the dice! To make sure we're on the up and up. You roll for the number of tries at the bowl. Hit the bowl with a copper and all the misses are yours."

"What do you mean?" Tora received the wooden objects and stared at them with a frown. They were crude but had not been tampered with. He handed them back. "They look like dice to me." He eyed the bowl, which was quite small and about ten paces away. The dirty ground around it was covered with copper coins. "I've never seen the game played like that, though."

Someone snickered, but the cook snapped, "Enough talking! Let's play!"

They were avid gamblers, but not particularly skilled at tossing for the bowl. Tora played judiciously, gauging the distance and the weight of the coins, slowly losing his pile of coppers before beginning to win steadily.

"Hey, you're getting good at this!" cried one of the men.

Tora boasted that he would not miss for the next ten tosses. They proposed a bet. Tora lost, but proposed other bets, which he won more often than not, until he sat before a small mountain of coppers, while his companions were dropping out of the game.

They sat with long faces. The cook glowered at Tora and muttered. Finally he snarled, "The bastard lied to us!"

Tora looked up from counting his coppers. "What did you say?"

The cook blustered, "You said you had no skill at the game."

"Did I not tell you that a buddy taught me how to play? Of course I know how to roll the dice," Tora said scornfully. "And I learned to toss pebbles when I was a kid."

"Well, you made it sound like you were green," whined another fellow. "We were just having a friendly game, and now you cleaned us out. What'll we tell our wives?"

Tora saw no reason why he could not succeed with the same method twice. "I tell you what," he said. "Just among friends and to show my appreciation for a pleasant game, why don't I use some of the winnings to treat you fellows to some really good wine?"

Their faces brightened instantly. "Here, runt!" shouted the cook to the smallest boy. "Run to the wine shop by the Left City Hall! They've got the strong stuff."

Tora scooped up his winnings, carefully counted out a generous amount and turned it over to the boy. "Get plenty!" he instructed, "and some tasty pickled radish to go with it."

There was a murmur of appreciation. The cook remarked that there were still some true gentlemen left in the world.

While they were waiting, Tora introduced himself as the new professor's servant and received, in return, information about the university, its staff, its professors and its students. The point of view on this occasion differed markedly from that held by the clerks. The kitchen staff and the groundskeepers and sweepers regarded students and faculty as inconsiderate nuisances who made their lives a constant misery. As soon as the wine, a very strong brew indeed, had made the rounds, their tongues loosened in the most helpful manner.

"I can see," Tora remarked to one of the sweepers, "that those youngsters are a lot of trouble to clean up after."

The man responded with a long list of abominations, but the cook snorted. "You think he's got trouble? The lazy rascal goes home at sundown. If you want to hear about trouble, it's me and my old woman you got to talk to. We're kept awake all night with the tricks those cursed students get up to."

"What sorts of tricks?" Tora asked, filling cups all around, but skipping his own.

"Oh, climbing the walls to get out. Smuggling in loose women. Breaking into the pantry and stealing food. Burning candles at night and setting the place on fire. You name it, they do it. Every night my old woman has to do a bed check, looking for their doxies."

"Doesn't trust you to do it, does she?" Tora remarked, grinning broadly.

This caused raucous mirth. One of the workers cried, "Him? He's so lazy, he wouldn't know what to do with a girl in his bed 'cept sleep. His old woman does the checking 'cause he's sacked out before the rest of us ever go home."

The cook glared, rolling his crossed eyes terribly. "Liar," he growled. "All day long I'm cooking to keep the little bastards' bowls filled! They eat like starved rats and beg for leftovers. Most of 'em don't have two coppers to rub together. Makes you wonder how they get the women! There's always a couple hungry enough to help out in the kitchen for a bit of extra food or a couple of coppers. It's my kindness! They steal more food than they're worth."

Tora thought this another example of how dubious a thing an education was. "If they are so poor, how come they get treated like gentlemen?" he asked.

The cook and the others looked at each other blankly. "Well," said the cook, "now that you mention it, it is funny. One day a starved kid comes begging to me for the scrapings of the stew pot, or offers to sell his gown for some rice. Out of the goodness of my heart, I give him a job. Then, a little while later, the same fellow is dressed like a prince in brand new clothes and looks down his nose at me like I was some slug under a rock when I ask him why he hasn't come to work."

"Yeah!" cried one of the boys. "I know the one you mean! Ishikawa! He used to fetch water from the well along with me last year. Now he wants me to call him *Mr.* Ishikawa."

"How'd he get rich all of a sudden?" asked Tora. "Some relative died and left him a fortune?"

"Naw," grunted the cook. The fat man's broad face was turning alarmingly red and glistening with sweat and he slurred his words. "Tha's what I thought at first. But tha' wasn't it. Eh, guys?"

They all shook their heads. The source of Ishikawa's wealth was a mystery to them. Anyway, the consensus of the group was that one couldn't understand the ways of students. They were crazy. All that reading was bad for the brain. Tora grinned.

"Take that Rabbit!" offered the cook.

"What rabbit?" asked Tora, looking around.

The cook saw a joke and began to giggle until tears ran down his fat cheeks. "Please!" he gasped, clasping his belly and wheezing with laughter. "He, he. Take the Rabbit! Har, har! You can have him." His companions joined in the laughter.

Tora looked blank until someone explained that Rabbit was the nickname of one of the cook's student helpers.

"Helper!" cried the cook, who had calmed himself somewhat with another draught of wine. "Useless as a blind man's lantern! Half the time I tell him sh . . . somethin' and he doesh shomethin' else. Jush las' night I tell him to put the rice on an' he forgets the rice and boils the empty steamers. Had to feed everybody leftover millet from breakfast. 'N when you talk to him, he shtands there with that shilly grin on his face an' his big ears flappin' or else a hangdog look like his mind is really shome other place an' you're no more'n a moshkito buzzing at him." He paused to peer up at the sun with his good eye. "Come to think, he's about due now. Musht be time to shtart up the fires again."

He heaved his bulk up with the help of his companions and stood swaying. "Damn good wine!" he muttered with a nod to Tora. "You're a pleashant fellow! Whash your name again?"

At that moment a terrible racket broke out inside the kitchen. Angry shouts rang out, followed by the crash of broken crockery. They ran to see what was going on.

Inside the long low kitchen they found two young men on the hard dirt floor, rolling about among broken dishes, assorted vegetables and a slimy gray substance which the outraged cook identified as millet gruel. One of the youngsters, a tall gangly figure who looked strangely familiar to Tora, was belaboring the other, shorter but more muscular, with his fists. "You dirty dog!" he gasped between blows, totally oblivious to his audience, "How dare you read my letter? How dare you make filthy insinuations! I'll kill you if you say one word about this to anyone!" He grabbed the other's shoulders and pounded his head on the floor to make his point.

"And I'll kill you, you worthless piece of dung!" roared the cook. He seized a broom and struck the gangly fellow furiously about the head and shoulders.

The combatants parted and staggered to their feet. The skinny one cowered under the cook's blows, protecting his head with raised arms. Tora recognized him as the student who had been working for the clerks. His appearance had not improved; plain of face at the best of times, with his long nose, protruding teeth, receding chin, and overly large ears, he was now covered with gruel and dirt, his hair knot had come undone, and his mouth hung open. With a horrified glance at Tora and the cook, he made a sound somewhere between a squeal and a sob, and took to his heels.

"An' don't bother to come back!" roared the cook after him, shaking his fist. "I'll have the damages outta your hide, you shnot-nosed, rabbitty bashtard!"

The other student meanwhile had been brushing himself off. He was Rabbit's age and, in spite of the pummeling, in reasonably good shape. Turning his round face and button eyes on the cook, he whined, "I have done nothing, Cook. I swear it! Rabbit jumped me all of a sudden. You saw I wasn't even defending myself. There I was, cleaning the radishes as you told me, when he threw the whole pot of gruel at me! Thank the gods it was cold. I could've been scalded. I tell you, he's mad! They shouldn't allow mad people to live amongst the rest of us. It's dangerous. And look at the terrible mess he's made of your kitchen. I don't know how a nice man like you can put up with such people."

Mollified the fat man collapsed on a stool, breathed hard for a while, then grunted, "Never mind, Haseo! One of the fellows'll give you a hand and we'll have it cleaned up in no time. Then you can start the soup. You're a good boy, and so I shall tell them in the paymashter's offish."

◆

Tora reported his discoveries with the greatest satisfaction. Akitada had just finished his noon rice (procured from the staff kitchen) and listened with flattering attention. He said, "Apparently, aside from the bed check by the cook's wife, there is no control of the comings and goings of the students or staff during the night hours. The gates are closed, but evidently anybody can climb over the walls or move about freely inside the grounds." He pondered this for a moment and frowned. "Of course that means that an outsider can get in also. It certainly widens the possibilities of potential blackmailers."

"For my money," said Tora, helping himself to some leftover pickled plums, "it's one of the students. Those poor bastards are half-starved and working part-time jobs to feed themselves. What about that fellow Ishikawa?"

"Ishikawa now has a job reading essays for one of the professors. That could explain why he no longer works for the cook, who is not, from your account, a nice man to work for. Also, Ishikawa is supposed to place first in the next examinations."

Tora snorted. "He'd better not count on it. According to the clerks, strange things happen in those examinations. You wouldn't believe what goes on!" He chuckled and explained the clerks' bookmaking operation.

Akitada's amused smile faded abruptly when Tora mentioned Nakatoshi's troubles after the last examination. He stiffened and cried, "What? Good Heavens! This goes far beyond a minor bookmaking operation by a few clerks! It sounds as if the examination results have been altered!" Jumping up, he started pacing. "It's shocking but nothing else fits. Nothing else explains the blackmail note so perfectly. And if it gets out . . . as it surely must with this abject poverty of students, staff and faculty . . . the emperor will have to take action. There will be a purge of the faculty at the very least."

Tora looked puzzled. "I don't see the point. Who cares about an examination? Now about Prince Yoakira's grandson . . ."

Akitada stopped his pacing. "What about him?"

"The kid was brought here by his uncle the night after his grandfather popped off. The clerk said he looked like he was sick. He thought it was strange they'd make him stay here."

"Yes, it is strange. I have the boy in one of my classes," said Akitada. "And I am worried about him. He really does not look healthy."

"You want me to go ask more questions about the kid?" Tora offered eagerly.

But Akitada's mind was again on the scandal involving the university and on vague suspicions that he did not yet dare admit to himself. "No," he muttered. "Go on home for now. I have to think about all this."

FOUR

SCHOLARS AND OTHERS

*A*kitada sat for a long time wondering what to do. For all its stern lessons he loved this university, and he had loved and idolized most of his professors. Now he wondered if his youthful hero worship had not been a form of self-delusion. It made more sense that a few human beings should be flawed than that the whole university with its solid, ancient virtues should have changed so completely in so short a time.

Clearly he should expose immediately the fact that university staff was engaged in making book on the outcome of the yearly examinations. But this must reveal to the world that someone had altered the examination results, either to manipulate the odds or in response to a hefty bribe. How many innocent people would be hurt by the scandal? What about the suspicion that must fall on Hirata and his colleagues? On the other hand, what about the student who had been cheated of his just reward? What of the guilty individual? Only one of the faculty, an examiner, could have altered the outcome of the most important examination in the country. Could this be allowed to happen again? Akitada's spirit rebelled at the betrayal of trust.

But the true cause of his distress was even more personal. If he was right, and the switch of winners was indeed the reason for the blackmail letter, then Hirata must have known, or at least guessed. Why had he withheld this fact from Akitada? If he had hoped to protect the reputation of the university, then Akitada must assume that Hirata had not trusted him. Why ask his help at all? Was he to find a cover-up for the scandal because he was in Hirata's debt? The thought was extraordinarily painful, and raised an even more dismal possibility. What if the blackmail note had been intended for Hirata all along?

In his anger and distress, Akitada thought of withdrawing from the case. His duty to his family demanded that he guard his reputation carefully, and being involved in covering up a former professor's misdeeds would certainly ruin his own career. But in his heart, Akitada knew he could not take this step. The past would forever shape his present; his duty to his mother and sisters was surpassed by his long and deep gratitude to this man, and by his affection for Tamako.

He recalled his first sight of her. Tamako had been a shy nine-year-old when he had walked into the Hirata household, a lost and confused boy on the verge of manhood. "I brought a house guest," her father had announced. "Make him welcome like a brother!" They had both made him welcome, and in time he had felt he was a part of them in a way he had never felt in his own family. He had been loved and comforted, a new sensation for him, who had been raised by servants, ignored by his beautiful and haughty mother, and systematically humiliated and thrashed by his father.

At fifteen he had done the unforgivable. He had turned on the man he was duty-bound to honor and respect, had snatched the bamboo cane out of his father's raised hand, and had threatened him with it. They had been in his father's study, a room which held such terror for him that he refused to use it to this day. The towering form of his father had loomed over him in the light of flickering candles, the handsome, cold features distorted by a rage caused by no more than an innocent remark by Akitada about his father's lack of military service, and he had experienced the sudden, overwhelming conviction that he could no longer bear the vicious beating he was about to receive. He had raised his hand and twisted the bamboo cane from his father's grip, shouting furiously about the intolerable injustice. When his father had backed away in total surprise, he had followed with the raised cane and stated his ultimatum. If his father ever touched him again, he would return the punishment tenfold. Then he had broken the cane and tossed it at Lord Sugawara's feet.

The outcome was predictable, though Akitada had not really thought about it at the time. His father had called in his wife and daughters, as well as the senior servants as witnesses, and had informed them that, since Akitada had raised his hand and his voice against him, he would henceforth no longer be a member of the family.

Dazed with despair, Akitada had walked out of his home and to the university, the only other world he had known. There Professor Hirata had found him, sitting on the steps of the law school, and had listened to his tale and taken him into his own household.

The memory of that time was still a wrenching pain in Akitada's belly, and it reminded him of the little Lord Minamoto. The Minamoto boy was younger and orphaned but, whatever the cause of the suffering, their experiences were similar. They had been abandoned to strangers, lost and friendless. Young as the Minamoto boy was, he had received an excellent education and could hold his own with the older students, but his mind was not on his work, and his eyes were red-rimmed. Probably he also grieved deeply for his grandfather. Why was there no other family member to care for him? What of this uncle, this Lord Sakanoue, who apparently could not even wait a decent time before getting rid of the boy? To judge by his name, the man must be related by marriage. Where was the rest of the Minamoto clan?

The boy had imperial blood in his veins, and it was clear from his reserve that he had been raised in the imperial tradition. Such an upbringing forbade familiarity and had made it impossible for

Akitada to approach the youngster. His every effort at sympathy had been rejected courteously but firmly, yet still Akitada's heart went out to the lonely child. He wished he could be another Hirata to the young lord.

At that moment, Hirata himself came in to announce that Oe had called a special meeting. While he busied himself adjusting his cap before the mirror, Akitada asked casually about the results of the last examination. When there was no reply, he turned. Hirata had turned pale and was looking at him helplessly. Akitada asked, "Are you quite well, sir?"

Slowly the older man nodded. "Yes, I . . . I see you have heard." He sighed. "Oh, dear! I am afraid it is quite true. A very mediocre student placed first. The young man who was expected to win had to accept second place."

"Were you not suspicious?" Akitada asked, surprised.

Hirata turned away. "Of course I was suspicious, but my hands were tied."

Akitada's disbelief turned to righteous shock. "Your hands were tied? How so?"

Hirata faced him. "You are young. You cannot understand." His voice was shaking.

Akitada steeled himself. He would have the truth now, even if it meant a breach in their relationship. "Since the matter touches on the blackmail, I think you owe me an explanation, sir," he said.

Hirata ran a shaking hand over his face, then nodded slowly. "Yes. Of course. I owe you that and an apology. I should have told you. Could we sit down?"

Akitada flushed a little at the humble request and gestured to a cushion. When they were seated, he said, "I need to know the extent of your involvement. Did you read the winner's composition and sit in on his orals?"

"I read his paper. It was superb. But, no, I was not invited to attend his orals. They were conducted by a mixed panel of senior professors and four high-ranking nobles appointed by the emperor. Oe, Fujiwara, and Tanabe represented the university."

"There must have been an outcry when the results were

published. What about the young man who was passed over? What was his reaction?"

Hirata's face looked strained. "He was poor and without family connections, as, indeed, are most of the faculty. Necessity often makes us suppress our views. He made no protest, and I convinced myself that nothing was wrong, that the other student had suddenly revealed hidden genius. One could not argue about the excellence of his paper."

Frustrated by Hirata's attempt to justify himself, Akitada lashed out. "But you knew better," he cried. "I have never known you to go against your principles. This is not what you used to teach your students. I thought better of you."

Hirata flinched. Regarding Akitada sadly, he said, "You are very young. Only young men think the greatest tragedy in life is suffering an injustice. There are worse things, but they happen to the old." He raised a hand to cover his eyes. When he had himself under control again, he continued, "Unfortunately, in this student's case, there was not even the consolation of a lesser assignment in the capital. He was assigned to one of the northern provinces as a teacher."

"Good heavens! That amounts to exile. And he accepted that?"

Hirata clenched his fists. "No," he said in a choking voice. "He committed suicide the day he was given the news."

Akitada sat speechless. The heavy silence hung between them like a wall.

After a long time, Hirata mastered his emotion and spoke again. "Now you know why I did not tell you the truth. This blackmail business has destroyed my precarious peace. For nearly a year I have tried to convince myself that the young man killed himself for other reasons, perhaps an unhappy love affair or money problems. I thought that no mere disappointment in the examination result could cause him to take his life when he had the talent and the youth to rise in the world in spite of it. I even blamed him for being too unstable to be worthy of first place honors, as if his suicide justified the examination results. I am deeply ashamed and beg your forgiveness for not telling you of this sooner."

Hirata's humility shook Akitada. "Er, of course," he stuttered, twisting his hands in his lap. "There is nothing to forgive, sir. Indeed, I . . . am very sorry for my rash words. I had no right." He paused, looking at the gray head bowed before him, and felt ashamed of his suspicions. He asked, "But how . . . ?"

Hirata's head snapped up. His face was haggard, his eyes hard. "How do I live with myself? Not well, I assure you. But I go on because I still have two obligations to meet."

Akitada sat aghast. He had not meant to cause such pain, had had no thought beyond his own self-righteous outrage. He cried, "Oh, I beg your pardon, sir. That is not what I meant at all. I wondered how it was done. How did the mediocre student write the winning composition? Did someone else take his place on the day of the examination?"

Hirata relaxed a little. His mouth quirked slightly. "Ah, Akitada! I should have known that you would look on the practical side. The answer is no; it would have been impossible. We know all of our students by sight and interview the few candidates who come from the provinces. The winner was one of ours. I saw him on the day of the examination, and I read his paper. It was in his handwriting."

"Could you have misjudged his earlier performances?"

Hirata grimaced. "No, though I certainly tried to think so. The winning essay was beyond anything he had ever done before. His approach to the complex question was original, his argument completely logical, his citations from the Chinese sources were abundant, accurate, and brilliantly appropriate, and his style was remarkable." After a pause, he added, "And this from a student who was not yet fluent in the Chinese language, had shown deplorable ignorance of the five classics on previous occasions, and could hardly make a great deal of sense when discussing current issues in his native tongue." Hirata ran a hand over his brow and shook his head. "Talking about it makes me ill. I should have demanded an investigation."

"Perhaps he memorized someone else's text, or a draft of the paper was smuggled in?" Akitada suggested.

"Neither. Memorizing would not have helped since he had no prior knowledge of the topic. Besides I doubt his knowledge of Chinese was good enough. As to passing him a draft, security, as you know, is very tight. The candidates are searched, led to their cubicles, and handed the examination topic and the sheets of blank paper by a faculty proctor."

"Then the proctor must have passed him the paper."

"Yes." Hirata's voice sounded dismal, but some color had returned to his face.

"I think the time has come for names."

Hirata sighed. "You would find out in any case. The student's name was Okura. I am thankful to say that he received a government appointment to a department where he can do no damage. There were four of us assigned as proctors, Takahashi, Fujiwara, Ono and myself. I was not the one who administered the question to Okura. Oe directed the whole affair, and it may be possible to find out from him who was assigned to Okura."

At this moment the door flew open, and Nishioka bounded in.

"There you are!" His bright eyes took in the scene and his nose quivered excitedly. "Important business? Or have you forgotten the meeting? The others are all there already."

"Thank you for reminding us," said Hirata dryly, getting to his feet.

They followed Nishioka to the *Nando-in*, the central hall of the school of Chinese classics. As Nishioka had said, most of the others were already assembled, clustered about in small groups or sitting in their places studying sheets of paper. Oe stood apart with Ono, apparently giving his junior last minute instructions. Near them hovered Takahashi with a murderous expression on his face.

Akitada made the rounds, bowing and exchanging pleasantries, without meeting anyone of interest until he recognized a familiar face. By now the most senior of the professors, the Confucian scholar, Tanabe, had seen him and was coming his way with a broad smile of welcome. He looked a little more frail and much grayer. Tanabe must be in his sixties by now, a small-boned man with pale, ascetic features and the bowed shoulders of the perpetual scholar.

"My dear Sugawara," he cried, acknowledging Akitada's respectful bow, "I am so very glad to see you again. Nishioka told me that you have joined our faculty. I have been following your career with great interest. You are to be commended on your connection with the Lords Motosuke and Kosehira. You have made a very promising beginning."

Momentarily taken aback that Tanabe should know about his friendship with the Fujiwara cousins, Akitada recalled that the old gentleman had a childlike admiration for the aristocracy and was well informed about all the important members of the ruling Fujiwara clan. The thought suddenly crossed his mind that such veneration could lead even a scholar of Tanabe's repute to compromise his principles if he were asked to do so as a favor to a high-ranking person.

But seeing the pure joy on the wrinkled face of his former teacher, he was ashamed and explained that his work rarely allowed him leisure to see his friends.

Tanabe looked disappointed. "Well," he said, "that is a pity, but here's another Fujiwara for you to meet." He waved over a tall, bearded man in a wrinkled green silk gown held together by an unmatched sash. The bearded giant approached and responded cheerfully to the introductions.

"The new man, eh?" he boomed. "Heard about you. Helped one of my namesakes out of a very sticky situation in Kazusa province." His eyes twinkled. "Not engaged in a similar mission here, are you?"

It probably was a joke, but Akitada gaped for a moment, much to Fujiwara's amusement. "My former mentor, Professor Hirata, has asked me to fill in temporarily for his assistant," Akitada said stiffly. He wondered if the big man's lumbering physique masked a very nimble mind. Then he remembered that Fujiwara had been one of the proctors during the spring examination, and, suddenly curious, he asked, "Are you related to Lord Motosuke?"

"Ho, ho, ho!" roared this Fujiwara. "Related? Me? No more

than China and Japan, or winter and summer. Different branches of the family altogether. We are the southern Fujiwaras, mostly small landholders in the provinces. Wouldn't the Fujiwara ministers, chancellors, counsellors and lords just love me for a cousin? Look at me, man! I'm a disgrace!"

"Surely not, sir," protested Akitada, embarrassed.

"Of course I am. I drink, I carouse, and I tell dirty jokes! I associate with disreputable characters and courtesans. My only saving grace is that I know a lot of interesting things about the history of China and about our own past, and the students seem to like to listen to me."

There was great charm in such honesty and modesty. Putting aside his suspicions, Akitada said warmly, "That is surely what matters most." On an impulse, he added, "Since you have a good rapport with students, perhaps you have some advice for me. I am very concerned about one of my charges, young Minamoto. He is withdrawn and seems troubled, but I don't seem to be able to talk to him."

Fujiwara became instantly serious. "Ah, yes. Poor boy!" He sighed. "Lost his grandfather recently. Weird story—you heard? Yes, of course." Again the shrewd eyes measured Akitada. "Since his parents and two uncles died during the last smallpox epidemic, his grandfather was raising him and his sister. The boy's too proud to show his hurt, of course. Thinks having imperial blood means being strong. Foolish but quite admirable in its way! Afraid I can't help you, though, Sugawara, having failed myself so far. But good luck!"

A bobbing and bowing Nishioka interrupted. "Very sorry to break in. Please forgive the intrusion! I had no time to pay my respects earlier, Sugawara. How do you find teaching?"

"I am beginning to find my way."

"Did I hear you mention the name Minamoto just now? Yes. I wonder if you found out what the boy is doing here?"

"He is a student," said Akitada curtly.

"Ha, ha. Yes. Of course. Everybody knows that. Ah, I see. You are not familiar with his story. You see, he is the grandson of the same Prince Yoakira who vanished into thin air under supernatural circumstances. The family claims it was a miracle, and His Majesty has graciously given them his support. But why is the boy here? His family has left town. Lord Sakanoue, who is said to have married the boy's sister, brought him here the very night after the grandfather's disappearance. A strange thing to do, don't you think?"

Fujiwara made a rude noise. "As usual," he boomed, "our own newshound Nishioka has smelled a story. Trust him to sniff around until he gets to the bottom of it."

Nishioka reddened, but defended himself gamely. "You like to joke, sir, but I make human behavior my special study. All of the sacred writings of Confucius and his disciples and commentators are based on nothing more than their profound understanding of personal relationships, and personal relationships can best be studied by observing people's actions and finding out the reasons for them."

Akitada looked at the nosy Nishioka with new respect. "I must confess," he said with a slight smile, "that I share your interest in people's behavior and am equally guilty of curiosity about the boy."

Nishioka clapped his hands. "There, you see!" he cried. "I knew we were kindred souls. We must put our heads together! I shall tell you everything I find out, and you shall do the same." At that moment his eye was caught by something across the room. He said hastily, "Please excuse me now. I must find out what Oe and Takahashi are snarling about."

Across the room, the two senior professors were engaged in some bitter argument as Ono stood by wringing his hands helplessly.

"Hmm," said Fujiwara, thoughtfully. "There is one difference between you and Nishioka, though. I think you ask questions because you care about people, while Nishioka only cares about a good story." He shook his head. "To most people he seems harmless enough, but the truth is, when that little fellow is about, nobody's secret is safe. Look at him! We'll have all the facts about that tiff between Oe and Takahashi in the twinkling of an eye."

As it turned out, it was to take longer than that, because Ono suddenly stepped on the dais and called everyone to order. Oe and Takahashi parted, and people took their seats, assigned by rank, department and seniority. Akitada found his own place behind Hirata, who was himself several seats removed from Oe who occupied the center of the semicircle facing the dais.

When Ono introduced Oe, he rose and ascended the dais majestically. His handsome face still flushed from the altercation, he looked resplendent in his blue silk gown, with every silver hair in place. He let his compelling eyes move across the assembly. "My friends and colleagues," he said, "allow me to take a little of your time to share good news."

"As little time as possible," muttered Fujiwara audibly.

But Oe was not to be rushed. His mellifluous voice weighed out the words like gold. "In our glorious past," he intoned, "our ancestors were accustomed to follow in the footsteps of the ancients."

Akitada found his interest wandering as Oe droned on and on about ancient rites and virtues, those long lost happy days when poets were venerated and rewarded. Instead he let his eyes roam among the faces of those men who might have altered the examination results.

Hirata, slightly in front of him, he saw only in profile. Deep lines edged his features and his chin rested on his chest. Only the hands moved restlessly, twisting and kneading the fabric of his robe.

Tanabe seemed to doze, a happy smile on his face, as innocent-looking an old man as Akitada had ever seen. By contrast, Takahashi, who sat next to him, was biting his lip, simmering with a fury that was about to explode. All of this fury was focused on Oe. He, however, was unaware of his audience as he lost himself in his own eloquence. Only Fujiwara listened, and he was clearly impatient.

"Alas," Oe was saying, spreading his arms for effect. "Those times are past. Our morals have declined as our aesthetic pursuits have become mere games for women and children. Those few of us who are serious poets toil in vain in the sterile soil of public apathy."

Fujiwara yawned loudly.

Oe shot him an angry glance, and continued. "But far be it

from me to dwell on our sufferings, for at last the fruitful rains of official approval are falling again. At last the revitalizing sun of imperial interest pierces the heavy clouds of indifference." Raising his voice triumphantly, he cried, "At long last, we shall have a poetry contest again!"

Since this was no longer news to anyone, only Ono jumped up and applauded.

Oe tried again. "And no ordinary contest either!" he cried. "It is to be a command performance on the first evening of the Kamo festival by request of several of the most august personages at court."

This time Tanabe woke up. "Hear, hear!" he cried. "The names of the august sponsors and participants, if you please."

Oe suppressed a smirk. "For the time being," he said, "I will only reveal that Prince Atsuakira will preside over the judges. However, we have been given permission to use the imperial pavilion in the Spring Garden for the occasion. And, since a certain anonymous benefactor is paying for everything, no expense will be spared."

Oe finally got enthusiastic applause from the faculty. He received it complacently, like an indulgent parent might accept his children's delight at an unexpected treat. Then, raising his hand, he cut the chatter short, and got down to business.

"You have been given a draft of the program. Please note particularly the selection of musical pieces and dances which will be incorporated. Does anyone have a question?"

Takahashi shot up, waving the program. "Yes. How dare you? I, for one, find it intolerable that I was not consulted about this," he snapped. "It shows the same unprofessional attitude towards your colleagues which caused me to reproach you earlier on another matter."

Oe reddened and his white hair seemed to bristle. He said acidly, "Someone has to plan these affairs and since it was I who worked tirelessly to gain support at court, it would hardly be seemly to turn this occasion over to someone who has neither interest nor talent."

Someone snickered in the audience. Glancing around at bland faces, Takahashi quivered with rage, then shredded his program and turned back to Oe. But before he could speak, Ono cried, "Pray do not allow personalities to get in the way of this remarkable achievement. Since it is a contest in the composition of Chinese verse, there can be no question as to who is the best man to plan it."

Takahashi flung around again. "Shut up, you silly, snivelling toady!" he shouted. "We all know you'd lick that conceited bastard's fat ass if he asked you to."

There were some gasps and a snort of suppressed laughter. Then Fujiwara's booming voice cut in. "Enough! I have better things to do with my evening than to listen to a couple of angry roosters crowing. Sit down Takahashi! Get on with it, Oe, and make it brief!"

For a moment Takahashi resisted the arms which were pulling him down, and Oe looked ready to walk out, but common sense prevailed. Oe got through the rest of his announcements with a minimum of flourish and self-congratulation, as Takahashi glowered silently. More papers were passed around by Ono without arousing much discussion. Only Tanabe could be heard muttering, "Splendid!" "Most gratifying!" and "What condescension!"

Akitada glanced at the sheet in his hand. It contained a list of noble sponsors and competitors. He did not share Tanabe's thrill, but recognized a name amongst the competitors representing the government, a Secretary Okura. He wondered if this could be the man who had placed first in last spring's examination.

The meeting broke up early enough for Fujiwara, who left arm in arm with Sato, talking loudly about a night on the town.

"Disgusting!" muttered Takahashi, who had been behind them and now paused to say to Akitada, "Such men should not be allowed to teach! They corrupt the young."

At this, Nishioka inserted his slender figure between them, saying, "Dear sir. Aren't you forgetting that that dissolute history professor is likely to win the contest prize away from Oe? I should

have thought you'd be more tolerant of his foibles under the circumstances."

Takahashi grunted and walked away.

"What do you mean?" Akitada asked Nishioka. "I thought Oe
was the favorite."

"Oh, no. There are any number of talented names on the list,
but the fact is that only Fujiwara is a true poet. Compared to him,
the rest are merely practitioners. If Fujiwara has a mind to it, or if
he is sufficiently drunk—the same thing in his case—he com-
poses like another Li Po. Oh!" Nishioka's face split into a grin.
"That earlier quarrel between Oe and Takahashi? That was about
a draft of a memorial to the emperor. Seems Takahashi composed
it and asked Oe's opinion. Oe gave it to the calligraphy professor
as scratch paper for his students."

Akitada's brows shot up. "Not intentionally?"

"Apparently. At least Oe does not deny it."

"What an extraordinarily rude thing to do!" Akitada said,
shaking his head. "No wonder Takahashi was furious."

Nishioka nodded happily. "Mark my words! This will not be
the end of it. Takahashi holds a grudge, and Oe cannot take any
injury to his pride. Oh, yes! There will be repercussions!" Rubbing
his hands, he walked away.

When Akitada left the building with Hirata, the sun was setting, and the cleaning crews were busy about the grounds.

"The Kamo festival is only two days away," Akitada remarked.
"How can Oe expect the participants to be ready for their parts in
such a short time?"

"He probably doesn't. Mind you, the musicians, like Sato, always have something prepared. The others . . . well, as long as Oe is
ready himself, he does not mind who makes a fool of himself."

Hirata was uncharacteristically caustic. Akitada put it down to
pressure. He asked, "Are professors always so hostile towards each
other, or is all this bickering due to what happened last spring?"

Hirata shuddered, hunching up his shoulders. "I cannot believe that it is public knowledge," he muttered. "No. The problem

is that we are more vulnerable to human flaws than ordinary people. If we were not, surely we would not be teaching. Saints make very poor preceptors. They don't know what it is to struggle with temptation."

He sounded so bitter that Akitada had to remind himself of the extraordinary tolerance Hirata had always shown for other men's shortcomings and vices. Such an attitude could, of course, be carried too far, and if such men ended up hurting others, it must eventually lead to self-recrimination. He recalled uneasily Hirata's strange remark that he only persisted because he still had two duties to accomplish.

They passed silently between the red-lacquered columns of the university gate and walked into Mibu Road. Directly across from them was the vast expanse of the park. Another gate, of rustic beams and with a thatched roof instead of lacquered columns and blue tiles, like the university gate, led into the *Shinsenen*, the imperial Spring Garden where the poetry contest was to take place. Flowering trees shimmered amidst the darker green of oaks, maples and pines, and the warm evening air was filled with the scent of blossoms. The picture of Tamako in her flower garden came to Akitada's mind.

"You must come to dinner again soon," said Hirata suddenly, as they turned north.

Akitada started. "Thank you," he said awkwardly.

"Tamako asks about you every evening."

"Oh." Akitada was at a loss for words.

They continued to the corner where Mibu Road ends at Second Avenue and their paths parted.

"Well?" asked Hirata, stopping.

"Yes. I should like to," stammered Akitada. "That is, if Tamako really . . . that is, I do not want to be a nuisance."

"Not at all. You would do us a favor." Hirata put his hand on Akitada's arm and pleaded, "You see, we live too detached a life. Especially Tamako. She needs to be with young people her own age. Usually mothers manage this sort of thing, but since my wife died . . ." He let his voice trail away uncertainly and sighed. "Some day I shall be gone and my daughter will be alone in the world. It is not natural for her to spend all her time with me."

Akitada's head spun. If he was not mistaken, Hirata had just implied that he would welcome him as a son-in-law. He could imagine what his mother would have to say to this! Suddenly anger at his circumstances seized him and he blurted out, "I always reserve a viewing stand for my mother and sisters to watch the Kamo festival procession. Would you and Tamako be our guests on this occasion, or are you otherwise promised?"

Hirata's drawn face brightened instantly. "Thank you, my dear boy! How very kind of you," he said warmly. "I cannot accept myself, because I am to join some old friends, but Tamako will be delighted. Please convey our gratitude to your lady mother for her great kindness to my child."

Akitada's heart quailed at this charge, but he said bravely, "Excellent! In that case, may I be permitted to escort her?"

"Of course, of course. What would be more suitable? And shall we say tomorrow night for dinner then?"

"Yes. Thank you. I am most honored, sir."

Hirata chuckled. "Why so formal, my boy? You are practically a member of my family. Good night!" He waved and walked away.

Akitada stood staring after him, wondering if this, rather than the blackmail note, had been the real reason Hirata had contacted him.

FIVE

DEATH IN THE SPRING GARDEN

$\mathcal{E}$arly the next morning Akitada paid a visit to his mother's apartments. He found Lady Sugawara taking her morning rice on the new veranda. When she saw her son, she waved the maid away.

Akitada's mother had once been a great beauty, but age and discontent had made her body gaunt and her face severe. Still, she greeted her son pleasantly and invited him to sit.

After having made his usual inquiries into her health, he reported on his preparations for the viewing of the procession of the Kamo virgin. His mother was pleased to approve. After an uncomfortable moment, Akitada said, "There is a matter on which I hope you will give your unworthy son your honored counsel."

Lady Sugawara raised her brows, then nodded. "Speak!"

"You may recall the kindness my former teacher, Professor Hirata, has shown me?"

His mother frowned. "It has been a great regret to me," she said, "that strangers should have taken the place of your own parents." After a short pause, she added, "Still, the man was respectable, and there was nothing unsuitable in the arrangement. You simply resided with your tutor."

"You know very well," Akitada protested, "that the arrangement, as you call it, was nothing of the kind. The Hiratas took me into their home out of the goodness of their hearts after I had been forbidden this house."

His mother looked away. "Always remember that you are a Sugawara. However, I expect Mr. Hirata is a very estimable person."

"He is the kindest of men and the father of a lovely and talented daughter." Akitada held his breath for a moment, but his mother merely compressed her lips and waited. "Her name is Tamako. We grew up together like brother and sister during the years I lived with them, but I had not seen her since my father's d—" He broke off, because his mother twitched her sleeve abruptly and frowned again. Taking a deep breath, he rushed through the rest of his speech. "Anyway, she is twenty-two years old now, the only child. He is anxious for her future. I believe he would welcome a proposal of marriage." There! It was out!

A long silence fell. Lady Sugawara neither moved nor looked at him. Finally she said, "I see."

"I," stammered Akitada, "I also would welcome . . . that is, I am naturally very fond of Tamako. You will like her. She is extraordinarily capable, reads and writes Chinese, having studied with her father along with me, and she is a wonderful gardener. You will have much in common!" This last was an outrageous lie, of course. The two women had nothing in common at all.

Lady Sugawara heaved a deep sigh. She turned to regard her son. "Well," she said. "You have passed your first youth and I have passed the golden years of age and count my remaining days in this world as unexpected gifts." She dabbed her eyes with the corner of her sleeve, then gave Akitada a tremulous smile. "It is time you took a wife, and I long to hold a grandchild in my arms before I die."

The weight of the world lifted from Akitada's shoulders. He almost could not believe he had heard right. "Thank you, Mother," he said fervently, making her a deep bow. "You are very understanding."

She waved away his thanks, and smiled a little. For a moment, she was quite beautiful again.

He said eagerly, "I am invited to dinner tonight and will give the professor my answer then. And you shall meet your future daughter-in-law on the day of the procession. I have invited her to join us on the viewing stand."

Lady Sugawara's smile faded abruptly. "You issued the invitation without consulting me?" she asked. "I have never heard of a more improper arrangement. It is customary to hire a go-between in these matters. You know how I dislike surprises! In the future, you will ask before introducing strangers into my presence."

Akitada apologized and bowed humbly.

His mother rearranged her gown, sniffed, then said, "Well. It does not matter. It is a respectable, but hardly important family. Naturally, you could do much better, but since I assume you are offering her a secondary position in your household, we can afford a certain informality."

Akitada's blood rushed to his face. "Oh, no!" he gasped. "I am afraid you misunderstood, Mother. A secondary position is completely out of the question! It would be the gravest insult after what the Hiratas have done for me." Feeling suddenly very angry, he corrected himself pointedly. "For *us*! Please remember that your highly-placed friends are fully aware of the circumstances which link our families!" His voice had become uncharacteristically sharp and his mother blinked.

"You have become very hard, Akitada," she said reproachfully. "I have always had only your own good in mind. The Hiratas can do nothing for your career. You simply must make a good marriage. I had thought of Takeda's daughter or one of the Otomo girls. Their fathers have considerable influence at court."

"I don't care!"

She shook her head sadly. "I know. That has always been the trouble with you. I, on the other hand, have a responsibility to my family. And I bear it alone! Your sisters are still unmarried."

There it was again. The guilt. His sisters' imminent doom was once again held over his head. His mother was fond of painting heart-rending pictures of their ending up as spinster aunts, running errands and nursing children and aged parents like unpaid servants. Should one of them find a husband, he would no doubt be a penniless, rude country bumpkin who would beat her. Or, worst of all, she might linger in misery as third or fourth consort of a nobleman under the cruel rule of the first wife.

He stiffened his back and said firmly, "No, Mother. I will not offer Tamako anything less than the status of first wife."

"Very well," she said with a sniff, and clapped for her maid. Akitada rose and bowed. His audience was over.

◆

He walked to his morning classes unhappily, thinking of his mother and of changes for which he was not ready. In the future, he would have to consider a wife, and eventually children, in every decision he made. There would be more financial constraints. He was taking on a new family at a time when he was scarcely able to provide for the old one.

He felt immediately guilty for his reluctance and reminded himself how lucky he was to win this slender, intelligent and lovely girl to share his life. And, in fairness, perhaps she, too, would be troubled at the prospect.

Caught up in his uncomfortable reflections, Akitada passed Mibu Road, the turn-off to the university, and absent-mindedly entered the greater imperial enclosure, turning his steps towards the ministry as if he were headed for his usual workplace. It was still early, but already clerks and scribes were rushing past him on their way to their various bureaus and offices. When he realized his mistake, he decided to look in on Seimei.

The old man was crouched over documents, taking rapid notes with his spidery brush strokes. He looked up anxiously, but brightened when he saw Akitada. "Good morning, sir." Rising, he bowed and said, "I found some records of the holdings of Prince Yoakira in the archives of the Bureau of Revenue and am making a copy for you. The papers must be returned before someone asks questions."

"Good man!" Akitada reached for the document and ran his eye over it. "Heavens!" he said. "Such wealth!"

"Yes. Five manors near the capital, one palatial in size, some thirty-five others all over the country, and huge rice acreage in the richest provinces, of which over two hundred acres are tax-exempt. I have made friends with a clerk in the Records Office. In time I may be able to consult the wills on file there."

Akitada nodded, leafing through the documents.

"But sir!" said Seimei, "I have become even more uneasy. Everyone at court is content to let matters rest. Lord Sakanoue, who has laid claim to a large portion of the estate as dowry of his bride, and who was never well liked before, has been received by both the emperor and the chancellor."

Akitada angrily tossed the papers down. "I am not surprised," he said grimly. "He married the granddaughter for gain and is said to be the grandson's guardian. All the more reason to keep on asking questions. Such wealth is a tremendous temptation to an unscrupulous man. It opens doors to him which would otherwise be closed. I want you to find out whatever you can." When he turned to leave, he remembered something else. "Oh, and also ask about a young man called Okura. He placed first in last year's examination, and must have received a good post in the administration."

"Okura? Wasn't that the name of the young gentleman who ran into Tora a few days ago?"

Akitada frowned. "Surely not! That silly fop? But I believe you are right! What an unimpressive figure he makes! Did he say he worked in the Ministry of Ceremonial? Well, see what you can find out about him! He may be connected with Professor Hirata's problem."

◆

Akitada's classes passed uneventfully. He had finally managed to accustom himself to his subject and charges and even enjoyed himself. With the late Prince Yoakira's wealth still fresh in his mind, he had set the class a topic on tax exemptions for members of the imperial family. This had produced some very intelligent and original comments from the students, but none more so than young Minamoto's, who had argued forcefully against the practice.

Still, many of his students showed a woeful lack of accuracy in Chinese. This was not his subject, but Akitada decided to stretch his legs by calling on his colleagues in the Chinese faculty.

He found only Ono and the student Ishikawa in the main hall. Both were grading student papers.

"The master is in the library," Ono informed Akitada, "but he is preparing for his poetry reading and must not be disturbed." He attempted to soften this news by many bows and profuse apologies, twisting his body, rubbing his hands together, and bobbing his head up and down, so that Akitada was forcibly reminded of Oe calling him "squirrel." Ishikawa watched the performance, a sneer on his handsome face.

"No matter," said Akitada. "It is nothing of great importance."

"Genius needs the utmost privacy," Ono insisted. "Perhaps Mr. Ishikawa or I may be of assistance?"

So it was *Mr.* Ishikawa now. Akitada glanced at the young man, who acknowledged his surprise with a raised eyebrow. Turning his back on him, Akitada asked Ono, "Is there some arrangement by which weaker students receive tutoring in Chinese? I am afraid I have discovered some dunces in my class."

"Oh," said Ono, "if they can pay, we can always find a senior student to work with them. Of course, if the student comes from one of the great families, he will have his own tutor already. But I hope you are not too severe? It is only rarely that we have someone as talented as Mr. Ishikawa."

Forced to acknowledge Ishikawa's presence, Akitada remarked to him, "Yes. I have been told that you are favored to win first place in the next examination. My compliments."

"Thank you," Ishikawa said complacently, adding, "Unfortunately that is still many months away."

Irritated by the other's assurance, Akitada nodded, saying, "Quite right! An uncertain business, apparently. I am told that the last favorite did not win after all."

Ono cut in, "Oh, that was a shock, to be sure! But it happens only rarely that a young man produces superior work so suddenly at the last moment. Surely it is not likely to happen this time. Not at all!"

Ishikawa smiled. "I'm not worried," he drawled. "After all, I have worked too hard and for too long a time to miss out now. Oh, no! I am quite certain of success."

Akitada did not like Ishikawa's tone. It was not so much his arrogant certainty that troubled him, as a hint of threat. After a trivial comment about the weather, he left to prepare the next day's lessons.

When Tora arrived with his master's good robe and hat, Akitada was still bent over his notes.

"You'd better change, sir," Tora cried. "It's almost time to leave for the professor's dinner."

"So late already!" Akitada rubbed his eyes and stretched. "Thank you, Tora." Suddenly the prospect of this evening's meeting overwhelmed him. He rose. "Help me out of this gown. And I suppose I had better wash my hands and face. See if you can find some water."

"Shouldn't you go to a barber?" Tora asked.

Akitada ran a hand around his chin. "Why? I never shave before dinner."

Tora grumbled but went for the water.

After Akitada had splashed his face and washed his hands, he patted down his hair before a mirror. Tora stood by holding the robe, his head cocked, watching Akitada with a broad grin. "You do look like a nervous suitor," he pronounced with a chuckle.

Akitada swung around. "How did you know?"

"Oh, it figures. First your lady mother insisted on selecting this robe. Then she had her maid sponge it. Then she mixed some incense and perfumed it personally. She said you're careless with your clothes." Tora chuckled and brought one of the sleeves to his nose. Inhaling deeply, he staggered a bit, cried, "Mmmm!" and rolled up his eyes comically. "The young lady will swoon! I can't wait to see it."

"Don't be ridiculous!" Akitada snapped, snatching the robe

away from him. "I am merely going for a dinner at the house of friends. And you are not needed."

"Sorry, sir." Tora grinned broadly. "Lady Sugawara's orders. You are to be accompanied by your servant."

Akitada glared at him, but Tora immediately put on an injured look. "Oh, very well," Akitada said grudgingly, slipping into the gray silk robe and belting it. Tora looked pleased and handed him the tall black hat.

Akitada slapped it on, saying impatiently, "Let's go then!"

Outside he strode out so quickly that Tora had trouble keeping up with him. "Wait," he cried, when Akitada passed through the university gate with flying skirts and his chin in the air. "There's no hurry if you're not going to stop at the barber's first."

Akitada came to a halt. Before him lay the green expanse of the Divine Spring Garden in the evening sunlight. On an impulse he crossed the street.

"Where are you going now?" Tora panted behind him.

"I want to take a quick look at the pavilion where the poetry reading is to be staged tomorrow. It will only take a minute."

But the rustic gate was guarded tonight, and the man barred their way. "I'm very sorry, sir, but the park is closed to the public today and tomorrow," he told Akitada.

"I am one of the professors," said Akitada, "and came to have a look at the preparations."

Eyeing the visitor's finery and his servant, the guard bowed and stepped aside. "In that case, since the gentleman is part of tomorrow's event, I am sure it will be all right."

The park was very beautiful at this time. The setting sun slanted through the branches, gilding the new leaves and spilling liquid gold on the gravel paths. Birds sang, the scent of flowers teased the senses, and the path took mysterious turns among fresh ferns and flowering azaleas. The haunting fragrance in the air reminded Akitada of Tamako and his imminent proposal of marriage. When he and Tora turned a bend, he saw that a gigantic wisteria had grown through a willow, mingling its heavy purple blooms with the pale green curtain of the willow's sweeping boughs. Suddenly his spirits lifted. Surely all would be well. They had been friends too long to make things awkward between them.

The next curve brought them within view of the lake and the emperor's summer pavilion. Akitada stopped to admire the scene. It was one of the prettiest sights in the capital. The fragile red-lacquered balconies and the brilliant blue tiled roof rose against the solid green of the park. Gilded dolphin finials and bells at the ends of the curved eaves sparkled in the rays of the setting sun. As they watched, a breeze stirred the tree tops and raised tiny wavelets of shimmering gold on the blue water.

"Amida!" gasped Tora at Akitada's shoulder. "This is what the gardens of the Western Paradise must be like. That lake is really big. Look at those boats. And there's an island with a temple on it, just like in that picture in your mother's room."

"It *is* pretty," said Akitada, thinking back to his student days when he spent hours fishing on the small island, and attended boating parties with friends on lantern-lit summer evenings. He saw that the preparations for the poetry contest had already begun. The boats were lined up on the shore, ready for tomorrow's guests. The expanse of white sand extending from the steps of the pavilion to the waterline was neatly raked, and on the broad veranda, already plunged into deep shadows, he could make out stacks of dark cushions.

Tora was more interested in the lake. "What are those buildings back there on the far shore?" he asked.

"One is called the eastern fishing pavilion. The other is the waterfall pavilion because next to it an artificial waterfall flows into the lake. There are two more just like them, but you cannot see them from here. On occasion the emperor and his court use all of them for their outings."

"Really?" Tora peered, then plunged into the undergrowth separating them from the lakeshore to get a better look, while Akitada waited, amused, on the path.

Suddenly he heard a cry followed by a colorful string of curses, and then Tora shouted, "Hey! Come here and look at this!"

Akitada entered the shrubbery more cautiously, moving the

brambles away from his silk robe. He found Tora bent over the sprawling figure of a young woman in a blue cotton robe. She lay on her side, her arms and legs flung carelessly among the reeds growing from the mud near the water's edge, and she looked very dead.

Akitada stepped carefully around the body on the soggy ground, saw the protruding tongue and purple cast of her skin, and recognized her instantly. She was the girl who had taken lute lessons from Professor Sato, and she had been strangled.

"Some bastard choked her to death," Tora said unnecessarily.

Akitada reached down and touched her cheek. It was soft, still childishly round, but dusted with a light coating of the white powder common among women of the upper classes and prostitutes. The skin felt faintly warm, not yet clammy. When he reached for her arm and moved it, it bent easily. The fingers were limp, skin and nails quite clean except for slight traces of mud where they had rested on the ground.

"Not long ago," he said, straightening up, and scanning the surroundings. The reeds around the body were only trampled where he and Tora had walked. "I wonder what she was doing in the park when it is closed."

"That killer may still be around," said Tora. "Shall I go have a look?"

"Yes, but don't go far."

Frowning, Akitada looked at the girl's body, then bent down to turn her fully on her back. As she rolled, her blue gown parted, revealing a dingy white cotton under-robe. He stood up again and began searching the ground between the body and the foot path, but found nothing. Returning to her, he squatted down again and gently lifted her chin. Deep red and purple streaks marked the white skin of her neck.

"Not a soul in sight," said Tora behind him, pushing through the reeds. He saw the body with its disordered clothes and cursed. "So he raped her first."

"I don't think so," said Akitada. "Her clothes are clean enough and uncreased. If she had been raped, she would surely have struggled."

"But her sash is undone! No respectable female walks around with her gown hanging open like that. If she wasn't raped, she was cooperating. And why would the guy choke her to death if she was willing?"

"A puzzle. Take a look at her neck! When a man strangles someone with his bare hands, he leaves finger marks. I read once that these can be measured and compared to the suspect's hands. But this woman was not strangled by hand; she was choked to death with a piece of fabric, possibly her missing sash. Did you see anything like it on your search?"

Tora shook his head. "A sash? No. You want me to look again?"

"No. The light is getting poor and the place is too large. I must go report the murder to the local warden. You stay here!"

At the gate, Akitada found the guard stretched out across the path, dozing. "Get up," he snapped, bringing the man stuttering to his feet. "There's been a murder committed within the past hour. Who has entered or left the park during that time?"

The man gaped and protested volubly that nobody, apart from Akitada and Tora, had been admitted or departed while he was on duty. "All the gates were closed two hours ago. Only authorized personnel are admitted, and only through this gate, sir," he cried. "You saw yourself that I stopped you and your man."

Akitada raised his eyebrows. "You did not seem to be very alert just now," he pointed out. "Are you certain there were no other visitors?"

"Yes, sir! And I was just sitting down for a minute. You may be sure I keep my eyes open at all times. This time of year the park is full of all sorts of riffraff."

"Then you did not see a young woman in a blue cotton gown going in? Medium height, about eighteen or nineteen, and pretty?"

The guard's eyes grew round. "Was it her that's been killed? Amida! I know the one you mean. She's a regular almost. Comes here quite often. Always comes alone and leaves alone." He placed a dirty finger on his nose and winked. " 'Course that's not to say she spends her time alone once she gets here, eh? The young gen-

tlemen from the university must have their fun! Hah, hah! Live
and let live, I always say."

Akitada said coldly, "Not in this case. So you did admit her
even though the park is supposed to be closed."

"Oh, no, sir! I didn't see her today. She must've gone in before I went on duty."

"Very well. Keep your eyes open and detain anyone who tries
to leave. The murderer may still be inside. I am going to see the
warden now."

The left division of the city administration, *Sakyo Shiki*, was in
the block just south of the university. It also housed the office of
the warden for this quarter. Akitada reported to a businesslike elderly man who immediately dispatched a runner to police headquarters, then sent a contingent of constables to the park before
taking down Akitada's statement. This took some time, and when
Akitada finally returned to the park gate, a group of red-coated
police were just entering at a trot. He walked in after them with a
nod to the gate guard, but suddenly there was a peremptory
"Halt!" behind him.

He turned. A tall, middle-aged officer in the uniform of a police captain, red robe, bow and quiver of arrows, was striding pur-
posefully towards him. The handsome bearded face was scowling.
"What are you doing here?" he snapped. "This park is closed.
Identify yourself and explain your business!"

Akitada obeyed meekly. The other man's glance sharpened,
but he did not relent. "So!" he said curtly. "I'm Kobe. Captain of
police. Show me the body!"

Akitada led the way. They found Tora and the policemen argu-
ing. Kobe barked an order, and his men retreated. Tora joined
Akitada as they watched Kobe making a preliminary examination
of the site and the body. When the captain was done, he walked
over to his men, gave some orders, and they dispersed. Then he
came back to Akitada and said, "Strangled, and not long ago. Two
hours, perhaps less." Again his sharp eyes studied Akitada, who
nodded. "I am having the park combed for the killer. You must
have found her shortly after it happened. Did you move the body?"

Akitada explained and, with Tora's assistance, demonstrated the girl's original position. "She looked as if she had been flung into the reeds," he said.

Kobe looked at the body, the trampled reeds and torn shrubbery and said sourly, "Too bad people feel the need to meddle. No telling how much evidence has been destroyed." After a moment's awkward silence, he added grudgingly, "But I suppose you didn't do too much harm. She's a commoner, but not a street girl, I think. About six or seven months pregnant."

"What?" Akitada flushed with embarrassment at his oversight. "I am afraid I do not have much experience in such matters," he mumbled, reddening even more at the admission. "She looked merely heavy to me."

The other man sighed. "Never mind," he said. "At your age I didn't know any better myself. You're not a married man, I take it?"

Akitada shook his head. "Not yet."

Kobe's lips twitched. Then he said, "Well, the coroner has to confirm it. Her sash is gone. I don't suppose you've seen it?"

"No. We looked in the immediate vicinity. It is probably red brocade, a particularly fine grade."

At this Kobe's eyebrows shot up, and Akitada elaborated. "I recognized her. She is a young woman I saw briefly about a week ago. At that time she was wearing the same sort of clothing, and I noticed the unusually expensive sash, because it did not match the rest of her clothes. I am afraid I do not know her name."

"Where did you see her? What was she doing?"

"She was leaving the music building of the university after a lute lesson."

"Lute lessons? From a music professor? A common girl like her?"

Not liking the captain's tone somehow, Akitada said stiffly, "Nevertheless, that is how I came to see her."

"What is this professor's name and where does he live?"

This would hardly endear him to Sato, Akitada thought. For a moment he was tempted to distract Kobe from the music professor by telling him what the gate guard had said about the girl, but he decided against it. A man as efficient as this one would natu-

HALF PRICE BOOKS

EST. 1972

Half Price Books #119
1075 East Golf Road
Schaumburg, IL 60173-4505
(847) 995-0240

07-01-21 1:10 PM
Store #0119 / Cashier MKoh119 / Reg 1
Sale # 373085

SALE TRANSACTION

Rashomon Gate	306834193U
1 @6.99	$6.99
The Adventures of Robin Hood	305772227U
1 @9.99	$9.99

2 Items in Transaction

Subtotal	$16.98
Sales Tax (10.0% on $16.98)	$1.70
TOTAL	$18.68

PAYMENT TYPE

Cash	$20.00
CHANGE	$1.32

Thanks for shopping at Half Price Books!

H 0 2 0 1 1 9 0 0 1 3 7 3 0 8 5 4

HALF PRICE BOOKS

YOUR FAVORITE LOCAL BOOKSTORE. EVERYWHERE.

WHEN OUR STORES ARE CLOSED, JUST OPEN YOUR BROWSER. SHOP HPB.COM FOR MILLIONS MORE TREASURES ONLINE.

JOIN THE HPB EMAIL LIST AT HPB.COM/JOIN & GET A 10% OFF COUPON TO SAVE ON YOUR NEXT PURCHASE IN STORE.

STORE RETURN POLICY

Cash refunds and charge card credits on all merchandise are available within 7 days of purchase with receipt. Merchandise charged to a credit card will be credited to your account. Exchange or store credit only for returns made with a gift receipt within 30 days of purchase date. Exchange or store credit will be issued for merchandise returned within 30 days with receipt. Cash refunds for purchases made by check are available after 12 business days, and are then subject to the time limitations stated above. Please include original packaging and price tag when making a return. Proper I.D. and phone number may be required where permitted. We reserve the right to limit or decline refunds.

Gift cards cannot be returned for cash, except as required by law.

The personal information you provide is confidential and will not be sold, rented or disclosed to a third party for commercial or other purposes, except as may be required by law.

HALF BOOKS

rally interrogate the guard. "His name is Sato," he said. "I do not know his address."

"Hmm." Kobe thought for a moment, looking at the body of the girl again. "It gives us a place to start. I don't suppose any of the faculty are still about at this hour?"

"I doubt it."

"Sir?" Tora was becoming restive. He pulled Akitada's sleeve, whispering, "It's getting very late. The Hiratas are waiting."

Akitada recalled himself to his own problems. "Yes, of course, Tora. I forgot." Turning to the captain, he said, "If you don't need us any further tonight, I am late for an important appointment."

Kobe looked Tora up and down and asked, "Tora? Are you the one your master picked up on the highway after someone tried to rob him?"

Tora grinned. "The very same, sir," he said proudly.

Akitada stared at Kobe in speechless surprise. "How could you know about that?" he asked.

Kobe's eyes twinkled suddenly. He clearly enjoyed the effect he had created. "Oh," he said, "in my business it's a good idea to keep my ears open. In fact, the only reason I didn't arrest you two on the spot was that I recognized your name. There was a lot of talk in this city about the way you handled those renegade monks." The corner of his mouth twitched again and he almost smiled. "But don't let me keep you. I shall know how to find you if I have further questions."

"Oh," stammered Akitada, "I see. Yes. Thank you."

They hurried away. Near the gate they ran into a group of constables who were dragging along an old ragged beggar. Worried about their lateness, Akitada rushed past them, but Tora hung back to ask a question.

When he caught up, he said, "They found that beggar hiding in some bushes near one of the gates and arrested him. Seems like he had a woman's sash in his sleeve."

Akitada stopped and looked back at the group. "That old man? Impossible! He looks too frail to lift a baby, let alone a full-grown pregnant woman."

He started towards the constables, but Tora grabbed his sleeve. "No, you can't! You have promised the Hiratas and your mother. Besides that captain looked smart enough to figure that out for himself."

Akitada nodded reluctantly.

When they had left the park and were rushing along Second Avenue, Tora said, "So she was pregnant! I thought so. I wonder what that means."

Akitada did not answer.

"That fellow Sato? Her teacher? You suppose it's his kid?" Tora persisted.

"Hmm."

"Maybe he killed her because she was blackmailing him."

"What? Will you please be quiet, Tora? I am thinking!"

Tora grinned, barely refraining from another quip about anxious suitors. They covered the rest of the distance without talking. Akitada's face wore a distracted, anxious look, and he had started to perspire, more from nerves than their rapid walk.

As it turned out, he need not have worried.

The minute he knocked on the Hiratas' gate, it flew open. Tamako herself stood before him, holding up a lantern and peering up at him anxiously. In the golden light, her slender figure looked like an apparition against the darkness of the garden behind. She wore a fine gown, but in the glow of the lantern, Akitada saw that her face was pale and tense.

"Thank heaven," she cried. "Here you are at last! I've been waiting forever. Where have you been?"

As her tone did not imply a flattering impatience to be with her future husband, Akitada was taken aback. "Has something happened?" he asked.

"No. I must talk to you."

Akitada sent Tora along to the kitchen quarters and explained the reason for their delay.

Tamako stood, her head lowered, swinging the lantern a little. "Oh," she said when they were alone. "Please forgive me! How terrible! The poor girl. I did not know."

"How could you have known? What is wrong?"

"Oh, Akitada!" It was a mere breath. She was standing close to him in the darkness, both of them enveloped by the fragrance of wisteria, peonies and a thousand nameless other blossoms. She was trembling, and he felt a powerful urge to touch her. But when he put his hand on her shoulder, she stepped away from him quickly.

"Please!" Her voice was tight and urgent. "I know that Father has spoken to you about marriage. But you must not do it. I beg you, if you care for me at all . . . like the sister you said I was to you . . . do not make an offer tonight, or ever! Oh, Akitada, I am so sorry, but I simply cannot marry you."

"But why not?" Aghast, he stepped closer but she flinched away again.

"Do not ask me why. I beg you to make this easy for me, and I shall always be grateful."

SIX

THE KAMO PROCESSION

*T*he rest of that evening would always hold a vaguely nightmarish quality for Akitada. He had informed Hirata that there would be no marriage, taking the blame upon himself by claiming the uncertainty of his future and his obligation to his family. Hirata had accepted his refusal without comment.

The subsequent dinner was a dismal affair. Tamako sat beside Akitada with downcast eyes, pushing her food around and eating very little, while her father looked sadly at them, sighing deeply from time to time.

At home another confrontation awaited him. His mother was still up and received the news as a personal insult.

"May I ask who broke off the engagement? And why?" she snapped.

Akitada's heart sank. He foresaw problems when his family met Tamako on the occasion of the Kamo procession. "I presumed on our friendship," he said. "It was completely my mistake."

"I see. Then *your* offer was rejected. What an affront! And to think that a Sugawara consented to marry a mere Hirata!" His mother's eyes flashed with anger.

"It was not like that," Akitada protested. Fear for Tamako caused him to add more sharply, "And I hope you and my sisters will remember tomorrow to treat Tamako with the respect due to a friend of the family."

His mother drew herself up stiffly. "Do not take it upon yourself to teach me manners! My grandfather was a direct descendant of Emperor Itoku, and I have served in the palace. I shall always know what is due our guests. You may leave! It is past my bedtime."

◆

The morning of the Kamo procession dawned splendidly. It was a holiday, dedicated to the guardian spirit of the capital city, and an excuse for high and low to enjoy the final days of spring. Tora had rented the high-wheeled ox cart at sunrise and was now backing it up to the veranda of the main house so that the Sugawara ladies could enter it without dirtying their skirts in the courtyard.

Akitada's sisters emerged first, preening in their prettiest gowns and chattering excitedly. They were not twenty yet, and a mystery to Akitada who had spent many years away from home and only remembered them as a couple of round-faced children who seemed to follow him everywhere. Since his return he had decided that they had become silly but good-hearted girls. Today he met their exuberance without so much as a smile. The sight of their brother's joyless face caused them to fall abruptly silent and climb into the carriage without further ado.

Not so Lady Sugawara. She arrived dressed in a gorgeous rose-colored Chinese robe embroidered with peonies, a part of her dowry, but came to an abrupt halt when she saw the plain, woven carriage.

"You do not expect me to ride in this, do you?" she asked Akitada icily. "We have never attended a public affair in a rented conveyance. Our own family carriage with our crest was always drawn up behind our viewing stand."

"We no longer have the privilege of a private carriage, mother," Akitada pointed out wearily.

"And it appears my son no longer has friends who will oblige him with theirs," his mother shot back nastily.

Akitada sighed inwardly. He had offended and would have to soothe his mother's temper. "My sisters have looked forward to this treat for years," he reminded her, "and without you neither they nor our guest will be able to attend the procession."

Lady Sugawara tossed her head, but entered the carriage without further protest.

Akitada saw his family off before turning his own steps towards the Hirata residence.

The weather, poised between spring and summer, made the Kamo festival an occasion for romance. Even the most strictly raised young ladies were permitted light flirtations with young gentlemen without incurring censure. As Akitada walked, he saw young couples strolling towards First Avenue, where the procession would pass on its way from the emperor's palace to the Kamo shrines outside the city. They were dressed in their best finery and wore hollyhock blossoms, sacred to the Kamo virgin, on their hats and in their hair.

Akitada wished he had arranged for a sedan chair. Until last night he had looked forward to the privilege of walking beside Tamako as her acknowledged suitor. Now the arrangement was awkward for both of them, but all the chair bearers were long since committed,

Tamako was ready when he arrived at the Hirata house. She had never looked more beautiful. The many-layered silk robes, reds and pinks under shades of gradually darkening greens, suited her slender, elegant beauty. In her hand, she carried the straw hat with the veil worn by all women of good family when walking in public, and her glossy black hair brought out golden tones in her face. Akitada recalled that Tamako spent much time in the sun, tending to her garden. It was unfashionable, but he admired the healthy glow of her skin. Then their eyes met, and both looked away simultaneously.

"Good morning, Akitada," Tamako said, bowing formally. "It's very kind of you to come. Are you certain you don't mind taking me along?"

"Of course not." He managed a smile. "You look very elegant. I am sorry but I did not get a chair. Will you mind walking?"

"Not at all. It is a beautiful day. Shall we go?"

In the willow above them, a bird burst into song, and behind her the garden shimmered in the morning sun.

Akitada nodded miserably. They had never spoken to each other like strangers.

Tamako paused at the gate and bent to an earthenware pot which held bunches of flowering hollyhocks.

"I did not know what color your robe would be," she said, "so I cut some of each color. I think this white one will look well. What do you think?"

"Yes. It was kind of you to remember. I forgot that also."

"Don't be silly. I have a whole garden full of hollyhocks!"

She reached up and fastened the white blossoms and green leaves to his court hat while he bent his head. Tamako was tall for a woman, and her face, intent on the task of arranging the blooms, was close to his. Akitada's eyes were on her lips, very pretty lips, slightly open so that he could just see a tip of her tongue between the white teeth. A subtle fragrance escaped from her sleeves and Akitada closed his eyes. A fierce wave of despair seized him and he stepped back abruptly.

"Oh," she breathed, her eyes flying to his.

He bent and caught up a cluster of pale pink blossoms. Uncertainly he looked at her hair, gleaming bluish-black in the sun and caught on her back with a broad white silk bow. "Where should I . . . ?"

"I think in my sash. The hat would crush them in my hair. Here, I can do it." She took the hollyhocks from his nerveless fingers and tucked them in her sash. Putting on the hat and tying it, she arranged the veil and said, "All ready."

They walked most of the way without saying much. Tamako commented on the delightful weather, and Akitada agreed that it was so. He really wanted to ask her why she could not marry him. All night he had lain awake wondering. Was there another man, perhaps? It was the most likely explanation. At the thought he felt his stomach twist with helpless anger. He had been a fool not to ask her himself months ago. But would not her father have known of another attachment? Perhaps he was too poor? Too tall and gangly? Too ugly with his heavy, beetling brows and his long face? He walked beside her in silent misery.

Two blocks later he pointed out the antics of some children and Tamako remarked that it was a very happy time for the youngsters. The thought threw them into an even deeper depression until the passing of an elegant carriage caused both of them to speak at the same moment, to apologize, and to fall silent again. The invisible barrier between them made their time together extremely distressing to Akitada. When they finally arrived at the viewing stand, he felt more relief that their walk was over than worry about his mother's reception of Tamako.

Lady Sugawara and his sisters had been watching their approach. Akitada made the introductions, and Tamako stepped forward to bow deeply before his mother. She said, "This humble person is quite unable to express her feelings at your ladyship's goodness."

"Not at all. Not at all. Welcome, child!" Lady Sugawara's voice was warm, and she smiled in the kindest manner. "I see," she said, "my boorish son has neglected to provide you with a sedan chair. I apologize for him. Please come and sit with us!" She patted a cushion which had been placed between herself and her daughters.

Tamako thanked her and bowed again before greeting Akitada's sisters and taking her place beside them.

Having seen her installed, Akitada cast an imploring glance at his mother, who looked back blandly. He made his excuses, claiming that he had to meet friends, and escaped. It was a cowardly act, but he consoled himself that his mother would have resented his presence as a sign of distrust.

Miserably he wandered along First Avenue towards the gate

through which the procession would leave the city on its way to the shrines on the banks of the Kamo River. Neither he nor his family intended to follow it the whole way.

The viewing stands stretched along the entire length of the parade route and were already well filled with onlookers. Above some flew banners with the crests of the ruling families of the realm. Between the stands or behind them, elegant painted and gilded carriages of the nobility had been placed side by side, the oxen unhitched and the shafts propped up on supports. From beneath the woven shades the scented and many-colored sleeves of court ladies protruded. Passing dandies guessed at the occupants and made flattering comments on the color combinations in hopes of eliciting a giggle or even a wave with a fan.

The crowds thickened near the palaces of the great nobles along the southern side of the street. Here and there the imperial guard was in evidence, mounted on prancing horses, their bows and quivers slung over their shoulders.

Suddenly Akitada saw a familiar face. Young Minamoto was seated on one of the stands. Next to him was a tall man in his thirties. The stand was draped with the Minamoto crests, and Akitada wondered if the tall man might be Lord Sakanoue. On an impulse he crossed the street. He saw that the boy was wearing particularly fine robes, but his face was pale and set. He seemed to look at the spectacle in the street with blank eyes. The man next to him wore a haughty and forbidding expression. The slitted eyes and impassive features seemed to belong to a statue rather than a living, breathing human being.

Then the boy saw Akitada and rose to bow. Turning to his companion, he said, "Allow me to present one of my professors. Doctor Sugawara, my lord."

The impassive eyes flicked Akitada with a glance. The stony head barely nodded.

"This is Lord Sakanoue, my guardian," the boy explained.

Akitada bowed, saying with a smile, "I had hoped to make your acquaintance, my lord, to tell you what a fine student your ward is. Now I am glad to see that you are giving him a day's out-ing. He deserves it. He has been working very hard."

"It is his duty to work hard," said the other curtly, in a surpris-ingly high, nasal voice. "It is also his duty to attend official events. As his teacher you should know this."

Akitada found the man's words offensive and therefore did not acknowledge them. Instead he turned to the boy again, saying, "You must be enjoying your visit with your family."

The boy colored. "My sister could not attend," he murmured, "and there is no one else."

"You may continue your conversation some other time," barked the high voice of Sakanoue. "The procession is about to start. It is very unseemly to stand about chatting when people have come to observe."

The dismissal was as rude as it was final. Akitada bowed and withdrew without another word. But he saw the tears of shame in the boy's eyes and blamed himself for having provoked the un-pleasant scene with his impulsive action.

He continued his stroll along the stands worrying about the boy, following the rest of the sight-seeing and socializing crowd ab-sentmindedly until the noise in one place caused him to look up. He saw four stands, elaborately decked out with flags, greenery and hollyhocks and filled with a large crowd of boisterous celebrants in silk robes of every shade and pattern. The Fujiwara crest flew gaily in the breeze above all four stands. Akitada scanned the faces. Somewhere in the middle he found the rotund figure and smiling face of his friend Kosehira. Evidently he had strayed into a party hosted by Kosehira, and he ducked his head and passed by quickly.

But Kosehira had already seen him. He was shouting, "Aki-tada! Akitada! Up here!" When Akitada turned, Kosehira had climbed upon his seat and was waving excitedly. "By all that's holy! It *is* you! Come up here, man!"

Akitada feigned pleased surprise and clambered up. Kosehira made room next to himself, found a pillow for Akitada, intro-duced him around and insisted he stay for the procession. In the distance sounded the great drum, and they could hear the runners' first shouts to "make way." Akitada settled down to enjoy himself.

The procession came their way so quickly that there was little time to exchange news with Kosehira. In the vanguard walked the Shinto priests in their white robes. They were followed by officials in bright yellow silk who carried large red and gold fans on long poles.

Someone pressed a lacquer box filled with elegant snacks into Akitada's hand, and Kosehira urged him to eat. Just then flag bearers passed, followed by an ox-drawn carriage covered with blooming wisteria branches. Their sight and scent reminded Akitada of Tamako and he closed the lacquer box on his lap. He had no appetite.

"Isn't he magnificent?" asked Kosehira, pointing to the huge ox. "He belongs to Sakanoue, who has donated him to the Kamo shrine. Rumor has it that that there have been bad omens about his marriage."

Sakanoue again! Akitada glanced at the beast, heavily garlanded with wisteria, draped with orange silk tassels, and led by a handsome youth in a colorful court robe. It was more likely that the arrogant man he had just met was more concerned about currying favor with the emperor than buying off the gods.

Immediately behind the ox rode the emperor's messenger to the Kamo deity. A handsome young man in costly robes, he sat his horse well. The spirited horse was a rare dappled gray and elicited cries of admiration. He pranced, causing the red silk tassels hanging from his head to bounce, and the young man on his back laughed out loud. When his eyes fell on Kosehira's stand, he flashed a broad smile towards them and waved before passing on.

"The empress's brother," Kosehira shouted into Akitada's ear over the applause of the crowd. "Not at all bad, considering he was up most of the night with us, drinking and reciting poems." The rest of his words were drowned out by the rhythmic booming of the great drum which made its appearance next. It travelled on another decorated ox-drawn carriage and was beaten by a muscu-

lar giant of a man, stripped to the waist and already glistening
with perspiration in the cool morning air.

Akitada was glad there was no need to make conversation. He
had fallen into a depression, and Kosehira's reference to the poem-
composing nobleman had reminded him of this evening's competition in the Spring Garden, which in turn called to mind the
brutal murder of the girl, his assignment at the university and his
unease about Hirata.

The drum passed, followed by a group of beautifully gowned
and masked dancers who paused briefly before their stand to give
a performance. Kosehira leaned towards him again. "I hear you are
teaching at the university now," he said. "Your talents are wasted,
my friend. Heaven knows there is too much trouble in the world
for a man of your ability to pass his time in the schoolroom."

Akitada sighed. "I don't know what trouble you are thinking
of, but even at a university there may be the occasional puzzle to
solve."

Kosehira raised his eyebrows comically. "A puzzle? You don't
mean it?" he cried, slapping Akitada on the back with a chuckle.
"Wonderful! I want the whole story when it is all done. But look!
Here comes the virgin! Gorgeous litter, isn't it? I'm told the little
princess is the prettiest creature. Some lucky man will take her to
wife some day and make his fortune to boot."

They watched the litter, borne on the shoulders of twenty
young noblemen in matching pale green and light purple robes,
sway past in its gilded glory. Only the virgin's sleeves, many layers
of gauzelike silk, shaded from the palest cream to deepest red,
showed under the decorated curtains which hid her from view.

Akitada's mind was on another young woman and his failure
to take her to wife. He sighed.

"Why so glum?" asked Kosehira. "Is it the problem at the university?"

"That, and other matters."

"Can I help?"

"No. Thank you. But tell me, are you acquainted with Lord
Sakanoue?"

An expression of extreme distaste crossed Kosehira's normally cheerful, round face. "Certainly not. Don't like the fellow," he said. "There's talk that he forced Prince Yoakira's granddaughter to marry him. People say he plans to do her little brother out of his inheritance."

"Is this common gossip?" Akitada asked, surprised.

"Well, yes and no." Kosehira looked uncomfortable. "Some of us who knew the old prince are very concerned. You see, the old man never liked Sakanoue. Sakanoue is not a nice person. I myself witnessed an incident the other day where he pushed ahead of old Lady Kose, the late emperor's nurse. She cried out in alarm, and he said something very rude about senile old hags. I was shocked."

"He is definitely not nice," Akitada agreed. "I just had a taste of his lack of manners myself. The grandson is one of my students, by the way."

Kosehira's eyes widened in surmise.

Akitada added quickly, "No, no. He is not the reason I am at the university. Besides, a man's lack of manners does not necessarily prove that he has criminal intentions."

Kosehira shook his head. "In this instance I don't agree with you," he said. "But in any case it is a very good thing you're there. If anyone can get to the bottom of the affair, it is you. Just be careful! Sakanoue may be dangerous. Incidentally, he is some kind of cousin to the family. There was some talk after the old prince's son died, that he planned to adopt Sakanoue, but he evidently decided against it and raised his grandson instead."

Akitada would have pursued the matter, but Kosehira's other neighbor asked his host a question. On the street, a group of musicians was passing and at that moment they raised their flutes to their lips and played an ancient melody. Instantly Akitada was entranced. This was even better than Sato's lute playing, and it looked a great deal easier. For a moment he considered whether Sato might consent to teach him the rudiments, but that reminded him again of the murdered girl and her relationship with the music teacher. Sato must certainly have been interrogated by the police by now. Perhaps he had even been arrested.

With the flutists, the procession drew to its close. A final group
of white-robed priests passed, and then the spectators fell in behind, following on foot or in their carriages. The stands were
emptying rapidly, and Kosehira turned to Akitada.

"Will you join me in my carriage?" he asked.

"No. I must see my family and a guest home. Besides I have
made the journey many times."

They parted with promises to meet again soon, and Akitada
hurried back. But before he reached their viewing stand, he was
hailed. It was the police captain he had met the day before.

"Glad to run into you," the man greeted him. "If you can spare
the time, I'd like you to come to the jail with me. We have arrested
a suspect in the park murder. He had a woman's red sash on him;
I'd like you to identify it."

The picture of the old beggar flashed through Akitada's mind.
If he was the suspect, he would have to try to get him released, but
first he must see to his family and Tamako. He explained his
dilemma to Kobe and promised to come as soon as he could.

To his surprised relief, he found that Lady Sugawara had invited Tamako to share their noon rice.

"And we will send her home safely in the rented carriage," she
told her son, "since you cannot be trusted to extend the proper
courtesies to a young lady."

Akitada's eyes went to Tamako. She looked calm and nodded
with a little smile. "I told your mother how pleasant our walk
was," she said, "but she insists that I must ride home in style. I am
sure you must be very busy, and we are having a lovely time talking about you."

Akitada's sisters broke into giggles, and his mother smiled in-
dulgently. Somewhat dazed, Akitada saw the ladies into their carriage and gave Tora instructions about taking Tamako home.
Then he hurried to the prison.

The municipal jail was only a few blocks away. He found Kobe
pacing in the guard room, a bare hall primarily decorated with
chains, whips, handcuffs and leg irons hanging from hooks on the
walls.

"Ah. There you are," Kobe said in lieu of a greeting. On a rickety and scarred wooden table lay a bulky paper package tied with cord. Kobe tore it open, and took out a wrinkled length of bright red brocade with a small pattern of flowers and birds in many colors. "Do you recognize it?"

Akitada stepped closer. "It looks like the one the girl wore to her lesson," he said, touching the fabric. The creases were particularly deep in two places. It looked as if the sash had been looped around something, and then pulled and twisted sharply. He glanced at Kobe. "This must have been used to strangle her."

Kobe nodded. He picked up the sash, refolded it, and put it in his sleeve. "Follow me!" he said, heading out the door.

They passed down a long, dingy corridor with many cell doors. Haggard faces appeared at the grates, but none of the prisoners spoke. At the end of the corridor a door opened onto a veranda which looked down into the jail's courtyard, where a dismal group awaited them. Two brutish-looking guards jumped up and jerked a bedraggled figure between them erect. With a thin cry of pain the old beggar staggered to his feet. Because his ankles were chained and his hands tied behind his back, he lost his balance and fell against one of the guards, who immediately clouted him over the head. The old man sagged to his knees again. His chin sank to his chest and he whimpered.

"Why are you holding this poor old man?" Akitada cried.

Kobe shot him a glance. "He is the suspect in the murder."

"Impossible! And what have you done to him? There is blood on his clothes."

"He has been whipped. Such methods are used when suspects refuse to cooperate."

"But he is only an old man. How could he have had the strength to kill that young woman, let alone—"

Kobe interrupted sharply, "May I remind you that we are not alone?"

Akitada flushed. "Why did you bring me here?" he said as sharply.

"I wanted you to hear what he has to say. At first we thought he was simply stubborn and facetious, but I have since had second thoughts." Kobe turned to the group in the yard and shouted, "Umakai? Look at this!" Removing the brocade sash from his sleeve, he held it up.

The beggar continued to sag between the burly guards. One of them kicked him. "Pay attention, you piece of dung!" he snarled. The old man slowly raised his face to look up at the veranda. Akitada's stomach contracted with pity. The old face was bruised and bloodied, and tears ran down the wrinkled cheeks.

"Tell this gentleman who gave you the pretty red sash!" shouted Kobe.

The beggar trembled and shook his head violently. The guard to his left raised a whip, but Kobe stopped him. "Don't worry, Umakai!" he called. "You will not be beaten if you tell us what we want to know. This gentleman was in the park and may have seen the same thing you saw."

The old man looked at Akitada, thought about it, and shook his head again. Kobe frowned. "Listen to me, Umakai," he roared. "I don't have time to waste. Either you talk, or I'll send for the bamboo switches. Do you understand?"

Akitada moved. "Captain Kobe," he said through clenched teeth, "I will not watch an innocent man being beaten. If you wish me to remain, I suggest we go inside, dispense with those two fellows, and give the old man something to drink to loosen his tongue."

Kobe suddenly smiled, his white teeth flashing from his bearded face. "But of course," he said smoothly. "Why not?"

The beggar was taken to the guard room, untied, and settled on an old cushion. Kobe produced a pitcher of wine and poured him a cup. Umakai moved clumsily because his wrists were swollen, but he managed to raise the cup to his mouth and empty it in a single gulp. He gave a deep sigh, and Kobe refilled the cup. The old man drank again. This time he burped and clutched his stomach.

"Are you in pain?" Akitada asked anxiously.

"Not bad, not bad," the old one muttered, giving him his attention for a moment. "Is it true you saw him?" he asked. His eyes were curiously unsteady, shifting about between Akitada, Kobe and the objects in the room.

"I may have," Akitada said cautiously. "What did he look like?"

"What did he look like? Why, he looks like all of them. They all look alike, don't they?"

Akitada thought for a moment. It occurred to him that the beggar must have seen a guard or a policeman. "You mean he wore a uniform?"

Umakai chuckled. "A uniform? I guess you could call it that."

"It was a red coat, wasn't it?" Akitada shot a glance at Kobe, who raised his eyebrows.

The beggar stared at Akitada. "No, a red hat," he said. "Don't you know anything?"

"A red hat!" Akitada looked at Kobe again, who grinned back broadly and nodded.

"But . . . nobody wears a red hat," Akitada protested.

"Oh, I don't know," said Kobe, studying the ceiling. "Ask him the name of the fellow with the red hat!"

Feeling foolish, Akitada turned back to the beggar and asked, "Did he have a name?"

Umakai gave him a pitying look. "Of course! Everybody knows his name. Stupid question! There are hundreds of them all over the place."

Akitada sighed. Kobe must be playing an embarrassing joke on him. The old beggar was clearly mad. But he decided to play along. "Please tell me. I seem to have forgotten it," he said.

He received a sympathetic glance from the old man. "So you've got that trouble too. My head hurts fearfully some days, and I can't remember where I slept the night before. But I would never forget Jizo."

"Jizo?" Akitada turned to Kobe, who was grinning and nodding his head. "Does he mean the god Jizo? The one who protects travellers?"

"And small children," said Kobe. "In fact, that is why mothers sew red hats and bibs for his statues."

Umakai cried, "Now do you remember? He had his red hat on and he gave me a present. Did he give you a present, too?"

"No," said Akitada. "I wish he had. Where did you meet Jizo?"

The old man frowned. "I don't know. Someplace. There's one on the corner of Third Avenue. Third and Suzaku. You go and ask him! Ask him for a present too! And tell him Umakai says hello."

"Thank you. I will. Did you ask Jizo for the pretty red sash?"

"No. I just stuck out my empty bowl as he was passing. And right away he put the pretty red silk in it."

"I see I must get myself a bowl," said Akitada with a straight face. "But isn't the bowl for food? A man can't eat silk when he is hungry."

"Wasn't a bit hungry. Had some bean soup at city hall. The clerks there are my friends. Would you tell them about me?" Umakai's eyes were filling with tears again. "Tell them to come get me! And tell Jizo they took my present away and beat me!"

Akitada turned to Kobe. "Surely . . ." he said.

Kobe walked over to the beggar and helped him up. "Come, Umakai," he said. "We'll find you a nice place to sleep and some hot food. By tomorrow you'll feel much better." He clapped his hands and when a constable appeared, he told him, "Take him away. Give him bedding and see that he gets some food, but lock him up!"

The guard led the shuffling Umakai out.

Kobe turned, smiling broadly. Akitada met his eyes in stony silence.

"I must congratulate you," said the captain, rubbing his hands. "Your method worked. Yesterday the tale sounded like a rigmarole. Now we know that someone in a red hat or cap gave him the sash. He is too simple to make up such a tale."

Akitada could not remember ever having felt so angry. "Since it is now apparent to you," he said icily, "that the man is innocent of the murder and told the truth all along, what other torments can you possibly be planning for him? Any normal man would have been distraught at having put another human being to the torture, but you are evidently saving him for another day. You will either release him immediately with profuse apologies, or I will personally bring charges against you."

Kobe's eyes had narrowed. He remained silent for a minute. Then he said stiffly, "I have been aware of the fact that you disapprove of my methods. Perhaps I should remind you that these methods are mandated by law and depend on the circumstances. Umakai was found on the scene of a crime. In fact, he was the only person there, with the exception of yourself and your servant. Furthermore, he had the weapon, such as it is, on his person. Last night it was not obvious that he was simpleminded. I was afraid that he was shielding an accomplice. Criminals often work with beggars. In any case, I followed the prescribed procedure as I am sworn to. As to your demand that I release him now: It should have occurred to you that he is our only witness to the identity of the killer. Beggars do not, as a rule, have a permanent home. They sleep wherever they happen to find shelter, this time of year often in the street. If I released him, we would not find him again. And the killer might."

Akitada saw the force of the argument. He was about to apologize, when a sudden thought struck him. What if Kobe had arranged this interview not to get Akitada's help, but because he wanted to see if the beggar would identify him? He said brusquely, "Very well. You must do as you think best. Excuse me, but I have delayed my own business too long," and left.

The interview with Kobe and Umakai was a fitting culmination to a day which had been dismal in most respects. In a dark mood, Akitada walked to the university. Beating helpless people who happened to have the bad luck to be in the wrong place struck him as an example of how far a flawed legal system would go to protect the privileged classes. Yet even his own relatively privileged life was no protection against misery—witness his own childhood and his present disappointment. How could he have hoped to find personal contentment with Tamako? He was a great deal better off alone.

He reached the gates of the university in a mood of self-pity and hopelessness. There were no gatekeepers today, but on the steps sat one of the senior students who occasionally ran errands for Hirata and himself. The young man was staring rather fixedly at the park across the street. He was a very plain and gangly fellow, with protruding teeth and round, frightened eyes, and a tendency to startle and drop things. Akitada searched his mind for a name and finally came up with "Nagai." Calling out a greeting, he climbed the steps and stopped before the student.

The youngster stumbled to his feet, looked at him wildly, and bowed. There was a sickly greenish cast to his face and dark circles under his eyes as though he had not slept for weeks.

"Are you feeling quite well, Nagai?" Akitada asked, concerned.

"Yes. Yes, I'm well," stuttered the student, his eyes downcast, his hands clenching and unclenching convulsively at his sides. "Quite well. Thank you, sir."

The young man looked absolutely wretched and was trembling even as he talked. "Had a bit too much to drink in celebration?" Akitada asked sympathetically, recalling some of his own youthful excesses.

The other jumped a little and looked horrified. "Celebration?" he squawked. "No, no celebration. Oh, God, no!"

"Well, don't be foolish! I hope I am not such an ogre that you have to be afraid to tell me. If you'll come with me, I'll brew you some of my tea. You will find it a little bitter, but it will settle your stomach and head. Are you going to the poetry contest in the park tonight?"

Nagai practically shrank into the gate column. "In the park? No! I couldn't go in there! Please excuse me, I'm not feeling well!" He turned and ran off in the direction of the dormitories, leaving Akitada to stare after him.

SEVEN

THE WILLOW QUARTER

*A*fter Tora had seen his master's lady friend home, he returned ox and carriage to the rental stable and walked into town. It was only mid-afternoon and, like most of the other inhabitants of the capital, he had the rest of the day and night off.

Crowds of people were strolling, shopping or sampling food in restaurants or at open stalls. On Suzaku Avenue, smiling celebrants passed back and forth in their best clothes, hollyhock blooms everywhere: in their hats, their sashes, on the saddles and in the bridles of their horses, draped about the horns of their oxen and threaded through the curtains of their carriages. The "good people" rode to parties or picnics, and the commoners walked towards the markets or the Willow Quarter. And everywhere there was merriment: old men sat on temple steps, smiling and nodding to passersby; normally sober officials walked with jaunty steps; and young lovers giggled, holding hands and looking into each other's eyes.

Tora approved but felt lonely. He looked wistfully after the pretty girls with their young admirers. There had been a coy little maid at the Hirata house who had given him a long appraising look when he had helped her mistress down. He had winked back, but she had only tossed her head pertly and flounced away. He wished she were with him now.

On an impulse, he decided to buy her a little gift. Such things could pave the way to future friendly relations.

Strictly speaking there were two markets in the capital, one west and the other east of Suzaku Avenue, but they were open on alternate weeks as a rule. Today, because of the festival, both markets were open and bustling with crowds. Each covered a whole city block, enclosed by permanent one-story shops facing inward. Access was through four gates, and the large central space was filled with temporary stalls, tents, and anyone who wished to spread a sheet and display his wares.

Tora browsed through the western market first, stopping before a fan seller. She had many cheap and colorful paper and bamboo paddles spread out on the ground before her, and there were others dangling from ropes stretched between two poles. He studied the fans, but decided the designs were too crude for a romantic offering. A shop, which sold combs, was also rejected because they were all made of boxwood and far too plain to impress a pretty girl.

With a sigh Tora crossed Suzaku Avenue and entered the other market through its tiled and painted gateway. Tantalizing food smells greeted him. Stands and ambulatory vendors dispensed bean dumplings, fried rice cakes, steamed seafood and noodles in fragrant broth. Tora's mouth watered, but he decided to conserve his limited funds for the evening. He stopped only to buy some pickles, a local specialty of radish slices with red pepper and seaweed. These he carried with him wrapped in a piece of oiled paper, chewing while he wandered about and peered at wares or eyed the girls. When the pickles were gone, he decided this market also had nothing suitable to offer. Enough time had been wasted. Already the setting sun slanted across the rooftops and it would soon be dark. He tossed the paper on a refuse heap near a vegetable stall and left for the Willow Quarter.

Walking northeast, he crossed Suzaku Avenue again and entered a more affluent merchant quarter. Buildings and shop fronts were wider and many of the wealthier merchants lived in large two-storied buildings above their shops.

Halfway down one street, Tora passed a very large silk merchant's premises. It reminded him of the murdered girl and her sash, and he thought he might find something here to please the little maid. He entered, slipping off his shoes, and stepped up to the raised platform of the sales area.

The shop's owner and several clerks were busy waiting on groups of seated customers. In the back a wizened middle-aged woman with a sharp nose and small, hard eyes was bent over ledgers and an abacus.

Tora sat down. The shop's owner, a short man in his early forties with a fleshy face and a thin mustache, glanced over and signalled to a young clerk who came to ask Tora's pleasure.

"I'd like to buy a sash for a young lady. Something bright," said Tora, craning his neck to see the fabrics in front of the other customers.

The young clerk hesitated. "How much was the gentleman prepared to spend?" he asked.

"Oh, you can go as high as twenty coppers," said Tora generously. He felt his lonely status very acutely.

The clerk did not quite sneer—Tora looked too tall and muscular for that—but he said coldly, "You will find the cheaper stuffs in the next street. This is Kurata's. We carry only fine silks and brocades."

"Well," asked Tora, "what's wrong with a small bit of brocade?"

The clerk shook his head. "Even a small bit would cost a great deal more than a string of coppers. We cater mostly to the 'good people' and even supply the palace."

Tora raised his eyebrows. "More than a whole string of coppers?" He looked about him. "You mean that flowered stuff over there might be made into clothes for His August Majesty?"

The clerk nodded.

Tora jumped up and strode to where two officials in their best robes and court hats were discussing several rolls of flowered brocade. Picking up a red one with golden chrysanthemums, he stared at it closely. The clerk ran after him with little cries of dismay, while the two officials watched with surprise.

"You would sell this to His Majesty, would you?" Tora asked the clerk, gathering a piece into his large fist to test its strength.

"Yes, yes," cried the clerk, wringing his hands, "but please don't do that. The fabric is very fragile. Rough hands can quite destroy it."

Tora relinquished the brocade reluctantly. "It's soft all right. Of course I like a bit more color. How much would such a thing cost?"

One of the officials burst into laughter. "He has good taste!" he cried and said to Tora, "Oh, just ten bars of silver. There's enough there for a court robe, if you like. Or perhaps you were thinking of a hunting coat?" His companion guffawed.

Tora regarded them with wrinkled brow. "No. I just want a sash for a little maid I've got my eye on," he told them.

This caused even more merriment. The other official cried, "Why, sir! In that case you may wish to purchase my ox and carriage to impress the lady when you pick her up." This time even the young clerk could not suppress a grin.

"What's going on here?" snapped a sharp voice behind Tora. "What does this fellow want?"

Tora turned and looked down at the shop's owner, or rather at his bald spot, inadequately covered by a topknot thickened with false hair.

"Oh," stuttered the clerk. "Nothing, Mr. Kurata. The gentleman was just inquiring about a sash."

"A sash? You're a fool, Yotsugi. This man cannot afford brocade." The shopkeeper turned to Tora. "A sash from this brocade costs twenty silver pieces, more than someone like you can earn in years. We have nothing for you or your woman. You'd better leave."

Tora looked at the man closely and did not like what he saw. There was meanness in the small eyes and compressed lips. Neither did he appreciate being made the butt of a joke. Turning to the two officials, he said, "I may take you up on your offer just as soon as I start collecting bribes like you fellows." Then he nodded to the clerk and departed.

In the next street he purchased a cheerful cotton sash in a pattern of white cranes flying above blue waves from a properly accommodating shopkeeper and tucked it in his sleeve. A couple of streets farther he found a baker of sweet rice cakes favored by the ladies. He bought an elegantly wrapped box of the most select sweets and put it in his other sleeve. By now it was getting dusk, and Tora turned his steps towards the river.

Between Fourth Avenue and Kyogo Street, along the Kamo River, stretched the Willow Quarter, named after the willows that grew on the bank. Here a lively trade catered to pleasures of the body, from the most basic of food, drink and sex to the more refined aesthetic delights of music and dance.

The sun was gone and twilight had fallen; the streets were already shadowed in darkness, while above still stretched a luminous violet sky with the first faint stars. Ahead Tora saw the gate to the amusement quarter. It sparkled with the lights of many-colored lanterns, and the first faint sounds of music reached his ears.

He increased his pace and passed into a fairyland of lights. They were suspended from the branches of the willows and the eaves of the wine houses, and swayed in the soft breeze which came from across the softly gurgling river. Warm colored light fell on the robes of pretty women who peered from doors and windows and caught the brilliant colors of the elegant robes of wealthy customers strolling along the river.

Tora looked and yearned for the expensive goods on display, but he could not afford the prices charged in the best houses of assignation, or in any houses for that matter. He consoled himself by engaging in lighthearted banter with the pretty girls behind the wooden grilles he passed.

The wine houses and restaurants were not all prohibitively expensive and quite good. Tora had become something of a regular at the Willow, unimaginatively named, but offering excellent value in food, drink and entertainment.

Here he was greeted by the gap-toothed auntie who arranged private entertainments with some of the best courtesans of the quarter.

"Tora-san," she cackled. "We have been expecting you, the girls and I. Surely on the night of the spring festival a strapping, handsome fellow like you will wish to enjoy the clouds and the rain?"

"Auntie-san," said Tora, bowing with a soulful look, "I am your most devoted admirer, but my station in life does not permit me to enjoy the company of ladies such as yourself or your companions. Please accept this insignificant present instead." He presented her with the box of sweets.

"Ooh!" Auntie received the box with delight and peered inside. "Foolish boy!" she cried, giving him a playful slap on the arm, "if you did not waste your money on stupid old women like me, you would warm your august implement in the grotto of a thousand delights tonight. Surely by now the poor bird must be quite worn out looking for its nest. Won't you let Auntie find it a cozy resting place? We'll just put it on account."

"Ah, in that case . . ." Tora leaned forward and whispered in her ear.

She burst into hysterical laughter, shook her finger at him, and cried, "One of these days, my pretty young cock, you'll meet a woman who'll take you at your word. Now run along! Your friends are waiting. Enjoy the food and wine. And maybe, if you like one of the pretties, Auntie will make it right for you."

Tora gave her a bear hug, much to her delight, and then went along the hallway and into a large room where five boisterous men were sitting around a brazier warming bottles of wine.

"You're late, Tora," cried a scrawny fellow with permanently bowed legs and a sunken chest. He was the *tatami*-maker Ueda, his physique the result of generations of Uedas sitting cross-legged and bent over straw mats. "We had to start without you. There's room next to Kichibei."

Tora grinned and flopped down next to a muscular, heavily tatooed porter, who shouted, "Bring more wine! A very thirsty fellow has just arrived."

"He's not the only one," grumbled a pudgy young man in the threadbare blue robe of a minor clerk, turning an empty bottle upside down.

"You'll never make a night of it at your rate, Danjuro!" teased his middle-aged neighbor who was a potter and never could get all the red clay from under his fingernails. "We've pooled our money, Tora. Fifty coppers will cover food, drink and the bounciest little bottom in the quarter."

"Sorry, Osada." Tora pulled the remnants of his wages from his sash and counted the coppers on the string. "Fifteen is all I can spare tonight."

After some cries of protest, Osada said, "Well, you can eat and drink, but it's not enough for any real fun."

Tora handed over the fifteen coppers with a sigh. "I was hoping to bring my own girl," he said, "but I couldn't find one in time."

"You should make your master pay you more," suggested Danjuro. "I plan to celebrate the festival of blossoms properly, among the local 'blossoms.' But then, they don't work for nothing."

"I prefer to do the work myself," Tora said. "You poor fellows must be so out of practice that you have to pay for the action." Danjuro joined in the general laughter and raised his cup to Tora.

"Well put, Tora," applauded the gray-haired man. "Never mind your empty purse!" he told Tora consolingly. "You just eat and drink your fill, and if you should pass out from too much wine, you'll never know what you missed."

"Thanks, Kunisada," laughed Tora. "That's good advice from a pharmacist. I'm parched and starving at the same time. Where's the food?"

A waitress arrived with more warm rice wine. After cheerful discussion, they ordered a feast which included eggs, fish soup, marinated *kisu* fish and boiled chestnuts among other delicacies.

Tora drank deeply from his cup, refilled it, and looked around at the shining faces of his companions. "Here's to good company," he cried. "May we enjoy each other for many years."

"What?" cried Danjuro, moving away from him in mock horror. "Are you mad? I don't care what you think about my prowess, but you are much too bony for my taste. My appetite's for female flesh. I hope you haven't decided to sleep with one of us."

Tora grinned, shaking his head. "Sleeping is about all I'm doing tonight. It's not been my day. I was looking forward to a pleasant afternoon browsing about the markets and shops, but got an earful from a snooty merchant and a couple of crooked officials."

"What happened?" asked Kunisada.

"Any of you fellows know a silk peddler called Kurata?"

"You mean the big shop in Sameushi Street? Everybody here knows Kurata," said Kunisada.

Danjuro confirmed it. "Kurata! Now there's a lucky fellow with lots of money for women! They say he's had every charmer in the quarter at least once."

The potter burst out laughing. "You haven't heard! Kurata won't be back for a while," he said. "His old woman caught him with one of her maids and beat them both black and blue."

There was general laughter. Danjuro moaned, "Poor bastard! The old hen who lays all the eggs won't let the rooster at the pretty chicks any more."

The porter muttered, "Serves him right! He's a mean bastard! Beats the girls."

"Why doesn't he tell his old woman off?" asked Tora.

"That shop is the biggest in town," cried Ueda, "but it's the wife that owns it."

"How come?"

"He's adopted. Old Kurata's only daughter was so mean and ugly they couldn't find a guy willing to marry her, especially since the old man let it be known that she would keep the property. When she took up with the shop assistant and turned up with child, her father was so pleased he adopted the assistant, giving him his name along with his daughter. Lucky bastard!"

Danjuro sneered, "What's lucky about it? That old hag owns the place and she's at least fifteen years older than him and as ugly as a dried prune."

The waitress arrived with food and served them. Then the door opened again and three elegant female musicians slipped in. The one in front was a little older than the other two, perhaps in her thirties, but still quite handsome in her pale green silk gown with deep red under-robes. She carried a lute. The two girls with her were pretty, one particularly so, thought Tora. They had zithers and wore lilac silk and cream brocade respectively.

The men greeted them with pleasure, and the women bowed. Then they took their seats decorously against one wall and began to play.

Tora was not particularly fond of music, but could not take his eyes off the girl in the lilac gown. When she smiled at him, her cheeks dimpled charmingly. They played a selection of fashionable and popular songs which were well received. Kunisada offered them wine, which the older woman refused politely. Instead she asked for requests, and the company became very jovial. Several more rounds of wine were ordered, and Tora exchanged soulful glances with the pretty zither player. Then Danjuro asked the ladies to dance for them, but they shook their heads, the two girls giggling. Tora looked at his girl and folded his hands in entreaty. She nodded ever so slightly, glancing toward the door. Danjuro was showering all three women with suggestive compliments and, being more than a little drunk, ended up propositioning them. At this point, the older woman rose abruptly and signaled to the girls. All three bowed deeply and were gone.

"Now see what you've done, Danjuro!" grumbled Kunisada. "You have the manners of a pig. Don't you know a respectable musician from a streetwalker? You have insulted the famous Madame Sakaki."

But Danjuro only laughed and shouted for women. Immediately the auntie shoved in a gaggle of brightly robed and heavily made-up girls. In the confusion of shouting men and squealing females, Tora slipped from the room.

He caught up with the musicians as they were preparing to leave. "Wait, little sisters!" he called.

They stopped at the door, and the older woman said sharply, "I beg to be excused, sir. We have another party to play for."

Tora bowed to her. "Madame Sakaki," he said imploringly. "Please forgive the rude behavior of my friend. He was quite drunk with wine and your beauty. It is too bad he has no ear for music. As for me," he lied, "I only came to hear you play. Please allow me to invite you all to a nice dinner after your work is done. I want to make up for the unpleasantness."

Madame Sakaki smiled a little, but shook her head. "It is kind of you, sir, but quite impossible."

Tora hung his head. "I understand," he said. "It was a pleasure to hear a true artist. I have heard of a lute player who takes lessons from a professor at the university. Could it be you?"

Madame Sakaki flushed and drew herself up sharply. "No," she snapped. "That is Omaki. Now you must excuse us." She bowed and hurried off. The two younger women followed, the pretty one with a wink.

Tora looked after them disappointedly. Now what was he to do?

"Well?" The auntie had come up behind him. "Did you like the little zither player? I told her you admired her."

"Oh. I didn't know." Tora was crestfallen.

"You mean you let her go?" The auntie threw up her hands. "You must be stupid."

"Never mind, Auntie," sighed Tora. "Tell me about this girl Omaki. Is she here?"

"That one? You can forget her! She's taken. And I've washed my hands of her. Took her on because the professor asked me to, but she's unreliable. Always looking to catch a man."

"What do you mean, she's taken?"

"Never you mind! She's not here and I'm busy and don't have time for silly fools. Go away!"

Outside the lanterns glimmered in the scented darkness like fireflies among the trailing willows. Revellers crowded the streets in holiday garb and lovers embraced in the shadow of the trees. Tora spent an hour strolling about, smiling at the few unaccompanied girls. None proved free and easy company. His spirits low, he finally leaned against one of the willow trees and pondered what he should do. It was too early to go home. He had bragged about his plans, and the other servants would tease him unmercifully. On the other hand, he had not enough money left to go to a cheap brothel.

"Tora-san," whispered a voice at his shoulder. He turned, and there stood the pretty zither player, clutching her instrument to her chest and smiling at him. She said shyly, "I am finished for the night."

Tora's eyes widened in joyous surprise. "Sweetheart," he cried, "I was just making a wish and here it is already come true! I was wishing for you."

"Oh, go on!" She blushed and giggled. "We only met tonight."

"That's the way it hits some men! Like lightning! Nothing we can do about it, but suffer. Unless . . ." He looked at her beseechingly.

"You shouldn't say such things to a girl, Tora."

"You know my name, but I don't know yours. How can such a thing be?"

"I'm Michiko. And I know your name because the auntie at the Willow told me."

Bless the auntie, thought Tora. He liked Michiko and her artless manner. "Let's walk a little, Michiko," he said, "and if we see a good place to eat, let me buy you supper. You must be hungry and tired by now."

She smiled up at him. "Yes, thank you, Tora."

But all the restaurants and wine houses were too crowded by now and the private rooms were taken. Since Tora had designs beyond dinner, he began to feel frustrated.

"Why don't we buy some food at one of the stalls and take it back to my place?" Michiko suggested when she saw his glum face. "I live close by."

Tora brightened instantly. He purchased fried shrimp and a large pitcher of wine, and they left the pleasure quarter. Michiko rented a room behind a bamboo blind–maker's shop. The family was already asleep. So they tiptoed down the long hall and entered a small room which was no more than a flimsy wooden shack added to the back of the house. It was perfectly clean and tidy.

Michiko took a rolled-up reed mat from a shelf and spread it across the bare wooden floor. Then she set out dishes and cups which had been stored in a simple chest. They sat down. She placed the food in bowls and Tora poured the wine.

The girl was starved. Tora, who was full, watched her eat, passing her his own portion when she had finished hers. He liked a girl with a healthy appetite. Close up she was even prettier; her eyes began to sparkle as her hunger and tiredness vanished, and her moist lips looked full and inviting. Finally she stopped eating, burped in a ladylike fashion, and gave him a big smile. "Thank you, Tora," she said with feeling. "That was very good."

Touched, Tora reached into his sleeve and handed her the sash with the crane pattern. "Here," he said. "It's not much, but it's for you if you like it."

She spread it out on her lap. "Oh Tora!" she whispered, touching the fabric reverently. "It is so beautiful. I had no idea you bought me a present. Did you know I'd come back to you?"

Tora had the grace to blush, but thought that, on the whole, it would be kinder not to confess the truth. "I told you I had made a wish," he said.

Michiko flung her arms around him and pressed her cheek to his. "I'm so glad," she cried. Then she jumped up and started putting away the dishes. Tora got up to help.

"Do you happen to know a girl called Omaki?" he asked, handing her one of the shrimp bowls.

"Oh, yes. She used to be my friend."

"Used to?"

Michiko knelt, poured some water into a large bowl and rinsed the dishes. "She got snooty. Taking lessons from a professor who comes to the Willow a lot. He made her think she was better than the rest of us. Then she got sick to her stomach a lot, and when I asked her if there was something wrong, she snapped at me to mind my own business." She pointed to a neatly folded length of cheap cotton. "Do you mind drying?"

Tora obliged. "That wasn't very nice of her."

"No, and of course it made me think. She must be pregnant. And I bet that's why she wasn't working today. The auntie probably told her nobody wants to look at a pregnant musician."

"Any idea who the father is?" asked Tora, stacking the clean dishes on the chest.

"My guess is it's the professor's," said Michiko, pouring the dirty water out the window, and putting away the bowl. Then she turned, giving Tora a thoughtful look. "Why are you asking? Don't tell me you've fallen for *her*?"

"Never, my sweet!" Tora said fervently, stepping closer to stroke her cheek with his finger. "I don't even know the girl. Someone said she was a good lute player, and I thought Madame Sakaki was her. What a charming neck you have."

Michiko giggled and caught his hand in hers. "Omaki can't touch Madame's playing. She's the best. And she hates Omaki." She nuzzled Tora's hand, and said wistfully, "I'm sorry I can't play the lute, Tora, but I know lots of other games."

"Really?" Tora pretended ignorance. "Like what?"

"Like 'bamboo bridge to the pavilion,' " she whispered, tracing Tora's jaw with her finger and fluttering her eyes at him, "or 'cicadas clinging to a tree,' or 'monkey swinging from a branch' or 'bouncing the infant.' "

Tora's eyebrows shot up. " 'Monkey swinging from a branch'?" he asked, astonished. "What sort of game might that be?"

She moved quite close to him. "Silly! Don't you know anything? Haven't you ever visited the ladies of the Willow Quarter?"

Tora made a grab for her and pulled her down onto the mat. "No, you hussy," he muttered, fumbling for her sash. "And you shouldn't know such things either."

She giggled, twisting in his arms. "The girls tell us all about their work. They make good money, but I prefer to take my pick of the handsome fellows."

"Do you now?" asked Tora with a broad smile, tossing aside the sash and pushing her gown off her shoulders.

"Wait," she cried. "Let me make up a bed first!"

Tora stumbled up, cursing under his breath. He was taking off his robe, while she brought out her bedding and unrolled it on the floor. Her loose gown gaped enticingly, revealing glimpses of bare skin—a slender thigh, high breasts, a flash of well-rounded hip and . . . She slipped off the gown, folding it neatly away. Tora gasped and began to tear at his loincloth.

In a flash she was by his side to help. "Oh," she cried, "how large! It is truly like a tree for monkeys to climb." She gave a little screech. "This little monkey is afraid," she cried and jumped under the covers, giggling.

Tora dove under himself. "Forget the monkeys," he groaned. "This tree must be planted quickly before it dies."

Michiko was not only a compassionate girl, but also a very good teacher. Tora learned all about swinging monkeys and other entertaining games that night.

EIGHT

THE POETRY CONTEST

)t was the hour of the cock, about two hours before sunset, when Akitada entered the Divine Spring Garden again. For the occasion of the contest the gate had been festively decorated with banners, and two foot soldiers from the imperial guard stood at attention on either side. Akitada presented his invitation and was waved through. Ahead of him he saw Nishioka walking side by side with the student Ishikawa, but he made no effort to catch up to them.

He had been downcast all day, and his depression deepened as he passed the spot where they had found the girl's body. When the imperial pavilion burst upon his eyes, filled with hundreds of elegant guests in colorful robes, the scene was almost painfully bright in the afternoon sunlight, a shocking contrast to his dark mood. Vermilion columns and balustrades, emerald roof tiles, gilded ornaments, many-hued silk cushions and colorful robes of contestants and guests, painted boats on the white sand of the lake which lay like molten gold in the setting sun—it all seemed for a moment completely unreal. Akitada felt that he had walked into a place quite separate and distant from the work-day world of normal people. It was certainly a world which was remote from that of the dead girl and the old beggar, and both had intruded into it at a cost.

Filled with an irrational anger at those who lived "above the clouds" like the very gods, Akitada climbed the steps to the veranda. It was already nearly filled with chattering and laughing guests. None of them, he thought, would care that a young woman had died only a short walk away.

At the top of the steps he paused briefly before the dais of the presiding judges to make his bow to Prince Atsuakira and the other imperial personages. Then he turned towards the left where he saw other members of the faculty and found his place somewhere in the back. After a moment, Hirata appeared by his side. He looked tired but smiled.

"I have not been home all day," he said, sitting down. "Did the ladies enjoy the procession?"

"I believe so." Akitada had to make an effort to smile back. "My mother invited Tamako to share their midday rice. I had to leave—a matter having to do with the murdered girl—but Tora was to take your daughter home in the hired carriage."

"That was most kind of you and your lady mother," said Hirata warmly. "Please express to her my deep gratitude for the honor she has done my insignificant daughter."

Insignificant? Honor? Kindness? The words of polite convention were as false as the ridiculous affair he was about to witness. Akitada nodded and turned away to look at the nobles and ranking members of the government seated to the right of the stairs. It suddenly struck him that even the cushions people sat on distinguished them by rank, as if a noble behind must not be insulted by an inappropriate support. The princes sat on purple brocade; the nobles had deep red, green or blue silk cushions; and he, along with the rest of the faculty and students, was provided with a gray cotton one. Never once forget your place in the hierarchy!

Strange, he thought, in the dusk last night the stacked cushions had all appeared the same. A trick of light, or of darkness rather.

The thought teased him, as if this trivial matter had some hidden significance, but he did not pursue it. The ceremony was beginning.

Prince Atsuakira rose and stepped forward on the dais, and silence fell. His brief opening address was followed by others, last but not least by Oe, who made the most of his opportunity to shine before such an eminent audience.

Oe was wearing another splendid blue brocade robe, and his white hair gleamed under the formal black court hat. After bidding the guests welcome in the name of the combined faculties of the university, he explained the rules and sequence of the competition.

Akitada knew already that there would be four segments, compositions celebrating special occasions, travel poems, drinking songs and love lyrics. Each segment would be separated from the next by musical interludes and dance performances, after which each winner would be declared.

As Oe's voice droned on, Akitada looked out over the lake. A group of ducks came paddling around a bend, paused, seemingly astonished at the brilliant congregation of humans at the pavilion, then burst into disgusted quacking and rose from the lake in a clatter of wings and sparkling drops of water.

"The beauty of this day," said Oe, "will give birth to genius and affirm the greatness of His Majesty's reign." The nobles across the way applauded, and Akitada, idly glancing, recognized a face.

There, if he was not mistaken, sat the fellow Okura, the weak-chinned dandy who had quarreled with Tora and who had, against all probability, placed first during the recent examinations. He was one of the contestants. Akitada began to take some slight interest in the proceedings.

When Oe finished to general relieved applause, Hirata leaned over and whispered, "Did you notice anything strange about Oe's manner?"

"No. Why?"

"I hope I am mistaken, but I could swear the man was drunk already. He was slurring his words." Hirata shook his head. "I would have thought winning would be too important for him to risk embarrassment."

Akitada said dryly, "If you are right, he will not last long. I see they are beginning to pass the wine around." It was customary to toast each composition with a cup of wine, and from the size of the program it was clear that it would be a long evening and night.

The first presentations passed without great surprises. Occasional verses were the specialty of court officials who were forever dashing off lines in honor of imperial birthdays and esoteric ceremonials. Okura competed in this segment, and Akitada watched him with interest. He appeared composed, even complacent, reciting a short composition which seemed, to Akitada's untrained ear, surprisingly competent, certainly no worse than the rest. Could Hirata have misjudged his ability?

Hirata grunted. "His style has improved amazingly."

Okura retired to mild applause. Suddenly a voice hissed into Akitada's ear, "Well, well! Our esteemed colleague sells his talents to the highest bidder!"

Akitada turned his head and looked into the hooded eyes of the turtle-headed Takahashi. "I am sorry, but I don't understand you," he said coldly.

"Of course not. You are not as familiar with Oe's turn of phrase as the rest of us, to our misery. His style, if you can call it that, is quite unmistakable. He is the one who wrote Okura's poem. Okura could never do it himself."

Akitada stared. "How can you be certain? A student often imitates his teacher's style."

"Well, Hirata," Takahashi asked, "am I right?"

Hirata nodded reluctantly. "It may be so," he said.

"And what's more," continued Takahashi, "our 'great man' has been drinking all day, and wine does not make him amiable. He has already lost his temper twice with that poor fish Ono. I don't see how that man can show his face in public after today. The names Oe called him! And in front of any number of influential people. It was shocking!"

New applause broke out, and Takahashi left to talk to Fujiwara who was arriving late, still wearing the same disreputable silk robe and unmatched sash Akitada remembered from the faculty meeting.

Hirata put his hand on Akitada's arm and nodded towards the stage. Oe, his face flushed, had stepped forward again. He had developed a rather strange manner of rocking on the balls of his feet. Instead of facing the judges, he was looking across at the gathering of government and court officials. "Again you find us gathered so," he began in his mellifluous voice, "again the sun sets bright." He waved an expansive arm towards the bright lake, and received a smattering of applause. "The same that shone a year ago," he lowered his head sadly, "but, oh, how changed we are tonight."

Akitada rather liked the sense of nostalgia and the appropriateness of the images, and waited expectantly for Oe's star performance.

To his surprise, Oe's head jerked up to look again into the gathering of officials, and he concluded sharply: "Some break the rules by which the game is played, / And gain reward where none is due, / While others find their hopes betrayed. / For time and change please only few." He bowed jerkily and returned to his seat, leaving his audience dumbfounded. There was some dubious applause, but most people whispered, shaking their heads in confusion.

"What can he have meant by that?" asked Hirata. "It's almost as if he had accused the judges of awarding the prize to the wrong poet."

Akitada frowned. Surely Oe would not accuse the noble judges. Was he referring to another matter? The charges were uncomfortably apt for the compromised examination. The matter was completely puzzling, and Akitada promised himself a frank talk with the great Oe as soon as possible.

A winner was declared—it was neither Oe nor Okura, but one of the officials—and the servants walked around with trays of wine cups. A gorgeously costumed child, the young son of one of the court nobles, now took the stage and performed an elaborate dance. It told the story of an ancient emperor who had won a battle against insurmountable odds by disguising himself as a fierce dragon warrior.

There was a generous burst of applause when the child finished. Oe shot up from his seat and, before he could be stopped, recited another poem. To everyone's relief, it turned out to be in praise of the grace of this scion of a noble family and predicted greatness for his future. This time, Oe reaped generous applause. Most of the guests were under the impression that they had just witnessed a brilliant extemporaneous composition, but Akitada was convinced that Oe had come prepared. It made the previous poem even more puzzling.

The second segment passed without incident. It featured, among others, Ishikawa, who won a prize. An interlude of flute music followed; Akitada gave it his full attention. He stretched to see if Sato was playing but found that the performer was a stranger. Sato's absence caused him to wonder about the police investigation. He hoped Kobe had not decided to arrest the music professor. Recalling the beating given to the old beggar, he felt uneasy about having mentioned Sato's name to the captain. When the flute player stopped, Akitada got up to stretch his legs. He strolled along the veranda to the rear of the pavilion.

On the ground below was a great bustling of waiters who were heating flasks of wine in large braziers and running back and forth with trays of cups. Akitada leaned on the balustrade to watch. Directly below him, a group of servants unpacked large colored paper lanterns. It would not be long till night, for the brilliant sunlight had turned a muted gold and the deep blue of the sky was changing to the pale shade of wisteria blossoms. Soon in the darkness, hundreds of colored lanterns would gleam.

Occasionally one of the guests passed below, perhaps to relieve himself after all the wine. Akitada stretched and decided to walk down, when he suddenly noticed the student Ishikawa. He stood near the corner of the pavilion, talking angrily to someone hidden by one of the lacquered columns. Suddenly Ishikawa lunged and pushed. A tall, broad figure in blue staggered out from behind the column. Oe. He had lost his hat and his face was nearly purple with rage. He roared something and attacked, slapping Ishikawa across the face so violently that Akitada could hear the sound above the noise of the waiters. Ishikawa recoiled, touching his face, then reached down and raised what looked like a broken oar. He looked absolutely murderous. Akitada leaned over the balustrade and shouted a warning. Ishikawa froze and looked up; his eyes met Akitada's. He dropped the oar, said something to Oe, and disappeared around the corner. Oe stood a moment longer, staring up at Akitada. Then he, too, turned and stumbled away.

When Akitada returned to his seat, he asked Hirata, "Do you know of any reason why Oe and Ishikawa should get into a fight?"

Hirata frowned. "A fight? You must be exaggerating."

"No. I just saw them."

"Remember, Oe has been drinking. Come, Akitada, it is a beautiful evening. Let's enjoy it while we can. Look! The *Dengaku* dancers are performing."

Akitada glanced at a group of young women on the stage. He found Hirata's lack of interest irritating and said, "I thought you wanted me to get to the bottom of this matter. Here we may have a clue to your blackmailer and you don't want to discuss it."

Hirata flushed and looked over his shoulder. "Ssh! Not so loud." He leaned closer. "You are quite right to be angry. It is true that I have had second thoughts about the wisdom of involving you in this matter. I think it will be better for you not to pursue it further. Please forgive me for causing you all this trouble, especially now that . . ." He broke off delicately, but Akitada knew that he referred to the failed marriage plans.

So Hirata had merely wanted a husband for his daughter. A cold fury seized Akitada and made his stomach churn. "Unless you have discovered the answer yourself," he snapped, "in which case you owe me at least an explanation, the situation remains as dangerous as before. Or are you telling me now that the letter was a mere subterfuge to invite me to your house?"

Hirata paled. "No," he said stiffly. "I asked you because of the danger to the university." He paused and looked at his hands, which lay in his lap. "It is true that I had hoped our working together might lead you and Tamako to discover affection for each other again."

And the plan had worked perfectly well in Akitada's case, though not for Tamako! Akitada felt a wave of nausea. Whether or not the note was real, Hirata had just admitted that he had really wanted something far more personal. Little did he know that his daughter had refused the bridegroom her father had chosen for her, the one man he could count on because of the debt he owed them. Akitada turned away.

The older man sighed deeply. "Don't be angry, dear boy," he pleaded. "I was afraid you would misunderstand. Now I wish I had bitten off my tongue before mentioning the note to you."

Akitada wished it too. He said through clenched teeth, "Never mind. I understand."

There was a lull in the performance, and a certain stillness had fallen over the park. The last light was fading in the sky. Akitada searched in his mind for the right words so that he might leave.

Then the poetry recitals began again. Akitada listened absent-mindedly to some poorly scanned lines in praise of wine and emptied his cup quickly. A waiter replaced it with a full one, and Akitada emptied this also.

"About Oe and Ishikawa," said Hirata suddenly. "Last year Ishikawa began to assist Oe with minor chores. They seemed to get along well until just recently. Ishikawa's arrogance became more pronounced. He often showed a great lack of respect when he addressed Oe, who was his senior professor. But can his bad manners really be significant?"

Akitada forced himself to reply. "Uncharacteristic behavior is always suggestive. Something happened to change their relationship. Was this around the time of the examinations? Perhaps Ishikawa learned that Oe had helped a student cheat."

"Oe?" Hirata looked stunned. "Surely you are wrong. Oe is too highly thought of to do such a dangerous thing. Ishikawa is another matter. He has always been arrogant and might well engage in blackmail. But not Oe. You said yourself that Oe's blue gown could not possibly have been confused with my green one."

"Perhaps Ishikawa is colorblind."

But Akitada did not think so. He had a feeling that there was a much simpler explanation for the mistake, but his mind was growing fuzzy.

Below the first lanterns glimmered on in the blue dusk. They raised sudden flashes of jewel tones from the robes of poets and musicians and made rainbows of the painted boats. The sky still retained the faintest tinge of lilac, and a thin line of gold rimmed the dark mass of the western mountains.

The mood of the company had changed. Loud laughter and shouts accompanied verses celebrating inebriety. But all became quiet when Fujiwara stepped forward and bowed towards the dais. The crowd was expectant.

Fujiwara's voice sounded deep and compelling. Syllables rolled off his tongue like distant thunder. The poem was long and spoke of human needs beyond fame and fortune, of friendship between men which becomes most tender when wine loosens the tongue and true feelings break down the barriers of social convention. And it was far and above the most moving verse Akitada had ever heard. As he listened, his thoughts recalled lost friends, and tears rose to his eyes. The crippled giant Higekuro and his daughter Ayako, once so close to his heart and now lost forever; the handsome Tasuku who had left the world because it had become a place of sorrow; all those who had been his childhood friends and were gone, either through death or distance. Tamako, too, was quickly slipping away from him. In life there was a great need to hold on to friends.

A brief silence fell when Fujiwara finished. All that could be heard for a moment was the rustle of paper lanterns in the evening breeze and the distant voices of waterfowl on the lake. Even the servants had fallen quiet in the hush of the audience. Then the applause came, general and thunderous. Soon every man was on his feet. People were bowing to Fujiwara, shouting their approval, even walking over to embrace him.

Suddenly a single shrill voice rose over the rest. Oe was standing, waving his arms about, shouting, "Stop this vulgar display! Sit down, everybody! This rudeness must stop immediately. The rules do not permit it, and the contestant who invited this rude outburst by his unseemly subject must be disqualified. His lack of decorum is more suited to the revels of derelicts and whores!"

The crowd gasped. All eyes were on Oe and Fujiwara. Hirata jumped to his feet, muttering, "I must stop the fool," and started toward Oe. But it was already too late. Everyone, from His Imperial Highness to the lowest ranking official, had heard the insulting words. Hirata and Ono between them managed to pull Oe down on his cushion, but he continued to struggle and shout unintelligibly.

Fujiwara surprised everyone. In his booming voice he made a clever joke about the potency of wine and poetry. It set everyone laughing and calling for refills.

With peace thus reestablished, another contestant took his turn, and Fujiwara walked over to the small group gathered about Oe, which by now included Nishioka. The tall, broad-shouldered Fujiwara leaned down, put his arm around Oe's shoulders, and lifted him to his feet. Ono took the other side, and between them they walked the babbling Oe away from the gathering, Hirata going ahead to make way and Nishioka following behind with Oe's belongings. When the group had disappeared around the corner of the pavilion, Akitada saw Ishikawa rising to follow.

As the last contestant finished his verse, Fujiwara returned to his seat, dabbing at his cheek with the sleeve of his robe. He was bleeding from a large scratch.

Unfortunately the bloodied cheek could not be glossed over, for when the prince called the name of the winner, Fujiwara had to rise. Prince Atsuakira himself walked over to congratulate him and present him with a fine silk robe. As Fujiwara knelt and bowed, blood dripped into his beard. The prince murmured something, but Fujiwara smiled, saying, "Just a clumsy collision with a branch, Your Highness."

After another dance interlude, the boats were launched into the lake, their lanterns sparkling on the dark water like the stars in the sky above. Other lights blinked on along the lakeshore, among the trees, and even on the island. It was a magical scene, in its own way more splendid than the brilliant colors of the afternoon.

Now the servants passed along the veranda with lighted lanterns and attached them to the eaves with long poles. Across the way, where the nobles sat, the lantern bearers had not yet begun, and the darkness had turned the colorful cushions of the nobles, abandoned for boat rides or strolls in the park, a uniform black. Akitada remembered how the stacked cushions had all seemed the same color to him the evening before. They had been in the shadow of the veranda. He had assumed they were all blue, because one blue cushion had caught some light. Of course! The same thing must have happened the night the blackmailer delivered his note. Blue and green would have been indistinguishable, and both Oe's and Hirata's robes had had white designs around the sleeves. That must have been how Ishikawa had made his mistake.

Already completely out of tune with the beauty of the evening, Akitada had no desire to hear the next segment of the competition. He felt too heartsore to listen to love poems, and was on the point of leaving when Hirata returned, looking upset.

"What happened?" Akitada asked him.

"A terrible scene. Oe attacked Fujiwara with his bare hands and would have hurt him seriously if we had not all thrown ourselves on him." Hirata shook his head. "I never realized how strong a man can be when he is out of his mind. It was a serious insult to Fujiwara who was only trying to help. We finally calmed Oe down enough for Ono and Ishikawa to take him home, but I fear he is completely unbalanced. He was weeping when I left. I never imagined wine could do this to a man."

"Not wine, but guilt—and the knowledge that he is in the power of an unscrupulous man who plans to ruin him."

"What?"

"The note *was* intended for Oe. In the dark there is little difference between green and blue."

"Are you sure?" cried Hirata. He thought it over. "If that is the case, what shall we do?"

"We will confront them both as soon as possible. Once their guilt is established, you can take whatever action you please."

"Oh, let us wait and think about this first."

Akitada rose. "No. I am anxious to be done with the whole affair. After tomorrow I shall consider the matter closed as far as I am concerned. Now, if you will excuse me, I am going home. Good night."

Akitada walked away, leaving Hirata to stare blindly at the gaily lit scene on the lake.

NINE

TEAR-DRENCHED SLEEVES

The next day was also a holiday because it was the day when the Kamo virgin returned from the shrine to her palace. Akitada called on his mother, as he did most mornings. He found her at breakfast with his sisters and asked how they had enjoyed their outing the previous day.

"Tamako is a most charming person," cried his younger sister Yoshiko. Remembering her brother's ill-fated courtship, she blushed a little and added, "She stayed quite late with us and promised to return soon. We were delighted to have her company."

Akitada's heart sank. He had no wish to face any more embarrassing encounters with Tamako. "I am glad you had a pleasant day," he said and glanced at his mother.

"It appears the young woman gardens," Lady Sugawara informed him. "She had a number of helpful suggestions for us. As you can see," she waved a careless hand towards the lush growth surrounding her new terrace, "this place is overgrown like an abandoned ruin. It is too bad that I must rely on chance encounters to get things done."

"I thought you liked the garden this way," said Akitada, hurt in spite of the fact that he knew his mother was still angry with him for other reasons. "All you have to do is ask, and I will have Tora see to some trimming and replanting."

"Hmph! That fellow is gone more than he is here," grumbled his mother.

"Last night he did not come home at all," volunteered his sister Akiko.

Akitada's mother cast her eyes to heaven and sighed deeply. "No doubt he is in jail at this very moment," she said. "To think what I have come to. A dilapidated home and a bandit for a servant! This was once a great house, bustling with well-trained servants. Now we exist like exiles condemned to the wilderness of a distant province."

"I am sorry you are so downcast today, Mother." Akitada rose and bowed. "I shall visit again when you are feeling more cheerful."

Lady Sugawara did not bother to reply.

◆

The university was nearly deserted today because there were no classes or lectures. Akitada stopped by Hirata's room, but found it empty. The holiday was causing problems. He was anxious to get their meeting with Oe and Ishikawa over with, but could do nothing without Hirata.

In his own room a stack of student papers lay on his desk. He wondered whether he was obligated to read them before leaving, or if he should spend his last day gathering up his belongings. Postponing the decision, he took a stroll over to the students' dormitories with the vague idea of asking Ishikawa a few questions.

Things were a bit livelier here. Some of the youngest boys were gathered in a grove of pine trees where they were noisily occupied with large sheets of colored paper. Akitada approached curiously and realized that they were building kites.

He glanced up at the clear sky. Fluffy clouds travelled quickly on the breeze. It was perfect kite flying weather. Watching the boys, he saw the first trial kite rising from the line of a madly dashing youngster. It soared briefly, then made a sudden plunge, and became entangled in the top of one of the pines.

Akitada walked over. The pine looked like a good climbing tree. On an impulse, he took off his robe and fastened the legs of his full trousers around his knees. Pulling himself up to the lowest branch, he began to climb. But the kite was too far up. The weaker branches near the top would not hold his weight. As he paused to ponder the situation, something plucked at his trousers.

"Excuse me, sir," said one of the boys, peering up at him. "Would you mind if I passed you? My kite is stuck up there."

Akitada moved aside and watched as the agile little monkey reached the kite, plucked it loose, and let it down to his waiting comrades.

"Excuse me, sir," said the boy again, passing him on the way down.

Feeling foolish, Akitada watched him scramble quickly back to the ground. Had the boys not realized that he had been trying to get the kite? What had gone through the child's mind when he saw one of the masters climbing a tree? Humbled, Akitada descended more slowly and put his robe back on. Climbing trees after kites was clearly no longer proper at his age.

At one of the dormitories he found an older student sitting on the steps, mending his shoes. Akitada asked him, "Can you tell me where I might find Ishikawa?"

The young man stood politely and bowed. "He is not here today, sir. I saw him leave before dawn. He was carrying a bundle, so I assumed he was going on a short trip."

More delays! Ishikawa would not be back till late. Akitada strolled back towards the boys with their kites. Suddenly his eyes fell on the small figure of young Minamoto, sitting quietly on the veranda outside his dormitory room. He appeared engrossed in a book, but stole surreptitious glances at the other boys. For a moment Akitada wondered why he was not with them; then he remembered that rank and recent bereavement probably prevented him from joining in games that should have been a natural part of his young life. The young lord's continued isolation from the other children pained Akitada.

Shaking his head helplessly, he left the enclosure by its north gate and crossed the street to the school of music. Sato must be in, for he could hear the sounds of his lute. This time the melody was even more lilting than on the last occasion. As Akitada walked towards the music, a second lute joined in. Another student? No. From the delightful harmony which ensued, it was clear that two master musicians had met.

Akitada approached quietly and seated himself on the veranda outside Sato's room to listen. He wished, not for the first time, that he could play like that. It was wonderful to become lost in music. All one's cares seemed to drop away. As a youngster he had briefly practiced the flute, and he had had some lessons as a student, but then more important matters had taken up his time and he had neglected his practice and given up.

After a little, the music ended and there was some subdued talk. Embarrassed, Akitada rose, cleared his throat and went to greet the music teacher.

Sato was again with a woman, this one older and more elegant than the murdered girl. They had not heard him, and this time surely there was no doubt that the teacher and his visitor were lovers. Both were seated cross-legged, their lutes resting in their laps, and their heads inclined towards each other. But it was more than their physical proximity to each other. They exchanged soft glances and the woman reached out to caress Sato's cheek.

Taken aback, Akitada retreated, but he had already been seen. The couple jerked apart, staring at him. Making a bow, Akitada apologized for his intrusion. The woman blushed and assumed a more decorous kneeling posture. Her beauty, though mature, was poignant. Akitada explained lamely, "I heard the music and could not resist it."

"It's a holiday," snapped Sato angrily. "Don't you have a private life?"

The woman got up with her lute and slipped out without a word or gesture to either of them.

"I am sorry," Akitada said again, looking after her. "Believe me, if you are worried about my complaining about your private lessons, your secret is safe with me. But this lady played so well that she can hardly be your pupil." He flushed, thinking how this must sound to Sato.

Sato looked at him without expression. "She is a fellow musician and acquaintance who dropped by for a chat," he said. When Akitada made a move to leave also, Sato became hospitable. "Will you take some wine?"

Somewhat surprised, Akitada accepted readily. Sato was an interesting enigma. Akitada sipped his wine and said, "I assume the police captain has talked to you about the girl who was murdered in the park. Could you provide him with a name?"

"Yes. Her name's Omaki. I had to go and identify her body. Poor little wench!" Sato took a big gulp of his wine. "I suppose I've got you to thank for the police interest?"

Akitada met his eyes calmly. "I am afraid it was unavoidable. My servant and I found her, and I remembered meeting her with you."

Sato looked away. "Yes, I see. I suppose it couldn't be helped. She was a silly girl, but she didn't deserve to die so young." He grimaced. "It was a bit embarrassing, though. I met her in the Willow Quarter."

"She was a prostitute?"

"Not everybody in the Willow Quarter is a prostitute," snapped Sato angrily. But he calmed down quickly and sighed. "Poor Omaki. She was training to become an entertainer. If you ask me, she was on her way to becoming a prostitute when she died. It was her karma. Her father's a poor man, an umbrella maker called Hishiya. They live in the sixth ward. The mother had died and he remarried. It's the usual story: the second wife did not get along with the grown daughter. The girl threatened to sell herself to a brothel rather than stay home as a servant to the new wife. The father, who's a decent man, came to me one evening. Told me the girl played the lute and asked if I could get her a job. I listened to her play. She was untrained but not bad. The long and the short of it was that we made an arrangement by which I got her a job in a place I know, and she paid me for a few lessons. She learned quickly. Anyone else would have succeeded. But for her? All wasted! Poor silly chit!"

He filled his cup again, drank deeply, and stared out the door. Akitada sipped his wine slowly. He did not believe either the sentiments or explanations. Sato had become positively chatty. The man's behavior, his reputation, the fleshy, sensuous lips and soulful eyes—all were at odds with the detachment he pretended. No, Sato was a womanizer, perhaps a murderer, not a humanitarian.

"Did you know of anything that might help the police find her killer?" Akitada asked.

Sato shook his head. "I doubt it. I knew she was with child, foolish girl. That meant the end of her career just as it was starting. But she didn't seem to care. When I asked her about the child's father and her plans, she closed up. Actually, if anything, she seemed more cheerful, or excited, than before." He paused and thought. "There was one thing I told that captain. I saw her with one of the students here. Maybe that young rascal was the father of her child. He used to moon about the place where she worked. Damned youngsters ought to keep their heads in their books! Though this particular one was hardly a dashing figure. Can't imagine what she saw in him!"

There was a sharp twanging sound, and Akitada's eyes went to the music teacher's hands. They were clenched tightly around the neck of the lute. Sato followed his glance and immediately relaxed his long fingers. They looked powerful from twisting tight lute strings, and agile from many hours of practice. Powerful and agile enough to twist a piece of silk around a woman's neck and strangle her to death?

"Oh, I can see what's going through your mind," Sato said angrily. "It wasn't my brat and I had nothing to do with her death. And having said that much, I have no intention of pursuing the subject."

Akitada reddened, disclaimed such suspicions, and changed the subject to the previous evening. But his comments about Oe's argument with Fujiwara seemed to irritate Sato more. He growled, "I wasn't there, and I don't care a monkey's fart what that bastard Oe does. Serves him right, if he made a mess of himself." Grasping his lute, he got to his feet.

It was a signal that the conversation was over. Akitada rose also and left to return to his room, where he found a bleary-eyed Tora waiting for him.

"You look terrible," Akitada said sourly, eyeing Tora's unshaven chin, his dishevelled hair and the bloodshot eyes. "Where have you been? Have you had any sleep?"

"None at all!" Tora grinned. "Sleep isn't everything. As you'd find out if you tried it. You know, you should sleep with a woman more often. It may not be restful, but it's a great deal better than sleeping alone. Not having a woman saps a man's vital essence after a while. I may look worse than you, but my vital essence is in top shape, thanks to the prettiest and most talented female you ever saw. Oh, what a body that girl has . . . and the things she does with it! There's a position she calls 'monkeys swinging from a branch' where she—"

"Enough!" Akitada roared in a sudden fury. "Watch your tongue when you speak to me! And spare me the details of your sordid affairs! Seimei is quite right. I have spoiled you. Your excessive familiarity is beginning to grate. And now you are becoming insolent. Not only do you lack all respect for your betters, but you don't seem to do much work. Why did you not return to the house last night and report to your mistress for your duties this morning?"

Tora gaped at his master speechlessly.

"My mother complained about you," blustered Akitada, "and I did not know what to say. Be careful! If you try my patience too much, I shall abandon you to the streets."

Looking pale, Tora scrambled to his feet. "I'll go right now, sir," he mumbled, eyes averted and his voice tight with shock.

Immediately ashamed of his outburst, Akitada bit his lip. "Well, er, maybe you'd better wait a little before showing up at home. Er . . . do you know anything about building kites?"

"Making kites? Of course! And flying them! When I was a kid, I was champion in my village two years running. Why?"

"Some of the younger students are making kites in the dormitory courtyard. I think they must plan to fly them today. There is a good breeze for it. I want you to go over and talk to the Minamoto boy. He is probably still on the veranda pretending to read a book. You might see if you can get him interested in kites."

"A boy who's not interested in kites? You must be joking!" Tora paused abruptly and said, "I beg your pardon, sir. I'll take care of that right away." He rushed out, then stuck his head back in. "Oh, I forgot. I've solved your other case for you. The dead girl's name is Omaki. She played the lute in one of the wine houses in the Willow Quarter until she was fired."

"I know, and that hardly solves the case," Akitada said. Tora's face fell. Hanging his head, he turned to leave, when Akitada added, "All the same, it was good of you to ask around. We'll talk about it later."

When Tora was gone, Akitada sat down heavily and stared at the spray of white hollyhocks that survived, somewhat crushed, in a wine cup full of water on Akitada's desk. Perhaps Tora had a point. A man was not meant to spend his life alone unless he was a monk or hermit, and Akitada had no interest in the contemplative or spiritual life. What was it Sato had said? He had asked if Akitada had a private life. Against his better sense, he closed his eyes and thought of Tamako in her Kamo finery. It was a revelation how enchanting her face seemed to him now, since he had really never realized it before. And she had a very graceful figure, slender, with elegant shoulders and a most enticing neck when she turned her head. The image of that white neck with a delicate rosy ear half hidden by the silky black hair was extraordinarily erotic, and he called himself to order sharply, ashamed that Tora's tussle with a common prostitute should have caused him to think with physical desire of the young woman who had been like a sister to him. He reached for the student papers.

Professor Hirata stopped by when Akitada was halfway through the stack of essays. He complained of not being able to find Oe. "Have you spoken to Ishikawa yet?" he asked.

"No, he left early this morning. It is a holiday, and he may be visiting friends." Akitada found it difficult to behave normally around Hirata and had to force himself to carry on a conversation. "How did the rest of the contest go?"

"I left after the final competition. They tell me that the party went on into the night, with boat rides on the lake and impromptu poems praising the moon. Incidentally, Fujiwara won another prize in the love poetry category and was declared this year's poet laureate. Oe will be furious when he finds out. He has expected that honor for years now. For all we know he will contest the results on the grounds that he was forcibly removed by Fujiwara before he could present the rest of his work."

Akitada smiled thinly. "Surely he has been embarrassed too thoroughly to show his face in public for a while."

Hirata nodded. "Besides there is the matter of the last examination. We can exert a certain amount of control over him in the future. I have thought about that. It will surely be enough if we confront Oe and Ishikawa with our knowledge. We will insist that Ishikawa stop his blackmail demands and that Oe remove himself from judging future examinations. I admit it hardly punishes their behavior, but there is nothing we can do to rectify what happened in the spring. The damage is done, and we cannot bring back that poor young man who killed himself. Besides, reversing the results at this time will permanently damage the reputation of the university." Hirata looked at Akitada anxiously.

Blackmail begets blackmail, thought Akitada. But he said, "Certainly. As you wish."

There was a pause. Hirata bit his lip. His face betrayed surprise and worry at Akitada's lack of interest. He was about to pursue the subject, when Tora burst into the room.

"You'll never guess what just happened!" he cried. "The police arrested one of the students for the murder."

"No!" cried Hirata. "Who is it?"

"It's Rabbit." Tora looked at Akitada. "You know, the fellow I told you about. The one who got into a fight with another student in the kitchen that day." Tora fumbled in his sash and produced a crumpled piece of paper. "Here!" he said, extending it to his master, "he wrote you this note."

Akitada unfolded it. It was short, stating simply that the author was innocent of the crime, implored Akitada's help, and offered to pay for it. It was signed Nagai Hiroshi. He passed the note to Hirata.

"Poor boy!" cried Hirata, looking shocked. "That nice, awkward youngster. Who could possibly believe him capable of murder? There must be some mistake."

Akitada recalled the brief encounter at the gate the afternoon before, and had the sinking feeling that there was no mistake. "What about this fight you saw, Tora?" he asked.

"I think the other fellow had been making fun of his crush on a woman. But I'll lay you a bet, sir. If Rabbit was that girl's lover, I'll give up women for good!"

Amused in spite of himself, Akitada murmured, "I don't want to create difficulties for the young man, but I am tempted to hope you would lose."

Tora looked hurt. "I know I'm right. She was a good-looking skirt, and he looks like a cross between a mangy rabbit and a crane. He walks like some long-legged bird that's stepping on broken reeds, and his big ears are flapping in the breeze while his teeth are looking for his chin. Believe me, no pretty girl in her right mind would be seen with something like that!"

"You exaggerate," said Akitada, but he recalled Sato's words about Omaki's unlikely boyfriend. "I met the young man at the gate yesterday. He looked very ill."

"Hah!" cried Tora. "Maybe he did fall for her! Anyway, the police searched his room and found a bunch of stuff he had written. They took it all away with them." A thought struck him. "That just goes to show the trouble you get into with an education. It's his writing poems about the girl that got the fellow arrested."

Akitada's eyes met Hirata's. They smiled. "What do you think I should do?" Akitada asked the older man. "I hate to meddle in Captain Kobe's business again so soon after we had words over the beggar he arrested."

"What about the beggar?" Tora interrupted.

Akitada frowned at him and continued, "Besides there is our own problem. You know I want to get that matter settled as soon as possible. Getting involved with this student may keep me here indefinitely."

Hirata avoided his eyes. "Your fame as a righter of wrongs seems to have spread to the students," he said lightly. "Of course you must try to help Hiroshi. A young man's life and his family's honor are at stake. Even the reputation of this university is less important than that." He paused. "I recall meeting Hiroshi's father when he brought the youngster. Mr. Nagai is a poor schoolmaster in Omi province. The boy is the only son of five children, and I am sure the family is making many sacrifices to pay for his studies."

A scenario not so different from that of the student who had committed suicide. But there was little point in resenting Hirata's hypocrisy or his relief that Akitada would be trapped into staying on after all. He could not refuse the student's appeal. Akitada sighed. "Very well. I shall go to see him."

"What about me?" asked Tora. "You will need me to investigate, but the young lord is waiting to go buy paper and bamboo sticks for our kites."

Akitada turned to Tora with amazement. "You mean you have already won the boy's confidence?" he asked.

"Oh, it was easy enough. For all he's a lord, he was dying for someone to talk to. When I told him about the kite I won my first district contest with, he couldn't wait to try to build one like it."

Akitada clapped Tora on the shoulder. "Excellent!" he cried. "You did better than any of us! I have been trying for many days now to talk to the boy and failed miserably. You must have a special touch with children." Tora preened a little. "Under the circumstances," continued Akitada, "you must keep your promise to Lord Minamoto. But later today, when you are done with the kites, go to see the girl's family. Professor Sato tells me that Omaki was the daughter of an umbrella maker called Hishiya. They live in the sixth ward. She was unmarried and pregnant, as you know, but apparently not particularly worried about her future. Perhaps you can find out something about the men in her life."

◆

When Akitada got to the municipal police headquarters, he discovered to his relief that Kobe was out. Even better, one of Kobe's men recognized him and took him to see the student Nagai.

He found him sitting on the dirt floor of a small, damp cell, lit by a single slit of a window near the ceiling. When the door opened with a rattle of locks and keys, Nagai raised red-rimmed eyes. Akitada was startled anew by the pathetic ugliness of the boy's features, wet and swollen with weeping. Akitada, ashamed of his reaction, greeted the boy with a smile.

The young man stumbled to his feet, but the chains which bound his wrists and ankles made this difficult.

"Please sit down!" Akitada said quickly and seated himself on the bare floor. "I received your note. Exactly what sort of trouble are you in?"

"I am accused of having killed Omaki." The youngster swallowed hard, a prominent Adam's apple bobbing disconcertingly in his long neck. "As if I could!" he cried. "I worshipped her! But things look very bad for me. Only you can help me, sir! They say you have solved many difficult cases. Please, for the sake of my family, clear my name! I don't care anything about myself, but my poor parents and sisters . . ." Tears started down his cheeks. He sniffled, and wiped ineffectually at a running nose with a sleeve already wet with tears.

Akitada regarded him with pity. Tora's estimation had been cruel but correct. The homely face, now red-splotched, the dripping nose and lax mouth made him a most unlikely romantic hero. Such a young man must feel deeply the hurt of rejection by the one person he idolizes. And a girl like Omaki, pretty, pert, ambitious, would have considered the adoration of this youngster, with neither looks nor fortune, a tedious joke. Had she taunted him, tried his patience and devotion too far until he had killed her?

Was he the student she had been in the habit of meeting in the park? Or had he followed her and, finding her with another student, lashed out in anger at her betrayal?

"What made the police fix on you as a suspect?" Akitada asked.

"They talked to some of the students and my name came up." Nagai hung his head again. "One of them found a poem of mine and told the others. I was angry at the time, but perhaps it was very foolish of me to think that such a pretty girl could like me. When we first met, she was really nice to me. And she seemed to enjoy going for walks in the park. She told me all about her music, and I told her about my family."

Akitada's heart went out to the poor infatuated youngster. But pity would not clear Nagai of the charges against him. He said, "Your name being mentioned by the other students explains why the police talked to you, but it does not account for your arrest. What else happened?"

Nagai sighed and gave Akitada an imploring look. "We quarrelled, Omaki and I. The day she . . . before she was found. Someone overheard us. And then, when the police searched my room, they found the poems and my diary." He hung his head, twisting his red, bony hands.

"You quarrelled in the park?"

Nagai looked up. "Oh, no!" he cried. "We did not go to the park that day. We talked in the university, just inside the dormitory enclosure. She had finished her lute lesson. I usually waited for her there."

"What did you quarrel about?"

There was a pause. Then Nagai said, "I asked her to marry me. I know I should not have asked her without my father's permission. My family counts on me to do well in the examination. But I was afraid they would forbid it, and I couldn't wait. Well, I thought Omaki needed someone . . . and I thought if I could take the next examination instead of waiting my turn, I might pass. Even if I did not do very well, I could still become a schoolmaster back home. And Omaki and I could live with my parents. She could help my mother, while my father and I could run the school." He shook his head sadly. "I should have known I was being foolish."

Akitada said dryly, "I take it she was not overjoyed by your offer."

An expression of acute pain passed over the young man's face. "She laughed at me! She wanted to know how we would live until I passed the examination. When I suggested that she might give lute lessons or play for guests just a little while longer, she got angry and called me names. She called me r . . . rabbit because of my ears and teeth, and . . . ugly toad and worse things." He flushed and looked at Akitada earnestly. "She was not herself. You see, she was expecting a child. I am told women become very high-strung in that condition."

"Was it your child?"

Nagai hesitated, then shook his head. "No. We didn't . . . it must have happened before we met. I never asked. Some unprincipled person must have taken advantage of her and then deserted her. When she first confided in me, I got the idea that she might consider being married to someone like me."

He looked so completely humiliated that Akitada's heart contracted with pity and he felt increasingly angry with the dead girl. Finding herself pregnant, she meant to marry the infatuated student, but later decided he was not good enough. This change of heart, if you could call it that, confirmed Sato's impression that she had seemed untroubled by her pregnancy and even pleasantly excited. Something had happened to make Hiroshi Nagai dispensable, so that she had felt free to mock and revile his unselfish and sincere devotion before sending him on his way. Her behavior gave him a strong motive to kill her. But Akitada wondered what had happened to change her expectations so drastically.

He told Nagai, "I will try to help you, but you must tell me all you know about her private life, her friends and her family."

The student bowed deeply and expressed his gratitude. Then he said, "I am afraid I don't know much." Looking a little uneasy, he confessed, "I met Omaki in the Willow Quarter. I know it is against the rules for students to visit there, but some of the others took me along one night. We climbed the wall. I was very nervous."

Akitada nodded understandingly. No doubt the lonely, unpopular youngster had accepted the invitation eagerly, even against his better judgment.

"Omaki had a job playing the lute in one of the wine houses we went to. She played as beautifully as she looked." He smiled a little at the memory. "I kept going back there as much as I could, and one day she noticed me and smiled. After her performance I got up the nerve to talk to her. We took a walk by the river. I thought she was wonderful. She talked about herself, how poor her family was and how very unhappy she was. Her stepmother beat her and made her rise before dawn to do all the work, even when she didn't get home from her job in the wine house until very late. She told me many times she wanted to run away or kill herself." Nagai sighed deeply.

"What about the people where she worked? Did she tell you about them?"

"Not much. The auntie at the Willow was always wanting her to sell herself, but Omaki wanted to be an entertainer. I know some people have said bad things about her, but that proves she was a decent girl, doesn't it, sir?"

Akitada did not share this conviction, but nodded. "Who said what about her?" he asked.

"Oh, some of the fellows I went out with. But they were lying. They were always making fun of me." With a bashful glance at Akitada, he said, "I thought maybe they were jealous of me."

"I see. Was there anyone else who knew her well?"

"She was taking lute lessons from Professor Sato. Professor Fujiwara and Professor Sato often go to the Willow. The first time I saw them I was frightened, thinking they would turn us in, but the others told me that I had nothing to worry about. Anyway, Professor Sato being an instructor of the lute, I pointed him out to Omaki. She managed to get him to take her as a private student. That was wonderful, because then I got to see her during the day.

We'd always meet after her lesson and sometimes we'd stroll over to the park. Until that last day." He sighed and wiped his eyes again.

"What about other people? Friends, coworkers, regular patrons?"

"There is another lute player at the Willow, but they did not get along. Omaki said the woman was too proud. And the girls were silly and common."

"What about men friends?"

"Omaki had no men friends!" He was emphatic. "She was not a loose woman. I don't care what they say! There were no other men after we met."

They looked at each other. Hiroshi held the gaze defiantly, but Akitada did not know whether the agony so eloquent on the homely face was due to better knowledge, to grief, or to rejection. He sighed and rose. "Very well. It is not much to go on, but I shall try to find out more. Meanwhile, if you can recall anything else, something she said or any gossip about her which might point to other relationships, send me a message."

"This useless person is deeply grateful, sir," said Hiroshi fervently, prostrating himself with a great clatter of chains and knocking his forehead on the ground.

Akitada stood for a moment longer, staring down at the ungainly figure. The deep sadness which filled his own heart seemed to spill over, flooding the small cell and drowning its unhappy occupant and himself. With a shudder, he turned and walked out.

TEN

KITES

𝒯ora collected the young lord, and together they walked companionably into the city to buy paper and string. The boy's drawn face brightened and his eyes went everywhere when they reached the shopping district. Only his sense of his own importance kept him from stopping in front of every shop to gape at all the goods on display. Eventually, to cover up his unseemly curiosity, he began a conversation with Tora.

"They certainly have a lot of fans in this shop," he would say, and pause to look.

Tora would shoot a careless glance towards the fans, agree, and walk on.

"Do people really eat all those rice cakes that the baker has stacked up on that shelf?"

"Mostly," said Tora. "What he can't sell, he eats himself or donates to a temple for gifts to the deities."

The boy stopped to eye the cakes hungrily. "Isn't that a big waste?" he asked. "Especially when they are jam-filled cakes? Surely the gods don't care much about jam-filled cakes. Do you suppose the monks eat them and pretend the gods have done so?"

Tora, who had perforce stopped also, looked down at the young lord in surprise. "Don't you believe in the gods?" he asked.

The boy turned away after giving the cakes another longing look. "I don't know. I have never seen one eat, or do anything useful." They walked on. "How much do those jam-filled cakes cost?"

"Three coppers. And you can't see gods, because they are spirits." A thought struck Tora. "It's really strange to hear you talk that way about the gods. Is it because they took your grandfather away from you?"

The boy flung around and glared at him. "It was not the gods who took my grandfather!" he cried.

Tora raised his hands. "Sorry! Forget I asked." He did not know what to make of this outburst, but felt guilty for having touched on a painful subject. Belatedly he realized why the boy had asked about the cakes. "Come," he said. "Let's go back to that baker's shop. I'm hungry all of a sudden, and those cakes did smell real good. I like the ones with jam myself. How about you?"

The boy put on an indifferent face and said, "I don't care. You may suit yourself."

Tora went inside, purchased two fragrant cakes, and returned, offering one to the boy.

The little lord accepted the offering without comment or thanks, and bit into it with a good appetite.

"Mmm," muttered Tora through rice crumbs and bean jam. "They *are* good. That jam . . ." he took another huge bite, making the jam spurt out and dribble down his chin, "is delicious."

The boy stared at him and began to giggle. "It's on your nose!" he pointed out, almost choking on his next bite.

Tora cleaned his face. "It's delicious anyplace," he said firmly, licking his fingers. But the boy's eyes had already become fixed on a display of painted paper umbrellas.

"Look," he said. "Aren't they colorful? I have never seen paper parasols before. The only ones I have seen were made of silk. The emperor is carried under a very large one. And they have them in the temples for the abbots. Sometimes my great-uncle gets to walk under one. But these have flowers and birds painted on them.

Could we make kites out of them? They are made of paper and wood ribs. All we would need is some silk cord."

"Silk cord?" Tora looked down at the boy with raised brows. "Hemp will do much better and is cheaper. Unless you plan to pay for our stuff, we'll make do with plain paper and hempen cord. We'll pick up the bamboo sticks on the way back. I know where there's a bunch on an empty lot." He shook his head. "The very idea! To make a kite from an umbrella! Why, there's not a whole sheet of paper in the whole thing. It would rip apart in a moment. And think of the money! Don't you know anything?" Seeing the sudden hurt in the boy's eyes, Tora reached out and squeezed the small shoulder gently. "Never mind. You'll learn in no time!"

But Lord Minamoto hung his head and scraped a toe through the dust of the street. "It is very good of you to show me how to build a kite," he muttered. "Naturally I shall recompense you for your expenditures as soon as I receive my allowance."

"Forget it," laughed Tora. "I'm going to enjoy this. Besides, my master'll give me the money if I ask. He's the one that suggested you and I build kites together."

The boy looked up, startled. "Why would he do that?" he asked.

Tora grinned at him. "He likes little kids, I guess. And maybe he wishes someone had taught him when he was your age."

This information preoccupied Lord Minamoto until they found the shop they were looking for. Tora quickly purchased two large sheets of cheap mulberry paper and two rolls of hemp line on wooden spools. Then they walked to an open area where a stand of bamboo in the first fresh green of spring swayed gracefully in the breeze. Tora quickly gathered a bundle of dry, broken canes and added them to their bundle, explaining the proper sizes and varieties for kite building.

They walked back happily discussing Tora's kite flying recollections. Then the boy suddenly said, "Your master is a nice man, but do you like working for him?"

"Of course I like it. I wouldn't be doing it, if I didn't like it. Though there was a time when I thought he was one of those per-

fumed lordlings that think common hard-working folk are nothing but stinking dung. I would not have worked for one of those
worthless bastards for a bag of gold. Worthless and evil is what
they are! Devils!"

The boy's eyes flew to Tora's face. "What do you mean?" he
cried, his eyes wide and angry and his fists clenched.

Tora glanced down at the outraged little lord. "Oh, sorry." He
grinned, not at all intimidated by the boy's ferocious expression.
"I forgot you're one of them. Anyway, that's what I thought then.
My master turned out to be a good man. In fact, he's not really
much different from us ordinary people. Maybe you, too, will
grow up to be like him."

The boy opened his mouth to protest, but decided to think
this over. After a moment, he asked, "What makes you hate the
good people so much?"

"The 'good' people, you call them?" Tora gave a derisive laugh.
"The 'good' people took my parents' farm and my parents starved
to death, while I was away fighting the 'good' people's wars for
them."

"That must have been terrible," said the young lord, "and I am
very sorry for you. But surely such things rarely happen in this country. I know all of our own peasants are very happy on our lands."

"And how would you know that? You're just a kid and live in
the capital. You have never lived like one of your peasants. Where
I come from back east, a lot of farmers have had the same kind of
thing happen to them that happened to us. They work the fields
from sunrise to sunset, planting, tending and reaping. They grow
rice, millet, hemp and beans, and just when they think they got
enough to make it through the winter, the tax man comes and
takes half of it for the lord. And when they go back to the fields to
grow some winter vegetables to ease their hunger, the lord needs
a pond in his garden, and he sends for the poor farmer to dig it.
Then he wants a mountain moved to the pond, and guess who'll
do it? Then roads must be built, and the lord wants a fine temple
erected to honor his ancestors. All the while the farmer is working

for the lord, his wife and children starve and tend the fields. And when the farmer finally gets home, the lord starts a war and the farmer has to report for duty with a halberd and whatever armor he can afford to buy. And while he's away fighting, another lord's soldiers come and kill his family and burn down his house." Tora broke off, breathing heavily. Belatedly he recalled his companion and looked at him anxiously. But young Lord Minamoto was staring into the distance.

The boy was silent for a long while. Then he said solemnly, "You do not understand. Someone has to look out for the common people. We are raised to take care of the peasants, just as the peasants work for us. It is a fair exchange. We fight wars to protect you people, and we die for you in battle. We also plan for your future by storing grain for bad years, and we administer the law, catch criminals and keep good order among you. And building a temple is for the good of all people, as are the roads."

Tora stopped, placed his large hands on the child's frail shoulders and said, "A fair exchange, is it? Look around you! Whose life is better? Who has plenty of food? Who rides the horses and carriages instead of walking? Who wears the silken clothes? Who can afford many wives and concubines? Who has time for hunting and games and silly poems?"

The boy shook off Tora's hands angrily. "You are blind!" he raged. "You only see things your way! You've never been a lord. How would you know our troubles?"

Tora nodded. "You got me there. You know, you're pretty smart for your age. By the way, how old are you?"

"I am in my eleventh year, but age has nothing to with it," the boy snapped haughtily. "I know such things because, unlike you, I have been raised to use my intelligence."

"Ah," said Tora, keeping his face straight, and looking thoughtfully up at the floating clouds. "In that case, you should have no trouble building your own kite, my lord." With an exaggerated bow, he presented the bundle of paper and string to his lordship. "I am supposed to take care of some other business anyway."

The boy put his hands behind his back. "I do not carry bundles like a common person. You carry it. Besides, your master has ordered you to teach me."

Tora laid the bundle on the ground between them. "You remember asking me if I liked my master?" When the boy nodded reluctantly, he said, "Well, the reason is that he treats me with respect. I can leave any time I want to, and if I decide to work for his mother—who is a terrible old woman, by the way—I do so because I want to. In the same way I agreed to help you build a kite because I wanted to. But it is clear you don't want me."

"That is not true!" The boy's anguished protest hung between them for a moment. Then the little lord turned away and started walking, his shoulders drooping and his eyes on the ground. Tora watched him for a while, then snatched up the bundle and followed.

At the gate to the university he lengthened his stride and caught up. "All right," he said. "This time I'll forget it, but don't do it again. Friends don't talk like that to their friends."

The boy's pale skin turned a deep red. He nodded wordlessly. They proceeded towards the dormitories and sat down on the veranda. Tora undid the bundle and checked the contents. He frowned and said, "We forgot the knife. Got to have a knife. Come, let's go borrow one from the cook."

"That fat, filthy animal?"

Tora nodded. "I see you've met. Yes, him. Unless *you* happen to have a knife?"

"No, but I have a sword." The boy disappeared into his room and returned carrying a long package wrapped in lustrous red silk and tied with gold-trimmed white silk cords. Unwrapping this carefully, he produced a beautiful sword in a wooden sheath covered with gold-dusted lacquer and inlaid with mother-of-pearl birds in flight. He drew the slender blade of blue-black steel by its hilt, which was heavily ornamented with silver and gold chrysanthemums and bees. This he extended to Tora. "Here!"

Tora looked at the sword, then at the child. He knew the weapon was a family heirloom, something that is passed from father to eldest son, and kept enshrined on the family altar. He had never seen anything so beautiful, and jerked his hands behind his back. "I can't touch that," he said. "It is much too fine. You should not offer it to people to use for cutting bamboo and paper."

The boy nodded. "I know that. But you said you were my friend. And . . . and I have nothing else to offer you. You may use my sword, Tora."

Tora's face broke into a smile. "Thank you, my friend," he said with a bow.

The little lord smiled shyly. "My friends call me Sadamu."

"Thank you, Sadamu." Tora wiped his hands carefully on his robe and accepted the sword. "It is very beautiful, and I appreciate your allowing me to hold it and look at it." He turned it this way and that, tested the sharpness of the blade with his thumb, performed a few slashes at the air, and then replaced it in its sheath and returned it with another bow. "We will get a knife from the cook. Your ancestors would be upset if we misused this fine weapon."

The cook, who was seated on the floor of the kitchen, resting his broad back against a barrel, greeted Tora with a grin which faded when he saw Lord Minamoto. "Thought you'd come for another game," he muttered. "I've been practicing."

A bowl stood in the middle of the floor, surrounded by heaps of coins, pebbles, radish heads, beans, stale rice dumplings and other unidentifiable kitchen waste. The cook's assistants rushed about doing their chores, giving him and the bowl a wide berth.

"Some other time," said Tora. "I came to borrow a knife. We're making kites."

"Ho, ho. Kites, is it? For a moment I thought you needed protection against murderous maniacs like that Rabbit. But they got him safely locked up. That'll be the end of him, strangling girls in the park! I always knew he'd come to a bad end. Why, remember the day you and I caught him beating up poor Haseo? He could have killed both of us, if you hadn't been along." He cocked his head and thought a moment. "You'll ruin my knife, cutting bamboo," he said, "but in gratitude for saving my life, I'll let you have one." After shouting an order to one of his men, he turned back to

Tora. "I hear your master's been to see Rabbit in jail," he said. "Tell him he's wasting his time. Haseo's been to the police and told them all about Rabbit and the girl. Did you know they used to meet on the sly and they argued the very day he killed her?"

Tora asked, "How do you know this Haseo wasn't lying? Looks to me like he'd use a chance to get back at Rabbit for his drubbing."

The cook cackled. "How do I know? Well, let me tell you. That day I was fixing the noon rice, wondering where those lazy bums were, when Rabbit arrives, with this terrible look on his face and muttering to himself. I can see he's not going to do much work and am thinking of firing him, but Haseo comes in and tells me about Rabbit having a fight with his girl. Seems like she told him off—like what girl wouldn't? Rabbit hears us laughing about it and gets this wild look in his eyes. I tell you, I was afraid he'd strangle Haseo right then and there. So I made him go and clean out the storage shed, figuring that'd keep him busy all afternoon." The cook shook his head. "But did his face ever look horrible! Trust me. He killed that girl all right. He's a lunatic."

Lord Minamoto stepped forward and stared down at the fat cook with disdain. "You are a lying piece of dung," he pronounced calmly. "I know the student you call Rabbit, and he is not like that at all. If you and that disgusting fellow Haseo don't stop slandering him, I'll have you both arrested and whipped."

The cook's mouth fell open. Tora snatched the knife from the hands of the gaping worker and, taking the young lord by the arm, said to the cook, "Thanks. You'll get it back when we're done." They hurried out.

"Lesson number one," Tora told the boy outside, "never insult a man you want a favor from. Insult him after you get what you want."

"Sorry. He made me angry."

"You liked the ugly student?"

The boy nodded. "He's one of the few who talked to me. Besides, I watched him. He is a kind and gentle person."

When they reached the veranda again, they settled down to the building of the kites. Tora showed the boy how to split bamboo into thin, flexible lengths and tie them with hemp into an oddly shaped framework of lightweight, strong "bones." "For the spine, always point the bamboo downward so the heavy end is on top," he explained, "and the ribs at the top are heavier, too." Together, they built two bamboo skeletons. Next Tora cut sheets of the paper to cover the two frames, overlapping them slightly. The outlines now resembled those of soaring birds of prey.

"Night hawks," said the boy, studying the shapes critically, "or rather kites. They are large but much too plain. Can't we paint the paper?"

"We've got no paint! Besides I'm not much of an artist," said Tora. "Never mind! As long as they climb higher than anyone else's." He shot a pointed glance at a gaggle of boys who had gathered at a distance and were watching them.

"I have paints and ink," said the boy. "And I can paint bird feathers. Wait!"

He dashed off and returned with two brushes, water, ink and a box of paints. He rubbed the ink with a little water and mixed some red powder into a paste. Then he began to paint two round ferocious eyes and tinted them bright red. The small body feathers followed, scalelike, black on the brown paper, with a few red dots here and there. The wing and tail feathers were last, broad and boldly striped. After watching him for a while, Tora took up the other brush and began to paint, glancing over at the boy's paper from time to time to compare. He sighed with pleasure as he saw eyes, beak, wing and tail feathers take shape on his own kite. "Very realistic," he said. "I bet they'll scare the little birds away."

"How did you meet your master?" the boy asked.

Tora told of their encounter with highway robbers and how Akitada had subsequently rescued him from a murder charge. The boy stopped painting, engrossed in the story.

"That's what I was talking about earlier," said Tora. "I thought my master was one of those tax-grabbing officials from the capital, but it turned out he was on the way to uncover a vicious crime. He's good at that. And now he's going to help Rabbit too."

That, of course, raised more questions and produced more tales, and the sun was already low before the kites were finished, the ends of the framework inserted through the slots in the paper and secured with string, the wing tips and tail feathers cut out, the beaks sharpened and the bridles carefully measured, fastened and attached to the lines.

The moment of trial had arrived. They walked away from the buildings into the large open area between the dormitory and the stand of pines. "A mountaintop or a beach would be better," said Tora. "But this will do for practice." He explained, then demonstrated, and his kite rose sharply and triumphantly on the breeze as he let out the cord on its spool.

Lord Minamoto laughed aloud at the sight and clapped his hands. "Look at it soar!" he cried. "It looks exactly like a giant kite. Oh, it is beautiful!"

Tora grinned, then tied his string to a sturdy shrub. "Now you," he said. "Here, hold it like this. Heavens! It's taller than you! Are you sure you can run with it?" The boy nodded, his teeth catching his lower lip, and his free hand clutching the spool of string. "All right! Run that way, as fast as you can. When you feel the kite pulling, start releasing the cord."

The first try ended in failure. Boy and kite took a hard fall. But Lord Minamoto was back on his feet instantly, brushed away dirt and blood from a nasty scratch on his cheek, and took off again, short legs flying. This time the kite rose, jerkily at first, then more smoothly, when Tora rushed up to lend a helping hand. Cheers and applause rose from the group of watching youngsters, but neither man nor boy heard them. Their eyes were on the soaring paper bird high above them, rising ever higher with every tug on the line. Together, their fingers touching, Tora's large dark hands next to the boy's small pale ones, they felt the power of the kite as it rose on the wind, the pull upward, skyward. They sensed its thrill of flight, the utter freedom from the human condition.

"Oh, it is so strong," cried the boy. "Can it lift me up? Could it carry me over the trees? All the way to the mountains?"

Tora laughed with joy. "Never! Too dangerous! I'd not let it happen. Besides you're stronger than your kite. Here, you try." He released the line.

The kite swooped up, performed a perfect arc, and dove steeply earthward.

"Oh!" cried the boy and instinctively pulled in the line. The kite leveled, completed the circle and rose again. "Did you see what I made it do?"

"Yes. And I haven't even had time to show you that trick. Let me get my kite, and we'll make them chase each other!"

This involved the finer points of maneuvering and steering their kites. As Tora demonstrated attack and evasion, the paper birds swooped at each other, passed and soared apart again. The boy's face was flushed, and his eyes shone with excitement.

"Did you know that you can have a contest?" asked Tora.

"How? Please show me how!"

"You cross strings with your opponent, and then pull back hard to make his kite tumble."

The boy eyed the soaring kites and quickly moved behind Tora and past him. "Like this?" he cried when the lines touched.

Tora grinned. "Right! Now jerk hard!"

The little lord pulled back so hard that he sat down, and Tora's kite made a sudden dive.

"Careful! It'll go into the trees!" shouted Tora, reeling in line frantically. His kite struggled and began to rise a little again. Behind him he heard a loud giggle, and then he saw the boy out of the corner of his eye, up and running with all his might back toward the dormitory. The lines snagged again, and this time Tora's kite plummeted to earth.

"I won! I won!" cried Lord Minamoto, jumping up and down.

"So you did," said Tora, grinning broadly as he went to pick up his kite.

It was getting dark. They had not noticed the sunset, and dusk had fallen swiftly. Above, the sky was still bright and the boy's kite caught the last golden rays on the tips of its wings, but down below all was getting dark. "Better bring it in," cried Tora. "It's getting late."

To his surprise the boy obeyed without argument. "You will come back tomorrow?" he asked, when he had reeled in his kite.

"I doubt I'll have the time," said Tora, winding up string. They carried their kites back to the veranda. There a small huddle of boys awaited them.

"Can we see your kites?" asked the biggest one.

"You'll have to ask Sadamu," said Tora. "They're his."

They clustered around Lord Minamoto, looking and admiring. "Would you teach us, Sadamu?" asked another boy shyly. Tora watched with a fatherly grin. When the discussion became technical, he interrupted. "I've got to go now," he said.

The little lord came to him immediately and they walked a few steps. "Thank you for your help, Tora," said the boy, making a little bow. "I would consider it a great honor if you would come to visit me again when you have time."

Tora reached out a hand and tousled the boy's hair. "I'll be back, Sadamu. Whenever I can. You take care of yourself and remember what I taught you."

The boy nodded. Then he looked up at him, a strange expression on his face. "How much money does your master pay you?" he asked.

"He's not a rich man," said Tora. "But I live in his house and eat his food, and besides he gives me what I need for clothes or wine. I'm satisfied. Why?"

The boy's eyes had widened in surprise and satisfaction. "Oh, I just wondered," he said vaguely, adding, "I think you have many useful talents," and ran back to his new friends.

Tora chuckled, shook his head, and left.

ELEVEN

THE SACRILEGE

Akitada returned to the university in a somber mood. Ishikawa was not back yet, and so he went to his room again and settled down to reading his students' papers. But his mind was not on his work. He pushed the essays away and stared at the wall. The problem of clearing Nagai of the murder charge was not all that troubled him. There was also the continued absence of both Ishikawa and Oe.

It was not, of course, unusual for either to absent himself from the university. Ishikawa might well have decided to spend his holiday visiting friends, and Oe was probably too embarrassed to show his face. Still Akitada felt vaguely uneasy.

Since he could not concentrate on his work, he decided to look in on Seimei at the ministry, but just as he was leaving, Hirata arrived.

"I was coming to see you," he said. "How are things with young Hiroshi?"

Akitada gave a brief summary of his talk with Nagai.

"Poor foolish boy," sighed Hirata. "By the way, I cannot find Oe anywhere. Knowing how anxious you are to settle this matter,

I went to his home, but his servants say that he has not been seen there since yesterday. I asked them if he might have gone out of town to his summer place, but it seems he would not do that without taking them. I must say, it is most unlikely. Oe is much too lazy to live there like a hermit and do for himself. What do you suppose he is up to?"

"You know the man better than I. Could he be hiding with friends until the talk dies down?"

Hirata raised his brows. "What friends?" he asked.

"Well," said Akitada, "there is nothing to be done until he reappears. I am on my way to check on Seimei at the ministry, but will return later to finish some student papers."

◆

Seimei was bent over Akitada's desk copying manuscripts. Neat stacks of document boxes stood next to him, and his brush flew across the paper. He greeted his master with an expression which managed to be both pleased and sympathetic. Laying down his brush in its wooden rest, he rose to bow to his master.

"It is kind of you to think of me when you have so much on your mind," he said with an earnest look. For a moment Akitada wondered how he had heard about Nagai's arrest already, but Seimei continued, "You must feel the disappointment deeply. I need hardly say how glad I was when I heard that you had chosen your wife. And such a very suitable match! I well remember meeting Miss Hirata when I used to carry messages between the two houses. You were both still children, but even then I used to think how perfectly matched you were." He sighed. "Ah, fortune and misfortune are truly like the twisted strands of a rope."

Akitada turned away. The old man meant well, but sometimes he wished for a little less garrulousness. "Thank you, Seimei," he said, staring at the shelves as if he were checking on their caseload. "You are right. It was . . . is a great disappointment to me." For a moment a powerful sense of loss gripped him and something in his chest contracted painfully. He cleared his throat, covering an involuntary gasp, turned back and said briskly, "Well, I shall soon

join you here again. Hirata's problem at the university is just
about resolved. Have you made any progress about Prince
Yoakira?"

Seimei looked smug. "I am afraid it has been more difficult
then I thought. After all even a thief takes ten years to learn his
skill, and he is only stealing property. I am looking for plots and
stratagems."

Akitada raised his eyebrows. "Where did you pick up such
high-flown language?"

"The recording clerk of the Bureau of Records is a very interesting man: a man of letters, as it were. We have much in common." Seimei smiled complacently.

"I am happy to hear it. What does he have to say about the
prince's will?"

The old man looked shocked. "Sir, I could not ask him such a
blunt question!"

"Oh. Was there some other reason you mentioned him?"

"We have fallen into the habit of meeting after work. He is a
widower and lives by himself. It appears we share a passion for
chess."

"Really? I had no idea you were such an avid chess player,"
Akitada said with a smile.

"I find it exercises the mind. One sits and thinks about the
next move. Sometimes both players pause and empty their minds
by speaking of trivial matters."

"Trivial matters?" Fascinated, Akitada waited.

"Matters such as the recent gossip about the prince's peculiar
disappearance might easily be mentioned in passing." Seimei cast
a sly glance at his master. "It is natural to theorize about heirs and
successors when great men die. It is also natural to express disbelief at the extraordinary wealth of some people."

"Most natural."

"I am to see the documents in question tonight. My chess
partner expects to win a small wager."

Akitada made a face. "I see you are a master at the game. How
much?"

"One piece of silver."

Fishing around in his sash, Akitada produced the coin. "Go on."

"He did imply that most of the property is settled on the grandson, with a large dowry for his granddaughter."

"Aha! What about appointments? Are there any rumors about who will take his position?"

"That is common knowledge by now. The crown prince's younger brother will succeed to Prince Yoakira's post. But the position he vacates is mentioned for Lord Sakanoue, since he is the late prince's grandson-in-law."

"Better and better! Enough to tempt even that proud gentleman!"

Seimei cleared his throat. "By the sage Master Kung's definition, such a one is no gentleman," he said primly. "Besides the master taught that men should beware of coveting riches lest heaven send calamities to them."

"The sage Confucius has been wrong in this instance," Akitada remarked bitterly. "So far the calamities seem to have befallen the innocent."

Seimei ignored this criticism of his favorite idol. "You also asked about Secretary Okura. People positively enjoy talking about him. It turns out that he is a low class individual, being merely the only son of a wealthy land speculator, a tradesman."

Akitada suppressed a smile. Seimei had the typical snobbery of the hereditary retainer. "What do they say?"

"They make jokes behind his back about his common background. It seems he is spending money lavishly on entertainments to impress the 'good people' while they amuse themselves behind his back at his lack of refinement. There is a particularly shocking rumor that he is so desperate to be accepted that he has been spending nights with the daughter of a high-ranking nobleman in his mansion in the Sanjo ward. A marriage announcement is imminent. The lady is no longer young and said to be extremely unattractive." Seimei paused to let this sink in, then continued, "You will be particularly interested in some talk that he has bought his first place in the examination. People like to embarrass him by asking him to explain Chinese verses."

Akitada sighed. "So much for protecting the reputation of the university. But I must say, I am relieved that he has not been able to fool anyone. It means that he has gone as far as he can in the government."

"A tadpole can only turn into a frog," Seimei pointed out with great satisfaction.

"Yes." Akitada glanced at the document boxes. "How are the case reviews going?"

"All is well. No new business has come in since you left, and I can keep up easily with the ongoing work."

Akitada touched the old man's shoulder. "Well done, old friend! I don't know what I would do without you. I especially admire your handling of the clerk from records. I'm afraid I have to go back now. Professor Hirata and I are hoping to confront the culprits in the blackmail scheme." He walked to the door, then added, "By the way, one of the students has been arrested for the murder of the girl in the park. I believe he is innocent and have promised him some help."

He left before Seimei could ask questions.

◆

Akitada's optimistic expectation of a rapid disengagement from Hirata's problems and the Hirata family was doomed to failure. When he passed the gate leading into the courtyard of the Temple of Confucius, he became aware that something was wrong.

It was a flash of red that caught his eye first. He stopped to look and saw a group of red-coated policemen guarding the temple steps against a handful of curious spectators.

With a strange sense of being about to confirm a nagging fear, Akitada joined the onlookers just as a glowering Captain Kobe emerged onto the veranda. He saw Akitada immediately and his expression turned even grimmer.

"I knew you would show up sooner or later," he growled. "Come up here!"

Akitada thought Kobe's manner more than usually rude, but complied. When he reached the top of the steps, he asked, "What has happened here?"

Kobe did not answer. Instead he walked to the open door of the temple hall, where he looked back and said, "I was told that you came to the jail to see the student who killed the pregnant girl."

Akitada was beginning to lose his temper. "You have the wrong man again," he snapped. "Nagai is as innocent as the beggar."

Kobe drawled, "Of course! Like a newborn babe! Follow me!"

The temple hall was plunged into a general gloom. The corners were in deep shadow, and the red-lacquered columns looked black. A strange smell hung in the musty air. Akitada wrinkled his nose, wondering if a dog had got in and relieved himself. On the raised platform against the far wall loomed the life-sized statues of the sages, looking more massive and ghostly in the murk.

In front of the central figure of Confucius stood two people. Akitada recognized the frail Tanabe, who was leaning on Nishioka's arm.

"What is going on?" he asked Kobe again as they approached the group. The smell was strong and repulsive. There was something horribly familiar about it.

Nishioka turned and said in a tight voice, "It's Oe! What a dreadful thing!"

"Oe?" Akitada followed Nishioka's glance to the statue of the sage and saw for the first time that it seemed to be draped in a voluminous, bulging blue robe. It also seemed to have grown a second head, drooping forward across its chest, and another set of arms, hanging limply. Then he saw the blood. Of course! He had smelled it, and excrement. The blood had streamed down from beneath the second head, a broad band of dark brown across the front of Oe's elegant blue robe. Blood and excrement mixed in a large puddle on the floor between Oe's neatly shod feet, and blood had run to the edge of the platform and dripped down, forming a second, smaller puddle on the polished floorboards. Shockingly,

Oe's robe had fallen open. Apart from his white silk socks and black slippers, the dead man was completely nude underneath.

Kobe's sharp voice cut across Akitada's shock. "Two murders in two days," he said. "Within steps of each other. This one happened last night. I believe we have the killer already in custody. Not even you could believe that there are two separate homicidal maniacs loose in the university, Sugawara."

Akitada did not reply. His mind was reeling. Stepping up to the monstrous statue, he lifted the drooping head by its white topknot. Oe's sightless, bloodshot eyes stared back at him, his features distorted in death. The blood had poured from a deep gash nearly severing the head from the body. It was also apparent now what held the body upright. The killer had passed Oe's sash under his victim's armpits and slung it around the neck of the wooden figure of the sage. In death the body had slumped forward and the knees had buckled, but to a casual passerby its presence might not have been immediately noticeable in the dim hall.

As Akitada glanced down, he was struck again by the incongruity between the fine robe and neatly shod feet and the indecently exposed bulging stomach, the sagging folds of skin and the thin soiled legs with their varicose veins and age spots. Nudity, especially that of the elderly, negated the image of power and rank. Behind the pomp and circumstance was the reality of human frailty and imperfection. Someone had been at pains to reveal the real Oe to the eyes of the world.

Turning to his colleagues, Akitada asked, "Who found him?"

Tanabe was very pale and trembled. His lips moved but produced no sound. After a moment, Nishioka said, in an unnaturally subdued tone, "I did. It was a shock. Since there are no classes today, Professor Tanabe and I planned to spend the morning working on a new glossary for the *Analects*. I passed through the hall twice without noticing anything amiss. Then, the third time—I was returning a document to the library—I saw an odd reflection in a spot of sunlight." He looked at the shadowy dais. "It was midday then and the sun was just right. It came in through the open door. Anyway, something glistened. When I came closer, I noticed the smell, and then I found the blood on the dais. And . . . and then I looked up to see . . ." He broke off with a shudder. Tanabe patted Nishioka's hand with his own trembling fingers.

Akitada moved the body's arms and hands. They felt quite cold, and the stiffness which follows death had passed away already. The blood on the floor had congealed and no longer reflected light, and that on the robe was quite dry. Kobe was right. Oe had died during the night. Akitada turned to the captain. "I don't suppose you have had time to question people," he said briskly. "We must find out who was the last to see Oe alive."

Kobe, arms folded across his chest, looked grimly amused. "Since I am a mere police officer, I have been waiting for you. No doubt you will tell me how to proceed," he said, "whenever you are quite finished with your own investigation."

Akitada flushed. "I beg your pardon," he said stiffly. "I realize this is your case, but there are some things. . . ." He stopped. Perhaps it was better not to mention the details of Oe's involvement in the examination fraud or the blackmail letter at this time and in front of witnesses, so he continued, "Well, I have taken an interest in the student Nagai whom you seem to hold responsible for this murder also. Oe attended the poetry contest yesterday and became quite drunk and quarrelsome. He was led away early by his assistant Ono and a graduate student called Ishikawa. My colleague Professor Hirata was with them before they left the pavilion."

Kobe regarded him fixedly. "Your two colleagues here have already informed me of those facts. As you maintain your conviction that Nagai is innocent, can you provide a motive for the murder of this man?"

Akitada forced himself to meet Kobe's hostile eyes calmly. "I cannot suggest anything at this time. But your theory that Nagai has somehow run mad and killed the girl one day and his professor the next does not make sense. For one thing, the young man was quite lucid when I talked to him this morning. For another, the girl was strangled, while Oe's throat was slashed. That suggests two different killers, particularly since a sash was available in this instance also. Look." Akitada pointed to the brocade belt which held the body up. "This sash was used in order to create a macabre and shameful public display. The other sash was removed from the scene, and the girl was hidden in the reeds. Surely that suggests two very different mentalities."

Kobe was unimpressed. "Not necessarily. The first crime may have made the killer feel so powerful that he decided to show off a little the second time. As to the slashed throat, Oe is much bigger and stronger than the girl. A knife or sword was a safer way of killing him than strangulation."

Akitada saw the reasonableness of the argument. Pulling his earlobe, he nodded slowly. "I still don't see Nagai acting in this fashion, but I suppose you are right about Oe's size," he said grudgingly. "Even drunk he would not stand still for a strangler. But why would the killer remove the man's trousers and string him up like this?" Akitada wandered to the back of the statue to look at the knot in the sash.

"Exactly!" Nishioka cried.

Kobe scowled at him, and Nishioka's mouth snapped shut. Kobe remarked, "A perverted sense of juvenile humor, I would say."

Tanabe spoke up for the first time. "It is a frightful sacrilege to the temple." His voice quavered. "Who would dare dishonor our patron saint in this fashion? It must have been the act of a madman or a depraved person."

Akitada nodded. "It is quite extraordinary behavior. I wonder what happened to Oe's trouser skirt . . . and his loincloth. He was in formal court dress last night." He glanced around the hall, then said to Kobe, "No doubt you will order a search, and you had better speak immediately to Ono and Ishikawa. They were closer to him than any of the rest of us, apart from being the last to see him alive. Incidentally, I have promised Nagai that I will help him, so I expect we will meet in the future."

Kobe's face was flushed with anger. "Are you finished?" he asked in a tight voice. "Or are there more instructions?" He stepped up closely to Akitada and glared into his face. "You have no authority here, and I will see you when you are needed in the investigation, not otherwise. Is that clear? I don't need your advice, now or in the future, and you are wasting your time on Nagai. I've got him for the murder of the girl, whatever turns up on this case. And if you think he's clear because the beggar Umakai didn't recognize him, don't be too sure. The old man is senile. He probably just dreamed the whole Jizo thing."

However much he resented the dressing-down, Akitada was most troubled by the news that Umakai was free. "I shall refrain from making any more suggestions," he said stiffly, "but I am concerned about the old man's safety. You yourself pointed out that the killer may find him. Can your men keep an eye on him for a few days more?"

Kobe threw back his head and laughed aloud—the sound echoed in the silent hall, and Tanabe jumped a little. "You forget. There's no need: we've got the girl's killer in jail. Besides, the police have better things to do than follow every beggar around."

Akitada was about to respond sharply, when a new voice interrupted.

"August heaven! What an abomination!" Wrinkle-faced and skeletal, Takahashi inserted himself into the group and stared up at the bloody body suspended from the neck of the sage. "It is absolutely grotesque! But how typical. Even in death Oe had to make a spectacle of himself."

"Who are *you*?" growled Kobe, glaring at Takahashi.

"Oh, I'm Takahashi. Mathematics. I suppose you have taken Fujiwara into custody for the murder?"

"What?" roared Kobe. "Who the devil is Fujiwara?"

"Oh, you mean they haven't told you?" Takahashi looked from Nishioka and Tanabe to Akitada, shook his head and *tsk*ed. "That was not very forthcoming of you, gentlemen," he said. "After all, in a case of murder one has a duty . . . however, I digress. Fujiwara is another of our little group of academicians. Professor of history with a flair for poetry, drinking and brawls. The latter hobby is what will interest you, Captain. He and Oe slugged it out last night. Or rather, Oe slugged Fujiwara. In public." Takahashi nodded towards the body. "One assumes Fujiwara settled the score later."

Kobe looked at Akitada. "Is that true?"

"There was a minor incident," Akitada said, "but Fujiwara made it quite clear to everyone that he did not consider Oe accountable. Oe was too drunk to know what he was doing. You can ask others." Akitada shot Takahashi a disapproving look, and added firmly, "In my view the incident was too minor to be a motive for murder, and Fujiwara is hardly the type to commit this kind of assault."

"Is he another one of your protégés? That certainly tells me something. And I don't bother with what 'type' a man is," snapped Kobe. "A simple person like myself is quite satisfied with motive, opportunity and perhaps a few pieces of hard evidence."

Nishioka bristled. "But you cannot simply ignore—"

"Hush!" Professor Tanabe squeezed his arm, and then told Kobe politely, "Captain, we have notes to put in order before tomorrow. May we be excused?"

Kobe hesitated. He looked at all of them suspiciously, then said, "Very well. You can all go for the time being, but no one is to leave the university without my permission. I'll get to the bottom of this in spite of all of your interference."

Back at the law school, Akitada found Hirata waiting for him. He was pacing back and forth, looking anxious. Akitada suppressed his distaste when he saw the older man's strained face. Hirata asked, "Have you heard the rumor? Oe has been murdered."

"It is no rumor. I am just coming from the Temple of Confucius. Someone slashed his throat and tied his body to the statue of Confucius. It must have happened last night, after he left the competition. Captain Kobe is in a filthy mood. I suppose he thinks there is some sort of conspiracy brewing here, and that I am in the middle of it. He did not take kindly to my visit to the jail and I managed to irritate him more."

"Oh, dear! Tied to the statue of Confucius, you say? It is incredible!" Hirata wrung his hands. "Does he suspect anyone in particular?"

"Poor Nagai is still his prime suspect—on the theory that both murders must have been committed by the same person. I tried to change his mind, but I am afraid that my attempt merely made him suspicious and added all of us to his list of possible assassins."

"Well, it certainly cannot be Hiroshi. Oe never paid the least attention to the poor fellow. He thought him too ugly and ill-born to be of any consequence or promise. And what motive could Hiroshi possibly have? There are other people who had much better cause to kill Oe."

"Precisely. And it won't take Kobe long to work that out. Do you have some wine or tea? I am parched."

Hirata led the way to his office. It was one of the small rooms under the sloping eaves, between the classroom and the veranda overlooking the gravelled courtyard. Here Hirata had gathered all his teaching tools: law books, rolled up maps and diagrams, the Chinese classics, the *Analects*, Prince Shotoku's legal reforms and innumerable stacks of student essays. These were labelled by year, and Akitada could only guess at the devotion of a man who preserved the efforts of generations of students.

Hirata pointed to the cushion lying near his low desk, and brought a small pitcher of wine and two cups. On the desk stood a pale porcelain vase with a single pink peony blossom. Its scent filled the small room.

Akitada held his cup, staring at the flower, its ruffled petals perfectly shaped, its color deepening to rose near the center. Tamako must have selected and cut this flower for her father only this very morning. A lump formed in his throat. Resentful that everything seemed to conspire to remind him of her, he drank deeply and then said, "In any case, the student could not have killed Oe. He is not strong enough."

Hirata looked surprised. "Not strong enough to slash a man's throat? I grant you he is thin, but young and sinewy."

Akitada shook his head. "The killer tied the body to the statue, and Oe was not only tall; he was a big man. As a dead weight he would have been too heavy for Nagai."

Hirata looked shocked. "What an extraordinary thing to do! It is like an insult to the whole university! A student once tied a hat on the sage for a prank; he was dismissed instantly. Who would think of such a thing? And why? It seems inconceivable."

"I know, but it may help us find the killer. Certainly a number of people were openly hostile to Oe, and some of them may have had strong enough reasons for murder, but not all of them could have killed Oe. Takahashi certainly hated Oe and is unpleasant enough to be capable of anything. However, he is past middle-age and lacks the muscle to lift Oe. Ono, on the other hand, is still young and, as Oe's assistant, has suffered continuous abuse from his superior. He seems meek, but sometimes grudges fester until only violence can even the score. But here again, he is too short, unused to exercise, and thus clearly not up to it physically." Akitada sipped more wine and continued. "Now Sato, Fujiwara and Ishikawa are all strong enough and all have reasons to hate Oe. Sato, however, does not have a very strong motive to kill Oe, who merely disapproved publicly of him. And that leaves Ishikawa and Fujiwara, both of whom had a violent physical altercation with Oe shortly before the murder. It won't be long before Kobe arrives at the same conclusion. Takahashi has already accused Fujiwara."

"Oh!" cried Hirata in a frustrated tone. "I almost wish it were Takahashi. He is the unkindest man I know. And Fujiwara is one of the best. Heaven forbid that Kobe should make such a mistake! We must hope that the murder was committed by an outsider."

Akitada raised his brows in disbelief. "It is difficult to see how an outsider would have known where to find Oe on that particular night, or why he would choose to display the corpse in this particular fashion."

"But Kobe could have a point about this murder being connected with the girl's death," Hirata said stubbornly. "And the girl was from the city, from the common people."

Akitada sighed. Hirata was not without the snobbery of his class. Under normal circumstances a kind and gentle man, he nevertheless held on to the belief that the "good people" were incapable of committing a crime, while, regrettably and understandably, the poor citizens often got involved in violence. Akitada said, "I do not know what to think at this point, but you will have to tell

Kobe about the blackmail note. In a case of murder you cannot hope to cover up an incident which may point to a motive. No doubt Kobe will appear shortly to ask his questions. Be prepared."

Hirata stared at him. His breathing became agitated. "Oh, good heaven! I had not thought of that." He held his head, moaning softly, "What a misfortune."

The door opened a crack and Nishioka stuck his head in. He looked better, having regained color and some of his normal spirits. "May I come in?" he asked. They nodded, and Nishioka entered, seated himself, and accepted a cup of wine. "Thank you. I'm afraid I have had a terrible shock, Doctor Hirata. I suppose you have heard that I was the one who discovered the unfortunate victim."

Hirata, still looking quite ill, made a sympathetic comment.

"Thank you. I will get over it, no doubt. I came along to warn you both about that police captain. The man is clearly lacking in the most basic understanding of human behavior. In fact, he even brags about it. Since he was quite rude to me, I have decided not to share my ideas with him. Apparently, and quite perversely, he has already made up his mind that it must have been poor Rabbit."

Akitada nodded. "I am afraid Kobe's attitude is not exactly promising at the moment."

Nishioka brightened. "I see you have formed the same impression. Let's put our heads together and find the killer ourselves! Don't you feel that there was something very nasty about the way the murderer tied Oe up on that statue of our honorable Master Confucius?"

Akitada and Hirata both nodded, and Nishioka continued eagerly, "That is exactly the sort of thing the captain is too dull to notice. Now I, for one, wonder what went through the killer's mind to cause him to do such a thing. Clearly he must be a man without respect for the scholarly tradition the great sage represents. On the other hand, he does appreciate symbolic gestures. Do you agree?"

Again Akitada nodded. Nishioka smiled. "There! I can think of only two people who have the right mentality. And perhaps a third, though I don't know him well enough to be certain." He paused, looking at his companions expectantly.

Hirata cried, "Who are they?"

Nishioka shook his head. "It would be premature to make accusations, Doctor Hirata. At this point, one waits and watches." He looked at Akitada. "I wonder. Are we thinking along the same lines?"

Akitada said, "I have not formed an opinion yet. If you have strong suspicions, you had better mention them to Kobe. As long as the killer is free, he is a dangerous man."

"I refuse to speak to that man. He is rude and ignorant. And I assure you that I am a very careful person. I merely observe quietly, perhaps ask some harmless questions. Believe me, I am so subtle that the object of my interest is never aware of my motives." Nishioka smiled, nodded once or twice, and went on, "Take for instance the evening of the contest. Why, I could have predicted Oe's murder. The evidence was all there for anyone to see—and hear." He asked Akitada, "You noticed, didn't you?"

"If you refer to the incident with Fujiwara," said Akitada, "you have heard me say that I don't think the man capable of this murder."

Nishioka's eyes sparkled. He said, "Fujiwara? Ah, perhaps not. Though you never know with phlegmatic characters like him, or even volatile ones like Sato. But then, any man is capable of murder if provoked sufficiently. All men have at least one sensitive area in their lives which they will not allow to be tampered with."

Akitada regarded Nishioka suspiciously. "What about Sato?" he asked, before Nishioka could go off on another tangent again.

There was something slightly superior about Nishioka's smile. "So you missed that one too, eh? Oe's been talking about petitioning the president of the university for Sato's dismissal. I overheard him telling Ono that he finally had proof of Sato's depravity and planned to write to Sesshin. I expect he found out that Sato has been entertaining prostitutes in his room here."

"Who is Sesshin?" Akitada asked.

Nishioka's eyes widened. "He is the president of the university. I thought you knew."

Hirata interrupted, "I am sure that charge is malicious slander! I am surprised at you, Nishioka, for passing such rumors about. Poor Sato is guilty of no more than giving a few private lessons to earn some additional income." His face had an unhealthy flush, and he gasped a little after speaking.

"Oh, no, Doctor Hirata. It must be more than that, for Oe has known about the 'lessons' for quite a long time." Nishioka emptied his cup and got up. "But I must run along. I want to catch Fuji-wara before Kobe gets to him. Thank you for the wine."

When Nishioka was gone, Hirata said irritably, "How can he talk that way about Sato? He is getting almost as bad as Taka-hashi."

Akitada looked at the door through which Nishioka had left and frowned. "I confess he makes me very nervous. If he really no-ticed something that points to the murderer, he is being very fool-ish. But about Sato he may well be right. I have found the man with two women. The first was the murdered girl. The other one was a very handsome woman his own age. To be sure, both women were playing the lute at the time, but clearly they also were on very familiar terms with him."

"I cannot believe it of him. He is a married man with children."

Akitada gave the older man a pitying look and watched him redden. He said, "Remember that Sato is quite strong, especially his hands."

Hirata poured down the rest of his wine before asking, "You really think he strangled the girl and then killed Oe to protect his position here?"

Akitada did not reply right away. He could imagine Sato com-mitting Oe's murder. The music master was unconventional and, in anger at his treatment by Oe, might have decided to mock the insti-tution's sacred canon by leaving its most famous representative tied around the neck of the patron sage. And removing Oe's trousers might be the gesture of a man who had been accused of sexual im-propriety himself. But he was still not convinced the murders were connected. Finally, he said, "I do not know what to think."

Hirata twisted his hands. His fingers trembled. "I hope it had nothing to do with the note."

"Yes. Ishikawa's continued absence is worrisome," agreed Aki-tada. "Are you feeling quite well?"

"Yes, yes. Just some indigestion," said Hirata. "Ishikawa is a big, strong fellow all right. I am ashamed to admit that I never liked him very much. I had much rather he were the killer than Fujiwara, or even poor Sato. But why would Ishikawa kill Oe? It was Oe who had reason to kill Ishikawa."

"I am afraid we won't know that until we speak to him. He must have at least part of the answer about Oe."

"Who does?" asked a sharp voice. Kobe pushed the door back on its tracks and strode in unceremoniously, followed by a clerk carrying writing utensils.

Ignoring Hirata's greetings and offer of wine, Kobe sat down with a grunt and gestured to his clerk to do likewise.

"Well?" he persisted, looking from Akitada to Hirata and back.

Akitada answered. "Professor Hirata and I were concerned about the disappearance of one of the students. His name is Ishikawa. He is a graduate student who used to read Oe's papers for him. He should be in his dormitory, but seems to have left very early this morning. Since he is one of the last people seen with Oe, I thought that he must have valuable information."

Kobe's eyes went to his clerk who had set up a small portable desk and was rubbing a worn block of ink across a wetted stone. The sound was irritating in the quiet room. When the man finished and reached for his brush, Kobe turned back to them. "This Ishikawa. Full name, place of birth, name and hometown of parents, profession of father and appearance of suspect!"

"Suspect?" stammered Hirata, but he supplied the information. When the clerk had written it down, Kobe asked, "Is this Ishikawa likely to have gone off with the fellow Ono?"

Akitada stared at Kobe. "Why Ono? Is he gone too?"

Hirata said, "Nonsense. Ono must be at home with his mother. She is crippled. They live on Takatsukasa Street west of the palace."

Kobe shook his head. "One of my men checked. He is not at home, and his mother does not know where he went. She is not even sure he came home last night."

Hirata and Akitada looked at each other in dismay.

Kobe said impatiently, "Well? Is this Ishikawa all you have thought of? He's the right size for it apparently. But so is Fujiwara."

"I see you have had second thoughts about poor Nagai being guilty," said Akitada with a grimace. "He simply is not strong enough. But it is only fair to add that neither Professor Hirata nor I think Fujiwara a likely suspect either."

Kobe snapped, "I have not eliminated anyone. The killer may have had an accomplice." He paused to let this sink in, then continued, "As to Fujiwara, he had a motive and is strong enough to haul the body about. Perhaps you should know that your colleagues have been quite forthcoming about each other and the late Oe. It appears that just about everybody here hated the man. To save you the trouble of protecting your colleagues, let me fill you in. Ono hated Oe because he was an abusive tyrant; Sato was about to be dismissed on charges brought by Oe; Tanabe was being forced into retirement, because Oe thought he was senile; both Fujiwara and Takahashi had been publicly shamed by him. Takahashi, by the way, is a positive waterfall of information about the faculty's various and varied offenses." Kobe grinned unpleasantly. "Do either of you have anything to add to the list of motives for murder?"

Akitada avoided looking at Hirata, who had started breathing hard again. He shook his head. "I see you have not wasted any time."

"In that case," said Kobe, "I will now hear your stories. Names, ranks, places of residence and relationship to the murdered man first. You start, Hirata."

Hirata gasped his way through the information, and Akitada followed suit. When the preliminaries were out of the way, Kobe asked, "When did you last see Oe alive?"

Akitada repeated what he had told Kobe earlier. Hirata confirmed it and added that he had accompanied the group that had removed Oe from the gathering as far as the gate to the park and then returned to his seat in the pavilion.

"Where were Ono and Ishikawa taking him?" Kobe asked Hirata.

"I assumed to his home. It is in the western part of the city."

Kobe grunted and sat lost in thought. Then he asked, "Can anyone confirm the time when you returned home?"

"What?" cried Hirata, flushing. "Surely you cannot think either of us—"

"You had better tell the captain what he wants to know," said Akitada soothingly. "I expect he asks everybody. As for me, I left before the last segment of the contest, but spent the rest of the evening reading in my room at home. I had no cause to speak either to my family or any servants."

Hirata stammered, "I went home after it was all over. It was late. But my daughter may have heard me come in."

The clerk was writing busily while Kobe sat, staring at the ceiling with pursed lips.

"Er," said Hirata awkwardly, "perhaps now that we are done, you will take a cup of wine, Captain?"

"I do not drink during an investigation," said Kobe coldly. Then he looked at Akitada and remarked, "It occurs to me that you are tall and strong enough for the job yourself, Sugawara."

Akitada's jaw dropped.

Kobe let his narrowed eyes move from Akitada to Hirata and back again.

He said, "I am told that you two are very close. You, Sugawara, owe Hirata a lot. In fact, you are like a son to him, because he raised you."

Akitada flushed with anger. "Not precisely. What is your point, Captain?"

Kobe did not answer. His eyes went back to Hirata, and he said, "Takahashi says that you have been on bad terms with Oe since the last examination."

Hirata flushed guiltily. "That is not true," he blustered. "Oe and I were not exactly friends, but we were certainly on speaking terms."

"Hmm," said Kobe thoughtfully. "I have an idea that something was wrong with that examination. And then there is the matter of Oe's new summerhouse." He shook his head. "It smells of blackmail, and blackmail makes a very good motive for murder."

Hirata had turned absolutely white and was grasping his chest. He gaped at Kobe in horror and gasped, "Are you accusing me of having Oe killed?"

Akitada snapped, "That is absolutely ridiculous!" But he knew that Kobe's mistake made it impossible now to tell him of the note. It would be interpreted as a desperate attempt to put the blame on a dead man.

The captain looked pleased. "Let's say I am considering possibilities. Of course," he said, studying his fingernails, "Hirata's not young or strong enough to accomplish it unaided, but then he has an assistant who certainly is." And now he looked fully at Akitada.

Hirata was scrambling to his feet, crying, "It is outrageous to suggest such a thing . . . all lies!" Then he groaned, his legs buckled, and he collapsed. Akitada jumped up to go to his aid. Hirata's face was covered in perspiration and his lips were turning blue.

"What is it, sir?" Akitada asked, slipping his arm under the older man's head. "Shall I send for a doctor?"

Kobe said, "A convenient spell. I expect the good professor will recover as soon as I leave."

Hirata twitched in Akitada's arms, muttering, "No. It's nothing. It'll pass." But he was still gasping for air, though a little color was seeping back into his face.

"Calm yourself, sir," Akitada said through clenched teeth as he helped Hirata sit upright. "The captain is playing with us, like a fisherman who hopes to catch his fish by dangling a special bait before him. Hardly what one would expect of a gentleman, of course, but the police evidently have their own methods." He gave Kobe a furious look.

Kobe bared his teeth in a nasty smile, then got up. "I told you," he said, "I have eliminated no one. You may both go home now, but do not leave the city."

TWELVE

THE UMBRELLA
MAKER'S HOUSE

*P*leased with his kite-flying success, Tora left the university for his second assignment. It occurred to him belatedly that he had spent far more time playing children's games than was justifiable for an investigator of crimes, particularly since he also hoped to look in on Michiko. Although his grumbling stomach reminded him that it was time for his evening rice, he ignored the hunger pangs and his aching legs and walked briskly to the sixth ward where he asked directions to the house of the umbrella maker Hishiya.

The light was fading, but he found the street easily. The poorer sort of artisans lived and worked here. Small, narrow houses were crammed together, eaves touching eaves. Tora knew such places well. Behind this block of houses would be a bit of open ground, sometimes made into a tiny garden, but most often just an alley collecting debris and starving dogs.

He saw the umbrella maker's sign, but walked past the house, getting a general impression of the neighborhood and hoping for a bit of gossip with one of the neighbors. He had reached the end of the block without seeing a soul—most people would be eating—when he heard a door opening and then the angry voice of a woman and a cry of pain. When he turned to look, he saw that a small servant girl had come from the umbrella maker's house and was scurrying off with a big basket on her arm. In the doorway stood a buxom female, shaking her fist.

Tora waited until the woman had gone back inside and then ran after the little maid. He caught up with her at the next corner.

"Good evening, little sister," he cried, falling into step beside her.

The little girl—she could be no more than ten or eleven years old—jumped and turned a tear-stained, homely face up to him. She was a pale and very thin child, and her eyes were filled with fear. "Excuse me, sir," she whispered, "I must hurry," and started to run.

"Wait!" Tora persisted, lengthening his stride and straining his sore muscles. "I'll walk with you. You work for the umbrella maker, don't you?"

She slowed down. "Yes," she said, looking up at him uncertainly. Seeing his friendly smile, she relaxed a little.

"I'm sorry if I frightened you, little sister," Tora told her. "I heard you cry out. Was that your mistress?"

Fresh tears rose to her eyes and welled over. She wiped them away with a grimy hand, leaving black smudges behind, and nodded. "She always beats me," she said. "I really try to do the work, but I am small and get tired easily, and I'm always hungry. I think if she'd give me more food, I'd be stronger."

The words had poured forth in one gulp and ended in a sob. Tora felt in his sleeve for his coppers. "Look, I haven't had my evening rice yet. How about you and me having a bowl of noodle soup together?"

The plain, bony face lit up, but she shook her head. "I daren't," she said. "I'm to fetch the vegetables for their dinner. She'll beat me even worse if I'm late."

"Come," said Tora, taking her small, sticky hand in one of his and relieving her of the large basket with the other. "I was on my way to see your master. I'll explain when we get back."

They walked to a neighborhood vegetable market near a small temple. Tora supervised the purchase, making sure she got the largest radish and the freshest mushrooms, before stopping a noodle vendor and ordering two large bowls of the hot soup.

The man carefully lowered his bamboo pole with the kettle and basket of bowls suspended at each end and ladled out two steaming servings of broth thick with fat noodles and bits of vegetables.

"Now let's eat. And take your time!" Tora told the frail child. "I'll speak to your master when we get back."

"Oh, the master's not home yet. Just the mistress and her guest." The girl stared at the food hungrily and licked her lips. Watching her, Tora was reminded of the little lord. They were about the same age, at the extremes of a rigid class system—but both were sad, lonely and fearful. His own life had been hard, but at least he had never lacked love or the joys of childhood play.

"Never mind. Eat!" he said gruffly.

They sat on the steps of the temple. It almost took Tora's appetite away to see how she gobbled her food. He waited until she was done and then asked, "Does your master beat you too?"

She shook her head. "Oh, no! He's kind, but during the day he goes to the big market to sell his umbrellas and I stay with her. Sometimes in the evening, he asks me if I get enough to eat or where I got a bruise, but she's always there and she looks at me like a devil, so I say 'yes' and 'I fell down the stairs.' And she says I'm a clumsy, stupid girl and she has to do all the work herself because he cannot afford to hire decent servants."

"And your parents?"

"My father's dead, and my mother couldn't keep me. Not with five younger ones to feed."

"Hmm." Tora poured the rest of his noodles into her bowl. "I'm not very hungry," he lied. When she had finished his portion also, he asked, "Don't the Hishiyas have a grown daughter? How about talking to her?"

"She got murdered a couple of days ago," said the little girl in a matter-of-fact tone. No doubt, her own troubles overshadowed any concern for others. "She was never home, anyway. Only to sleep, and sometimes not even that. She was the master's daughter. The mistress is his second wife."

"I expect they were very sad when they found out," said Tora.

"Well, Master cried." She took his bowl and stacked it into her own. "But not her!" She spat. "When he was gone she danced a little dance and sang all day long."

"Really? Was there bad blood between them?"

The girl nodded. "They quarreled all the time. Master would leave to get away from them."

"What did they quarrel about?"

"The young miss had pretty things, and the mistress was forever borrowing them. The young miss didn't like it. And then the young miss would talk about the guests, and the mistress would get very angry."

Tora pricked up his ears. "Your master had many visitors?"

"Not the master." She stood up and took the bowls back to the vendor. When she returned, she said, "We must go now. Thank you very much for the good noodles." Reaching for the basket with the vegetables, she added, "I feel much stronger now and can carry the basket very well."

"Not on your life," said Tora, snatching the basket away. "How would it look if a strong young fellow like me let a little lady like you carry such a very large radish by yourself?"

She giggled. "I'm no lady. And you shouldn't be carrying vegetables, sir," she protested.

"I'm not proud. Come, we'll chat as we walk. What about those guests?"

She suddenly looked wise beyond her years. "Oh, they come to see the mistress. There's one at the house now. She says they're cousins from her village, but I've seen them around town."

Tora whistled a few notes of a popular salacious ditty, then asked, "And the daughter? Did she entertain guests, too?"

"Oh, no. The mistress would not have allowed it. She was that jealous of Miss Omaki. Specially when Miss Omaki started getting all the presents from her gentleman."

Tora looked down at the little maid fondly. What a very useful child she was! "Was she going to get married then? What sort of fellow was her betrothed?"

The term puzzled the girl. "Her betrothed? I don't know that word. I've never seen Miss Omaki's gentleman. The mistress only called Miss Omaki names, like 'slut' and 'whore.' I know what those mean, and I don't think she would've done that if Miss Omaki was about to get married, do you?"

"No, I expect not. Well, here we are!" Tora paused before the umbrella maker's house and looked it over. "Did they give you Miss Omaki's room?" he asked.

"Oh, no. I sleep in the kitchen. Miss Omaki's room is upstairs in the back. The mistress has locked it up, because Miss Omaki's things are still in it." The little girl looked nervously at the upper part of the house. "I don't go up there. A dead person's spirit stays in the house for forty-nine days and nights, and I bet Miss Omaki's spirit is angry the mistress is wearing her things."

Tora felt his own hair bristle. He wished the girl had not mentioned spirits. "Well, come on," he said gruffly.

The little maid gave him an anxious look. "You will talk to her so she won't beat me again? You promised."

"Yes."

She took the basket and opened the door. They stepped into the dark front room of the house. The little maid struck a flint and lit an oil lamp. The room was deeper than it was wide. To their left was a kitchen area. Its floor was bare earth and the customary two plaster ovens with their rice steamers were built into the side wall of the house. A fire under one of the steamers was nearly out. The girl exclaimed and, dropping her basket, she ran to put more wood on and to blow at the glowing embers.

On the right side, a raised wooden platform held neat stacks of materials for making umbrellas. Bamboo shafts, rolls of oiled and painted paper, pots of glue, hemp and dried grasses for tying were all kept in tidy bundles and rows. On one side lay a pile of half-finished umbrellas.

In the back, a steep stairway climbed by way of stacked storage cabinets to a loft, and beyond this a narrow passage led to the rear. There was no one about.

"Oh, mistress?" shouted the girl, rising from her efforts with a fresh coat of ashes and soot on her pinched face. Her voice echoed from the smoke-blackened ceiling rafters.

"What do you want?" a shrill voice responded from somewhere beyond the stairs. "You're late! Get busy with those vegetables!"

"There's someone to see you," cried the girl.

After a moment's silence, there was the sound of a door and some whispered conversation. The door slid shut, and soft steps padded towards them.

"You should have said so right away, girl!" said the lady of the house, emerging from the dark passage into the faint light. She pulled some shimmering yellow garment around her and peered towards Tora uncertainly. He stepped forward into the light and bowed. Taking in his neat blue cotton robe with its black belt, and then his broad shoulders and slim hips, his handsome face and his neatly tied hair, she reached up to touch her own hair. "Oh!"

Tora eyed her with equal interest. The yellow garment seemed to be a fancy embroidered jacket, and she wore it over a thin under robe. She appeared to be in her thirties, her face somewhat coarse but not unattractive, and her body well-padded.

She asked, "Would the honored gentleman like to order an umbrella?" and came towards him with mincing steps, swinging her hips from side to side. Pointing to the platform, she said, "Please to be seated, while I get the patterns." Slipping dirty feet out of straw sandals, she stepped onto the platform to lay out a cushion for Tora. As she bent, he could see that she was naked under her robe.

"Do not trouble," said Tora, tearing his eyes away from her heavy breasts and seating himself on the edge of the platform. He gave her an admiring smile, showing off his white teeth, and said, "I came to speak to your husband, ma'am, but on another matter. Your little maid was kind enough to show me the way. I'm afraid I made her late, because I had some business to take care of first."

The woman waved the apology aside, saying, "Please don't

worry! There is plenty of time. But my husband will be late." She glanced nervously at the darkness outside the window, then smiled at Tora and asked, "Can I be of some assistance?"

"Ah." Tora stroked his small mustache and eyed the lady appreciatively. "It is my very good luck to find his beautiful lady instead."

"Oh!" She batted her eyes and touched her hair again. "I'm afraid you caught me at my worst. I was taking a nap."

"You look elegant. Your husband is a lucky man. At least he shows his appreciation!" Tora touched the hem of the yellow jacket admiringly.

"Oh, this? My husband didn't give that to me. He's an old man who has no interest in such things. Besides he barely scrapes together enough to put food on the table. I married beneath my station." She noticed the little maid, who was still standing there, clutching the basket of vegetables and watching the exchange open-mouthed. "How filthy you are, girl! Go wash your face!" she cried. "And get on with the laundry while you're at it!"

"But you said to fix the vegetables for the evening rice. . . ." One look at her mistress's face, however, made her set down the basket and scurry along the passage and out the back door into the yard.

"Please excuse this humble and uncomfortable place," the woman said, kneeling down near Tora. "Will you take a cup of wine?"

"You are very kind," said Tora, stealing another look at her charms. "I wish I could, but I'm on duty. But perhaps you can help me."

Her eyes widened. "On duty? How can I be of service to the honored gentleman?"

"I came to ask some questions about your daughter Omaki."

"Omaki?" Her face stiffened and a wary look came into her eyes. "She's not my daughter. She's my husband's. Besides, she's dead."

"I know. That's why I'm here. A very unfortunate case. You certainly have my deepest sympathy."

She quickly lowered her eyes, nodded, and raised an embroidered sleeve to her face.

"I'm attached to the Ministry of Justice you see," Tora continued, pleased with himself at the choice of words. She looked up at
that, clearly impressed, and he decided to stretch the truth a little
further. "Since Captain Kobe of the metropolitan police is following up another lead, we have been asked to investigate this end of
the case."

"You don't look old enough to be with the Ministry of Justice,"
she said dubiously.

Tora gave her another brilliant smile and bowed. "Thank you,
ma'am, for the compliment. Actually I'm just a 'junior junior,' so
to speak. I got lucky with a case in the provinces and was trans-
ferred here. Now I'm trying to make my way in the capital. I don't
like to trouble folk when they're mourning a loved one, but you
surely want the killer caught, and I'd be glad to get some help." He
looked at her pleadingly.

"Well," she said, frowning. "I don't know. . . . Haven't they
caught the killer already? That student she was seeing? I expect it
was his child she was expecting. Or maybe not, and that's what
made him mad enough to kill her."

"There," cried Tora. "That's exactly what I need. A woman's
impression of what was going on. I knew right away that you
would have a sharp eye and a fine understanding. Look at the way
you knew I was too young for my job. I don't believe you miss
much when it comes to sizing up people and their feelings. So you
knew Omaki was seeing the student?"

"Yes. He walked her home from work a few times. A silly, ugly
thing with ears like handles on a jug. Even Omaki made fun of
him. I thought she didn't like him, but I guess I was wrong about
that."

"Well," said Tora, "we're not supposed to talk about a case with
the people concerned, but since you already know . . . Omaki
used to visit him at the university, and he wrote poems about her."

She moved a little closer to him, listening avidly. "Poems? You
don't mean it! So maybe it was his kid after all. Does his family
have any money?"

"I don't think so."

"Then Omaki must've been mad to mess around with him. And look what it got her!"

"Actually," said Tora, "it looks like he didn't kill her. Could there have been another man?"

She thought, chewing her lip. "I suppose it's possible," she said. "She met a lot of people at her work. Sometimes they'd even give her presents."

"Could you find out about that?" He smiled at her and stroked his mustache, letting his eyes travel slowly to her large, dark-skinned breasts, half exposed where her jacket gaped.

She looked down, and pulled her jacket together. Flushing, she raised her eyes to his. "I might need a little time," she murmured, shifting her round hips a little and smoothing the jacket over her knees. Her eyes moved to his lips, his shoulders and his broad chest. "Could you come back?"

Tora nodded. "Tomorrow? Maybe a bit earlier than this?" He let his eyes go to her breasts again. "No point in disturbing your husband's dinner." This time she smiled and leaned towards him, the dusky globes straining from the fabric. A warm, unwashed smell came from her body.

Tora had rarely felt less desire for a female, but an investigator's work sometimes required acting skills, and he forced himself to whisper, "How delightful!" Pretending to recall his purpose, he cleared his throat. "Did your daughter ever mention any admirers to you?"

Her smile faded. "I told you, she's not my daughter," she cried petulantly. Tora apologized profusely, and she said grudgingly, "Well, she kept to herself a lot, you know. It's hard to be a second mother to someone your own age." She patted her hair and gave Tora a sidelong glance to see how he took this. He nodded sympathetically, and she went on, "And then Omaki thought she was much too fine for us after she became an entertainer in the Willow Quarter. Though in my opinion, that's not much better than being a whore."

"Ah! So she may have taken customers?"

The woman looked away. "I wouldn't go that far. At least you'd better not mention it to my husband. The old fool thinks she was a saint. And here she brought home all those expensive things! I ask you, who'd give a simple girl a fine jacket like this," she held out an embroidered sleeve, "for playing a lousy lute?" She paused. "Say! Is it true that the murderer and his family have to pay blood money to her relatives? I mean, if the killer was found, would you people make his family pay up for what he's done to us?"

Tora nodded. The woman placed her hand on his arm familiarly. "I can make it worth your while to look after our interests," she said, squeezing gently. "Humble folk like us don't know our way around police and the courts, but you, being with the Ministry of Justice, could keep your eyes and ears open and help us make our claim."

"Oh, I don't know that I can agree to be an informant to someone connected with a case," said Tora, frowning. "It's against the rules and might cost me my career, maybe even my job, to do such a thing."

"Oh!" she cried, "I wouldn't expect that. Only to get what is rightfully ours." She crept close to him on her knees and murmured, "I'd be very grateful. We are poor people and Omaki was our entire hope in our old age."

Tora raised his eyebrows. Apparently she could adjust her age from girlhood to senility at a moment's notice. He had noted that this was a skill peculiar only to the middle-aged female.

She misinterpreted his astonishment. "The girl had a brilliant career ahead of her," she cried. "Think of the money she would have earned; think of how she could have taken care of her old parents! Is it justice that all of that should be taken from us?"

"Hmm," Tora pretended to consider her claim, "there is something in what you say. I'll think about it. Of course, you are not likely to get anything unless we find the killer and he turns out to have some money."

Before she could answer, there was a loud and angry thumping noise from the back of the house. Mrs. Hishiya jumped a little and got to her feet. "It's getting late. I must see about dinner. My husband will be here any moment. Maybe you'd better not talk to him tonight. Come back tomorrow afternoon."

He knew she was eager to get rid of her impatient lover before her elderly husband returned home from the market. He nodded with a big smile and took his leave.

Outside, he walked around the block and up the dark alley, counting off roofs until he was behind the Hishiya house. A patch of light fell from the open door on a small yard where the little servant was hanging washing over a bamboo fence.

Tora remained in the shadows and studied the rear of the house. The small yard was full of the umbrella maker's materials and debris. A rain barrel leaned against one corner of the house and propped up a stack of firewood. This reached halfway up to a ledge under a single shuttered loft window. Omaki's room must be up there. Satisfied, Tora nodded to himself. There was plenty of time to go to the amusement quarter and pay another visit to the Willow.

◆

When Tora entered the wine house, he found the auntie surrounded by her girls. She was giving them their appointments while she kept a careful eye on the entrance.

"Well, my young friend," she asked, greeting him with her gap-toothed smile, "are you ready for some serious battling on the silk mats? How many of my precious flowers can your little soldier defeat?" A chorus of giggles came from her girls.

"No, no, Auntie!" cried Tora, ogling her. "I came only to see you!" The girls hooted with laughter, and she snapped open her fan and hid behind it like a shy maiden. "Besides," he whispered in her ear, putting an arm around her broad waist, "I have only enough to buy a cup of wine for each of us. You know I'm a poor man."

She chuckled when he squeezed her a little and shook a finger at him. "Come, a handsome fellow like you? I'd soon make your fortune for you. There's many a lonely wife who wouldn't mind having a bit of what her husband gives my pretty flowers."

Tora released her abruptly. "I am shocked at you! Does that mean you aren't interested in me?"

She laughed and pinched his arm playfully. "All right! All right! I have a few minutes." She waved a waitress over and told her to bring some of her special wine to her office. "My treat," she told Tora.

When they had settled down in the cubicle where she kept her rosters of girls, her appointment books, her accounts and money boxes, she asked, "Did you find the young chicken I sent you last night to your taste?"

"Ah!" Tora looked dreamily at the low ceiling. "A very tasty morsel, no doubt, but I am still a starving man! I met her outside, complimented her, and offered to walk her home. But she's a very proper girl!" He sighed.

Auntie burst into a loud cackle and slapped at him. "Liar! I saw her face today. If she got any sleep, I'll be a monkey's mother."

Tora made a grab for her and pinched her buttocks. She squealed, "What did you do that for?"

"Just feeling for your tail, Auntie dear."

They burst into laughter as the waitress walked in with the wine. She looked at Tora with new respect. When they were alone again, Tora sipped, smacked his lips appreciatively, and said, "The chicken told me you fired the pretty lute player because she was breeding. I've been wondering who's been playing her 'lute'?"

Auntie's smile disappeared. She narrowed her eyes. "That girl's been found murdered," she said. "What is it to you?"

Tora decided that lies were inadvisable with this shrewd woman. "It happens," he said, "that my master takes a great interest in crimes, and he's promised to help the young fellow the police have arrested. He doesn't think the boy did it. I'm in a bit of trouble at the moment and thought the master might forget the matter if I could find out something useful about the girl's friends."

"So you're trying to pin the murder on one of my customers, eh?"

"Auntie, I swear the student couldn't have done it. He's pathetic. As ugly as sin and twice as naïve as a baby. The fool met her here, and she made him think she liked him. Then she dumped him. He's been going crazy ever since."

"Him? Yes, I saw him. No money there! Dry as last week's rice cakes and less appealing, I told her, but she said she wouldn't mind being a scholar's lady some day."

"Well, she turned him down," said Tora. "I figure she found a better prospect."

The auntie looked thoughtful and pursed her lips. "That girl was always secretive. And she never carried on with the customers while she was working, I'll give her that. She could have done a good business, that one, but she wanted to be a famous entertainer."

Tora got impatient. "Come on! There had to be a man."

"Well, she took lute lessons from one of the music masters at the university. The man spends most of his nights in the Willow. Maybe the kid was his. I expect that's the way he got paid for his lessons."

There was a loud gasp from the door. "That's a horrible lie!" cried Madame Sakaki, white-faced with anger. She pushed the door wider and came in. "How can you say such things? Why must you ruin a man who has never hurt you? For all you know this person will tell the police what you said, and they'll arrest Sato. And once they have him in their jail, they'll torture him till he confesses, and then . . ." She slumped on the floor and burst into tears.

The auntie *tsk*ed, got up and went to kneel beside the weeping woman. "Now, now." She put an arm around Madame Sakaki's shoulders. "Do not fret. You've been working too hard, dear, playing every night, and then going home to take care of your parents and husband, and the little ones. This is only Tora, a good friend of mine. He won't get your precious teacher in trouble."

Oh, won't he? thought Tora, when his eye fell on the open door. Michiko was hovering outside. His face broke into a broad smile, but she put a finger to her lips. Tora rose, nodding to the auntie, and went out, closing the door behind him.

"I've missed you, sweet," said Tora to Michiko, nuzzling her neck. "See? I couldn't stay away even one night."

"Not here," she hissed. "I'm working. Come to my place later."

She ran past him into the well-lit front room, where she bowed deeply before an arriving guest in an expensive brown silk robe, and cried, "Kurata-san! Welcome! The Big Willow lost all its fine leaves when Kurata-san stopped coming, and the songbirds were about to fly away from the winter of your absence."

Tora stared, anger rising inside him. He recognized the haughty silk merchant even in these luxurious clothes and the formal hat. The man patted Michiko's cheek and then put his arm around her shoulders. Tora was about to intercede with a well-placed fist when the auntie pushed past him and made a great outcry over the new guest. A bevy of pretty women materialized, and they all walked down the hallway. Tora followed, scowling.

"But Kurata-san," purred Auntie, "what happened? We have been so worried about you. Priceless Pearl wept because she thought you were ill, and Precious Jade has refused all her customers. I hope you weren't angry with us?"

"No, no." The man's voice was high and sharp, and his small eyes undressed the women. "I was merely preoccupied with private affairs."

"Private affairs?" wailed Auntie. "What a faithless fellow! And to think that my beauties suffered sleepless nights over you!"

The merchant laughed and reached out to run a thin, yellow finger along Michiko's slender neck. "I see," he said, eyeing Michiko speculatively, "that I must try to make up for it. Fortunately I have taken a special tonic tonight and feel strong enough for all your nieces, Auntie." Without taking his eyes from Michiko, he asked, "Is my usual room available?"

At that moment, the auntie turned and caught sight of Tora's murderous expression. Leaving Kurata to Michiko and the other girls, she barred Tora's way. "Private party," she snapped.

Consumed with fury, Tora retreated to the front room. He hung around the restaurant for another hour without seeing either Michiko or the auntie again. Finally he left in disgust and walked to the market, where he ate his supper and bought a cheap lantern. Then he returned to the alley behind the umbrella maker's house.

All was dark and quiet. Tora eyed the house. No doubt Mrs. Hishiya had long since dismissed her "cousin," fed her unsuspecting husband his supper, and retired with him. Poor craftsmen and their families were fast asleep at this hour. And so were starving little maids, Tora hoped. He was not, in any case, worried about real, flesh-and-bone people. It was Omaki's restless spirit which he was afraid to meet. Then he thought of the revelers at the Willow on the other side of town and got angry enough to suppress his fears.

There was a quarter moon out, which shed just enough light for Tora to find a thin sliver of bamboo among the debris, creep across the small yard, and climb up the barrel and stacked wood to the ledge. He accomplished this with a minimum of noise and walked carefully along the ledge to the shuttered window. This he found latched so carelessly that the bamboo strip inserted between the panels opened them at the first try. He listened, muttered a brief prayer, and stepped over the sill into darkness.

When he straightened up, his head crashed into an overhead beam. The noise reverberated and fiery flashes exploded inside his skull. He froze and whispered, "Omaki, do not be angry! I am trying to help! I will find your killer, if you don't hurt me."

Somewhere down below a window opened. Tora opened his eyes and sucked in his breath. He had woken someone. There were the sounds of a muttered conversation, then Mrs. Hishiya's sleepy voice cried, "Shoo! Damned cat!" and Tora heard the sound of something heavy being thrown. Then the window slammed shut and silence fell.

Tora breathed a sigh of relief and softly closed the shutters. He struck a flint with trembling fingers, and lit his lantern.

He was in a small space, right under the eaves, no more than three mats in size. Four stacked clothes boxes, a roll of bedding, and a lute hanging from a nail proved that he had found the dead girl's room. It was blessedly empty of both the living and the dead. He checked the door and found it locked.

It did not take long to search the room. There was little in it beyond the contents of the four boxes and a few small knick-knacks on a cross beam. The boxes contained the girl's clothing, separated by season of the year. Tora was surprised when he discovered that two of the chests, those for spring and summer, contained not only some plain, serviceable cotton robes but also silks. In the summer chest especially, he found silk under-robes, two bolts of glossy pale blue and peach-colored silk, and a gown in a bright shade of plum blossom red. He put everything back the way he had found it, and turned to the knickknacks. Omaki's everyday comb of plain wood, with a few teeth missing, lay next to a small lacquered one with a design of golden chrysanthemums. There were several fans, most serviceable paper and bamboo, but one was silk, painted with a pair of ducks under a spray of cherry blossoms. A small brocade envelope next to the fans contained visiting cards, black brush strokes on red paper covered with gold dust. Tora looked at these, raised his eyebrows whistling softly, and pushed the envelope inside his robe. He glanced around the room, bowed deeply to the unseen presence of the dead girl, then blew out his light and quietly climbed out and down again.

Once back in the street, he breathed easier. He could not resist the urge to check on Michiko at her place. Somewhat to his surprise, he found her there waiting for him.

"So," he snarled, scowling ferociously, "are you finally done pleasuring that bastard from the silk shop?"

"What? Kurata? Are you mad? I was engaged to play for a party of rice dealers."

"I saw him touching you. He wanted you all right. And you went with him to his room."

"I did not. I went along only as far as the back door. There's a shortcut to the restaurant behind the Willow. The rice dealers were waiting there. But I admit Kurata was acting a bit strange tonight. He's never paid any attention to me before. Anyway, I don't like him. He's not a nice man."

"Then you should've told him off!" Tora grumbled, eyeing her doubtfully.

Michiko opened her mouth to defend herself, then began to giggle. "Oh, Tora! You're jealous!" Her voice became husky with emotion. "My big tiger! Don't you know I shall never want another man as long as you want me?" she said and slipped into his arms.

THIRTEEN

THE PRINCELY MONK

*A*s Kobe had predicted, Hirata's strength seemed to return as soon as the captain left them. He rejected Akitada's offer to take him home, claiming that he had some work to do. "Do not worry," he said, bustling around his office, "I have these bouts of cramping every time something irritating happens. My stomach cannot take aggravation any longer. Fortunately it never lasts very long. Please do not mention the matter to Tamako."

There was little chance of that! Akitada had no intention of making a nuisance of himself by playing the heartbroken suitor before her. But he watched his old friend worriedly, saying, "I don't like your color. You need a long rest. These foolish tricks of Kobe will continue. Why not go home and stay there for a few days? I can easily meet your students and set them some essay topics."

But Hirata was adamant. There was nothing wrong with him but a little occasional discomfort, and Kobe had surely done his worst already. Since he knew he was innocent, he would not concern himself further with Oe's murder. That was much the best way.

So Akitada acquiesced.

The following day Akitada still stewed about Kobe's outrageous accusations. But he reminded himself that the police captain was not as stupid as he pretended to be. He had found out much more quickly than had Akitada that the examination results had been tainted, and he had linked the matter immediately to Oe's murder. Left to himself, he would surely uncover the rest of the mystery. No doubt his accusations had been tossed about indiscriminately in an effort to gain more information. The method had worked quite well.

Akitada ate his morning rice and then paid the customary visit to his mother, whose manner showed that he had not been forgiven yet. After the usual polite inquiries, he returned to his room where he found Tora chatting with Seimei, who was laying out Akitada's formal gown and cap.

"Good heavens, man," said Akitada when he saw Tora's tired, bloodshot eyes. "I don't believe you slept last night either. Must you celebrate quite so enthusiastically?"

"Sorry, sir." Tora grinned. "I'll try to catch a nap today. It was all in a good cause. I hear you got another gruesome murder to solve. There must be a demon loose at the university."

"Captain Kobe is handling the matter, and I have been discouraged from meddling. I am working on Nagai's case. What did you find out?"

Tora reported first on the kite-flying adventure. "He's a bright little kid and very quick to learn," he said in a surprised tone. "I'd never have believed one of those pampered nobles can run like the wind."

Akitada smiled. "Boys of his class have a good deal of training in sports. They are taught to ride, shoot arrows, use a sword and play football. What about the girl Omaki?"

Tora gave a detailed account of his conversations with the little maidservant and with the umbrella maker's wife. His description of the latter's lifestyle and dubious charms was so lurid that Seimei looked scandalized and Akitada snapped, "Enough! Stick to the facts! It seems to me that she is not likely to be guilty herself, because she could have killed her stepdaughter more conveniently at home. And her single-minded interest in getting paid makes her an unreliable witness. Try to speak to her husband instead."

Tora looked relieved. "Phew! Thank heaven; she's not my type. Well, afterwards I went on to the Big Willow and talked to the auntie there. She knew Omaki had been seeing Rabbit and also that she'd been taking lessons from that lute teacher. She told me the child was Sato's, but just then one of the entertainers, a Madame Sakaki, walked in and got all upset. Come to think of it, the same woman was acting kind of strange the night before when I was asking questions about Omaki and Sato."

"Really? What does this Madame Sakaki look like?"

"Oh, she's a good looker for all she's not that young any more. In her thirties, I'd say. Kind of slim, but not too slim, if you know what I mean. Nice hair, in a bun. Michiko says she's a fine musician, and the auntie seems to like her. Keeps her on because she's married with children and some aged parents to support. After that I had to leave because that swine of a silk merchant came, and all the women rushed to greet him like he was the emperor himself. He has money to spend and so they all made up to him, especially since he'd stayed away a few days. Rumor is he's so henpecked at home that his wife beats him when she catches him chasing skirts. I hope so. Serves the coward right!"

Akitada was getting impatient. "Could we just have the pertinent facts about the murdered girl without your description of the life of prostitution?"

Seimei snorted.

"Well," Tora reminded him, "you sent me there yourself. I was just trying to find out stuff for you. Maybe you should go there yourself and get the whole picture. Anyway, I went back to the umbrella maker's. They'd all gone to bed and I climbed into the dead girl's room." Tora described what he had found and produced the brocade card case with a flourish.

Akitada was pleased. "This looks like the same brocade as the sash she was strangled with," he said. "Too fine and expensive a fabric to be anything but a gift from a wealthy man."

"I know," nodded Tora. "That bastard Kurata threw me out of his shop when I tried to buy some for a friend of mine. Seems riffraff like myself can't touch stuff like that."

Akitada raised his brows. "The man was rude. Ignore him." He opened the case and shook out the crimson cards. "Quite good writing," he muttered.

"I couldn't read it," said Tora, who was watching him eagerly. "They look like some of those fancy visiting cards you carry about. I thought they might be her lover's. Can you make out the name?"

Akitada chuckled and, passing the cards to Seimei, said, "I am sorry to disappoint you. I expect you thought you had found the murderer's cards. Actually the girl Omaki used these to advertise her skills as a lute player. She refers to herself as the 'Willow Tree Warbler' and says that she can be reached in the wine house by that name."

Seimei returned the cards. "Very improper for a female, and of that particular class," he said with a sniff. "Such cards are to be used only by gentlemen of rank."

Tora picked up one of the cards and stared at it. "She wrote these?"

Akitada shook his head. "Hardly. The writing is in a scholar's hand and in Chinese. But I must say it was very enterprising of her. Evidently she expected to play only in the best houses. I expect young Nagai wrote them. The strange thing is that they were useless. She lost her job and she got rid of Nagai. I don't suppose you picked up any rumors about marriage?"

Tora shook his head. "Not likely. According to the little maid, the stepmother called Omaki a slut."

Akitada pulled his earlobe pensively. "Why is it that she should have given up her career, her job and a marriage offer from poor Nagai without seeming in the least troubled about what was to become of her?"

Tora nodded. "Me and the auntie wondered about that too. Michiko said Omaki looked really cheerful about something before she died."

"I think," said Akitada, "we must look for the father of Omaki's unborn child. The pleasure quarter is the most promising place. And I apologize for snapping at you. You have done very well. Next time you go there, find out if any of the customers showed a special interest in the girl."

Tora jumped up eagerly.

"Wait!" said Akitada. "There is another matter, and it is more urgent. Do you remember the beggar Captain Kobe arrested for the murder?" Tora nodded. "He has been released, and I am worried about his safety. We must find him and bring him here. They might know where he is at the municipal hall for the eastern city. He visits there."

When Tora had left, Akitada said to Seimei, "I am sorry I complained about a lack of excitement in my life! Suddenly I am involved in three murders without having the least notion of how to proceed in any of them."

Seimei was holding out Akitada's gown for him to slip on. "*Three* murders? There have been only two: the girl and Professor Oe."

Akitada took off his house robe and put his arms into the sleeves of the formal gown. "You forget Prince Yoakira," he said, tying the sash.

Seimei looked unhappy. "I do wish you'd forget about Prince Yoakira," he muttered. "It is too dangerous. And I see no reason why you can't leave the other two cases to the police."

"At the risk of sounding like one of my more irritating colleagues," Akitada said, "it is a question of the killer's personality. Kobe is simply not interested. I doubt he fully understands what led to Oe's murder. In any case, Nagai has asked for my help and has no one else to speak up for him, so I shall do my best."

Seimei handed his master the hat of stiffened black gauze. "Remember," he warned darkly, "it is said that if you chase two hares, you will lose both."

◆

At the university, normal activity had resumed in spite of the murder. Hirata was back in his classroom, looking more like himself. Akitada spent the morning teaching, not an easy task because of continuous whispers among the students. He finally dismissed his last class of the morning, hoping to stretch his legs by going home for his midday rice, but when he was putting his books away, he became aware that one of his pupils was still sitting quietly in his place.

"Sadamu?" Akitada felt tentative about using the boy's given name. He was somewhat hazy about the proper protocol under the present circumstances.

But the boy did not seem to mind and bowed.

"Was there something you wished to say?"

"Yes, sir. I wished to thank you for lending me your man. It was extremely obliging. I found him very skillful with kites, and he provided excellent entertainment."

Akitada suppressed a smile at the boy's formal manner. "I am very happy to hear it. Tora has spoken equally highly of you."

The boy's face brightened. "Did he really? I should like to hire him if you can spare him. I expect to get my allowance soon, and he will be very well paid."

Akitada was momentarily taken aback. "You surprise me," he said. "You will have to speak to Tora about this. He is free to choose his own master."

"Yes. I understood him to say that he had come to you only recently or I would not make the offer. He told me how you met." The boy gave Akitada a surreptitious glance and added, "He seems very loyal."

"Tora has many excellent qualities."

"But loyalty is a most important quality in a servant, don't you agree?"

"That and affection."

This thought appeared to be new to the little lord. He pondered it and then nodded. "Such emotions place a master under an obligation," he said. "The obligation to protect his people."

Akitada was beginning to feel uncomfortable with the direction the conversation seemed to be taking. Was the boy reminding him that he was too poor to afford a man like Tora?

But young Lord Minamoto went on in a voice that suddenly shook with passion. "When my grandfather died, that obligation passed to me. How am I to carry out my duty to my people when I am kept a prisoner here without a single retainer or even servant at my command? Not so much as someone to bring me my clothes or my food?" Clenching impotent fists, he cried, "How will I protect my people?"

Akitada sat speechless at this outburst. After a moment spent looking into the boy's agonized eyes, he said hesitantly, "Surely your people do not expect you to take on this burden until you are older. Meanwhile others will take care of your family business for you. And personal servants or armed retainers are not really permitted here in the university."

The boy jumped up angrily. "You don't understand! My rightful place has been taken by Sakanoue. He is the one who keeps me here. It was not my grandfather's wish that things should be this way. I had private tutors. Heaven only knows what that evil man is doing to my people . . . and my sister." He swung around towards the nearest wall and pounded his fists against the boards in helpless rage.

Akitada waited until the boy calmed down and was standing still, his chin on his chest and his arms hanging limply at his sides. "Do you have any proof," he asked quietly, "that Lord Sakanoue is not carrying out your grandfather's wishes?"

The boy turned around, his eyes blazing through tears. "I need no proof. I have my grandfather's word for it! My grandfather hated him. He called him an upstart and suspected him of stealing from us. He warned me never to give him any power."

Akitada sighed. "Lord Sakanoue has been appointed your guardian," he reminded the boy. "In order to change his guardianship, you will need to go to court against him, proving his unfitness—and since your grandfather is not here to testify, it will be your word against his."

Silence fell between them. The boy sat back down, biting his lip. After a moment he said, "Tora says that you solve crimes no one else can solve. I want you to solve my grandfather's murder. Can you do that?"

It seemed to Akitada that he had waited for this moment since the first time he had heard of the peculiar circumstances of the prince's death. Forcing himself to conceal his surge of excitement, he said quietly, "I don't know. Perhaps you had better tell me what happened."

"Then you agree that it was murder?"

"It is more likely a murder than a miracle."

The boy's eyes shone with relief and excitement. "What do you want to know?"

"Everything you remember about the time before and after your grandfather's disappearance. I gather you suspect Lord Sakanoue. Perhaps you had better start with him."

"Yes." The boy straightened his shoulders. "Sakanoue was our bailiff. His father before him held the same position and his father's father. It was hereditary. My ancestors and my grandfather had always trusted the Sakanoue family, and they, in turn, were well rewarded. But when Sakanoue started to buy land while reporting shortages in our rice crops, my grandfather became suspicious and called him to the capital with the accounts. I know this, because my grandfather told me about it. That was when he warned me against him. My grandfather was quite angry, but I think Sakanoue talked his way out of the shortages, for my grandfather was going to send him back to the country. Then, the day before my grandfather died, they had a terrible argument. It concerned my sister."

Akitada interrupted, "How do you know this? Were you present?"

The boy shook his head and stared at the clenched fists in his lap. He swallowed and said, "I had my own quarters in my grandfather's house. That afternoon I was in the garden. I could see servants rushing about. Then my grandfather came from his rooms and ran along the open gallery to my sister's pavilion. I could tell he was very angry, so I stood and waited, and he came right back, shouting for someone to get Sakanoue." The boy paused and looked at Akitada defiantly. "I went to listen on the veranda outside my grandfather's room. He was shouting at Sakanoue, but I could not make out the words. Then Sakanoue came out, and he looked . . . like a devil would look, I think."

"I see. What about your sister? Did you have a chance to speak to her?"

"No. I have not seen my sister for more than a month. I do not know if she is alive. Sakanoue claims she has married him." The boy almost choked on the words.

"Yes. That is what people say. Now you had better tell me what happened next. Why did your grandfather travel to the mountain temple when there was trouble in his family?"

"When my father died, my grandfather had a dream. In the dream my father appeared to him and told him that he must pray for him on the first day of the fourth month at sunrise, or the family would die out with me. My grandfather has carried out those instructions every year since then."

"Good heavens!" said Akitada, staring at the boy. "Do you plan to continue the tradition?"

"Of course!" The boy hesitated. "If I live to do so."

A heavy silence hung between them. Of course. The child stood between Sakanoue and one of the richest estates in the country. For a fanciful moment, Akitada wondered if the prince had actually performed the prescribed ritual on this occasion. He asked, "What were you told about the events at the temple?"

The boy tossed his head. "They came back with this story that my grandfather had gone into the shrine hall and stayed there. When he did not come out, Sakanoue and the others opened the door. My grandfather had disappeared. They all said the gods must have come for him, for there was no other way for him to leave."

"They?"

"My grandfather's companions. Besides Sakanoue, there were retainers, servants, and some of his friends."

"I shall need their names. Did they all watch and witness the disappearance?"

"Yes. Or so they said."

Akitada pulled his earlobe. "You know that they would have

been investigated carefully before the emperor would lend his support to the story of a miracle?"

"His Majesty has been bewitched by Sakanoue," said the boy. "I wish I had been there! I wish I had stayed up to see my grandfather leave! I wish I had spoken to him one last time, but I expected to see him the next day. I was to ride with him in his carriage. He sent a message that I was to go to bed early to be ready for the journey."

Akitada was startled. "Journey? What journey?"

"We were to move to the country the next day. Grandfather wished to supervise the estates himself to make certain there were no future shortfalls."

"This plan to remove to the country, was it sudden?"

"Yes. The servants were all complaining about it. You never saw such a bustle of packing. There were boxes and chests everywhere, and the yard was full of wagons, clothes hampers and crates of bedding when I got up in the morning."

"So you were up when the news of your grandfather's death arrived?"

"Yes. General Soga, one of the gentlemen who had accompanied Grandfather, came shouting and knocking at the gate. When they let him in, his horse was all lathered up and he almost fell off in his hurry. I had heard the noise and I ran out to see what was happening. He saw me and took me inside. Then he told me that Grandfather had disappeared. Later Sakanoue arrived with the others. He said the gods had taken Grandfather to be with them, and we must be happy about it and build a shrine to his memory. He also said that he was my elder brother now, since he had married my sister. I told him he was lying and spat in his face. That's when he hit me and locked me in my room. Later that day he came and brought me here."

"That must have been terrible. I am very sorry," said Akitada helplessly, putting his hand on the boy's shoulder. But the child moved aside, and Akitada let his hand drop.

"I know Sakanoue killed my grandfather," the boy said

fiercely. "You will prove it! Then I shall take control of my family and you will be rewarded."

Akitada said, "I shall certainly try."

"I was told by Tora that you are working on Nagai's case," the youngster continued. "I feel certain he is innocent, and his problem should not trouble you overmuch. Are you also helping with the murder of Professor Oe?"

"Not at the moment."

"Good!" The little lord rose. "In that case, you will be able to start investigating Sakanoue immediately. Remember the reward." He gave Akitada the tiniest of bows and was gone.

Akitada sat looking after him and laughed softly. Reward indeed! Young Lord Minamoto certainly knew how to put on the airs of the great man accustomed to giving orders. Still, the boy's awareness of his obligations was quite admirable and he had displayed considerable courage in his defiance of Sakanoue. On the whole, he thought, the young man showed much promise.

It was too late to go home, so he sent a servant to the staff kitchen for his noon rice and ate it alone in his room. When he was done, Hirata came in. Akitada saw with concern that the older man looked very tired and drawn again.

"How are you feeling today?" Akitada asked. "You gave me a scare yesterday."

"It was nothing. I am quite well again. Indigestion is one of the infirmities of old age. The reason I stopped in was to tell you that Sesshin has called a meeting. We had better be on our way."

Akitada was momentarily at a loss. "Sesshin?"

"The abbot of the Pure Water temple, but more importantly the director of the university. He is also our professor of Buddhism, a function he does not often carry out, because he prefers to live in his mountain villa which he intends to convert into a temple. He arrived about an hour ago; Oe's murder brought him back. No doubt he will disappear again as soon as he has appointed Oe's replacement."

"Hardly a testimonial of his devotion to the institution,"

said Akitada sarcastically, getting up and adjusting his hat and robe. Even at the best of times he had little respect for Buddhist clergy, and this one seemed lazier than most. "Isn't Ono back? Won't he take over for Oe?"

Hirata shook his head dubiously. "I have no idea. Ono has hoped for just this chance for a long time. I think it is the only reason he put up with Oe's abuse. But he is not the man Oe was, and Sesshin knows this."

They walked across the grounds to the Buddhist temple, discussing the effects of murder on their fixed routines. At one point, Akitada said, "Oh, young Minamoto spoke to me earlier. He has asked me to look into the matter of his grandfather's disappearance. He believes the prince was murdered by Sakanoue."

Hirata was so astonished he stopped in his tracks. "Lord Sakanoue? Oh, Akitada, please do not get involved in what is surely a mere child's fantasy. They say Sakanoue may become the next prime minister. If you let it be known that you support the boy in his charges, you will put yourself in jeopardy. You must speak to Sesshin about this."

Akitada laughed. "Speak to a monk? He is just about the last person I would consult."

Hirata shook his head impatiently. "I know all about your distaste for the religion, but in this case you cannot be aware of who Sesshin really is. He is another son of the Murakami emperor and the late Prince Yoakira's half brother. That makes him the boy's great-uncle."

Akitada's jaw dropped. He had assumed the boy had no male relatives left. "Sesshin is Sadamu's great-uncle?" he asked. "How could this man turn his back on the children? What sort of man is he?"

Hirata started walking briskly. "Come," he said. "That you must find out for yourself."

Crossing the street, they entered the temple courtyard. The doors of the small main hall stood wide open. Someone looked out and beckoned. They hurried in.

Akitada had forgotten how pretty the small temple was. It looked deceptively plain with its square, red-lacquered columns against the dark wood of ceiling and walls. Its only ornamentation was a lovely carved frieze of cranes, painted black and white with brilliant red patches on their heads. Behind the raised dais with its single cushion, covered in the imperial purple silk, hung five large scroll paintings of Buddhist deities. Before each scroll stood an elegant black-lacquered table with silver ceremonial implements.

Most of the others had already arrived and stood around chatting. In fact, apparently only the august personage himself was missing, for even the elusive Fujiwara and Ono had returned.

They greeted Ono first. Akitada had not expected grief, but the man looked both excited and smug. Akitada wondered if he had been confirmed as Oe's successor. They exchanged the conventional expressions of regret over Oe's death. Ono did not bother to explain his absence, and there was little point in pursuing the matter. Hirata turned to speak to someone else, but Akitada said, "You must be overwhelmed with duties. Will you rely on Ishikawa to give you a hand? I have not seen him since the poetry contest."

"I have no intention of employing that fellow," Ono said sharply. "He may know his Chinese, but his manners are unacceptable and he is completely unreliable. Would you believe it, he has taken off without so much as a note explaining where he went or when he planned to return?"

"I dare say Kobe will dig him up," said Akitada, and regretted his choice of words immediately. "You and Ishikawa were the last to see Oe alive that night, weren't you?"

Ono's eyes shifted nervously. "We only took him as far as Mibu Road. He insisted he had private business to take care of and ordered us to return to the competition to keep an eye on things."

"I see." Akitada decided to probe further. "I don't recall seeing either of you return."

Ono stiffened and glared at him. "I cannot speak for Ishikawa," he said coldly, "and I certainly don't feel I need to explain my actions to you, but I was quite unwell and had no desire to disgrace myself before the company, so I remained around the corner near the side stairs." Narrowing his eyes, he added, "For that matter, I saw you leave early, before the last competition started."

"My apologies." Akitada bowed. "I spoke thoughtlessly."

Ono acknowledged this with a curt nod. Akitada walked away, reflecting that the erstwhile worm was putting on the scales of the dragon already. Or had Ono always been a poisonous snake masquerading as a harmless creature?

He looked around and joined Nishioka, who was talking to Fujiwara. The latter seemed to have lost his booming good humor and merely looked tired and irritated.

But Nishioka's eyes sparkled. He was more cheerful than anyone else here. Tucking some loose strands of hair back into his topknot and scratching his lantern chin, he said to Akitada, "I was just telling our friend here that he need not worry about being arrested for Oe's death. I have thought about it and decided that his particular personality disqualifies him from all but the most brutal of murders, and then only if he were provoked upon the instant and carried out the deed without regard to his own safety."

"Thank you for that testimonial," said Fujiwara dryly. His cheek showed the ugly marks left by Oe's nails, and he had not bothered to change. Akitada noticed the blood stains on the sleeve of his robe and wondered if he only owned the one garment. "But," continued Fujiwara, "how will you convince the police captain that I did not have another quarrel with the man in the Temple of Confucius and lost my temper?"

Nishioka shook his head. "Impossible! You would not have bothered to tie him to the statue. You would have smashed a few things and run off to get drunk."

Fujiwara choked back a laugh. "I see my reputation is well established. Well, who, in your opinion, has the correct personality?"

"Oh, at least two people." Nishioka smiled slyly. "Though in one case I have not yet worked out how it was done unless he had an—" He broke off as a sudden hush fell in the hall.

A side door had opened and His Reverence entered. The noble monk was hardly a prepossessing figure. Very fat, he was dressed in a black silk clerical robe; a green and gold embroidered stole was slung across one shoulder and his paunch. He padded with a waddling gait to the raised dais and plopped down on the cushion with a grunt.

They all bowed deeply. Akitada risked a surreptitious look and saw a moon face with small deep-set eyes under heavy lids and a small, soft mouth. Sesshin surveyed the bowed backs impassively. To Akitada there was a sort of naked grossness about the man which was not entirely due to his shaven head. His smooth, round face had hardly any eyebrows and rested on a triple chin. The ears were enormous, with pendulous lobes which rested on fleshy shoulders.

Perhaps it was due to his natural and learned dislike for Buddhist clergy, but it seemed to Akitada that appointing a man such as this as president of the university, a spoiled member of the imperial family who had renounced his worldly career in order to devote himself to leisure and luxurious living, was another example of the weakness of the current government.

The fat monk cleared his throat and said in a soft, dry voice, "Thank you all for coming. Please be seated." With a general shuffling of feet and rustling of robes they obeyed.

Sesshin looked over their heads and spoke in the same low, soft voice. "Recent events require my presence here and I take this opportunity to make a few announcements." The silence in the hall was profound as they all strained to hear. Akitada thought irritatedly that the man was even too lazy to raise his voice. "Because of the unfortunate death of our colleague, certain disruptions of my routine and yours are unavoidable, but we must attempt to carry on. You will, of course, meet your students as usual and cooperate fully with the police. Ono will temporarily see to the lectures on Chinese literature. I will send him a suitable assistant. As usual, when I am in residence, I will conduct a series of lectures on the scriptures. This time I will give a commentary on the Great Wisdom sutra. It will take place every afternoon immediately after the noon rice. You may announce this to your students. That is all." He nodded to them, rose with another grunt, and padded out.

That was all? For a moment Akitada sat stunned, while his colleagues got up and began to chatter. Then cold and irrational fury seized him. How dare the man? Before he was fully conscious of what he was doing, he was up and striding after the figure of the priest.

He passed through the door into a long dark corridor where the distant faint daylight gleamed on polished black boards. Ahead of him moved the large figure of the monk. Sesshin stopped at a door, disappeared into the room behind, and closed the door after him. Akitada opened it again and walked in.

"I want to speak to you," he snapped, adding lamely, "Your Reverence."

Sesshin had his back to him and was removing his stole. Turning slowly, he looked at Akitada. After a long moment he said, "You must be Sugawara. If I remember, abruptness was always a failing of the Sugawaras. Please be seated."

Akitada was still fuming. This man had deserted two helpless children. "What I have to say will not take long. I have just been told that you are the brother of the late Prince Yoakira."

Sesshin calmly folded the embroidered stole and draped it over a stand. The room contained little more than that, a pair of cushions and a small low table upon which were set a wooden rosary, a beautifully decorated sutra box and a brazier with a teapot. The monk lowered himself to the cushion next to it. "Forgive me for sitting down myself. I am an old man. I would offer you a cup of tea, but it is not customarily consumed while standing. You young fellows do not allow yourself enough leisure. All is haste and intensity for you."

"I am afraid that most of us do not have the privilege," Akitada said tartly. "I apologize for the abrupt intrusion, but I won't keep you from your leisure long. Your great-nephew, Lord Minamoto Sadamu, is presently a student here, and I had occasion to speak to him at some length this morning about a situation which is disturbing, to say the least."

Sesshin remarked placidly, "I hope the young scamp has not given you cause to complain of him?"

Akitada steadied his breath. "Not at all. Quite the opposite. He is extremely bright and has a sense of responsibility beyond his years. That is why I have acceded to his wish to investigate his grandfather's death."

Sesshin sighed and reached for his beads. He neither responded nor changed his calm demeanor. If anything, he seemed more indifferent than before. The heavy lids drooped over his deep-set eyes until he looked almost asleep.

"Have you nothing to say?" cried Akitada. "I had hoped that you would take an interest in your brother's grandchildren. They are quite alone in the world and, if I am not mistaken, in danger of their very lives."

There was no reaction from the monk, and Akitada turned to leave. "I am sorry," he said. "I was mistaken."

"A moment," said the soft dry voice. Akitada paused with his hand on the door latch and looked back over his shoulder. The smoldering black eyes were fully on him now. "You intrude most painfully into my hard-won peace," he said. "When I lost my brother, I nearly lost myself. My faith wavered and my very soul was drowning in tears. I returned to the world to conduct the memorial service, and was told on that occasion that the children were in good hands, that they had chosen their future paths freely. After the service I returned to the mountains to ask the Buddha's help in emptying my heart and mind of the memories. I do not tell you this because I owe you an explanation, but because I am grateful that my great-nephew has found a friend in his teacher. Now you may go in peace."

Akitada wished to argue but knew it would be both futile and dangerous to do so. He bit his lip, bowed, and left.

FOURTEEN

GATE OF DEATH

*S*ince Lady Sugawara decided it was time for the annual cleaning of the family storehouse, Tora could not leave for the city until late in the day. When he was finally free to look for the old beggar, he headed first to the office of the eastern capital near the university.

Tora stated his business at the gate, and the guard became excited. "Hey, fellows!" he shouted. "Here's someone asking about old Umakai."

Guards, constables, and clerks gathered around them. All expressed concern about the old beggar. Umakai was their special pet, and they had missed him. He was expected regularly for his noon rice. This the guards and clerks provided by passing his bowl around for everyone to contribute a small share of his own meal until the old man's bowl was filled to overflowing. The trouble was he had not been seen, except for a brief visit right after his release from jail, and they were all worried.

Tora asked if Umakai might be eating elsewhere, for instance with their colleagues in the western office, but they assured him that those people had hearts of stone and arrested beggars as vagrants and loiterers. In short, nobody knew where Umakai might have disappeared to.

Tora thanked them, promising to keep them informed. He began walking through increasingly busy streets, stopping from time to time to ask peddlers and street musicians about the old man. Some knew Umakai, but none had seen him around lately. It was not until he neared the market that Tora picked up a clue, and when he did, the news was not good.

He saw a middle-aged prostitute who was plying her trade on the street. No longer attractive enough to work in the Willow Quarter, she was reduced to accosting passing laborers and apprentices. Her eyes had assessed Tora, but his neat blue robe and black cap had convinced her that he was beyond her reach. Tora approached her. A woman like this would be familiar with the other street people who competed with her for a few coppers.

She was disappointed when he asked his question, but told him she did not know Umakai. When Tora turned away, she cried after him, "They fished an old man out of a canal this morning."

Tora's heart sank. "How do you know?"

"I was there, wasn't I? Bunch of people were looking, so I went to see what was up. He was dead all right. Small, skinny old guy. Looked down on his luck. Some old drunk, maybe. Stumbled into the water and drowned. Guess the warden thought so too. He just looked at him and then let his friends take him away. Could be it's your guy."

Tora nodded. "It could be. These friends? Do you know where I might find them?"

She laughed. "They're poor folk, like me. We don't have a regular place to go home to like you." She gave Tora's neat outfit an envious glance. "People like us live and sleep in the streets, or maybe in the western city in some shed or old ruin. But mostly we keep moving." She eyed Tora speculatively. "I don't suppose you'd be interested in a bit of pleasure?"

"Another time. I'm on duty."

She nodded in resignation and turned away.

"Wait! If you can describe the men who took the body away, there's ten coppers in it for you."

"Ten coppers?" She flushed with pleasure. "I can do better than that! It was Spike and Nail got the dead guy. Spike's a big brute. He lost a hand and put a metal spike in its place. His buddy's a thin little feller. Get it? Spike and Nail! Heh, heh. Anyway, I guess they knew what they'd find, 'cause they'd brought along a monk to say a few prayers."

Tora stared at her. The story sounded weird, but there might be something in it. "Thanks," he said and counted the promised coppers into her dirty hand.

She looked at the money, then closed her fingers tightly around it. Nodding towards a dirty alley behind her, she offered, "If you like, I could twirl your stem for you." She grinned and passed an agile tongue across her lips. "It won't cost you nothing."

Tora blushed. "No, thank you. I'm in a hurry to find out what happened to the old man." He turned to walk away.

"Bet they took him to Rashomon," she called after him.

Rashomon!

Tora shuddered. Of course. Everyone knew that the poor who could not afford a funeral left their corpses there for the authorities to gather and cremate on a common pyre. That was why nobody but cutthroats went to Rashomon after dark—and the light was fading rapidly.

Actually Rashomon was the great southern gateway of the capital. An impressive two-storied structure with immense red columns, blue tile roofs, and whitewashed plaster walls, it had been built as a fitting welcome for visitors to the imperial capital. As soon as they passed through its massive structure, they saw before them Suzaku Avenue, immensely wide and long, bisected by water and lined with willows, leading straight as an arrow to Suzakumon in the far distance, the entrance to the imperial city itself. And if you were leaving the capital, you walked through Rashomon and found yourself on the great southern highway which led to Kyushu and exotic foreign ports.

But Rashomon had fallen on hard times as, indeed, had the

capital itself. The gate was rarely guarded nowadays and had become a hangout for vagrants, crooks and undesirables from the surrounding provinces. After dark, ordinary people avoided the place, making it a safe haven for criminals. The police turned a blind eye, except that twice a week, in the pre-dawn hours, the city authorities sent crews to gather the corpses.

Tora dreaded a visit to the upper floor of Rashomon, where bodies were generally left, about as much as an interview with the king of hell himself, but the prostitute's story had to be checked out and his master expected results. It was not the first time since he had entered Akitada's service that Tora had faced what he feared most, the supernatural.

In this case his immediate decision was to postpone the inevitable. He went to the umbrella maker's house first. Omaki's father was in. Hishiya was in his late fifties, thin, balding and prematurely bent, with the gnarled and scarred hands of his profession. He smiled and bowed deeply, expressing his gratitude for Tora's interest in his poor daughter. To his further credit, in Tora's eyes, he made no mention of blood money. Unfortunately he seemed to know nothing of his daughter's friends.

When patient probing had produced no more than protestations of shock and puzzlement, Tora exclaimed in frustration, "But you're her father! How could you not care that she slept with men or who the father of her unborn child was?"

The elderly man bowed his head. "Omaki was a good girl, but we are very poor. She tried hard to make a living playing the lute. She was very talented; all who heard her said so. But the men where she entertained, well, they want more than a bit of music, and she had no one to look out for her. Who am I to ask questions or to blame her, when I am too poor to give her a dowry?"

"Sorry," mumbled Tora. "The trouble is, from all we hear, she was pleased about the kid. Like she expected to marry its father."

The man sighed. "Maybe. I wouldn't know. I'm gone so much, selling my umbrellas in the market and gathering bamboo for more. You'll have to ask my wife. Women have their secrets. Only she's not in right now."

Tora rose. "Never mind! It doesn't matter. I'll ask around."

He spent the next few hours in the amusement quarter. His day had been long and Lady Sugawara had worked him hard. He felt in need of a rest and liquid refreshment. Besides, the bright lights and sounds of laughter and music blotted out thoughts of the horrors awaiting him in Rashomon.

He drank liberally and asked his questions without getting any helpful answers. Omaki had not been well liked by the other women in the quarter. They thought her proud and secretive, and none of them knew anything of her private life. At some point the combined effects of his exertions and the wine caused him to nod off. When the waiter shook him awake, wanting his place for other customers, it was past the middle of the night, and Tora had no reason to put off the unpleasant business of Rashomon any longer. He reflected bitterly that murder investigations exposed a man to danger not only from killers, but also from the angry spirits of their victims. Rashomon, being a receptacle of the unwanted dead, must be teeming with disgruntled specters.

Casting an uneasy glance at the sky, he saw that it was clouding up, and the moon made only fitful appearances. The cool, clear days of spring were over. Soon it would be hot and the rainy season would start, but not quite yet. It was merely dark, an excellent night to search for abandoned bodies and encounter gruesome ghosts. It suddenly occurred to Tora that he was totally unprepared for this undertaking and he headed for the market.

Most vendors had closed down, but he found a cheap lantern and then searched with increasing desperation for a soothsayer. He found this most essential individual in the form of a shrivelled old man who had fallen asleep over his stock of divining sticks, patent medicines and amulets.

"Wake up, Master," said Tora, shaking him gently by the shoulder. It did not do to offend one familiar with demons and spells.

"What do you want?" quavered the old one.

Tora explained his errand, and the old man nodded. "Wise precaution," he muttered, searching through his basket. "Last man went there after dark met a hungry ghost and had to give up his whole right arm to get away."

Tora shuddered.

The old man produced a wooden tablet with the crudely drawn image of the god Fudo. He threaded a string through its hole and knotted it. Next to this he laid a handful of rice. Finally he fished a sheet of cheap paper with some poorly written lines from the breast of his patched cotton robe and added this to the other two items. "Fifty coppers," he announced.

Tora blanched. He felt in his sleeve. "Do I need all that?" he asked.

The old man sighed. "The amulet you hold up before you if you encounter a demon. Fudo will strike the demon for you. The rice is to toss into a room before you enter; it drives hungry ghosts away. The paper contains the magical incantation of the virtues of Sonsho, who's Buddha's incarnation and protector against malevolent spirits. When you recite it, you will be safe even in Rashomon."

"I can't read," confessed Tora.

The old man sighed again. Taking the paper back, he said, "I'll read it; you repeat it."

The incantation was long and referred to some peculiar Indian names and terms, but Tora tried. The old man corrected him, sighed, corrected again, sighed, and finally nodded. "You got it! Practice it on the way."

"How much without the paper?" asked Tora.

The old man glared at him. "Fifty coppers," he said. "I should charge extra for the instruction!"

Tora bowed, mumbling his thanks for the generous price, turned over all but five coppers of his month's salary, and proceeded, only slightly fortified in mind, to Rashomon.

When his lagging steps finally brought him to the great gate, he found it nearly deserted. Only the hardiest, the most foolish or the most desperate of souls remained here after dark. A couple of beggars sat on the steps, hoping against hope for some late travellers entering or leaving the city. Inside, under the roofs of the vast structure, a few vagrants had taken shelter for the night. Tora surveyed them carefully.

An elderly couple in rags huddled against the base of a pillar, asleep and snoring. Near them an itinerant monk leaned against the wall, his straw hat covering his face, and his staff and bowl lying by his side. Monks of this type were a familiar sight on highways. They were not attached to any particular monastery and spent their lives travelling. This monk looked to be strong and healthy; at least he had muscular legs and large feet. Vagrant monks could be very unpleasant adversaries. Too often, they were wanted criminals in disguise. Tora watched him carefully, but decided that he, too, was fast asleep.

The sound of voices and laughter drew Tora to the other side of the gate. There, on the steps leading down to the highway, sat a group of men, engaged in a game of dice by lantern light. They looked like common laborers, their short-sleeved cotton shirts tucked into loose cotton trousers and their heads covered with knotted pieces of cloth. All chattered happily until one of them looked up and saw Tora in his neat blue robe and black cap. "An inspector!" he cried, and they all scrambled up and dispersed.

Tora chuckled. He had been mistaken before for one of the city officials who checked up on travellers. Since none of the men had fit the street woman's description of Spike or Nail, he would have to find the body himself. Tora turned back to enter the interior of Rashomon.

That was when he first noticed the armed man. He sat just inside the doorway leading into the building. His arms rested on his knees, and he had laid his head on them and gone to sleep. A big, brawny fellow, he had a sword slung over one shoulder and a bow and quiver of arrows over the other. Tora recognized the type. They were soldiers who served no master, but travelled from town to town looking for work which required the use of their weapons. If no such work was available, some became highway men, lying in wait for wealthy and unarmed travellers. This one was cautious enough not to take off his weapons even while he slept.

Suddenly, as if he felt Tora's scrutiny, the man raised his head slowly and looked at him. He was still young, about Tora's age, with a neatly trimmed beard and mustache, and cold steady eyes. They exchanged measuring looks. The armed man looked away first, spitting and scratching his topknot in a gesture of contempt.

Tora wished he had worn his old clothes and decided it was safer to avoid the armed man. He took the door on the opposite side instead.

It led into a large but empty guard room. Briefly, weak moonlight came through the door and a window, but a cloud extinguished even this. Tora lit his lantern; by its light he could barely make out the wooden stairs which ascended into the blackness of the second floor. A pervasive smell of dirt, rotten food, sweaty rags and, faintly, of decomposing flesh, hung in the dry, still air. From upstairs came soft rustling sounds. Hungry rats or angry spirits?

Tora shivered and touched the amulet tied around his neck. Murmuring a line from his protective spell, he started up the stairs slowly. When he was halfway up, a faint, flickering light appeared above, shifting weirdly across the dark beamed ceiling. A peculiar humming sound accompanied the light. Tora paused, feeling for the grains of rice in his sash. Suddenly a gigantic, grotesque shadow moved across the ceiling of the floor above. It belonged to a monstrous creature, misshapen and hunchbacked, with a claw-like hand that reached across the entire space, withdrew, and reappeared with a huge knife in it. Every hair on his head bristling, Tora tried to recite his spell, but his mind had become a complete blank. He tried to throw the rice, but spilled it on the steps. Then the knife above slashed downward, and Tora jerked back. Feet slipping on the spilled rice, he crashed down the stairway with a great clatter.

Above a woman's voice cursed loudly and with gusto.

Heaving a sigh of relief, Tora picked himself up. He could deal with low class females of the living variety. He rushed up the steps. When he reached the top, the light went out. At the same moment, a draft caught the candle in his own lantern, and all became dark.

Tora took a couple of steps forward into utter blackness and stumbled over a bundle, nearly falling flat on his face.

An eerie cackle from somewhere near his knee assailed his ears, and he smelled the stench of rotting gums. Whoever it was, he or she was right beside him. Tora moved aside quickly and promptly stepped on something soft and squishy. The cackle turned into a warning screech.

"Here! Watch what you're doin'! She won't holler, but you near put your big foot on me!"

"Sorry!"

He found his flint and relit his lantern. In its light, an old crone peered up at Tora. She was dressed in many layers of filthy rags, her long white hair draped crazily over hunched shoulders. In this light, her face looked like an animated skull. Gray skin clung to sharp bones, eyes disappeared in dark hollows, and a toothless mouth gaped in the rictus of a grin. She was cowering near the corpse of a naked female. Tora retreated with a curse when he realized that he had just stepped on the dead woman's arm.

The crone cackled again. "What's the matter? Afraid of the dead? Look hard, pretty boy! That's what your sweetheart'll look like soon enough!"

Tora had seen bodies before and glanced at the corpse. She was young and very slender except for her bloated face and abdomen. Short-haired and thin, she bore no resemblance to Michiko, whose every limb was plump and whose hair reached past her waist. The dead woman's eyes were open, turned up and showing only yellow-tinged whites. As Tora looked, a sluggish fly emerged from between the cracked lips. If the sweetish smell of corruption had not warned him that this one had been left here at the last possible moment, the purple discoloration in irregular splotches on the yellowing skin would have told him that she had been dead for a day or two. He shuddered and sighed.

"Pretty, ain't she?" The old crone cackled again. "If you want to lie with her, she's free. She won't give you no argument neither."

"Shut up!" Tora raised an arm as if to strike her. She scuttled away a few steps, dropping a long knife in her haste. Tora cursed and snatched it up. "What's that for, you she-devil?" he snarled, coming after her with the knife.

She backed against a wall, raising spindly arms to cover her face. "Nothing," she wailed. "There's no law against it. She'll not be needin' it."

Tora stopped. "What?"

The crone reached into her robe and stretched out a bony arm. From her fist dangled a long twist of black hair.

Tora cursed again and turned away. So she had come to rob the dead woman of the only valuable thing she had left. There was a good market for women's hair. The wealthy and noble ladies liked to augment their own thin or short tresses artificially; little did they know where their borrowed beauty came from. Glancing down at the dead woman, Tora saw that she might have been quite pretty once with her long and shining hair. His stomach twisted again with anger, but he restrained himself. The old one had to live too, and he knew well what poverty could make people do.

"I'm looking for the body of an old man," he said. The crone stuffed the hair back into her robe and picked up her lantern. "He's about a head shorter than me, skinny, big nose. A drowning victim. Have you seen anyone like that?"

"Gimme back my knife!"

He returned it to her reluctantly.

"What you want him for?" she asked slyly, shoving the knife into her belt. "Think he's got some gold on him?"

"No. He's a beggar."

Her eyes shifted past him. She muttered, "Don't know nothing. Gotta go." Kicking at Tora's lantern, she left him standing in the sudden darkness.

"Hey!" He cursed and groped his way forward, hoping he would not step on any more corpses or tumble down the stairwell. He touched a wall and moved along it cautiously. Somewhere ahead of him steps shuffled away. Then the wall ended. Tora decided to abandon his lantern rather than come in contact with the corpse again. A doorway opened into another room, dimly lit by moonlight coming through wooden shutters. Tora entered and threw the shutters wide. The room was empty except for a pile of refuse and a scurrying rat.

Back in the hallway, he found that he could see well enough now to make out several other doors opening into rooms similar to the last one. He stumbled over another body, which turned out to be still alive. He did not bother to check whether the person was drunk or dying. Checking rooms systematically while clutching his Fudo amulet, he finally found what he had come for in the fifth and last room.

A dark shape lay in the middle of the floor. When he bent to touch it, he found wet garments and went to open the shutters wide. The moon was about to disappear behind clouds again, and he quickly turned back to the corpse.

It was Umakai.

He had not been dead long when he had been fished out of the water. His face was blue; his eyes, their whites bloodshot, protruded; and his tongue showed between toothless gums. The wet rags notwithstanding, he did not look like a drowned man. Puzzled, Tora bent to check the dead man's throat the way he remembered his master doing with the girl Omaki.

At that moment the back of his head seemed to explode, and he fell into blackness.

◆

When he came to, he was lying on his side, his arms tied behind his back and his feet tied together and drawn up. There was an evil-tasting gag in his mouth, his head hurt blindingly and he felt nauseated.

Opening one eye, he peered cautiously at his surroundings and saw that he was still in Rashomon. The beggar's body was gone, but someone else had taken its place. A man sat cross-legged in the middle of the room, reading a book by the light of an oil lamp. The man looked familiar.

Slowly memory returned. It was the robber-warrior who had been downstairs earlier. His sword was still slung across his back, but he had laid the bow and arrows aside.

Tora decided that he was in an extremely unpleasant situation and surreptitiously tested his bonds. Not a chance! If it was his companion who had trussed him up, he knew his business. His legs were bent at the knees, and a short piece of rope connected the bonds of his ankles and wrists. The shoulder he lay on hurt like the devil, and something dug painfully into his ribs. He had lost sensation in one arm. But the gag was the worst. It was an evil-smelling rag, no doubt part of the refuse left after the grave robbers had picked their victims clean. A wave of nausea rose, and Tora concentrated on subduing it. If he were to vomit while gagged, he would suffocate. Slowly his stomach settled and he could breathe again.

The armed man turned to another page.

That a robber should read books in his spare time astonished Tora. The man looked to be about his size, but was more thickly built, with a broad chest and powerful arms. His face was slightly scarred, perhaps from superficial sword cuts. There was a daredevil handsomeness about his features, and the well-trimmed beard and mustache suited him. His clothes, too, were worn but clean and of good quality.

Steps sounded on the stairs outside, and the man quickly rolled up the book and tucked it inside his robe. He glanced at Tora and then at the doorway. Three men entered. Two of them were dressed like poor laborers; one of these was a big and clumsy fellow, the other not much more than four feet tall and very thin. The third man was a monk. Though he was bareheaded now, carrying the straw hat in his hand, Tora thought he was the same one who had been downstairs earlier, probably pretending to be asleep. He was still young, with a round, plain face and broad shoulders. The stubble of hair on his head and chin suggested that he was casual about his vows.

"Well, was it taken care of to your satisfaction?" asked the armed man.

The tall brute lumbered towards one of the walls and sat down. He gave a loud sniff.

"Stop sniveling, Spike!" said his short companion sharply. He had a high voice like a boy's and his face was smooth like a child's, but there were lines of age around his eyes and mouth. "Yeah," he answered the warrior's question, "we put our old buddy away neat and proper like we promised him. Dug a nice dry hole near the wall, and Monk here did the honors, saying some of his mumbo-jumbo while Spike wailed like a baby."

Spike sniffed again, and the monk asked in a deep, rumbling voice, "What about our prisoner?"

They all turned to stare at Tora, who shut his eyes quickly.

"Hasn't moved," said the warrior. "What will you do with him?"

"I should've killed the bastard!" quavered Spike. Tora's eyes snapped open. He now saw the pointed metal rod protruding from the man's right sleeve. No wonder his head felt the way it did. In fact, it was a miracle he was alive. His skull must be cracked.

The monk said, "No. There will be no bloodshed."

The armed man cleared his throat. "I think we've got a prob-lem. Since he's an official and has had time to memorize our faces,"—he broke off, jumped up and came over to grab Tora's collar and jerk him to his knees—"he'll have the police down on us before you can say 'Praise the Buddha's name!' There! I thought he was awake."

Waves of pain pounded the inside of Tora's skull. He shut his eyes and heard from a great distance the monk's voice. "He looks ill. Not much fight left in him. Why don't we loosen the rope a lit-tle? When he starts feeling a bit better, he can work himself loose. By that time we'll have gone to ground somewhere. Nail here knows a couple of places."

Spike made some outraged protest, and Tora opened his eyes cautiously. The room still spun a little and the rough boards un-der his knees seemed to move. He attempted a few pleading grunts.

The armed man regarded him with distaste. "I don't know, Monk," he said. "If you give an official enough rope, he'll hang an-other poor sot with it."

The monk choked back a laugh. "Well, we could just leave him for the scavengers."

Tora grunted again and tried to shake his head, but the room turned dark again. He barely managed to stay on his knees.

"I believe the fellow's trying to talk," the armed man remarked. "Take the gag out, Nail, and let's see what he has to say."

"He'll call for help!" Nail objected.

Tora shook his head again, and this time the pain was so acute that he sagged to the floor.

A hand grasped his arm and pulled him upright. The monk's deep voice asked, "How hard did you hit him, Spike? He looks very ill." He took the gag out of Tora's mouth.

Tora sucked in a big gulp of night air, spat out some stinking fibers, and straightened up as much as he could. "If you loosen the rope in back a little," he croaked, "we'll be able to have a comfortable chat."

The Spike cursed, but the armed man chuckled. "I like your spirit, official, but I think we'll leave well enough alone. What were you doing here?"

"I'm no official. I'm a retainer. My master sent me to find a beggar called Umakai. Turns out I was too late. A whore told me you picked up a drowning victim to bring him here. Then, just when I found old Umakai, some bastard knocked me out. That's all! Now why don't you untie me, so we can introduce ourselves properly?"

The armed man grinned. "Good try! I can see that you're going far. They tell me that all the officials take lessons in fake sincerity and the pretense of humanity. I think you've got a brilliant career ahead of you. You got the tone just right, but your lies need a bit more work. I gather your master is one of the good people. Why should such a one care about the safety of an old beggar? No, no! It's much too far-fetched."

"Yeah! The bastard lies," growled Spike. "Let's shut his mouth for good and get out of here!"

The other two waited in silence.

"All right," snapped Tora. "Have it your way! The killer ought to thank you for your help. First you bury the corpse and then you want to kill the one guy who could help you get the bastard. Fine friends the poor old beggar had in you!" He spat again.

"You're a filthy piece of cow dung!" howled Spike, coming to his feet, metal rod raised high. Without changing his position, the Nail extended a leg and tripped him. The Spike landed with a crash.

"Neatly done, Nail!" complimented the armed man. "Now sit down, Spike, and let the man talk. I'm beginning to get interested. All right, you! When the beggar was fished out of a canal this morning, the warden certified death by drowning. What makes you think he was murdered?"

Instead of answering, Tora graphically mimicked bulging eyes and a protruding tongue.

The armed man nodded slowly. "I wondered about that. So, who killed him?"

"I don't know, but it's bound to be the same bastard who strangled a girl in the Spring Garden. Old Umakai saw her killer and could identify the swine. That's why my master sent me to look for him as soon as he heard they had let him out of jail."

"You lie, dog turd!" growled Spike. "The police said it was old Umakai did the killing. They near beat him to death. Bet you're one of them, come looking for him to put him back in jail so you'd have someone to pin it on. Maybe you killed him yourself!"

Tora turned to look at the big brute. "No," he said slowly and clearly, as if he were speaking to a small child, "If I had killed him, I wouldn't come here. It was my master that cleared him of those charges. That's why the police let him go. And that's why my master worried about his safety."

"Who is this extraordinary master of yours?" asked the armed man with raised brows.

"Lord Sugawara." Tora's proud announcement met with blank stares. He snapped, "If you four weren't such dunces, you'd have heard of him. He's famous for catching criminals. In Kazusa province last winter, he uncovered a dangerous conspiracy against the emperor. And while he was at it, he caught three killers on top of that."

After a moment's stunned silence, the monk said thoughtfully,

"You know, I believe I've heard that story. This Sugawara is with the Ministry of Justice, I think."

The armed man growled, "That makes him a cursed official!" Glowering at Tora, he asked, "How is it that he solves murders for the municipal police?"

Tora's head started pounding again, and his back and shoulder muscles cramped. He sighed. "He doesn't. And he's not with the ministry just now. He teaches at the university. That's how come we found the dead girl in the park nearby. He called the police, and later we saw them arrest old Umakai. My master said right away that the old man wasn't guilty. The police chief wasn't listening at first, but my master proved it was so." Tora paused and glared at his captors. "I'm wasting my breath. With guys like you around, we would've been better off to keep our mouths shut."

A brief silence greeted that outburst. Then the monk said, "This Sugawara is a professor, a learned man who solves mysteries. Maybe we've made a mistake."

"Don't be a fool!" growled the armed man. "Those so-called academicians just put on a show. A good memory for some Chinese mumbo-jumbo and a hatred for everything Japanese will do the trick. It does not require intelligence."

Tora cried, "And where did you go to school? In a badger's hole?"

"Ah, Hitomaro!" laughed the monk. "He's got you there! All your reading's not going to help you without a proper teacher."

The armed man flushed. He was about to speak, but his eye fell on the window. "Never mind!" he said. "We're wasting time. It's almost dawn, and the scavengers will be here for the dead. What shall we do?"

"Let him go," said the monk quickly.

"Kill him," voted Spike.

The man called Hitomaro looked at the short fellow. "Well, Nail?" he asked.

Nail scratched his hair under the dirty rag he wore tied around it. "I don't know. He could be lying. But if he's telling the truth, there's a chance we could get the bastard that killed Umakai. I guess we'd better let him go, but make him swear first to bring the killer to us."

"Not much good," said Hitomaro. "If he's a liar, he'll swear to anything, and if he's an honest man, he'll swear to nothing he can't keep. I vote we let him go. We'll know soon enough what sort of man he is."

The monk got up, pulled a sharp knife from his sash and cut Tora's bonds. Tora straightened his legs and massaged his wrists with a grimace. "I'm Tora," he said, then asked, "Where did you put old Umakai? We'll have to dig him back up to prove he was murdered." He stood up, testing his legs cautiously. His head was feeling a bit better. "And where will I find you? There's bound to be questions."

"Don't tell him!" cried Nail. "He'll come back with the police to arrest us."

Hitomaro exchanged a look with the monk. Then he stiffened and turned his head towards the open shutters. "Ssh!" he said, getting to his feet and listening intently. "They're coming for the dead. Put out the light!" To Tora he said, "Umakai is in the old cemetery behind the West Temple. And you can leave a message for me by name at the wineshop next door to the temple."

The monk blew out the lamp. In the darkness, Hitomaro said, "If you turn us in, you're a dead man. You may get one or two of us, but the rest will find you."

Spike breathed down Tora's neck. "And it won't be pretty when we do," he snarled.

FIFTEEN

THE GHOSTLY MANSION

The next morning Akitada was up early, dressed for work and full of brisk purpose. Tora, on the other hand, presented himself holding his head and looking distinctly green.

"Good heavens!" Akitada stared at him. "This is the third day in a row that you show up here after a night of debauchery. Even *your* constitution is not going to keep up with this."

"It is said," remarked Seimei with a sniff, setting down a tray with Akitada's morning rice, "that with the first cup man consumes wine, with the second, wine consumes wine, and with the third wine consumes man." He peered more closely at Tora and added, "You truly look ill."

"It's not wine," muttered Tora, collapsing on a cushion. "My skull collided with a metal spike some fellow was using for a hand." He sniffed hungrily, eyeing the steaming rice gruel in Akitada's bowl. "And I've missed supper and breakfast both."

Seimei went to inspect the large swelling under Tora's hair and left, muttering, to prepare an herbal compress. Akitada pushed his bowl towards Tora. "Eat first and then tell me what happened."

Raising the bowl to his mouth, Tora tilted back his head and drank the rice gruel in large gulps. Lowering the bowl, he licked his lips. "Thanks. That's better," he said with a sigh of satisfaction. "Well, I found the old beggar, poor bastard. Someone had got to him before I did. He was strangled, dumped in a canal, pronounced an accident and buried in the cemetery behind the Buddhist temple west of Rashomon—all in a day's work!"

Akitada looked grim. "Explain."

Tora obliged in detail, while Seimei returned with another serving of gruel and a pungent herb pack which he applied to Tora's head, making clucking noises from time to time. It was not clear if he was commenting on the injury or Tora's story.

Akitada was deeply distressed by the beggar's death, but when Tora was done, he said only, "So! Our strangler again!" He got up and searched among his papers. "Here, show me on this map where the body was found!"

Tora pointed. "About there, from what I could make out."

"Hmm." Akitada pulled his earlobe and pursed his lips. "Between the river and to the east of the market."

"The business quarter. Merchant houses back up to the canal."

"Very strange. Not the kind of place to leave a body. Shoppers are passing back and forth, and the authorities keep an eye on things. More to the point, I cannot imagine what Umakai was doing there. They don't tolerate beggars."

"Well," said Tora. He scratched his head and dislodged the compress, causing another flurry of cluckings from Seimei. Tora ignored him. "The merchants close at a decent hour and go to bed. After that it gets pretty quiet at night. And I don't think many people would pass that way from the Willow Quarter."

"Regardless, the body must have been dumped at night, and even then the killer would have taken a chance." Akitada paused and considered. "Unless the murder happened inside one of the houses or in a courtyard." A vague idea began to take shape in his mind. Perhaps they had looked at the case the wrong way all along.

"Maybe," said Tora, "the killer was following Umakai and when he got to the canal, he strangled him, tossed him in the water, and walked away as if nothing had happened. It wouldn't take long with a decrepit old man like that."

"He would hardly get away with it in broad daylight. And where was Umakai all day? Nobody saw him after he left the city hall."

Tora had no answer to this problem.

"Merchants," said Akitada thoughtfully. "I wonder . . . Tora, as soon as you feel better I want you to go and find out who lives in the houses that back up to the canal. Seimei can take a note to Captain Kobe telling him where to look for Umakai's corpse. I hope the man has the sense to let the student go now."

"I feel fine," said Tora, getting up and losing the compress again. "And I can take the note on my way. I want to make sure old Umakai's friends don't get into trouble." He pressed the herbal pack into Seimei's hand.

Seimei protested, but Akitada said, "Leave him be, Seimei! I must say, Tora, you are unusually forgiving about the treatment you received. And conditions at Rashomon are getting appalling. The sooner the authorities are made aware of what is going on there, the better. This may just get them started cleaning out the riffraff around the gate."

Tora looked shocked. "You can't do that. Those guys let me go. I grant you Spike and Nail are a bit rough, but Monk and Hitomaro were very decent. They're educated men like you, reading books and everything. You can't throw people in jail for being down on their luck. You'd soon have nobody left to clean the streets and plow the fields."

Akitada grimaced. "You are right. Very well, I leave the matter in your hands." He rose and put on his hat. "Seimei, please make copies of the documents your chess partner promised to bring." At the door he paused and added, "Oh, and see if you can find out what tradesmen were supplying the wine, lanterns, cushions and so forth for the poetry competition. Try the housekeeping office in the Treasury and the office of the superintendent of the imperial parks."

Astonished, Tora and Seimei stared at each other.

◆

The mansion that once belonged to Prince Yoakira was only a short distance from the Sugawara residence. A tall plaster wall topped with tiles protected a compound covering an entire block. Behind the wall rose the tops of tall trees and the tiled roofs of many halls. A great silence hung over the whole area.

The heavy, studded double gate was securely locked, but a smaller gate beside it stood open. Akitada walked in and crossed an imposing entry courtyard. It was deserted. To the right and left rose buildings with deep verandas and wide roof overhangs. They were connected by covered galleries through which one could see other courtyards, some with trees and shrubbery, and more halls, roofs and galleries. Once the place would have thronged with visitors and bustled with servants. Now the emptiness and silence were oppressive.

Akitada passed by the main building, containing the ceremonial rooms used only for public functions or great family celebrations. Probably the service conducted by Sesshin had taken place there, but now the hall lay closed and brooding in the morning sun.

Beyond it was another courtyard, this one with a group of pines, dark and stiff guardians over the adjoining private residences. Which one had been the prince's? They all looked alike. Here must also be the quarters occupied by his granddaughter and grandson. Where had the boy stood when he saw his grandfather rushing across the compound towards the building belonging to his sister?

Suddenly Akitada felt uncomfortably like an intruder caught in the act. He turned quickly, scanning the surroundings. Nothing. Yet it was as if he had disturbed the peace of some immanent force, and a shiver ran down his spine.

But then his ear caught a reassuringly human sound in this ghostly place. In the distance, someone was raking gravel.

Following the soft, swishing sounds, Akitada went in search of the lone gardener. After a few wrong turns, he passed through a gallery into a small inner courtyard which was shaded by a huge old paulownia tree. An old man in a loose hempen shirt and pants was busy sweeping up the fallen blossoms and yellowed leaves.

"Good morning, uncle," Akitada called out to him.

The old man started and peered towards him uncertainly. After a moment, he bowed deeply, saying in a cracked voice, "Good morning, Your Honor. I'm afraid you have come at the wrong time. There's no one at home. The family lives in the country now."

The old-timer was bent with age, but strong and sturdy still, his sad face deeply tanned and wrinkled, like old wood cracked by time, his hair and beard nearly white. Akitada said, "My name is Sugawara and I come from the young lord, who is my pupil. He has expressed concern for his people, and so I thought to ask for news."

The old man's face broke into a smile of great sweetness. "The young lord?" he cried. "Oh, how is the young lord, sir?" Tears rose to his eyes and spilled over. "Oh, the sad change! Oh!" he murmured, shaking his head in sorrow.

"The boy is well enough, and a very good student. Come, let us sit down over there and talk. What is your name, by the way?"

"I'm Kinsue, Your Honor." The greybeard carefully leaned his bamboo rake against the trunk of the old tree and followed Akitada to the veranda steps. "The old woman and me, we stayed behind to take care of the place." He stopped uncertainly. "But won't you come inside?"

"No, no." Akitada sat down on a step. "It is a beautiful day and I would much rather be in the fresh air. Young Lord Minamoto is concerned about the well-being of his sister and of the servants. Can you tell me about them?"

Kinsue remained standing respectfully. "Not much, Your Honor," he said. "You see when I came back from the mountains, the wagons were all packed to go. The young lady and all the other servants left soon after. There was to be no mourning, because the master had been transported to Nirvana, you see. Lord Sakanoue said it was a matter for rejoicing." He looked down at his hempen outfit, traditionally worn by a dead man's servants, and brushed the fabric awkwardly. "It seemed disrespectful." Gazing across the courtyard, towards the tree, he wiped his eyes. "Forgive me, sir, but I'm an old man," he said brokenly, "and I cannot help weeping. To me it was dreadful, the day we lost our master. Lord Sakanoue took the young lord away and when he came back, he told me and my wife to stay behind. We were not wanted. He took the last wagon to the country himself."

"But he is back in the capital. Does he not reside here?"

"No. He went to see everyone settled and then came back alone. But he doesn't live here. There's talk of ghosts, you see. It's only me and the old woman who live here and look after the master's home." The old man sighed. "You can't blame Lord Sakanoue. The soothsayer warned us. He said evil would befall this house. But the master had him whipped from the gate. Now the master's dead and the halls are without life. Even this tree is dying. My wife and I, we say our prayers for the master's spirit every day. The forty-nine days will be up in another week. Maybe then he will have rest. May the Buddha grant it." He bowed his head and let the tears drip unchecked into the gravel.

Akitada did not know what to say in the face of such grief and superstition. His eyes went to the pile of yellow leaves under the tree. It was early summer still. Why was the tree losing its leaves? He looked up at the dense crown above. There was an astonishing number of yellowing leaves amongst the green. It must be the hot, dry weather. Soon the summer rains would come. Surely the old tree would recover then.

As if he had shared his thought, the old man before him began to talk again. "We try to keep his place the way he would like it," he said. "Every day I put fresh flowers in his room and offerings of fruit and rice. When I am there I talk to him a little. Nothing much. About the weather and what part of the house we are going to clean next. I shall tell him what you said about his grandson being such a fine scholar. He will be so pleased; he loved the young lord. He was a very good master." Again Kinsue brushed awkwardly at his wet face with a gnarled hand. "Would Your Honor like to see the master's room?" he asked timidly.

Akitada accepted and found that he had been sitting on the steps leading to the prince's pavilion. Kinsue climbed the steps and opened a finely carved door leading into a large, bright space divided by means of painted screens into three smaller areas. One of these, the old man explained, had been where the prince had slept. It was now bare of mats and bedding. A fine low writing desk and shelves with a few books occupied the next space. Here, in a niche with a hanging calligraphy scroll, Kinsue had placed his offerings: a sheaf of purple irises in a porcelain vase, and two bowls of food, one of oranges and another of rice. Set carefully beside these traditional offerings to buddhas and spirits of the dead were a pair of new straw sandals and a small pile of copper coins.

Looking searchingly at the old man, Akitada pointed to these and asked, "Do you not believe the story of the miracle? If your master is with the Buddha now, he will not need such things."

Kinsue shrunk into himself. "I don't know about such things," he muttered miserably. "Here it's like he speaks to me, and he's . . . not happy."

Akitada shivered involuntarily. The atmosphere in the room was certainly more intensely unsettling than it had been outside. "Did you say you went to the mountain temple with him that day?"

"Yes, Your Honor. I was his driver and I saw it all, everything that happened."

Akitada narrowed his eyes. "Everything? You saw your master get into the carriage here and you saw him get out at the Ninna temple?"

The old man nodded. "That I did. And he was a splendid sight in that fine purple robe. His train was so long it was dragging up the steps to the temple hall."

Akitada pursued that thought. "Did he have problems getting in and out of the carriage?"

Kinsue frowned. "The ox was acting up, and I wasn't looking, but I don't think so. My master was wonderfully well for a man of his age, almost like a young man sometimes. I remember thinking so when he ran up the steps to the temple. So eager to worship the Buddha!"

"Then he was in a good mood? Smiling, talking to his friends?"

"Oh no. They were with the horses both times. I was the only one there, holding the ox when he got in the carriage and again when he got out later."

Akitada sighed. It was becoming clear that the old man prided himself on his powers of observation and attention to his master, but had been prevented by his duties and the darkness from seeing everything that was going on. "And Lord Sakanoue? Did he ride with the prince in the carriage?"

"Oh, no. Lord Sakanoue rode a horse."

"In front of the carriage?"

Kinsue shook his head. "The ox is slow. Sometimes the gentlemen passed us, and sometimes they were behind. But I know that, coming back, he was out in front." He scratched his head and frowned, but said no more.

"I see." Akitada turned to look through the open doorway, picturing the nighttime bustle of departure, the carriage drawn up at the foot of the steps, the waiting riders. Again he had an eerie sense of something intangible, of an unseen presence listening, waiting. "How many went with the prince that night?" he asked.

The old man thought. "Let's see. There was me and Noro. Noro's the boy that rode on the ox. Then there was Lord Abe and General Soga, and Lord Yanagida and Lord Shinoda in front. Yes, that's all. The others had to stay to pack for the trip to the country."

Four witnesses besides the driver and the boy! Akitada shook his head and said, "It seems strange that your master should suddenly have decided to remove the whole family to the country on the very day of his annual visit to the Ninna temple."

Kinsue shook his head sadly. "Who can say? The soothsayer cursed us," he muttered. "It was an evil day when the master had him whipped from the gate. That's what I told my old woman, when there was the trouble with the young lady we weren't supposed to know about."

That confirmed the boy's account. Akitada returned to the events at the temple. "You say you saw everything that happened at the temple. Were you not tending to your ox?"

"No. That's what the boy was there for. I was sitting down by the wall, watching the gentlemen on the veranda and listening to the master praying."

"Are you sure you could hear and see?" Akitada asked in disbelief. "It was surely dark, and you were across the courtyard if you were sitting by the wall."

"It's only a small courtyard, and the sky was getting light."

"Very well. Go on. Tell me everything you saw and heard from the moment you arrived."

Kinsue got a faraway look in his eyes. "After His Highness got out," he said, "I untied the ox and told Noro to take it to the next courtyard and feed it. Then I sat down to wait. His Highness had already gone in and I could hear him chanting. The gentlemen were sitting on the veranda outside the door. After a time the sun started coming up over the mountain. Then the monks rang the great bell of the temple, and the master stopped chanting. Lord Sakanoue got up and walked to the balustrade to tell me to bring the ox, which I did. I remember Noro and I were talking about being back in town in time for a good breakfast. We hitched the ox to the carriage, and then we all waited. The gentlemen were still standing on the veranda. They were talking, but I couldn't hear what they said. Some of them came down to get their horses. Then Lord Sakanoue went to the door and knocked, crying, 'Your Highness! Everything is ready!' But my master did not come out. One of the gentlemen and Lord Sakanoue talked and then they went in. Me and Noro stood staring up, wondering what was wrong. The other gentlemen came to look, too. Then Lord Sakanoue came back out, and he was carrying the master's purple robe and he was weeping. He said the master was gone."

The old man let his head drop to his chest and he wiped his eyes again. "I never saw my master again," he muttered. "The monks came then, and the abbot, and they all searched and searched. Then they brought an exorcist and a medium. The

medium went inside and when she came out, she said that the master had been reborn in paradise because of his devotion in reading the sutra and in wishing to be with his son. I suppose it must be so." Kinsue stopped, exhausted.

Akitada gave him time to recover. Then he said, "You must have wondered what happened. Did you not think your master might have just walked away? Or that someone might have abducted him or even killed him and hidden his body?"

Kinsue shook his head. "It was impossible," he said stubbornly. "I watched. The gentlemen watched. Lord Sakanoue made all of us come up and see that there was no one in the hall, and there was no way the master could have left. It must have been as the medium said."

"Kinsue," cried a faint, quavering voice outside. The interruption was so startling that both men jumped a little.

"My wife," explained Kinsue.

"I would like to meet her."

Akitada followed Kinsue out. Under the paulownia tree stood a short, fat old woman who was staring at the rake and the pile of leaves as if her husband might suddenly materialize. When Kinsue called out to her, her face lit up until she saw Akitada. Her husband made the introductions. Getting awkwardly down on her knees, she bowed rapidly several times.

Akitada said, "Please get up. I wondered if you might have some message for Sadamu from his sister. He is worried."

The old woman began to cry. "Oh, my poor little lady," she sobbed. "All alone now. May Amida protect her!" She fell to praying, eyes closed and lips moving soundlessly.

"Hush, old woman!" cried her husband, scandalized. "Do you want to frighten the young lord?" He turned to Akitada to explain. "My wife took the young lady her morning rice before she left for the country. The young lady's maids were busy loading the carts, and so she was allowed into the young lady's quarters. The young lady was weeping terribly, but it was a bad time, what with the sad news. I am sure the young lady is quite well by now. Being married to Lord Sakanoue, she is now number one lady of the household. That is something, isn't it, when she is but fifteen years old?"

Fifteen? She was a mere child then. "Was there really a marriage?" asked Akitada, looking at Kinsue's wife. She nodded, her eyes unhappy.

"But I thought Prince Yoakira had refused to give his consent," Akitada said.

The two old people looked at each other, puzzled. "But they must be married," said the old woman. "His lordship spent the night with her three nights running, and I baked the wedding dumplings myself on the third day." Her face crumpled again. "It was the day before the master went away to heaven."

Kinsue shook his head in wonder. "What a day! So many things happening!"

"Yes," said Akitada. "It must have been. Thank you both. I shall tell Lord Minamoto what you said."

The old woman scrambled up to whisper something in her husband's ear, then wobbled off at a half-run. Kinsue said, "My wife went to fetch something for the young lord."

Akitada nodded and turned to look up at the prince's quarters. Here the quarrel had taken place after Yoakira had discovered to his shock that his granddaughter had, willingly or otherwise, become Sakanoue's wife. No wonder he had been furious! What had passed between the old nobleman and his new grandson-in-law? Had he acknowledged the marriage, or refused to countenance it? Akitada thought he knew the answer to that. It was the motive for the murder of the prince. Poor children, both at the mercy of an unscrupulous man. He tried to imagine what the girl must have felt, must be feeling now.

Lost in thought, he walked up the steps again and stood in the doorway looking in. It must be a marriage as empty and desolate as this room. He thought of his parents, their formality with each other, the absence of any signs of fondness, of physical familiarity. But his mother had always been a strong character, well able to cope with an autocratic husband. Was this what had frightened Tamako?

Had she been afraid that he would be a distant husband, leaving her to the cold demands of her mother-in-law? He sighed unhappily. That mystery would never be solved, but the strange disappearance of the man who used to occupy these rooms would be, if he could help it.

As he thought this, Akitada felt his hair bristle. It was as if something spoke to him with a terrible urgency.

He looked around. Not so much as a clothes chest remained, only the outline where one had stood, obliquely, near the door. Packed and ready for transport to the country? Why had they removed the prince's things? he wondered. He had been gone by then and would hardly need his clothes.

Someone had inexpertly scoured the wooden floor after the chest had been removed. The marks had dulled the deep gloss of the floorboards. Kinsue, no doubt, in his fervent desire to keep the master's room spotless.

The calligraphy scroll caught Akitada's eye. Idly, he deciphered the Chinese ideograms, feeling strangely as if he were hearing the words in his head. "Seek the truth and thou shalt find it! Neglect the truth and it shall be lost forever! The seeking is within thy power, but the finding is in the hands of heaven. Thou must search the truth within, for thou shalt not find it without." The words were attributed to Meng Tse.

With a sigh Akitada turned away and went out into the courtyard. Kinsue and his wife awaited him.

"Tell me," he asked them, "what has become of the prince's clothes and other things?"

"Oh, they've been taken to the country," the old man said. "Lord Sakanoue took them himself in the last cart."

"I see. Well, I see your wife has returned, and I must be on my way. Thank you for telling me your story. Lord Minamoto will be glad to know that you and your wife are taking such good care of his home and are thinking of him."

Kinsue's wife shuffled up. With a toothless smile splitting a round face that resembled a dried yam, she bowed and extended the small box tied with a bit of hempen string towards Akitada.

"It's sweet dumplings," Kinsue explained for her. "The young lord is partial to them."

"Thank you," said Akitada, accepting the parcel, "and thank you also for your explanations. Should either of you remember anything else, even if it seems unimportant, send for me. It may help the young lord to understand."

Kinsue nodded. "There's nothing else, sir," he said, "except the horse, but how can that matter?"

"Horse?"

"Lord Sakanoue's horse, the one he took to the mountains. It wasn't his and it wasn't one of ours. I know all of our animals, sir."

SIXTEEN

ROASTED WALNUTS

*I*n spite of the brutal murder of its most famous scholar, the university was open as usual. Akitada arrived just in time for his first class. He was relieved, because that meant that he need not exchange pleasantries with Hirata. Their relationship had become unbearably strained, not only because Akitada still resented the way Hirata had trapped him into a marriage proposal—one which had turned out to be unwelcome to Tamako—but also because even the briefest encounter with the father reminded Akitada painfully of the daughter. Striding quickly through the main hall, he went directly to his own classroom.

His students sat waiting, their faces turned eagerly towards the door as he entered, their smiles welcoming him before the fifteen blue-robed backs and the fifteen black-capped heads bowed low before their master. His heart warmed with gratitude. He considered for the first time that a teacher had a blessed life. Encouraged by his reception, he spent the morning expounding the laws governing provincial administrations and was pleased with their patience.

In fact, Mr. Ushimatsu, the middle-aged student, outdid himself, having not only memorized the names of all the provinces, but volunteering to point them out on the map. He also supplied fairly accurate information about crops, industries, towns and temples, until even his peers looked impressed. When Akitada praised him, Ushimatsu's eyes sparkled with pleasure. He murmured shyly that he dreamed of being sent to one of the provinces as a recorder or junior clerk on the staff of one of the governors. Therefore he had thought it wise to prepare himself by studying all the possible assignments ahead of time.

One of the young nobles snorted. "You want to leave the capital for some godforsaken place?" he cried. "And as a mere clerk? I have more ambition than that, I hope. Why bother to attend the university if that is all you want, Ushimatsu?" A chorus of supporters joined him, and it looked for a moment as though poor Ushimatsu would once again be cowed by his sneering comrades.

But Ushimatsu bowed to his critic. "Forgive me, Mokudai, but that is all very well for you. And for a lot of the others, too, I imagine. You have relatives who are great men here in the capital, and your Chinese is much, much better than mine." With a smile at the others, he added, "I am quite content to be a secretary to one of your cousins, or perhaps some day to one of you. As for leaving the capital, I quite look forward to that because it means that I shall get to see what the rest of the country looks like."

Young Lord Minamoto cried, "And I shall envy you, Ushimatsu. I wish I were free to see the world." For a moment a look of great sadness passed over the boy's face. "Oh, Ushimatsu," he said softly, "when you talked of the great snows and the bears in Echigo, I wished I could see them for myself. And I wished to sail the Inland Sea to see the monkeys in Kyushu, and travel the Tokaido Highway until I looked on Mount Fuji. But I know that I will probably never leave the capital as long as I live."

The critics yielded, and Akitada said quickly, "None of us knows what the future may bring. Many a great lord has been sent on missions of importance by His Majesty. We all serve where we can."

Akitada was inordinately proud of the progress Ushimatsu had made. If he kept up his pace, he would pass the next examination. Making a mental note to lend Ushimatsu some of his documents, he assigned an essay on the system of corvée to the class and dismissed them for their noon rice.

As young Minamoto passed his desk on his way out the door, Akitada remembered the present from Kinsue's wife. "Sadamu," he said, "I have something for you."

The boy's eyes widened with pleasure. "For me? What is it?" he cried, taking the box.

"It is not from me. This morning I went to speak to your grandfather's driver. He and his wife are the only ones left at the mansion."

"Kinsue," nodded the boy, his eyes suddenly intent. "What did you discover?"

Akitada hesitated. "Essentially Kinsue supports the official story. Your grandfather entered the temple hall, but did not emerge. When his attendants looked for him, he had disappeared."

The boy sighed. "Kinsue would not lie. He loved Grandfather. There must be an explanation. Will you go to the temple?"

"Yes. I will after I have talked to the men who were with your grandfather. I am told the Lords Abe, Yanagida and Shinoda, as well as some general, accompanied your grandfather. Do you know any of them?"

The boy nodded. "I know them, but not well. They came often to the house, but I was not present when my grandfather entertained them. The general is called Soga. I am sorry I cannot help you any more."

"It does not matter. By the way, I am amazed you know the names of your grandfather's servants. There must be many of them."

The boy smiled. He was weighing the box in his hand and shaking it slightly. "Of course," he said. "But especially Kinsue and Fumiko. Fumiko is Kinsue's wife. Are they both well? Is this present from her?" Somehow the string had come undone. His lordship raised the box to his face and squinted at a crack under the lid, his nose twitching a little.

"Go ahead and look," said Akitada with a smile.

Instantly the lid came off. "Sweet dumplings!" cried the boy, doing a little skip and hop. "I was hoping it would be sweet dumplings.

She makes the best." He inhaled the smell ecstatically and extended
the open box to Akitada. "Please, sir, will you sample one?"

"No, thank you. It is time for my midday rice. Kinsue and, er,
Fumiko are quite well and wanted me tell you that they are taking
good care of your home in your absence."

The youngster closed the box, blushing a little. "It is very good
of them and I am glad that they are healthy and have not been dismissed. Do they need anything?"

Akitada marvelled again at the sense of responsibility this
eleven-year-old felt for his people. "No," he said, "I don't believe so.
They grieve, of course. For your grandfather and because you are
not with them."

The boy blinked. "I am glad they are at the old place, because
that is where my grandfather's spirit will be until his forty-nine
days are up," he said, his voice choking a little. "Is there any news
of my sister, sir?"

"None, I'm afraid. She is in the country. By the way, where is
your country house?"

"Near Mount Kuriko on the Nara Highway."

"I have also spoken to your great-uncle, Bishop Sesshin. I don't
suppose he has sent for you or changed your living arrangements?"

"No, sir. My great-uncle is a priest. He takes no interest in
worldly things."

It was said matter-of-factly, but Akitada's heart contracted for
the lonely boy. "Well," he said with a forced smile, "enjoy your
dumplings!"

He was rewarded by a big grin and watched with a chuckle as
the boy skipped out, clutching his precious box. It took so little
to make a child happy. Even the dim memories of his own past
included moments of sheer bliss.

His smile faded a moment later, when he was interrupted in
his childhood reminiscences by Nishioka, who stuck his long nose
in, asking, "My dear fellow, aren't you having your noon rice today? I'm on my way to my office for mine. Come, be my guest! I
am anxious to share my new theory with you and give you a taste
treat at the same time."

Akitada was about to decline, when he saw Hirata's gaunt face appear behind Nishioka. Sighing inwardly, Akitada accepted the invitation. Hirata nodded to both of them and withdrew again.

Nishioka chattered away as they walked together towards the Temple of Confucius. Akitada, feeling guilty about Hirata, said little. It was uncomfortably hot for the first time this year. Glancing up at the sky, Akitada thought the weather was changing. An oppressive heat haze hung over the city, and hardly a leaf stirred in the trees.

"Master Tanabe took off today on my urging," Nishioka said when they reached his room. "I'm a bit worried about him. He's getting too old for all this excitement. The sooner the police arrest the killer, the better for all of us."

Thinking of how frail and ill Hirata had looked, Akitada agreed.

Nishioka confided excitedly, "I think I have worked it out. We agreed it is all a question of the murderer's personality, and by that premise I have narrowed it down to a single person. Of course, if it were not for the fact that it takes a very strong man to tie a body the size of Oe's to that statue, the field would be much larger. But let us discuss it over our food."

They settled down on the veranda outside Nishioka's cramped and cluttered study to a meal of rice and pickled vegetables delivered from the staff kitchen. Akitada eyed the food with little interest or appetite. "A taste treat, did you say?"

Nishioka's eyes sparkled. "Later," he promised and returned to the subject of Oe's murder. "It seems to me that we should consider everybody who had a motive, eliminate those who could not have done it, and analyze the psychological traits of those remaining. Agreed?"

Clearly this would take a while. Unhappily, Akitada nodded, brushing away a few beads of perspiration from his brow. He was not particularly hungry and ate listlessly.

"Let us begin with ourselves," said Nishioka, waving his chopsticks. "No, no! Don't shake your head. We must be systematic. System is everything in scholarly research. I, Nishioka, did not like

Oe. He was quite rude to me on several occasions. I also did not care for his lack of respect towards Master Tanabe. But dislike is not a strong enough motive for murder. You, unless you inform me otherwise, would not have known the man long enough even for that. Am I right?"

Akitada gave Nishioka a long look. Then he put down his chopsticks and rice bowl and said bluntly, "You may have had a stronger motive than dislike. The police captain seems to think that Oe was threatening you over certain gambling activities."

Nishioka's jaw dropped. He turned absolutely white. "K . . . Kobe said that? How could he? What did he say?"

"Nothing specific. He picked up the information among a lot of gossip about the faculty."

Nishioka relaxed a little. "It's a silly story. Vastly exaggerated. There is really nothing to it. A couple of clerks in administration were taking bets on the outcome of the last examination and they asked me to hold the money for them. Nobody would have said anything about it, if we had not had some sore losers. You see, the favorite did not place first."

"So I gathered," Akitada said dryly. He had noted the shift in pronoun from "they" to "we," and wondered just how culpable his host had been. Everybody needed money, and assistants, as Akitada knew, were paid a pittance. He asked, "How much money was involved?"

Nishioka fidgeted. "All in all about five hundred pieces of silver."

"That much!" Akitada stared at him. "Who won?"

"There was only one winner. Ishikawa."

"Ishikawa! You don't say! If he got that much, why was he reading Oe's papers?"

Nishioka put on an irritatingly mysterious look and merely said, "Ah!"

Akitada took up his bowl and ate a bite. "Please continue your analysis of the murder," he said curtly, after he had swallowed some very dry rice.

His host, disconcerted by Akitada's tone, stammered, "Oh. Yes. Motives. Well, er, as far as your friend Hirata is concerned, he

seems to get along with everybody. I could not discover a motive.
Master Tanabe also was always very patient with the man. I think
we can eliminate both of them. Fujiwara, on the other hand, is
more complicated. He's another easygoing fellow, but Oe hated
him and never missed an opportunity to malign Fujiwara publicly
or privately. The incident at the poetry contest may have been the
last straw for Fujiwara. A definite motive of revenge, I would say."

Akitada ran a finger between his stiff collar and his neck. Perspiration made the silk cling to his hot skin. "You are guessing," he
said. "Hirata, or I for that matter, may have had a motive you
know nothing of, and Fujiwara may be so easygoing that nothing
will ever push him to violence."

Nishioka looked offended. He snapped, "You must remember
that I know my colleagues a great deal better than you do." Gob-
bling a few bites of his vegetables, he muttered, "I suppose you will
next defend Takahashi. That man hates everybody and does his
best to make them suffer! Even you must remember that he was
practically incoherent with fury after what Oe did to his precious
memorial. I would call that a strong motive of revenge."

"I think," said Akitada, "that one should guard especially carefully against pinning a crime on a man one dislikes."

Nishioka put down his rice bowl with a distinct rattle. "Perhaps," he said, controlling his voice carefully, "you would honor
me with your views on the others?"

Well, thought Akitada, it serves me right. Why can't I keep my
temper under control and my mouth shut? There was nothing he
could do, except comply and hope that Nishioka would gradually
calm down. "I found Sato quite interesting," he said calmly, pretending nothing had happened. "He is outwardly quiet but has
things to hide. The private lessons are against university rules, and
there is gossip about scandalous affairs with women in his university quarters. I am sure that you know more about this than I."

Nishioka hesitated, but the temptation was too great. "Quite
right," he said. "And he could not afford to lose his position, for he
is poor and has a sizable family. Oe was about to pounce on him."

"Ah, self-preservation," Akitada said with a nod.

"Exactly! But don't forget Ono. As Oe's assistant, Ono has always hoped to succeed as head of Chinese studies some day. For that he put up with years of abuse and overwork."

"Yes, that gives him two reasons to murder: revenge and self-interest," said Akitada.

Mollified, Nishioka jumped up to fetch some wine. He filled their cups. Akitada drank thirstily with hardly a thought to this afternoon's classes. "Good," he said. "Is this the promised treat?"

Nishioka laughed. "No. Be patient! Well, what do you think of my reasoning so far?"

"It covers the faculty," said Akitada, letting Nishioka refill his cup. "But in fact, it could have been anyone else. Students, staff, visitors, friends, family."

Nishioka waved a dismissive hand. "Oe had no friends, and no close family to speak of. As for staff, they never had any particularly strong feelings about Oe, and Oe rarely ever bothered himself with them. The same is true of the students—with one notable exception: Ishikawa. Ishikawa is as poor as he is clever, and this spring he and Oe suddenly became uncharacteristically close. Ishikawa began grading papers for Oe. Very curious, that."

"Yes," said Akitada. "Particularly in view of the fact that Ishikawa had won your bets. Surely he did not need the money Oe paid him."

Nishioka dropped a piece of radish he had been raising to his mouth and flushed with irritation. "They were not *my* bets," he cried. "I wish you would not dwell on the matter."

"Sorry," murmured Akitada. "I think you suspect that Oe rigged the examination with the knowledge of Ishikawa."

"Of course he did. It was a clever scheme with no one the wiser about Oe's involvement. Ishikawa won the bet. But I think he turned over most of the winnings to Oe. Everybody noticed the change in Ishikawa after the examination. He became disrespectful to Oe, and Oe put up with it. There is even a rumor that Ishikawa attacked Oe. To me it smells exactly like a falling-out of conspirators." Nishioka's long nose twitched as if the bad smell had suddenly risen from his vegetables.

"Do you have any proof for that?"

"What proof? All you have to do is watch people's actions. I think Ishikawa blackmailed Oe. What do you think of that?"

Akitada had arrived at the same conviction quite a while ago. Unfortunately it did not seem to explain the murder. He said, "It was Oe who was killed, not Ishikawa. Why would Ishikawa kill the source of his income?"

"What if Oe got tired of Ishikawa's demands and was threatening him with expulsion?"

"Would he not have worried about Ishikawa revealing the whole scheme? That would have ended his university career."

"Oe had nothing to lose. He had already decided to retire."

"How do you know that?" Akitada asked, surprised.

"From what he said and how he said it. Remember, I keep my eyes and ears open all the time. Oe had the money from the bets and he detested his teaching duties. I expect he was getting ready to sell his position to the highest bidder." He paused and chuckled suddenly. "I wonder if Ono knew that. He is poor and that would certainly have given him another motive to kill Oe."

Akitada remarked, "Well, there seem to be enough choices, but hardly any facts to support your suspicions."

Nishioka nodded. "Fujiwara, Takahashi, Ono, Sato and Ishikawa. And facts are immaterial, provided you can eliminate all but one."

Akitada sighed. The vegetables had been very salty, and he drank deeply from Nishioka's wine.

Nishioka seemed inured to the food and heat. "As far as opportunity is concerned, Fujiwara certainly could have gone to the temple after the competition, and he is strong enough to lift the body, but he would have had to make an appointment with Oe beforehand. Takahashi is in the same position, and so is Sato."

"All of them could have run into Oe by accident and decided to act then," Akitada pointed out. "The university gate was neither locked nor guarded because of the holiday."

"I had thought of that, but it is not as likely. And I do not like coincidence. Ishikawa and Ono left with Oe and did not return to the contest. We have only their word that they separated at the gate. These two are the most likely for opportunity, either separately or together."

"Ono claims he returned, but go on." Akitada pushed his food away. He wished he could leave.

Nishioka rubbed his hands. "That brings me finally to our murderer's personality. Taking the less likely suspects first, Fujiwara is a talented but unconventional character. He cares nothing for appearances or personal fame and would therefore not be troubled by perceived insults. In that sense he is the exact opposite of Takahashi. Takahashi's motive becomes much stronger when you consider his vanity; however, he has an exaggerated sense of propriety which would counteract his desire for revenge. Sato, I confess, puzzles me. At times, I suspect, he has strong emotions, but at others he seems as uncaring as Fujiwara. Those two drink together quite a bit in the local wine shops, did you know?"

"The fact that a man enjoys the night life does not necessarily imply that he has no strong values." Akitada said sharply, increasingly irritated with the chatty, opinionated Nishioka and no longer intrigued by the promise of a mysterious treat.

"Very true. In any case, even given their different temperaments, none of the three has entirely satisfactory traits. Now let us move on to our prime suspects, Ono and Ishikawa. Ono is a repressed fellow who is capable of immense patience. But such men may explode when they see all their suffering wasted. Ishikawa on the other hand has a much stronger mind. He would plan, but without sacrificing face or safety. Instead of exploding, he would avert disaster by taking timely action. Either way, both Ono and Ishikawa would kill Oe. There, that ends my analysis of the case." Nishioka folded his arms with a triumphant smile.

"I thought you said you had narrowed it down to one man," Akitada protested.

"Ishikawa, of course," Nishioka cried, laughing heartily at Akitada's dismayed expression. "Don't feel bad that you did not discover the truth. Remember, I know these people and have trained myself to interpret their every action and word. You will learn."

"Thank you for the encouraging words," said Akitada stiffly, "but I suspect you blame it on Ishikawa because of his physical strength and the fact that he seems to have run off."

Nishioka chuckled. "That too. But there is a more important reason. Remember that the killer not only tied his victim to Master Kung, but took off his undergarments. Why?"

"A gesture of defiance?"

"More than that. An arrogant thumbing of the nose at the entire university and what it stands for. Ono is quite incapable of such a thing, not when this institution is his whole life and he hoped to be promoted to senior professor. Ishikawa, on the other hand, was always making cynical comments. It is exactly like him to flaunt his disdain for the establishment and for Oe as its representative in that fashion."

Akitada said stubbornly, "You may be right about that, but it hardly proves he killed him."

"Oh, well," said Nishioka, "it is enough to send the police after him. As for me, I've had my eye on someone else . . . which should prove amusing while we await Ishikawa's arrest." His eye fell on their bowls, his own empty and Akitada's abandoned long ago, and he recalled belatedly his duties as host. "You did not enjoy your food," he said. "Never mind. I have saved the best for last."

He jumped up and ran inside to rummage among his books. "Ah. Here they are!" he cried, coming back with a small wooden box which he carried tenderly in both hands. He lifted the lid and held it out to Akitada with a proud smile. The box was completely empty. They realized the fact simultaneously. Nishioka gaped at the box. "What . . . ? I cannot imagine . . ." He shook the box and held it upside down in the irrational hope that the contents would materialize after all. "They are gone!" he said in a stunned tone. "I could have sworn the box was half full last night. Well, it can't be helped. I was going to offer you some of my special walnuts to round out the meal. I know an old woman who makes them to perfection. It's a special recipe; she roasts them after they've been boiled in saltwater. They are my one weakness." He closed the box and tossed it carelessly back into his room. "I'll have to get a new supply and then you shall taste them."

Akitada expressed polite gratification.

Nishioka nodded. "Anyway, I intend to lay my deductions before Kobe this afternoon. It will take his mind off that silly gossip about the bets. Would you like to come along?"

Akitada shook his head and rose. "I have another class and a meeting," he said vaguely. Thanking Nishioka for his lunch, he walked back lost in thought.

Nishioka's summation of the case had not been without interest after all. Though Akitada had not agreed with Nishioka's interpretation, his own suspicion did not fit the facts too well either. However he certainly believed with Nishioka that Ishikawa was involved and had to be found.

When Akitada entered his classroom, he found a neatly tied package on his desk. It was addressed to him in Seimei's hand, and Akitada undid it eagerly. Inside was the list of merchants who had supplied goods for the poetry contest and a thick stack of papers concerned with the extensive Minamoto properties. A brief note by Seimei prefaced the latter. Young Sadamu was the principal heir. Seimei had not found any evidence of malfeasance, but many of the recent financial transactions bore the mark and seal of Sakanoue. Akitada put the Minamoto papers aside for later study and picked up the list of merchants.

Running his finger down the list, he found the name he had expected to see.

SEVENTEEN

THE BROCADE SASH

*D*uring the afternoon lessons, Akitada's mind kept drifting off to the three cases. Having seen Seimei's list, he was now anxious to get Tora's report to confirm the identity of Omaki's killer. Moreover, Nishioka's passionate pursuit of clues in Oe's murder caused in him a vague uneasiness which he could not explain, though he went over their conversation again and again. And every time he glanced at the bowed heads of his students, laboring mightily over a short essay, his eyes went to the little lord and he thought of the Yoakira puzzle. Why had Sakanoue ridden a strange horse?

When the big bell sounded the end of classes, the boys greeted its deep voice as eagerly as he. He watched them as they scrambled up, sketched their bows and rushed from the room.

Akitada straightened their desks and then his own papers. He was about to start home when Tora walked in.

"I was beginning to get worried," Akitada said, looking him over anxiously. "Are you feeling all right? And did you get the names of the merchants?"

Tora flopped down. "Yes, on both accounts," he said. "I gave your message to one of the constables at the gate and took off, figuring that they'd keep me there if I told the captain what happened in Rashomon. I don't trust those bastards. They would've wanted to know all about Hitomaro, the Monk and the other two. And you know I gave my word not to turn them in."

"Yes." Akitada frowned. "Are you afraid those hoodlums will come after you?"

"Them?" Tora looked shocked. "Never! They're all right. No, it's your law-abiding keepers of peace and order that scare the wits out of me. When they don't get the answers they want, they take it out of your hide."

Remembering the whippings the beggar Umakai had suffered, Akitada shuddered. "Surely not in your case," he said. "I would not permit it."

Tora guffawed. "And what could you do after they got through with me? Kobe'd tell you he was sorry his men made a mistake and got carried away a bit. Then he'd let you take me home for Seimei to put his salves on my raw backside. No thanks, I'm keeping my distance."

A brief silence fell. Akitada knew too well that the law practically obligated the police to use force during interrogations. Kobe was less cruel than most of his calling, but he prided himself on his effectiveness. He had ordered the bamboo to be used in questioning the senile beggar, and he would hardly hesitate to do the same with a young healthy fellow like Tora.

Tora took up his story again. "Anyway, after calling on the police, I went to the wine shop Hitomaro mentioned. Hitomaro and the Monk were sitting around looking hungry. I ordered some food and wine, and we had a nice little chat. I really like those guys. Especially Hitomaro. I figure he must be an ex-soldier like me. Or maybe even an officer, seeing he's got some class and book learning." Tora frowned. "Wonder what would make an officer quit the army. I asked him about that, but he got sort of cold and distant. Told me it was none of my business what they did."

Akitada said, "That was hardly polite when you were paying

for their food and drink. I thought you'd have better sense. Clearly they are criminals hiding some unsavory activities. I wish you would stay away from them in the future."

Tora shook his head stubbornly. "No, sir, you're wrong about that. They're my kind of people. Hitomaro is a very superior sort of person and Monk, well, he's really kindhearted. I grant you, what Hitomaro said made me wonder if Monk was really a monk, but I'd rather he weren't. You should see him, sir! He's got some huge muscles in his shoulders and arms. The old woman who runs the place needed to shift a stack of rice sacks. The Monk picked them up four at a time and carried them under each arm like they were puppies. She says he's always real helpful like that."

"Well, I suspect they are fugitives. But enough of that. What about the merchants near the canal?"

Tora took a crumpled piece of paper from his sleeve, flattened it out and laid it on Akitada's desk. "I went to the warden for this. He's the same guy that pulled poor old Umakai from the canal and certified it as an accidental drowning. At first the lazy bastard refused to help me, but I told him it was official business and we were checking into his handling of the drowning victim. He folded like a wet paper fan. Couldn't write the information down fast enough."

"You did not tell him you were with the police, did you?"

"Of course not. Ministry of Justice."

Akitada choked down a laugh and reached for the paper. The warden had drawn a rough diagram of the streets, the canal, and the rectangular business properties backing up to the canal. Each rectangle was marked with its owner's name. Fortunately the warden's writing was better than Tora's. Akitada's finger went to one of the larger rectangles. "Look!"

Tora peered and blinked; his reading skills were still very elementary. "I can't quite make it out."

"Kurata."

"Kurata? Holy Kwannon! Can it be? Oh!" Tora straightened up and hit his head with a fist. "I'm so stupid!" he cried. "I was in his shop myself! And I never recognized the place from the canal side. You mean it was him?"

Akitada nodded.

"He's the one that choked Omaki to death with her own sash?"

Akitada nodded again.

"The bastard! I suppose he took the sash away so nobody would trace it to his shop?"

"I believe so."

"But he gave it to Umakai. Why'd he do that? He's not the type who'd spare a thin copper for a starving man."

"He had to get rid of it quickly and made the fatal mistake of thinking that giving it to a beggar was the most efficient way of doing that."

Tora's face broke into a broad grin. "Blessed be the name of the Buddha! It served the devil right!" Then his eyes widened. "And what's more," he cried, "it was me that told you about him in the first place."

Akitada laughed. "It was indeed, Tora. I would have got nowhere without you. Come, mark the spot where the warden pulled the body from the canal, and then we'll take your information to Kobe."

Tora reached for his master's brush, licked it, and then touched it to a bit of drying ink. He carefully put an X in the canal behind Kurata's shop, and they smiled at each other with satisfaction.

◆

The captain was pacing up and down in his office when Akitada and Tora were shown in. His eyes passed over Akitada and went to Tora. "Are you the one who left the message about the beggar's body? Where the devil have you been?" he snarled.

Tora looked to Akitada who raised his brows and said, "He has been running an errand for me."

Kobe glared. "And I suppose you've come to gloat."

"Not at all. But I did wonder if you had any news."

"We dug him up. The coroner says it was murder. Someone

strangled him, just like the girl. He was already dead when he was dumped into the canal. Is that what you wanted to hear?"

"It is what I expected to hear," Akitada corrected him. "I am sorry it happened, but at least it helped Tora solve both murders."

Kobe stared at Tora and then back at Akitada. "You're joking. *He* solved the murders?"

"Why not?" They locked eyes. Kobe looked down first, and Akitada continued, "Since I was busy at the university, Tora has been working on the investigation. He has talked with Omaki's parents and her fellow entertainers in the Willow Quarter. Yesterday he went into the city to look for Umakai. He found him too late, but the old man did not die in vain. His murder finally proved who killed Omaki."

Kobe's fists clenched. "I'd like to know why your servant did not come here to report? If he found out anything about the girl's associates, he should have told us. Today we spent hours looking for him to ask him how he found the body."

Akitada said firmly, "As I said, I sent him for more information and he has just returned. We came as soon as we had anything useful to report. Now will you pay attention or are we going to waste more time?"

Kobe glared and growled, "What new information?"

Akitada spread out the warden's map on the desk and pointed to Tora's mark. "I believe this is where the beggar's body was recovered by the warden of the quarter?"

Kobe leaned over to look and nodded. "Yes. Just about there. Why?"

"Note the name of the adjoining property owner." Akitada placed Seimei's list of merchants next to the map. "And then take a look at this! These are the merchants who delivered goods for the poetry contest to the park the afternoon the girl Omaki died. The same name appears again."

Kobe picked up the list and scanned it. "Kurata." He glanced at the map. "You think one of his employees did it?"

"No. We think that Kurata killed the girl because she was expecting his child and demanded marriage, and that he killed the beggar Umakai because he could identify Kurata as the man who gave him Omaki's brocade sash."

Kobe laughed out loud. "Impossible! Kurata owns the best silk shop in the capital. Big merchants like him send their shop assistants and porters with the stuff. He'd hardly have carried it himself."

"I believe he went himself and even carried some of the silk cushions. It was an important order. Besides he had made a deadly appointment with the girl, and the porter's role was a good disguise."

"You are guessing."

"No. It is the only solution that fits all the facts. Omaki knew all about the park closing, but entered anyway. The guard saw her arriving, but forgot all about her because later he was kept busy admitting deliveries. You asked him about other visitors, and he only mentioned Tora and me. It never occurred to the man to include the deliveries. As far as he was concerned, they had legitimate business there. It follows that Omaki must have made an appointment with someone who was making a delivery."

Kobe thought about it and nodded. "I suppose that's possible."

Akitada continued, "When Tora visited the dead girl's family, he ascertained that she not only owned the costly brocade sash with which the murderer strangled her—a nasty touch, that—but also other gifts from his shop."

Kobe glanced at Tora. "But a man like that? A respected citizen? How would he meet someone like her?"

"Oh, he's a regular at the Willow," volunteered Tora. "The auntie there knows all about him. The Willow is the restaurant where Omaki played the lute."

Kobe stared at Tora, then turned back to Akitada. "So what if he did get her pregnant? Why didn't he buy her off? He's said to be wealthy."

Tora said, "Because his old lady frowns on his skirt chasing. And it's really her business."

"What?" Kobe started pacing again. "I suppose it could have happened that way," he muttered after a few moments. He went back to study the map and nodded. "So Umakai did see the killer after all," he said. "Why didn't the old fool tell us? He'd be alive today."

Akitada said, "He did."

Kobe straightened up and looked at Akitada. "He did not. All he gabbled about was Jizo. You heard him yourself."

"Precisely. The statues of the god Jizo traditionally wear red caps, because mothers make them as gifts when they are asking the god to protect their sons. Bearers also cover their heads with a piece of cloth when they carry heavy loads on their shoulders and heads. I think you will find that Kurata's people have red caps."

Kobe looked furious. "Have you known this all along?"

"No. But I believed that Umakai had seen something. I tried to find a connection between the Jizo story and the murderer. The deliveries to the park reminded me of the fact that bearers commonly wear some sort of cap. After that it was easy to guess what must have happened."

Kobe bit his lip. He grunted. "So you think the old man really recognized Kurata? Do you think he went to blackmail him?"

"No, I think Umakai must have glanced into Kurata's shop and recognized a manifestation of Jizo. I doubt he realized what he was up against. He probably told Kurata how he lost his gift. Perhaps he asked for another brocade sash. Of course Kurata could not let him live after that."

Kobe stared at Akitada for a long time. Then he cursed and sat down abruptly, putting his head in his hands and muttering, to Akitada's surprise, "So that heartless bastard killed an old man who thought he was Jizo! Damn it! It fits, and I should have seen it!" He jumped up again and pointed an accusing finger at Akitada. "But you and your servant should have reported sooner what you knew! If you had not been trying to be clever, we could have questioned Kurata days ago."

Akitada, stung by the accusation, said angrily, "Frankly, after you had failed to beat the truth out of Umakai, I had little faith in your methods."

Kobe flushed. "My methods are the only ones that get confessions," he shouted, "and without a confession the guilty go free. You had better leave the real work to the police in the future!"

Akitada retaliated with, "I cannot imagine that you are getting much help from honest citizens with that attitude."

Kobe glowered. "We manage," he snapped. "As for Kurata, we could check the man's whereabouts on the two days, and maybe we'd get results. But my way is to confront him now. A coward like that will confess soon enough, and if your servant is right about the wife, she'll be eager to help convict him when she hears the story."

"Good," said Akitada through clenched teeth. "Then we will leave the matter in your capable hands and be on our way."

But Kobe was not listening. The suggestion of a smile twitched at the corners of his lips. "We got the bastard," he said. "It's poetic justice really. We could never have convinced a judge using Umakai's testimony about the god Jizo giving him a brocade sash."

"Perhaps not," Akitada said over his shoulder as he was heading for the door. "But it is too bad he had to pay with his life to lead us to the killer."

"Not even you could have solved the case otherwise," Kobe said with a snort. His anger was gone, and he looked excited. "Where are you going? Let's go arrest the bastard!"

Akitada stopped. "You want us to go with you? Is that really necessary?"

Kobe had already taken his bow and quiver from the hook on the wall and flung them over his shoulder. "Probably not," he said with a grin, "but I want you to see how *I* work." Before Akitada could protest, he had flung open the door and was shouting out the names of five police constables who came up at a run, red-faced and adjusting their robes and paraphernalia.

"Fall in behind!" Kobe ordered, running a sharp eye over them. "We're on our way to Kurata's silk shop for an arrest." Turning to Akitada and Tora, he waved a peremptory hand for them to join him and then strode out.

Akitada sighed and said to Tora, "I suppose we had better go."

In spite of the evening heat which produced a general lassitude among the people in the streets, Kobe walked at such a pace that Akitada and Tora stayed a few strides behind. Their group attracted curious stares. Since Akitada and Tora were trying to keep up with Kobe and were themselves followed by five trotting constables, they looked like a pair of criminals being conducted to their well-deserved punishment. Akitada's upper class clothing caused particular interest, and by the time they reached Kurata's establishment, they had a following of about fifty people of all ages and types.

Kobe ignored them and strode into the shop, glanced around at the customers—staring open-mouthed at the sudden invasion of the red coats—and shouted, "Everyone out but the shopkeeper and staff!"

The customers scrambled up and ran, practically falling over each other in their haste to leave. Only Kurata remained, along with two shop assistants and a boy who had been carrying stacks of fabric and dropped them at Kobe's words, and a middle-aged woman who had been working with account books and an abacus in the rear. They stood or sat frozen, staring white-faced at the police.

The reputation of the municipal police force was such that anyone who found himself the focus of their interest immediately assumed that he or she had committed, however unintentionally, some terrible offense. Thus the boy burst into noisy tears, crying, "I didn't do it!" Of the two assistants, one attempted to slip away, while the other one was trembling so much that his teeth chattered.

Kurata, sleek in his silk robe, stood in the middle of the floor, opening and closing his mouth like a fish out of water. Only the woman with the abacus seemed in reasonable control of herself. She stood up, brushing down the black silk of her severe gown, and checked Kobe's rank insignia.

"What is your business here, Captain?" she asked in a harsh voice.

At that moment, one of the constables made a sudden dash and tackled the fleeing assistant, throwing him to the ground and sitting on his back. Kobe watched this expressionlessly before answering the woman's question.

"I am investigating a murder that was committed in this neighborhood two nights ago," he said. "Everyone in this house will be interrogated. Who are you?"

The woman bowed. "I am Mrs. Kurata, the owner." Casting a glance out to the street at the gaping crowd, she said, "Perhaps we had better talk inside," and pointed to a door in the rear wall.

Kobe nodded. "Lead the way."

"Someone will have to close the shutters or thieves will take the stock," she said.

Kobe snapped, "Don't be a fool, woman. No one is going to steal anything with my men on the premises."

She turned to lead them into the living quarters behind the shop. With the exception of two constables, who remained behind to keep the curious outside, they all followed her. Kobe seated himself on one of the cushions and invited Akitada to do the same. Kurata and his wife were going to follow suit, but Kobe snapped, "You stand!" On a sign from him, the three constables took up their positions behind the Kuratas. The shop assistants huddled together in a corner.

Kurata finally found his voice to make a protest. "What is this all about, Captain? This is my house and I am a respected—I may even say highly respected—citizen. I do business with the palace and the best people are my valued customers. Any number of them will testify to my good character."

Kobe looked at the sleek Kurata much like a cat studying the antics of a mouse, secure in the knowledge that there was plenty of time. His eyes went briefly to Mrs. Kurata, flicked over her bony physique, dwelt briefly on the sharp nose, the small, mean eyes, the thin lips and the gray-streaked, thinning hair before returning to Kurata. "Did you make a delivery to the Spring Garden the afternoon before the poetry contest last week?" he barked.

Kurata opened his mouth and closed it again. The question had clearly been unexpected. Kobe had announced that he was investigating a murder in the neighborhood, and Kurata had expected to be questioned about the beggar. He hesitated, then glanced at his two assistants for a moment, before admitting that he had. Akitada silently applauded Kobe. He had made it impossible for the man to lie or prepare an evasive answer in the presence of his employees.

"You were acquainted with the girl Omaki, a lute player who entertained in the Willow Quarter?" Kobe demanded.

Pearls of perspiration appeared on the man's face. Mrs. Kurata was standing quite still, looking strangely at her husband.

"I . . . I may have met her," Kurata stammered. "Why are you asking about . . . what does that have to do with—"

"Answer the questions!" snapped Kobe. "I don't have time for chitchat. Is it true that this Omaki was your mistress and that she was expecting your child?"

Mrs. Kurata made a hissing sound and clenched her hands in front of her stomach.

Kurata cried, "No! Of course not! I'm a married man and I have no other women. Someone is telling slanderous tales."

His wife asked Kobe abruptly, "This Omaki, is she the girl that was found strangled in the Spring Garden?"

Kobe looked at her. "Yes," he said. "I regret to inform you that your husband is a regular customer in a number of establishments of the Willow Quarter."

She nodded, and her eyes, inscrutable in their expression, fixed on her husband again. "What business did you have with that beggar two nights ago?" she asked him.

Kurata turned as white as bleached silk. "Wh . . . at b–beggar?" he quavered. "I saw no beggar. There was no beggar." His voice rose in panic.

His wife turned back to Kobe. Taking a deep breath, she straightened her shoulders, brushed her black silk gown down again with her hands, and said in a toneless voice, "Someone came late in the evening. I was in my room and heard my husband let him in. Naturally I got up to see who it was. I saw an old and ragged man talking with my husband. They were in the corridor.

I think the man was asking for red silk. My husband promised to give him some, and they went out the back way. A little later my husband came back. Alone."

Kurata wailed, "Don't believe her!" He fell to his knees, sobbing with fear. "She lies! She's angry because I had other women. That's why she's making up stories."

Kobe smiled. Again Akitada was reminded of a cat licking its whiskers in anticipation of a juicy meal. "Why the fuss?" he asked Kurata. "So you talked to a beggar. Is that any reason to start crying like a baby?"

Kurata wiped at his wet cheeks with a sleeve. "I . . . I don't know. All this is very upsetting. . . ." He staggered to his feet.

Kobe's smile widened. "I can see how it would be upsetting, when you are the one who strangled that beggar to keep him from talking."

"No, I—"

"Because that beggar," Kobe shouted suddenly, leaning forward to fix Kurata with his eyes, "was the one who saw you in the park the day you murdered the girl."

Kurata's eyes were wide with fear. He seemed incapable of looking anywhere but at Kobe. "No, no, I didn't . . . he didn't . . ."

"The girl Omaki. The one you gave the brocade sash to. Red *figured* brocade, remember! A pretty present for a pretty mistress. She wore it because you had given it to her. And you used it to strangle her."

Kurata's knees buckled and he collapsed on the floor, wailing, "No, no, no, no."

His wife looked down at him dispassionately. "You have dishonored the name my father gave you," she said loudly. "I shall petition the family council to rescind the adoption and expunge you from the family register. I also divorce you." Turning away from the moaning creature on the floor, she looked around the room. "You are all my witnesses."

Akitada was familiar with the legal terms of divorce and adoption; Mrs. Kurata evidently was also. She had, at this moment and in front of witnesses, divorced her husband and taken back the family name. That she had done so without hesitation or show of emotion, without any explanations, shocked him profoundly. He had believed women to be softer, more emotional, less coldly practical. Even years of grief from a faithless husband should not end like this, with a wiping out of every bond as if it had never existed.

Tora bent down to Akitada and whispered, "What a she-devil! I could almost pity that bastard."

Kobe was watching Kurata, who was Kurata no more, but a nonperson at the mercy of the law, even less likely to escape its full cruelty than the beggar Umakai.

Belatedly, the man became aware of his change in status and its implications. He raised himself to his knees and crept towards Mrs. Kurata, whimpering, "Take it back! Please, my treasure, do not do this dreadful thing! Remember our vows! Remember my years of hard work in the business! I have been unjustly accused."

She watched him approach until he came to a halt before her and touched the hem of her silk gown. Then she kicked his hand away and spat in his face.

Kurata recoiled. "My wife," he cried hoarsely, the tears running down his face mingling with her saliva, "I did it for you, for us. That girl, she was going to make trouble and come between us. I didn't want that to happen. And that old tramp, he saw me closing the shutters and started jabbering about Jizo and the park. I had to shut him up. You can see that, can't you?" He started towards her again, extending a hand pleadingly.

Mrs. Kurata had listened, stone-faced. Now she turned to Kobe. "Captain," she said, "you have your confession. Please remove this person from the premises. The sooner I can get back to work, the better. I have customers waiting outside. As a single woman, I cannot afford to alienate them. Kurata's has a reputation to maintain."

Even Kobe looked stunned at her words, but he nodded and clapped his hands. The constables surrounded Kurata and jerked him to his feet. "Chain him and take him away!" Kobe ordered.

Kurata started screaming. He was bound and dragged away, still screaming, and the sound receded slowly in the distance.

They waited silently. Then Kobe turned to look at Akitada. "Unpleasant," he said, "but I thought you should see how it's done by us. Shall we go?"

EIGHTEEN

THE PRINCE'S FRIENDS

*O*n their way home, Akitada and Tora stopped by the university to pick up some student papers Akitada had forgotten.

It was getting dark, though not noticeably cooler. Tora glanced at the sky and remarked, "We need rain. I haven't seen it this dry in years. It's a wonder there haven't been more fires."

Akitada nodded. The streets and courtyards of the university lay deserted, grass and weeds browned and dusty. The students were either in their dormitories or had left for visits with friends and relatives in the city. Guiltily Akitada remembered the little lord.

When he had gathered up the papers in his office he told Tora, "Let us pay a visit to Lord Minamoto. If he is not doing anything tomorrow, he might like to come for a visit."

They found the boy in his room, reading a book. He looked small and forlorn, but cheered up when he saw them. Bowing to Akitada, he said, "You are most welcome, sir. Have you come to report some news?"

Akitada smiled and sat down. "In a manner of speaking. We have solved the case of the murdered girl. It was mostly due to Tora's work. A silk merchant named Kurata was the culprit."

Lord Minamoto clapped his hands. "Oh, good for you, Tora!" he cried. Turning back to Akitada, he said, "So it was not poor Rabbit! I am glad you took an interest, sir. Is there no news about my case?"

"No. Not yet." Akitada looked around the small room. He thought again of the boy's great-uncle. Could the man not have done something for this child? Aloud he asked, "And you? Any plans for tomorrow?"

The boy's face darkened. "No, sir."

"Well then, perhaps you might like to visit us?"

The young face lit up. "Oh, could I? Thank you. Will you be there, Tora?"

Akitada answered for Tora. "Probably. Also my mother, my two sisters, and I."

Blushing, Lord Minamoto apologized, saying politely, "Please forgive my rudeness, sir. I am looking forward to meeting your family and having an opportunity to converse with you."

Akitada rose. "Good. Tora will come to pick you up right after your morning rice."

The boy stood also. "I shall be very happy to get away for a while," he confided. "There have been some new men working outside. They keep staring into my room and they give me the shivers. I think they look more like rough types, bandits or pirates, than servants. One of them was sweeping the veranda, but he does not know how to use a broom."

Akitada exchanged a glance with Tora. "How long have they been here?" he asked the boy.

"Since yesterday."

The thought that Sakanoue had sent thugs to watch the boy, or worse, crossed Akitada's mind instantly. Sesshin must have warned Sakanoue about Akitada's visit. Once again Akitada was reminded that only this child stood between Sakanoue and total control of the Minamoto fortune. It had been a terrible mistake to tell that old fake of a priest about his suspicions!

"Take a look outside, Tora," he said.

Tora disappeared and returned shortly. "A big rascal with an ugly face is out front. There's nobody out back."

"Sadamu," said Akitada to the boy, lowering his voice, "I don't like the idea of leaving you here until we have checked out the new help. I think we will take you home with us tonight."

The boy was on his feet in an instant, his face bright with excitement. Tossing a few books and clothes into a large square of silk, he knotted it and handed the bundle to Tora. Then he took up his sword and said, "I am ready, sir."

"Perhaps," said Akitada softly, "it would be better if you left quietly the back way. Tora and I are going out by the front. Tora will then double back and meet you at the back door."

The young lord's eyes flashed with the thrill of danger. He slung the strap of his sword over his shoulder, tested its readiness, and then took the bundle back from Tora, whispering, "I shall be waiting."

The maneuver was carried out with great success. Akitada and the boy walked quickly out of the dormitory enclosure and down the deserted street to the gate, while Tora lingered behind, making sure they were not being followed.

At home, Akitada installed his guest in his own room and went to inform his mother about their visitor. He was nervous about her reaction to the unannounced guest. It would be very awkward if she retaliated by refusing to receive Lord Minamoto.

But he should have known his mother better. As soon as he mentioned the boy's name, her eyes sparkled with interest.

"Prince Yoakira's little grandson? How charming! Finally you are cultivating the proper connections. You never mentioned that the poor fatherless child is your student. Nothing could be better! I shall ask him to consider this his home from now on. It is absolutely incomprehensible to me how his family could allow a boy of his background to mingle with unsuitable companions in a common dormitory." She made it sound as if young Sadamu had been condemned to live in an outcast village.

"It is a temporary arrangement only," said Akitada, "as is his visit here. I am merely giving the boy an outing, since tomorrow is a holiday."

"Don't be foolish!" snapped his mother. "This is your chance to become his private tutor. Then, as he rises in the world, so will you." She clapped her hands.

An elderly maid appeared and fell to her knees, waiting for her mistress's instructions with her head bowed to the floor. Akitada cringed inwardly. The woman, Kumoi, had been his nurse and his mother's before him. She was getting old and frail. His mother's insistence on proper respect struck him as unnecessarily cruel.

"Ah, Kumoi," Lady Sugawara said briskly. "Make haste to ready the large chamber next to my son's room for our noble guest. Have the maid scrub the floor and then move in several of the best grass mats from other rooms. Then you may go to the storehouse and select suitable furnishings. The best of everything—screens, scroll paintings, braziers, clothes boxes, lamp stands—you know what is necessary. And look for some games suitable for a boy of eleven as well. The bedding is to be of quilted silk only. Arrange everything tastefully and then return. Now hurry! I will inspect his room personally."

Kumoi wordlessly knocked her head against the floorboards and scuttled from the room.

"There was no need to burden the poor woman this way," said Akitada. "She is getting too old—and besides, young Minamoto is merely a child."

His mother fixed him with a cold eye. "Clearly you do not know what is owed to someone of that child's standing," she snapped. "Treat him well, and he may reward you some day. Treat him shabbily, and you have made an enemy for life. To people of his background, nothing is more disagreeable than low surroundings."

Akitada remembered the student dormitories and suppressed a smile. "Oh, I don't know," he said insidiously. "His lordship has become very fond of Tora since they flew kites together. He looks forward to spending most of his time with our servant."

His mother was taken aback. Then she snorted, "You should never have permitted that association! The boy's family will be shocked to the core. You will think up something to distract the child from Tora. Teach him football or something!"

Akitada smiled. "I hope to spend a little time with the boy," he said, adding as an afterthought, "In fact, the situation is a little like my own first stay with the Hiratas. I was not much older than he."

His year in the Hirata family was a sore subject between them, and his mother stiffened. With a frown she said, "That reminds me. Someone brought a letter for you from Tamako. She very properly enclosed it in a cover note to me. Here." She fished a slim, folded sheet from her sash and passed it to Akitada.

His heart skipped. The old pain, the many unanswered questions, were back in an instant. Struggling to maintain his composure, he said, "Thank you, Mother." The note he tucked, unread, in his sleeve, adding, "I had better go now and see to our guest." Bowing, he withdrew quickly.

Out in the corridor, he unfolded Tamako's letter with trembling hands. Whatever he had expected—and should not have expected in a letter meant to be read by his mother—he was disappointed. The note was extremely short and the form of address clearly put him in his place:

"Dear Honorable Elder Brother. Forgive this importunity, but could you look in on Father? His health is poor and we fear the worst. Your obedient younger sister."

Akitada refolded the paper in a state of confused unhappiness. He recalled guiltily the drawn face of Hirata and his repeated attempts to speak to Akitada. Could he be truly ill? Akitada blamed himself for the cold distance he had put between them the last few days. What if the older man's collapse had been more than indigestion? He really should have taken him home and explained matters to Tamako.

But seeing Tamako was more than he could face. It was impossible! It would open up too many old wounds. Akitada recalled bitterly that it had been her wish to discuss her father's condition that had started the whole miserable affair.

Twisting the letter in his hands, he wondered what to do. He walked out into the garden and started pacing. After some thought, he decided that Tamako intended him to look in on her father at the university. He would make it a point to see Hirata on the very next day of classes. Afterwards he could communicate the results to his "younger sister" by letter.

This problem settled, he tucked the letter in his sash and returned to his room and offered the boy some hot tea and sweet plums.

"Where is Tora?" asked Sadamu through a full mouth.

Tora! Akitada had forgotten all about him. What could have delayed him this long? He excused himself and headed for the courtyard to look for Tora. To his relief, the gate opened the moment he stepped out, and the truant slipped in.

Now that he was no longer worried, Akitada became irritated. "Where have you been all this time?" he snapped.

Tora was breathing hard. "They followed us," he said. "I saw them as soon as I passed through the university gate. You and the little lord had already turned the corner."

"Did you lose your pursuers?"

"Not right away. The bastards were good. And there may have been more than two. One of them is the big guy with the ugly mug who was outside the dormitory; another one is skinny, with a sneaky face and the longest legs I ever saw. I swear that rat can jump over whole city blocks. I must have spent the last hour running up and down streets and alleys. They almost caught up with me twice. I had to double back again and take another street. I think I lost them."

"You *think*?" Akitada felt a lump in his stomach. "I don't like this," he said. "Sakanoue means the child harm. If he felt any parental concern for the boy's safety, he could have contacted the university authorities." He paused. "We must consider what to do if they find their way here. This house is not safe."

Looking around the compound, Akitada saw that the mud walls were tall and in good repair, but an agile thief could climb them. The gates could be secured, but not against large numbers.

He shook his head. "I am afraid I may have exposed the child to much greater danger here than in his dormitory. Besides, I am jeopardizing the lives of my family. You and I are the only able-bodied men here. Seimei is too old and the boy too young to be much use against trained bandits. We must hire men to help us keep watch and, if necessary, defend the women and the boy."

Tora's face lit up. "I know the very guys, sir."

Akitada raised his brows.

"Hitomaro and Monk."

"Don't be ridiculous. After what they did to you? That is all we need, two known criminals inside our gates."

"They aren't criminals. They were only helping Spike and Nail because they thought the police had killed Umakai, and they figured I was one of them. Sir, they need the work and they'll do anything. They told me if they don't find some work quick, they'll have to eat what Monk can beg."

"It serves them right. If they had not broken some law, they would not be in this fix. Desperate men are capable of anything. Would you set a hungry cat to guard your fish?"

Tora's eyes flashed. "That's what Seimei said when I needed a job."

Remembering the incident, Akitada wavered.

Tora touched his arm. There were tears in his eyes. "Please, sir, trust me in this. At least talk to them."

Akitada was so astonished that his jaw dropped. "Very well. Bring them here and I will talk to them, but no promises. And I hope you know what you are doing."

Tora jumped up. "Thank you, sir! You won't regret it!" He dashed to the gate, slipped out and was gone.

Lady Sugawara chose to preside over the evening meal. Considering the short notice it was surprisingly splendid, including in addition to the customary rice and salted vegetables, steamed fish and eggs, and square rice cakes filled with vegetables.

She directed most of her conversation to their young guest, and her manner held an admirable balance between subservience to him as a person of imperial descent and motherly, or grandmotherly, warmth towards the orphaned child.

The boy accepted this as no more than his due, but had the good manners to compliment her on the food and the appointments of his quarters. He showed similar poise in chatting with

Akitada's sisters, who responded with monosyllables and subdued giggles. Everything considered, the evening was a success, and Lady Sugawara was charmed.

After everybody had withdrawn for the night, Akitada checked all the gates and informed Seimei of the situation. Typically the old man had a comfortable saying to fit the situation. "Virtue does not live alone," he said, when Akitada stressed the fact that Sakanoue could easily hire enough villains to overcome them and take or kill the boy. "It will always have neighbors. Do not worry! We shall find supporters." Also typically, he announced that he would keep watch all night outside the wing which housed the Sugawara ladies. Akitada decided to wait for Tora in the front courtyard.

It was a very dark night. The heat had lifted only slightly, and the stone of the well-coping against which Akitada was leaning was almost uncomfortably warm. All remained quiet. Finally, soon after a watchman had cried out the hour of the rat, there were footsteps, and then Tora's voice. Akitada went to open the gate.

The two men with Tora, seen indistinctly in the lantern light, seemed ordinary enough. They bowed politely, and the military looking fellow gave his name as Hitomaro, while the muscular man in the old monk's robe said he was Genba. Leaving Tora behind to guard the gate, Akitada led them to his room.

They sat down, looking appreciatively about at the books and calligraphy scrolls. The light was better here. Akitada saw two men of about his age, both fairly tall and well-built. Hitomaro, sunburnt and bearded, held himself stiffly at attention and his clothes and general appearance were clean and trim. He met Akitada's eyes with unsmiling directness. Genba, round-faced and clean shaven, but with a hard, muscular body, smiled broadly. He was not precisely neat, but his face was surprisingly gentle. Both bore Akitada's examination without protest or impatience.

Finally Akitada said, "Tora will have explained to you that we need your services for a few days only." They nodded in unison. "Has he explained your duties?" They shook their heads. "You will keep watch around the clock, but particularly during the night.

You will be given a place to sleep during the daytime when you can be relieved, also three meals and fifty coppers a day to share between you. Are those terms agreeable?"

The man called Hitomaro said quietly, "We accept."

"The fact is," added Genba enthusiastically, "we are very glad for the generous offer. We would have done it for food alone."

Akitada regarded him more closely. He was suspicious of such eagerness, but Genba met his scrutiny with bland cheerfulness and both men had the resolute expressions of having nothing to lose. So he said, "You are very honest, but I prefer to pay. I hope there won't be any trouble, but you must remain alert. Should something happen that you cannot handle, you may raise a general alarm. Your duty begins immediately." He prepared to rise, but Hitomaro cleared his throat.

"May we know what we are guarding?" he asked. "Tora did not specify."

"This property. That is all you need to know."

"As you wish. But I must point out that we can deploy our strength to better advantage and develop a plan of operation if we are at least informed where the valuable object is located."

"There is no object. You are guarding my family."

"Ah! From whom?"

Akitada rose impatiently. "Enough! You will arm yourselves and patrol the walls around the clock."

The two men also stood, but Hitomaro remarked, "It is said there are robbers on every road and rats in every house. May we assume that your servants are loyal?"

Akitada fumed. "Of course. Tora you have already met. My secretary Seimei will speak to you shortly. He has served this family since before I was born. You may discuss the rest of the staff with him."

They bowed and left. A few minutes later Tora slipped in. "Well, what do you think?" he asked, looking at Akitada anxiously.

Akitada sighed. He felt tired. Pulling at the neck of his robe, uncomfortably moist from the heat, he said, "We will have to hope for the best. The fellow Genba looks a bit too happy for my taste, but at least he appears to be honest. He told me they would have worked for food. But he is certainly no monk, for he did not object to arming himself. Now go and keep an eye on them, while I get some rest."

◆

The night passed uneventfully. Akitada rose before dawn to take over from Tora. His two new employees seemed competent, appearing at regular intervals on their patrol. Hitomaro looked surprised to see Akitada, but said nothing. Genba, however, paused occasionally to exchange a few words. Akitada encouraged this. The "monk" seemed curious about various sports, especially the annual wrestling matches for the emperor. But when Akitada, on his part, asked questions about Genba's background or that of his companion, he became evasive. He made few references to their past, and these entailed mostly humorous anecdotes about street characters and reminiscences of memorable meals. When Akitada became insistent, Genba departed on another round to check out a suspicious noise.

The sun rose on another cloudless sky. The daylight brought relative safety; attacks were highly unlikely at this time. Akitada told his two watchers to get some food and rest.

"Food!" Genba's face split into a joyous smile, and he trotted off eagerly in the direction of the kitchen, passing on the way the small figure of Sadamu, barefoot and in his white silk under-robe.

"Good morning, sir," the boy cried to Akitada. "What a fine day! Tora and I are making stilts today. Will you join us?"

"Perhaps later," said Akitada, tousling the boy's sleep-rumpled hair. His mother would be upset, but that could not be helped. He had more important errands today than walking about on stilts or playing football. Sadamu, at any rate, did not seem too disappointed. He waved and disappeared again.

The soldierly Hitomaro had gone to the well to wash his face and hands. He now sauntered back, casting a look around as the first rays of the sun gilded the tops of trees. Suddenly he gave an exclamation.

Walking quickly to Akitada, he said, "Look, sir! Over there! See that tall pine in the grove of trees? There's someone in it."

Akitada peered. The distance was too great to be certain. "I don't see anyone," he said.

Hitomaro shaded his eyes. "No. He's gone. But I swear I saw a small man for just a moment."

"Well," said Akitada, "even if someone climbed the tree, he need not have any designs on us. Go get some rest. Tora and the others will be up shortly."

Relieved that the night had passed peacefully, Akitada went to bathe and change into formal attire before paying his calls on Prince Yoakira's friends.

◆

Lord Abe's mansion was closest to the Sugawara residence. Akitada identified himself and was shown into a shady garden. An elderly man stood by a small fishpond, tossing bits of rice dumpling into the water. He had laid Akitada's card on the edge of the veranda nearby and glanced toward it when Akitada made his bow.

"Ah, hmm," he said, returning the bow. "Yes, er . . . Sado . . . Mura . . . what was it again?" He started towards the card on the veranda, when Akitada guessed at his problem.

"I am Sugawara, sir. Sugawara Akitada."

"Oh, of course. Sugawara. I had it on the tip of my tongue. Any relation of . . . no, probably not. And what was it that we were to discuss?"

"Prince Yoakira's grandson has asked me to look into his grandfather's disappearance. I hoped that you might give me your observations of what happened at the Ninna temple."

Abe's face broke into a smile. "The Ninna temple? Now there is a fine place! I remember it well. So many beautiful halls near the mountains! We enjoyed the most delicious plums there! The monks grow them themselves, you know. Ah, I must go there again some time. Since you want my views, I can recommend it highly. An absolutely wonderful place if you need a cure. I have trouble with my eyes." He leaned forward to peer at Akitada more closely and said, "Spots!"

An awful suspicion seized Akitada. "Do you recall Prince Yoakira?" he asked.

"Yoakira?" Abe smiled and clapped his hands. "So you come from Yoakira! How is the old fellow? I haven't seen him for ages." He paused, frowning. "What was it we were talking about?"

"I am afraid . . ." began Akitada, but Abe was peering into the fishpond. "Come, my little ones," he crooned. "Here's something good for you."

Akitada said loudly, "It has been a pleasure, sir. Many thanks for your excellent comments."

Abe looked up, smiled and waved a hand, "Not at all! Delightful! Er . . . Yoshida."

Akitada bowed and left. Poor old man. Even if he had still been in his right mind when the tragedy happened, he had no memory of it now. But a blissful loss of painful memories was perhaps the greatest gift of all, Akitada thought, as his eyes fell on some late blooming hollyhocks near the garden gate. His hand went to his temple where Tamako's fingers and sleeve had brushed his skin as she fastened the blooms to his hat.

◆

He attempted to see the retired General Soga next. But one of the general's servants informed him that his master had left the city for the cooler shores of Lake Biwa where he had a summer villa, and Akitada turned his steps to the house of Lord Yanagida.

There was nothing at all wrong with Lord Yanagida's recall of the last time he saw his friend. His problem was altogether different.

He received Akitada in a study which was primarily remarkable for the number of religious paintings on the walls and the presence of a small altar with a Buddha figure. Yanagida himself appeared to be an elderly version of this figure, having the same soft and fleshy physique, the same round features, clean shaven, heavy-lidded and smiling beatifically. He wore heavy silk robes vaguely resembling vestments and carried a rosary in one hand.

His lordship maintained a calm reserve until Akitada had

been seated and given a cup of chilled fruit juice. But as soon as Akitada explained the boy's concerns about his grandfather's disappearance, Yanagida became alarmed.

"Disappearance?" he gasped, fluttering his hands, the rosary beads swinging wildly. "You mean to say that no one has told the child about the blessed miracle? You must explain the idea of transfiguration to him. It was the most profoundly moving experience of my life! To be a witness to such a reward for devotion! I count myself blessed just for being there myself, a living testimonial! But I suppose you know that, or you would not be here. Oh, it was the holiest moment." Yanagida closed his eyes and sighed deeply.

Akitada's heart fell, but he asked anyway, "It would be most kind of you, sir, if you could give me an account of the events preceding the, er, miracle, so I can report to young Lord Minamoto."

Yanagida nodded. "Certainly, certainly. Nothing could be easier or more joyful. The whole scene is imprinted on my mind! It was still dark when Yoakira entered the shrine—for it shall always be a holy shrine now—and began his devotions. We went to sit outside, our minds caught up in the myriad things of this fleeting world, until he recited the sutra. We all heard him clearly. He was superb, never faltering, never missing a single line! It was inspiring, absolutely inspiring!" Yanagida fell to reciting the lines himself, counting them off on the beads between his fingers.

At the first brief pause, Akitada asked quickly, "Did you yourself examine the hall immediately after the prince was . . . transfigured?"

Yanagida placed the palms of his hands together and bowed his head. "It was my privilege and my blessing," he said. "It was when I realized that my friend had transcended this prison of eternal rebirth that I made my vow. I am preparing to put away my worldly self and take the tonsure, serving as a simple monk in that holy place where my friend achieved salvation. You may tell the child that from me."

"But how did you know it was a miracle? Could he not have left somehow?"

Yanagida closed his eyes and seemed to fall into a trance. There was the slightest hint of a smile around his full lips.

Akitada stared at him suspiciously. He distrusted demonstrations of religious fervor and wondered if Yanagida was covering up something, if he could possibly even have been Sakanoue's accessory. But he put the thought aside quickly. Yanagida, like the other three friends of the prince, enjoyed an excellent reputation and could not have known Sakanoue very well. Another glance about the room convinced him that he was merely dealing with a religious fanatic. Either way he would not get any help here, and he got up.

Yanagida also got to his feet, smiled at Akitada, his round face suffused with joy, and turning towards the altar, prostrated himself before the image. He began to declaim in a loud voice, "Life is impermanent, subject by nature to birth and extinction. Praise be to Amitabha! Only when birth and extinction have been eliminated is the bliss of nothingness realized. Praise be to Amitabha! . . ."

Akitada tiptoed from the room and sought out the last member of Yoakira's entourage, Lord Shinoda.

◆

Shinoda had escaped the midday heat by perching on the edge of a stone bridge in his garden and dangling his bare feet into the shallow stream below. He looked old and frail, with a thick head of white hair and a neatly trimmed white beard and mustache.

Akitada, seeing the unconventional occupation of the old man, was afraid that this friend of Yoakira's had also passed into his dotage. He found out quickly, however, that unlike Abe, Lord Shinoda was in full possession of all his faculties.

"So you're the boy's master," he said after Akitada had introduced himself and stated his business. He waved towards the space beside him and said, "Take off your shoes and socks and stick your feet in the water. It's much too hot for formalities."

Akitada obeyed meekly. The water was blessedly cool after the hot, dusty road outside.

"Glad to hear Sakanoue put the boy in the university," remarked Shinoda, catching a floating leaf with his toe and flipping it out of the water. "Much the best thing under the circumstances. The family was unsettled by this business." He shot Akitada a sharp glance from bright black eyes. "Are you sure you didn't come to satisfy your own curiosity? You have that reputation, you know."

Akitada flushed, startled that the old man had heard of him. He said, "To be frank, I did not believe the story of a miracle even before the boy asked me to find out what really happened. But I certainly did not put the idea in his head."

Shinoda's expression became veiled, his tone distant. "I cannot confirm your suspicions."

An ambiguous answer. Akitada tried to read the other man's mind. Shinoda was his last chance to find out the truth. "There are aspects of the incident which trouble me," he said tentatively.

Shinoda shot him another look. "Really? You will have to tell me what they are."

Akitada met his eyes. "I wondered why all of you assumed immediately that the prince was dead. Without a body, I would have thought a thorough search of the hall, the temple and the surrounding woods, as well as of the prince's various residences throughout the country was in order. Instead you announced almost immediately that the prince was no more."

Shinoda looked down into the water. "There was a search, but we knew he was dead."

Akitada stared at him. "Are you telling me that you found his corpse?"

Shimoda raised his eyes. "Certainly not," he snapped. "How could there have been a miracle if Yoakira had merely died in the middle of his sutra reading?"

"Then how—"

Shimoda said impatiently, "Trust me, young man, we had sufficient proof of death as well as of a miracle. Surely you don't think that we would trick His Majesty with some hocus-pocus?"

"Of course not, but . . ." Akitada realized belatedly that the emperor's sanction of the miraculous event would present an insurmountable obstacle to his investigation. Shinoda was not being merely abstruse or obstructive. He was reminding Akitada of the dangerous ground he was treading. But Shinoda and the others had seen something that convinced them of Yoakira's demise. He said, "I won't question the miracle, sir, but what did you find that proved to you Yoakira had passed from this life?"

Shinoda did not answer. He pulled his skinny legs from the water and started drying them with the hem of his robe.

Akitada put a hand on the older man's sleeve. "Please, sir. I am not asking out of idle curiosity. It is a matter of some urgency . . . of the child's safety. What did you find?"

Shinoda stood up and looked down at Akitada. "Young man," he said severely, "if I believed for one moment that what you hint at is true, I would hardly sit quietly in my garden soaking my feet. Since you appear to be one of those restless people who cannot leave well enough alone, you will no doubt look elsewhere. I wish you luck!"

"Sir," cried Akitada flushing with anger and frustration, "you may be helping a murderer escape justice to murder again. Think of your duty to your friend! Only the boy stands in the way of Sakanoue seizing the estates."

Shinoda's eyes widened. "How dare you?" he demanded. "You, sir, are accusing us of covering up a murder. Let me inform you that Lord Sakanoue never entered the hall while my friend was alive. He sat with us until the chanting stopped, and then we entered together and found . . . Yoakira gone. Furthermore, afterwards he was more eager to search the grounds than any of us. He was absolutely tireless! As for you, to my mind there has already been far too much idle and irresponsible gossip. First it was demons, now murder. Beware, sir, beware!"

And with that he padded off angrily, barefoot and indifferent to the sharp gravel on the path.

Akitada got up, angry with himself that he had ruined his last chance. He brushed the dust from his best robe and put on his socks and shoes over wet feet. Feeling slightly refreshed, but mentally more confused and frustrated than ever, he walked home thinking over Shinoda's words.

The complete lack of cooperation from all three men, though

for different reasons, had a troubling unanimity about it. Only Shinoda had given him an answer of sorts. He had seen something besides Yoakira's robe in the prayer hall, something which had proved to him and the others that Prince Yoakira had died there. What had he seen? Suddenly Akitada recalled vividly the admonition on the calligraphy scroll in the prince's mansion: "Thou must search the truth within, for thou shalt not find it without." He had wasted time talking to people in the capital, when he should have gone to the place where it had happened. Akitada now suspected that Abe and Yanagida had played an elaborate game with him. Yoakira's friends knew something they were afraid to reveal, afraid that it would feed more "idle gossip."

He was passing the university compound at that point and remembered Hirata's poor health. If only he could solve Oe's murder! That certainly would put an end to the stress his old friend was under.

On an impulse, he crossed Nijo Avenue. The grounds of the university were deserted and the heat hung heavily over the courtyards, baking the gravel and rising in shimmering waves above it. Not a branch stirred in the pines.

Akitada went to the Temple of Confucius and entered it. In the half light the hall was slightly cooler than the outside air. With the figures of the sages looming darkly above him, Akitada tried to get a sense of the atmosphere. On his visit to Yoakira's rooms he had felt the presence of the prince very distinctly. Here the walls and beams, the very floorboards under Akitada's feet were imbued with the mystery of Oe's murder, permeated with the images of violent death. Yet Akitada did not sense the spirit of Oe as he had that of the prince in the Minamoto mansion. What had these statues seen? How many people had been here the night Oe died? The victim and his killer, of course. And Ishikawa. Akitada was certain of this. But he did not think that Ishikawa had killed Oe. And he could not have been an accomplice. Ishikawa, the blackmailer, would have been a poor choice indeed. Had he been an unwilling witness? Or could he have come upon the body of his professor afterwards and decided on a whim to suspend it from the statue? That would have been in character. But Akitada could not see Ishikawa risking arrest by manhandling a newly murdered corpse. Quite apart from everything else, Oe's blood would have got all over Ishikawa.

Akitada stared at the polished boards at his feet. No, that was nonsense. If the body had been lying down, it would have left stains on the boards. And the blood in that case would have covered the victim's neck and shoulders only. Akitada raised his head to look up at Confucius. Oe's gown had had a broad band of gore running down its front, splashing into a puddle on the dais.

Akitada's eyes moved to the face of the sage. For the first time he noticed that the full lips, half hidden by mustache and beard, were smiling. With an angry exclamation, he turned on his heel and rushed out.

◆

Kobe greeted Akitada almost cheerfully. Apparently the arrest of Kurata had caused him to regard Akitada with friendlier eyes.

"You'll be glad to hear," he announced complacently, "that we got a full confession to both murders. Imagine, Kurata claims he cannot father children, and the girl was trying to saddle him with another man's child. He said it infuriated him so that he snatched back the expensive sash he had given her. That's when she started threatening him, and so he strangled her with it, tossed the body into the reeds, and the sash to the first beggar he passed."

"Umakai."

"Yes. Later the old man recognized Kurata in his shop and made a scene, talking wildly about Jizo and having lost the sash. Kurata told him to come back after dark and he would give him another. Instead he strangled the old man, carried the body a few steps to the canal and flung it in. Case complete."

"You are to be congratulated," Akitada said dryly. "That was certainly most efficient. However, I came about Oe. If you have kept the dead man's clothes, may I have a look at them?"

"Of course we have kept the clothes. That is an ongoing investigation." Kobe clapped his hands and gave an order to a young constable, who returned to place the bundle on Kobe's desk.

Akitada took up the embroidered sash and laid it out flat. Deep creases marked the places where it had passed under Oe's arms and been knotted around the statue. The center section was less creased but heavily soaked in blood. The material was heavy and lined on the inside. When Akitada turned it over, only a few traces of blood had soaked through. Next he spread out the robe.

"Just as I thought," he told Kobe, pointing to an unstained section of fabric on the upper chest, close to the neckline. He placed the stained sash over it. "Look! Do you realize what that means?"

Kobe leaned forward. His eyes widened. "Holy heaven!" he exclaimed. "He was killed after he was tied up."

"Yes. If he had been killed first, the sash would have protected the fabric of his robe at the waist, where it originally was. When he was tied up, the sash was passed around his chest and under his arms. That means the killer need not have been strong at all. Slashing the throat of a bound man is ridiculously easy." Akitada grimaced. "It is also a coward's crime."

Kobe scratched his head. "But how did he get his victim to agree to being tied up?"

"Remember, Oe was very drunk. Whether he was tricked into it or threatened in some way does not matter. I think he was too befuddled to realize his predicament."

"Hm," Kobe said stubbornly. "It may have happened that way, but that doesn't mean that Ishikawa didn't kill him. In any case, my men have been scouring the temples throughout the capital. Tomorrow they will start on those outside the city. I'll get that young villain eventually. He'll be sorry he ran."

Akitada almost hoped he had guessed wrong about Ishikawa's hiding place, but the foolish young man had brought this upon himself. He turned to go, saying, "I shall visit the Ninna temple tomorrow and save you the trouble of checking that."

Kobe's eyes narrowed speculatively as he watched Akitada walk from his office.

NINETEEN

THE TRUTH WITHIN

That night Akitada lay awake for a long time thinking about the Yoakira case. His decision to visit the temple had been intuitive rather than rational. Even now he had no idea what he was looking for in a place which must have been scrutinized over and over again after the event. He only knew he must go.

"Thou must search the truth within, for thou shalt not find it without," the prince's scroll had advised. He remembered the strange sense that a voice had spoken the words aloud as he was reading them. They referred to introspection, but could they not also be applied to the mystery? He had spent all his time looking for answers to the prince's fate "without," talking to the man's grandson and brother, and visiting his servants and friends. Now it was time to penetrate to the center of things, to the place where Prince Yoakira had ceased to exist as six men sat outside watching the door and listening to his voice.

Well before dawn Akitada and Tora got ready for the trip into the hilly countryside northwest of the capital. Since it was a workday, Akitada wrote a note to Hirata, excusing himself from his duties for one day and reassuring him about the Oe case. He gave it to Hitomaro to deliver at the university before the start of classes, feeling guilty about postponing further a visit with Tamako's father, but the danger to young Sadamu urged him to lose no more time in getting evidence against Sakanoue.

They left the capital on horseback. It was still dark, for which Akitada in his glum mood was thankful. The air was already warm and musty, and a faint stench of smoky cooking fires hung over the streets west of the palace. But as soon as they left the buildings behind, the smoke cleared and a light breeze sprang up, bringing the scent of warm summer grasses and the wildflowers which grew unseen by the side of the dirt road. They made good time, keeping their horses at an easy pace. The night was clear so that they could see the narrow band of road stretching gray before them. A breeze cooled their faces, and up ahead rose the black ridge of pine-covered headlands which lay between them and their destination. Now and then they passed another horseman, or a farmer with his cart, out before dawn; vague shapes in the darkness, or points of moving yellow lights if they carried lanterns. The carts did, as a rule, but men on foot or on a sure-footed horse relied on the faint light of the sky.

"You've got to admit," said Tora, coming up beside Akitada and breaking the long silence, "that Hitomaro and Genba are good fellows and have done exactly as you told them."

Akitada had been pondering Yoakira's journey to the temple and brought his thoughts back to the present with difficulty. "Fortunately they have not been put to the test," he said. "We have not had a single suspicious character show his face for the past two nights. But I intend to return to the city as quickly as possible."

"What do you really think of Hitomaro, sir?" Tora persisted.

"He does have some of the mannerisms of a military man. But I think he has a better education than the average warrior, though he tries to hide it. An interesting character."

"Yes, he acts funny sometimes. I offered him a stick-fighting match, but he said he'd never used them. Like he was above that sort of thing. And he wouldn't practice sword-fighting with me either." Tora sounded aggrieved.

"Never mind," remarked Akitada with a smile. "Your skills are much more appreciated by the young lord."

Tora grinned. "The boy's a quick learner. He got really good at walking on his stilts, but when I was about to show him a few simple stick-fighting moves, Lady Sugawara called me away to do some chores."

A vision of his mother's outraged face amused Akitada only for a moment. There were more important matters on his mind. "If Yoakira's journey was anything like this, I expect neither the driver nor the prince's friends would have been able to see each other clearly until they reached the temple," he suggested to Tora.

Tora glanced up the road, where an oxcart labored up the hill. "Not a chance," he said. "The riders probably passed the carriage and went ahead. Not much point in staying together. They'd all meet at the temple anyway."

"I seem to remember that the driver said those on horseback were sometimes in front and sometimes behind. I don't suppose Kinsue would have paid much attention even if he could see them."

"It doesn't matter. Nothing happened on the way. Now that we've solved the murders of Omaki and Umakai, what are you going to do about the university?"

"I am waiting to hear what Ishikawa has to say when Kobe finds him."

"You think *he* did it?"

"No, not really, even if Nishioka says so. There is another possibility, someone who has escaped scrutiny so far, but I cannot spare the time because it is more urgent to help young Minamoto. I am convinced Sakanoue murdered Prince Yoakira in order to gain control of the estates. He has already married the granddaughter and now only the boy prevents his owning all of it. He must have killed the prince at the temple, but all the witnesses say he did not. It would have been so much simpler if Yoakira had disappeared in his mansion in the capital."

The road began to climb, and soon they passed into the cool darkness of the forest. Above the branches of the pines and cryptomerias the sky gradually changed to inky blue and then a pale luminescent gray. When they reached the ridge, the sun was coming up over the eastern mountains, casting golden glints over the tree-tops and meadow grasses. A fox crossed the narrow road and disappeared in the brush, and the trees were filled with the song of birds.

Finally the view opened and they saw below them a broad valley. A river meandered through it, separating a small hamlet of thatched farmhouses from a vast complex of halls and pagodas that seemed to stretch all the way into the next mountain range.

The temple's proximity to the capital had made it the preferred choice of retirement for a number of emperors, most of whom had built their own palaces and shrines here. The site was picturesque, with religious buildings scattered amongst groves of trees and small hills.

Akitada and Tora covered the downhill stretch at a light gallop, easily forded the river, shallow in this dry season, and dismounted at the main gate.

Inside the gatehouse sat a monk who received them with little interest even at this early hour. Visitors were commonplace here, especially since the "miracle." Akitada signed the visitors' book and asked for directions to Prince Yoakira's hall. The monk gave him a rough map, asking that he return it on his way back.

Prince Yoakira's family shrine was at the far end of the temple grounds. As they rode slowly along the narrow road, they saw few monks and even fewer visitors. But when they passed an enormous lecture hall, its great roof thatched, its wooden supports, eaves and railings painted a brilliant red, they found the latticed doors thrown wide to the morning air, and inside they could see rows upon rows of seated monks listening to the sonorous voice of a reader. Groves of pines hid the temple halls and service buildings from each other, and narrow, pebble-filled canals carried bubbling mountain streams through the temple grounds. Everywhere there was a pleasant coolness and the scent of pine and incense.

When they reached the walled Minamoto shrine, Akitada peered through the rustic gateway. A single building, plain and square, was almost hidden behind the tall whitewashed mud wall.

Built of heavy timbers blackened by time, the hall was roofed with cypress bark and surrounded by a small courtyard. They dismounted outside the gate and tied their horses to the wooden posts provided for that purpose. As he and Tora walked towards the gate, Akitada explained that the prince's companions would have done the same and that Kinsue would have brought the empty carriage back here after the prince had entered the hall.

The courtyard was quite small, only large enough for one ox carriage, and at that the driver must have had a difficult time turning it around. Akitada and Tora climbed the wooden steps to the veranda. To either side of the hall, dense shrubbery closed in and blended with the forest. The heavy double doors, the only access to the interior, were closed. A plain balustrade surrounded the veranda, which extended only across the front.

Akitada paused here and looked around and back into the courtyard. On this veranda the prince's attendants—General Soga, Lords Abe, Shinoda, Yanagida and Sakanoue—had waited during the last hours of Yoakira's life. And somewhere down below, against the courtyard wall, Kinsue had sat peering up sleepily, listening to the disembodied voice of his master reciting the sutra inside the hall. There would have been only faint light when they arrived, for the prince was to begin his reading at dawn. The mountains around them would cast deep shadows, even after the first brightness was appearing in the sky. So much had happened in the dark. And inside this hall. Akitada turned towards the weather-darkened door.

The truth within!

Shaking his head, he pulled the door open. It creaked on ancient hinges. The hall inside was dim after the morning sunlight outside. Towards the rear wall stood a smallish Buddha figure carved from wood and painted in bright colors. It was seated on a raised lotus blossom, also carved from wood, and three small tables holding religious objects and ornaments were lined up before it. On either side, a tall iron candle stand, inlaid with gold and silver, held a thick candle. Akitada went to light both of them. The flames flickered in the draft from the open door, and weird shadows moved across the image and the simple prayer mat in front of it. Momentarily he felt again the touch of something ghostly—a sudden icy breath in the warm, stagnant air, raising the short hairs on his neck and leaving him dizzy. The sensation was not as palpable as it had been in the Yoakira mansion, but he shuddered nevertheless.

The walls appeared to be made from heavy posts and planks fitted without openings, and the roof, its thick rafters draped with cobwebs, rose steeply towards the massive ridgepole. The air smelled unpleasantly of incense and decay. Without windows, there was no circulation and the air felt heavy, warm and cloying.

Seen up close, the tables before the Buddha image were quite beautiful, gracefully constructed from some very dark wood and inlaid with mother-of-pearl. The trays and sacred vessels, their significance unknown to Akitada, were lacquered and gilded, and some of the bowls held flowers made from semiprecious stones and gold. A red plaque, inscribed with gilded characters, rested among these objects. Akitada read it and immediately bowed deeply. The inscription was by His August Majesty himself and commemorated the miracle.

Akitada felt anything but inspired. The atmosphere seemed to him almost repulsive, tainted and noxious somehow, and the darkness of the walls and roof gave the hall an oppressive feeling. Even the image seemed subtly evil. Akitada turned around to look for Tora and saw him at the open door, peering in. "What are you waiting for?" Akitada asked. "Come in! I need you."

"You think he was killed here, don't you?" Tora asked from outside.

"According to all accounts."

Tora's eyes searched the room. "Do you suppose his spirit is hanging about?"

"No. If it is anywhere, it's in his mansion in the capital. I have his old servant's word for it."

"Then maybe he was killed there." Tora walked in, wrinkling his nose. "They ought to leave the door open more often," he said.

Akitada gave Tora an irritated look. "It would certainly make my job easier if we did not have to investigate a disappearance from this hall," he said testily. "Never mind the smell. A lot of incense has been burnt here. Let's check the walls and floor for a hidden door." They started on either side of the door and moved along the walls, tapping the boards and checking the seams, until they met in the shadowy area behind the image. The walls were solid.

"Nothing!" said Tora, wrinkling his face again. "It really smells back here."

"It's either the incense or some small animal has died under the floorboards. I suppose there is little point in checking the floor. There is not enough space under the hall for a human being."

As Tora moved towards the door, Akitada cast one more glance around. When he turned to leave, he accidentally kicked the prayer mat out of place. It was an old one, but very beautifully woven and bound with embroidered silk around the edges. He bent to lift it and found the floor was solid underneath. "Well," he said with a sigh, "I did not expect to find anything. After all, they must have checked the building carefully. Come back here, Tora, and help me put the mat back."

Tora returned reluctantly and picked up one end. "Let's turn it," he said. "It looks better on the other side."

It was quite true. The mat was less faded, and the colors in the embroidery shone brighter. But it was slightly stained. Akitada knelt and looked at the stain closely. It was a small brown smudge, on the surface of the fibers only. He moistened a finger with his tongue and rubbed at it. A faint trace of brown appeared on his skin, and he smelled it.

"What's the matter?" asked Tora.

"Blood," said Akitada grimly.

"Hah!" Tora backed away. "So he died here."

"Perhaps. It is interesting, but there isn't very much of it. And it may not be Yoakira's."

"I bet it is." Tora glanced at the image and shivered. "What if something supernatural got him?" he asked.

"No."

"The blood! There are demons that tear people to pieces and eat them. Let's get out of here!" He started towards the door again.

But Akitada was staring at some white dust on the floor. "That was not here before," he said, pointing. "It must have fallen from the mat when we turned it."

Tora glanced back over his shoulder. "Some dirt. Monks are not good housekeepers, I guess."

Akitada crouched to investigate the dust. It was white and powdery. He rubbed it between his fingers and tasted it. "Rice flour," he said, straightening up.

"Maybe some of the monks brought it in," Tora called from the safety of the veranda.

"Hmm." Akitada wiped his hands on his robe and cast a last glance at the Buddha figure. He realized that it represented Amitabha. The carved face was painted in brilliant colors, the eyes a clear brown and the lips a deep red. Bright jewels encircled his neck and arms. Suddenly one of the jewels around his neck moved. Akitada stepped closer and saw that a very large fly, an iridescent bluebottle, sluggish in the stale warmth, was slowly rubbing its wings. No doubt the fresh air coming from the open door had roused it from its stupor. He waved at it with his hand, and watched it rise with an angry buzz. For a few moments, it droned around the image with bumbling, disoriented flight before settling again somewhere in the murky darkness. Shaking his head, Akitada blew out the candles and left.

Together they went down the steps into the small courtyard, but here Akitada paused to look back at the hall. "I wonder," he said, "what is behind the building. Let's go look."

Dense underbrush and trees grew up against the walls of the old hall. They fought their way through and found a narrow path that angled off from the hall towards the main temple complex. They followed this along the wall of the building until it reached the back and a deep gully which separated the hall from the hillside behind it. Here the path ended on a rocky ledge.

"What do you suppose that is for?" Akitada muttered.

"I don't know, but someone's been here recently." Tora pointed to broken branches on a shrub.

They looked out across the gully to the mountainside which

rose like a green wall, covered with vines, ferns and many small trees that clung precariously to small cracks in the rock. A lizard had been sunning itself on the ledge and disappeared into a hole with a sinuous curling of its tail.

"It's weird. There's nothing here but that funny flat slab of rock," said Tora. "Why would anybody beat a path to it?"

The slab was about the size of half a *tatami* mat and covered with moss and lichen. Akitada bent and touched a dark spot, rubbing the residue between his fingers. "Oil," he said, smelling his fingers, and added, "Cheap oil. We use a better quality in our lanterns. Someone has been here in the dark with an oil lamp." Akitada straightened up and scanned the ravine. Suddenly a strange idea occurred to him. It was so startling that he felt his stomach lurch, and for a moment he refused to believe it. "Tora," he asked, "can you make out that odd-shaped gray rock over there on the other side?"

"Looks like some kind of statue carved out of the stone. A Buddha, I think."

"Yes. The monks come here to worship, and at least once someone was here in the dark. Go back to the courtyard for a moment and listen."

"What for?"

"Never mind! Just go!"

Tora left, shaking his head, and Akitada wracked his brains for some lines from a sutra. His religious education left much to be desired at times. Well, anything would serve. Raising his voice a little, he recited the first poem that came to his mind: "The fires lit by the guards at the Imperial Palace gates, / Blazing bright by night, are damped down at daybreak: / So smolder my heart's thoughts . . ." He broke off, realizing that he had inadvertently quoted from a poem of unrequited love. It was a particularly apt description of pain, he thought bitterly.

Tora burst from the shrubbery, looking around. "What fire? Is there a fire?"

"No fire. I just wanted to know if you could hear me."

"Oh, I heard you. If I hadn't known better, I'd have sworn it was someone inside the hall."

"I hoped so," said Akitada. "Think about the miraculous disap-pearance for a moment. The only proof we have that the prince was here one moment and gone the next is that five witnesses, not count-ing Sakanoue, testified to his chanting the sutra inside the hall."

Tora's eyes grew round. "You think someone else was back here doing the sutra chanting because the prince was already dead? What did they do with his body?"

"I suspect the prince never came here. The murderer imper-sonated him."

"Sakanoue? How could he? The driver saw the prince get in the carriage and then get out again here."

"It was dark until the sun came up. Remember, we could not see the faces of those we passed on the way here. Sakanoue could have worn the prince's ceremonial robe and ridden in the carriage with no one being the wiser." Akitada paused, then muttered, "Ex-cept for the prince's white hair. That might have been seen even in the dark." Suddenly he slapped a fist into his hand. "Of course! That is what he used the rice flour for! Tora, I tell you, that is the way it was done. The prince was killed in his rooms in the capital." Akitada nodded vigorously and then took Tora's arm. "Come on! All we have to do now is solve a few minor difficulties."

They burst through the shrubbery into the courtyard, startling a young, red-cheeked monk, who had been looking around as if he had lost something.

"Oh, there you are," he cried when he saw them. "I saw the horses and wondered what had become of you."

Akitada said, "My friend and I were passing and decided to visit the famous site. It was most instructive. We have just been admiring the sacred figure behind the hall. Is it true that special benefits accrue from its worship?" He untied the reins of his horse.

"Oh, yes indeed, sir. You mean the image of Yakushi, the Heal-ing Buddha, I think," cried the young monk eagerly. Taking note of Akitada's silk clothes and his servant, he suggested, "If you like, you can arrange to have sutra readings performed in your ab-sence. May I show you the way to the recorder's office?"

Akitada accepted. The monk led the way, chattering about the wonders of the temple and the power of prayers said there. They followed, leading their horses, passing rows of monks' cells, where four or five young novices, stripped naked, splashed noisily in a large tub of water. Their guide proudly pointed out several halls of impressive size, the Great Buddha Hall and a beautifully detailed small sutra depository. Their destination was near the main gate and, to reach it, they had to pass by stables, noisy at this hour with the sounds of horses and grooms.

Akitada stopped. "Your stables are quite large. Do you by any chance supply horses to travellers here?" he asked the young monk.

"Oh, yes, sir. The stable is really a small post station. Horses may be hired as well as left. Such a service is very useful to pilgrims who wish to spend a week or more without having to provide for their own horses and grooms."

"How convenient," murmured Akitada thoughtfully.

Inside the administrative office they found the assistant recorder, an elderly monk with ink-stained fingers, bent over a large ledger.

"This gentleman is interested in sutra readings to the Healing Buddha," the young monk announced as proudly as if he were presenting a particularly large and juicy radish he had grown personally.

The old monk gave him a sour look and peered up at Akitada nearsightedly. "The Healing Buddha? *Tshk!*" he mumbled.

For a moment Akitada mistook this for a disparaging comment, but then he realized that the old man was toothless and had a disconcerting habit of sucking in his cheeks with a little smacking sound.

"What is the honorable ailment, *tshk*?" the recorder asked.

"What? Oh, er, it concerns a family member, not myself. It's a matter of, er, dizziness."

"Ah! That explains it, *tshk*. Young people rarely trouble with the Healing Buddha, *tshk, tshk*. May I ask the honored gentleman's name, the name of the ailing person, *tshk*, as well as the specific details?" He leafed through the pages of his ledger, mumbling and *tshk*ing. "Ah, here we are. Yes, *tshk*, I need the day, time and the reading. We recommend a chapter from the Sutra of the Golden Light as being most appropriate for Yakushi, but for a small extra charge we can include specific incantations for a case of light-headedness. *Tshk, tshk.*"

"It is for my mother, Lady Sugawara." Tora's jaw slackened, and Akitada bit his lip to keep from smiling. He told the monk, "I really don't know any details, but she said that the same reading was requested about a month ago."

The old monk looked astonished. "Sugawara? I don't recall any Sugawaras. Are you sure?" He scanned the entries and shook his head. "No, *tshk*. No one by that name. Is it really the Healing Buddha you want?"

"Yes. Mother sent someone else last time. Perhaps she gave another name. She does not want people to know she is ill."

Apparently Yakushi had no problem with pseudonyms, for the recorder merely asked, "And what name would that be?"

"Oh," cried Akitada in a tone of irritation, "how should I know? She never consults me! This is too frustrating! Let's just forget it if you cannot look it up!" He turned to leave.

"Just a moment, sir," the recorder said quickly. "There are not many requests for the Healing Buddha nowadays. Did you say a month ago? *Tshk*." He scanned the entries. "Here it is, the only entry in several months. The name was Kato! The Golden Light Sutra from the moment of sunrise. *Tshk, tshk*. Does the name ring a bell?"

"Kato," mused Akitada. "She has a cousin by that name. What day was it?"

The monk looked it up. "The ninth day of the third month."

Tora sucked in his breath, and Akitada shot him a warning glance. To the monk he said in a dubious tone, "It sounds right. What did this fellow look like?"

"*Tshk*. I really couldn't say, sir. Someone else made the entry."

"Well, how much did it cost last time?" Akitada asked, still frowning.

The recorder shuddered at this crude question, but said, "A generous donation of four silver bars was entered."

"Four silver bars!" cried Akitada, who did not have to pretend shock. "That does not sound right at all. My mother would never spend four bars of silver! No, I'm afraid I must have made a mistake. I shall have to consult with her before I make the arrangements. Thank you for your trouble."

The recorder sniffed and said, "Hmph, *tshk*. You are welcome, sir. Please hurry back!"

The young monk followed them out, looking disappointed. "Can I show the gentlemen anything else?" he asked. "Perhaps the gentleman's honorable mother might benefit from the sutra reading performed on the occasion of the archbishop's performance of the sacred rites. A very small gift to the temple would assure your mother's name would be included in the prayers."

The temple depended on such gifts for its livelihood, and the boy looked so hopeful that Akitada dug a handful of silver coins from his sash. "Will this be enough?" he asked.

The young man received the money with a smile and many bows, crying, "Oh yes, sir. Just a moment." He dashed back into the recorder's office and reappeared after a moment, carrying a receipt and announcing happily, "All is arranged, sir."

Akitada hoped that his mother would never find out. Then he remembered the fugitive Ishikawa, and asked, "Do you get many postulants your age here?"

The young monk looked surprised. "Not really, sir. Most of us come as children."

"I have an acquaintance, a very handsome and clever young man about twenty years old, who may have entered a monastery this past week. I wonder if he might have come here."

"Not this past week, sir. We have had no applicants of that age for many months now."

After they parted from their guide and got on their horses, Tora said with a grin, "You're getting pretty good at lying, sir. But who is this strange fellow? If he ordered sutra readings the same day the prince disappeared, he must be part of the plot."

Akitada decided to ignore the compliment. "Our friend Sakanoue has a weakness for impersonation. He paid four bars of silver, a considerable sum, to have the sutra chanted by a monk behind the hall at the time the prince always recited it inside." He added grimly, "It means that Sakanoue plotted the murder days before it happened. What I still do not understand is why Yoakira's friends assumed the prince was dead. How could they have known?" Suddenly he reined in his horse. "Tora," he cried, "the flies! There were flies near the image of the Buddha. Let's go back!"

With a groan, Tora followed. They returned at a canter to the shrine. Akitada rushed up the steps two at a time. When Tora caught up with him in front of the Buddha figure, his master was holding up one of the candles and tapping the carving with his fingers.

"Should you do that?" Tora asked nervously.

A fly buzzed lazily up from behind the figure's head, circled the flame, and then settled down on Buddha's nose. Akitada walked around to the back of the statue. "Come here!" he called to Tora.

Tora found him staring down at the floor. One of the dark boards had a small pale gash in it. Akitada squatted and probed with his fingers. "Give me your knife," he said.

When the blade was inserted into a crack, a section of flooring about a foot square came up, releasing a strong stench and several flies. They peered down into the dark space under the floor. It was not deep. Within arm's reach lay a box slightly smaller than the opening. Beside it was a pile of incense sticks.

"It's just storage for some sacred stuff, incense or scrolls or some such," suggested Tora.

"Neither of which would attract flies," said Akitada and reached down to lift the box. Immediately more flies rose into the air. The box had held the incense at one time. Akitada opened the lid.

"Holy heaven!" cried Tora, recoiling. "What is it?" He held his nose and slapped at angrily buzzing flies. "Some dead animal? It's crawling with maggots."

Akitada sighed. "It is a human head. The head of an elderly man with white hair," he said. "I think it used to belong to the prince." He replaced the lid and gently put the box back under the floorboards. "Sakanoue brought it here."

Tora had turned pale. "But why—and where's the rest of him?"

Akitada said nothing for a minute or so. "The driver mentioned his master's stiff robe," he finally said slowly. "It is easy to hide a man's head in such a garment. The murderer intended it to be found as proof of death, but Shinoda, who went inside with Sakanoue while the others waited outside, decided to hide it."

Akitada thought back to the day he had visited the prince's friends. Abe, clearly impaired by age, had been as confused about the events as about Akitada's name, while Yanagida had been overwhelmed with religious fervor by the miracle he had witnessed. Only Shinoda had treated the temple story rationally. In his mind, Akitada saw Shinoda again, soaking his feet in the stream, his sharp eyes gauging his visitor's purpose. He heard the old gentleman again, firmly allaying suspicions and finally warning him off sharply when he had persisted. And suddenly he understood the events of that night as if he had been present. He knew now that Shinoda had hidden the truth from him as he had hidden Yoakira's head that morning. Unlike the senile Abe, or the devout Yanagida, or the general who would not have countenanced tricking the emperor, Shinoda had both the quick intelligence and the nerve to create a miracle in order to protect his friend's memory. So that was the truth, finally, the truth inside. The head had lain here, hidden inside this hall, all along, just as the truth had lain hidden in Akitada's memory.

He sighed. "Yes. Shinoda hid the head, but he did it out of love for his friend, not to protect a killer. He certainly could not suspect Sakanoue, who had been in his plain sight the entire time. As for the body, that was left behind in one of the trunks, I suspect." Akitada rose. "Come! We have seen enough."

◆

They rode homeward at a steady pace. Akitada was still lost in frowning thought.

After a considerable silence, Tora ventured a question. "What will you do now?"

Akitada looked at him bleakly. "I have no idea, except that I must somehow protect the boy. We are dealing with a very devious mind, and one that has carefully and quickly plotted a crime which was so extraordinary that people called it a supernatural event because there was no rational explanation for it. And because a foolish old man decided to hide the head, the only proof that Yoakira had died violently, though not at the hand of demons, the emperor himself declared the case a miracle."

"You mean, if they had left the head it would have been blamed on demons?" Tora asked. "It makes sense. People would figure the prince had done something evil. The same thing happened to a bad man years ago in the palace grounds. Everyone knows that story."

"Yes, everyone knows that story," nodded Akitada. "And Sakanoue counted on that. No doubt the incident of the soothsayer's evil omens and his curse after the prince had him whipped from his gate gave Sakanoue the idea to stage the demonic incident. Nothing more likely in popular superstition than that demons should have punished Yoakira for his disrespect. It was timely also. Yoakira had just discovered his fraud. As soon as Sakanoue had insinuated himself into the granddaughter's bed, with or without her encouragement, the prince's life was forfeit. Instead of ignominious dismissal, he saw suddenly a way to wealth and power. The prize was worth any risk."

Tora thought it over. "I understand about Lord Shinoda, sir, and I see Lord Sakanoue's motive, not that we haven't known about that for a long time now, but I don't see how he hoped to get away with it. He might've been caught at any moment."

"Not really. There were only two dangerous moments. The first one was during the impersonation, just after he left the carriage and entered the hall. He had to be quick, for though Kinsue had left again, the prince's friends would enter the courtyard any moment. I remember Kinsue talking about the amazing speed with which the prince ascended the stairs. But once inside, what Sakanoue had to do took only a moment. He lit a candle and some incense, stripped off the robe and left it, along with the bloody head, on the prayer mat. Then he slipped back out, closing the door behind him, and waited in the dark for the old gentlemen to seat themselves on the veranda. When they saw him, they were too tired from the journey and lack of sleep to wonder where he had come from. He was expected, and he was there. Soon after they all settled on the veranda, the sun rose and the chanting began. All four men on the veranda and Kinsue in the yard saw Sakanoue sitting among them while the sutra chanting was going on. Both Yanagida and Shinoda were adamant that he was there from beginning to end. He had a perfect alibi, and the world another supernatural event."

Tora shook his head in wonder. "What was the other time?" he asked.

"Sakanoue's second problem was a horse for the return trip, but that was easily accomplished while the whole monastery was running about searching for the prince. After all, horses were readily available in the stables. In fact, old Kinsue, the driver, was puzzled by the fact that Sakanoue's horse had not been one of their own."

Tora nodded reluctantly. "All right. I can see how it could be done. It was the middle of the night and they were all old men. Probably couldn't see the hand before their eyes by daylight. But tell me this: how did Sakanoue get rid of the body?"

Akitada sighed. Retracing Sakanoue's clever plot was one thing, but the body left behind in the prince's rooms, stashed headless into one of the bedding trunks, brought with it the knowledge of sudden violent death. He pictured again the room, recalled the scratches on the otherwise immaculate floor, and felt the unearthly presence of the dead man's spirit. Perhaps the murdered man had tried to tell him then. He summed up bleakly, "The corpse was taken to the country in one of the trunks."

Tora looked dumfounded. "To be unpacked?"

"No, of course not. According to Kinsue, Sakanoue drove the

last cart himself, and it was night again. He probably dumped the body someplace on the road. A headless corpse is not readily identifiable."

Tora cried, "No, sir! He didn't have to do that. He passed through Rashomon! They bring their dead there at night. You could leave the chancellor himself, and nobody would think anything of it."

"Rashomon? But surely the men who pick up the dead would report a headless corpse?"

"Maybe they would and maybe they wouldn't," Tora said darkly. "Things happen to dead people in that place, and not all of them are done by the living." He shuddered, then added more cheerfully, "Congratulations, sir! You've solved the case."

Akitada nodded glumly.

"What's wrong? You got that bastard Sakanoue. I thought that's what you wanted."

"You and I may know he killed the prince, but we will never prove it. The emperor himself has put his seal on Sakanoue's safety."

They had reached the top of the ridge and caught their first glimpse of the capital spread across the vast plain below them. In the heat of the midday sun, a haze hung over the great city, and only the blue-tiled or black-thatched roofs of the imperial palaces and government halls were clearly visible. From there, Suzaku Avenue stretched southward, its willows fading in the distance as into a fog. They both looked for the tiled roofs of the distant Rashomon, but the great gate was lost somewhere in the blue vapor.

Tora cried out, "Look! There's been a fire! I thought I smelled smoke this morning." He pointed at heavy streaks of charcoal gray hanging over the northwest quadrant of the city. "I knew it would happen in this weather. Poor bastards! Thank Heaven it's a long way from home!"

Akitada thought of his family and the young boy who was their visitor. He spurred on his horse. They made the descent rapidly and were soon close enough to see the location of the disaster more clearly. The fire had been brought under control. Only a

slight dark haze was left over a particular grove of trees and
rooftops, while the black smoke was slowly drifting away in the
blue sky.

Akitada reined in his horse with a jerk. "Merciful heaven! I
hope my eyes deceive me." He pointed. "Look, Tora! Isn't that gap
among the charred trees where the Hiratas' house used to stand?"

Tora came alongside, glanced at his master's white face, and
shaded his eyes. "Amida!" he muttered. "It is! Let's go!"

TWENTY

CHARRED EMBERS

𝒯he smell of acrid smoke greeted them blocks before they reached the Hiratas' street. It was almost palpable in their nostrils, burnt their eyes and felt greasy on their skin.

The street itself looked at first glance the same as usual. The Hiratas' garden wall stood firm, and the two willows by the gate swayed their graceful branches in the breeze. But the breeze also wafted gray filaments of smoke across the wall, and a gaggle of onlookers was gathered about the open gate.

To Akitada they seemed to peer in with the avid curiosity of people who, having been spared by disaster, savor their own luck complacently. Seized by a sudden furious hatred for them, he sent his lathered, gasping horse forward with a sharp kick to scatter them in all directions.

Inside the gate the scene was reminiscent of hell. He slid from his saddle and stood speechless, staring in horror and disbelief. Wet steaming mounds of charred rubble lay among blackened vegetation, and a bluish haze hung over the place where once the deep-gabled house with its attached pavilions had stood. Soot-darkened figures, their faces covered with wet rags, moved through the smoke like demons in search of lost souls, walking paths that had once meandered through Tamako's lush gardens.

Tamako! Akitada tried to call her name, but an icy fear made his voice falter and his tongue refuse to obey.

"You there!" shouted Tora, jumping off his horse behind him, "What happened to the family?"

One of the dark figures, a fireman, turned briefly and pointed. "Over there."

At the foot of a charred cedar there were two patches of bright color. A red-coated police constable stared down at a bundle covered by a blue and white cotton robe.

A woman's robe.

Akitada moved towards the cedar stiffly, forcing one foot in front of the other until he stood beside the constable and looked down on death.

The cotton robe had been folded back to show part of a human body. The charred remains were unrecognizable and looked surprisingly small, almost like a child's corpse. Bent double, arms and legs drawn up to the torso as if defending itself against the indignities inflicted on the dead, it was the first victim of fire Akitada had seen. That shrunken black mass of scorched flesh and bones could not be . . . but, oh, that robe!

The constable growled, "Hey! What do you think you're doing here?"

Akitada looked up dazedly. "Who is this?" he croaked.

" 'Was' is the correct word," said the man lugubriously. "They dragged him out of that pile over there."

Him? Akitada looked again at the corpse and saw that the back of the blackened head still retained remnants of a gray topknot. For a moment his relief was almost too intense to contain. Belatedly, Akitada looked where the constable had pointed. The rubble was what was left of Hirata's study, a pavilion separate from the main house. Oh, God! he thought. Hirata! Not Tamako, but her father. But where was she then? His brief hope died, as his eyes searched the debris, looked past the constables for other bodies, for there had been the servants, too. Were they all dead?

Tora walked up, stared at the corpse and asked, "Where are the others? There were the professor, his daughter and two servants."

"Three more?" The constable whistled. "I just got here. I guess they haven't found them yet."

Akitada's stomach knotted. No! Oh, no! Please, not Tamako too! Not his slender, graceful girl! Only the smoking ruins of the main house and of the two other pavilions remained. Nothing could have survived under those blackened beams and the burnt thatch of the roofs. Tamako's room used to be in the pavilion farthest from her father's study. Oh, Tamako! He swallowed, gagging at the memory of that twisted black corpse under the cedar, and started towards the steaming mountain of debris, forcing his trembling legs into a run.

"Wait," cried Tora, coming after him and snatching at his arm. "You can't go in there. It's still hot."

Akitada shook him off, and vaulted onto the remnants of a veranda, then flung himself on a piece of roofing and began to tear at charred timbers and kick away sodden thatch. Before he could make much headway, strong arms seized his shoulders and pulled him back. Tora and one of the firemen shouted at him. Struggling against their grasps, Akitada finally took in their words.

"The young lady's at the neighbor's house. The servants, too."

"Tamako?" He stared stupidly at Tora. "Tamako is alive?"

Tora nodded, patting his shoulder reassuringly. "She's all right, Amida be praised! Come along, sir. We'll go see her."

Akitada swayed with the relief. Barely allowing himself to hope, he walked with Tora to the adjoining house. When he knocked, an elderly man opened and looked at them questioningly.

"M—Miss Hirata? She's here?" Akitada stammered.

The man nodded and led them into the main room of the small villa.

Though the room was full of people, Akitada saw only Tamako. She was sitting on a mat, huddled under someone's quilted robe, her skin bluish white under the streaks of soot, her eyes huge and red-rimmed from tears or smoke, and she was shaking so badly she could not speak. Looking at Akitada, she only managed a long-drawn out moan: "O . . . h!"

"I–I came," he said helplessly.

She nodded.

"Are you hurt?"

She shook her head, but tears welled over and ran down her pale cheeks.

He wished to go to her, to gather her into his arms, to hold her to himself, offering himself for what she had lost. But they were not alone. And even if they had been, she did not want him. Had never wanted him. He gave himself a mental shake. Even so, she would have to accept whatever small comforts he could provide now.

His eyes swept around the room, taking in belatedly the man's wife, a matronly lady, the Hiratas' old servant Saburo and Tamako's young maid, as well as several wide-eyed children. He asked the wife, who was hovering near Tamako, "Is she hurt?"

The woman shook her head. "It's only the shock, sir."

"Tora!" When Tora materialized at his side, Akitada said, "Bring your horse and then take Miss Hirata and her maid to our home. Tell my mother to make her comfortable."

Tamako weakly moaned some objection. The neighbor woman bristled. "Who are you, sir?"

"Sugawara," snapped Akitada, his eyes on Tamako.

"But," persisted the woman, "what are you to Miss Hirata?"

Tearing his eyes from Tamako, Akitada finally understood the woman's concern. "It's all right," he said. "Tamako and I were raised like brother and sister. Professor Hirata took me in when I was young."

The woman's eyes grew large with surprise. "Oh," she cried, "then you must be Akitada. I am so glad you came for her. She has no one else in the world."

He nodded and went to lift the drooping girl into his arms. She sobbed and buried her face against his chest as he carried her out into the street where Tora waited with the horse. Lifting her onto the saddle, he told her, "Go with Tora, my dear. I shall take care of matters here."

She looked down, lost, hopeless, defeated. He wanted to tell her not to worry, to let him take care of her from now on, but those words he could not speak. Reaching up to adjust her robe over a bare foot, he stopped. The slender foot was covered with angry red blisters. His heart contracted at the sight and he raised his eyes to hers. He wanted to ask her again how badly hurt she was, but she spoke first.

"You hurt your hand."

He did not understand at first, then snatched it back. Like her foot, his skin was bright red and blistered under the soot. Dimly aware of pain, he realized that he had burned both of his hands pulling at the debris of her pavilion. Before he could deny the discomfort, Tora lifted the frightened maid up behind her mistress, took the bridle of the horse, and led them off. Akitada stood in the street, watching Tamako's slender figure next to the sturdier one of the maid until they disappeared around the corner. For a moment nothing else mattered than that she had been spared.

But his joy was short-lived. The old servant shuffled up to stand beside him sniffling. Akitada tore his eyes from the corner and sighed. "What happened, Saburo?"

"The master must've fallen asleep over his books," the old man said, weeping. "We'd all gone to bed. It was Miss Tamako's screaming that woke me in the middle of the night. And I saw the study was all afire, and the fire was in the trees and on the roof of the main house and the kitchen. Oh! It was dreadful! The poor master. We could see him lying in the fire. I had to pull Miss Tamako back or she would've run into the flames. It was such a long time before the firemen came, and then there was not enough water in the well and not enough buckets, and now all is gone." He burst into wracking sobs. "All gone!" he cried, hugging himself, "all gone! While I was sleeping!"

Akitada touched his shoulder, lightly, because his hands were painful.

They walked back to the ruins, where Akitada spent futile

hours trying to find explanations for what had happened. The professor had died, as one of the firefighters explained, because of an accidental spill of lamp oil. Seeing Akitada's disbelief, he added dispassionately that such things happened to scholars who fell asleep over their books. Saburo objected that his master had always used extreme care with fire.

Akitada wanted it to be an accident, but a black fear gnawed at his heart that it was not, and that it might have been prevented if he had spoken to Hirata sooner. Tamako had survived but she had lost everything. She had lost her father, her only support in this world. He cursed himself for the injured pride which had caused him to evade the older man for days. What if he was responsible for Hirata's death?

The twin demons of grief and shame pursued him all the way home, where he asked about Tamako and was told by his mother, unusually subdued for once, that Seimei had tended to her feet and had brewed a special tea for her and that she was now mercifully asleep. Then she completed his wretchedness by reminding him of the dismal future which lay ahead for a beautiful young woman left without a father or male relative to protect her.

◆

The day after the tragic fire Akitada kept to his room. Seimei, who brought his food and removed it untouched, thought that his master had not moved at all, so still seemed his sitting figure, so frozen his face looking down at the folded hands, raw and red where the hot embers had seared the skin.

Lady Sugawara came, as did Akitada's sisters, but he merely listened to their entreaties and sighed. Tora brought young Sadamu, hoping to cheer up his master, and left, shaking his head.

The following day, Akitada emerged from his room, haggard and unshaven, to tend to the most urgent business and to go to Hirata's funeral.

Hirata's colleagues and his students were there, in addition to many people Akitada did not recognize. Their obvious grief added to his burden of guilt, and he shrank more and more into himself.

He was intensely aware of a heavily veiled Tamako, seated behind the screens which also hid his mother and sisters. What must she think of him, who had betrayed his sacred duty to the man who had been a father to him, the "elder brother" who had forsaken them in their need, who had ignored her cry for help?

The journey to the cremation grounds, to finish what the fire had started, passed like a dream, as insubstantial as the black smoke which rose from the pyre of the man who had been more of a father to him than his own father. Afterwards he spoke to no one and returned home to disappear again into his room, where he remained for another day and night, his mind caught either in memories of the past or images of the disaster, eating nothing and drinking only water.

On the fourth day after the fire, still in the midst of his paralyzing despair, a messenger arrived from the university. He delivered a note from Bishop Sesshin, which Akitada unfolded with fingers still painful from the burns.

It said simply, "You are needed."

Outraged, Akitada tore it up and reached for a sheet of paper to write his formal resignation from the university. But something, duty perhaps or the remembered faces of his students, or the sheer pain of holding a brush, nagged at him to go in person. He called Seimei and, with his help, washed, shaved and changed into a clean gray robe.

"Please eat some of this rice gruel," Seimei said, his voice low, as if he were addressing an invalid.

Akitada ignored him and left.

When he walked into the main hall of the school of law, he found it filled with students, Hirata's and his own. Only young Lord Minamoto, still residing at Akitada's house for the sake of his safety, was absent. The students sat gathered in a semicircle around the large figure of Sesshin. The bishop wore a gray robe with a black and white stole to signify his mourning. The students were in their usual dark gowns, but their faces were sad and many eyes were red from weeping.

"Welcome, my young friend," Sesshin greeted him, his voice

rumbling. "We have been waiting for you. The students have talked to me about their memories of Professor Hirata, and I have told them that you were one of his special students once. Perhaps you will share some of your memories with us?"

Akitada glared at him. It was a dreadful request!

Cursing Sesshin in his heart, Akitada turned to the students. Ushimatsu was leaning forward slightly, his plain face filled with pity. Akitada looked at the others, wondering if his grief was so transparent to them all. There was Nagai, poor ugly Nagai, his eyes swollen with weeping and his mouth blubbering—at his age! He had not been this distraught in prison with a murder charge hanging over his head! But then Hirata had loved Nagai—like a son almost. Perhaps, not having had a son of his own, he had let his students fill that void. A new wave of misery washed over him. Hirata had loved them all, Akitada included! Tears dimmed the faces before him. He swallowed and tried to speak, but his throat closed up, leaving him mute. He made a helpless gesture to Sesshin, but the fat monk placidly nodded encouragement, pointing to a cushion by his side.

Akitada sat and somehow he found his voice, though later he could not recall what he had told the students. In a way, he had carried on a dialogue with himself about his life with Hirata. It had been a strangely purging experience, and he had wept. But he had found a measure of peace.

When he stopped, there was a long period of silence. Then Sesshin began to recite the soothing words of the Pure Land sutra. He closed by saying, "There is a difficult meditation practice in our religion, in which we submerge ourselves completely in nothingness. Only a few achieve success. But when we are successful, the mind is calm as the sea. Passion, hatred, delusion and sorrow fall away. False thoughts vanish completely. There are no pressures. We issue forth from our bonds and separate ourselves from all hindrances and cut off the foundations of our suffering. This is called entering Nirvana. It is a state of blessedness which can be achieved completely only through death. And it is where our dear friend now dwells forever."

There was the sound of soft sighs from the students, and then Sesshin arose, nodded to the students and to Akitada and walked out.

Akitada got up dazedly and followed. The old monk was waiting on the veranda, his hands on the railings and his eyes fixed on the roofs of the distant city. He did not turn as Akitada joined him.

"So many deaths," he said with a sigh, "in the midst of so much life." He gestured at the teeming city before them and back towards the lecture hall filled with quietly talking students. "I am forever reminded of the eight unavoidable sufferings: birth, old age, pain, one's own death, the death of a loved one, evil people, frustrated desire and lust. Sometimes I think I have had more than my share of all but one of them. Why are you so angry with me, my friend?"

"Your Reverence," Akitada said awkwardly, "I apologize for my unpardonable rudeness to you."

Sesshin's dark, liquid eyes passed over Akitada's face. "Never mind! I have been more foolish than you, and it is I who am in your debt. You opened your heart and home to a lonely child. Tell him from me to keep up with his studies."

Akitada stammered, "You know?"

Sesshin nodded. "I have had the boy watched since you came to warn me. My men reported that you took Sadamu away. They lost you briefly, but found your residence and verified that the boy was there." He added with a smile, "I hope he is not making a nuisance of himself?"

Akitada tried to control his amazement. "Not at all, but I wish we had known. We took him away secretly because Sadamu complained of two suspicious characters outside his dormitory. The one I saw was a vicious-looking brute, and Tora said the other fellow was smaller but the same type. We took them for Sakanoue's thugs."

Sesshin chuckled. "They have both been in my service for many years and, for all their looks, are quite gentle fellows. There was also a third man at the lecture hall to watch the boy during his classes. I should have told you."

Akitada felt foolish. "You could not have known that I would go to such lengths to meddle in your family affairs," he said contritely.

Sesshin sighed. "You did because I was negligent. I am grateful to you, you know."

Akitada hesitated, then said, "There are some new facts concerning your brother's death."

The bishop's face saddened again. "Not here and now," he said. "Come to me later." He bowed lightly and walked down the steps and across the courtyard.

Akitada returned to the students, realizing that he had changed his mind about resigning. Until new appointments were made, he would remain and cope with Hirata's pupils and his own. It would make up, in a small way, for his neglect of his old friend and mentor.

The students were subdued and grateful for his instruction. The concentration on the work took Akitada's mind off his grief until the bell sounded for their noon rice, and he was reminded to go home to check on his family, which was increased now by Tamako, her little maid and old Saburo, Hirata's servant.

Genba opened the gate to him. He was laughing at something and had a mouth full of food. His face fell and he swallowed when he saw Akitada, who caught a glimpse of rice cake in Genba's hand as it disappeared behind his back. Akitada gave him a nod and walked into the courtyard.

Tora and Hitomaro were sitting in the shade of the paulownia tree. When they saw him, they jumped to their feet. Both were dripping with sweat, and two long bamboo staves lay nearby. They had been practicing stick-fighting. Apparently Hitomaro had consented after all.

So! Life went on as usual for his staff. Akitada's resentment was mixed with a twinge of envy. He glowered, feeling an outsider in his own home, and it occurred to him that the services of Tora's new friends could now be dispensed with. He opened his mouth to tell them, when he saw Genba surreptitiously swallowing the rest of his cake and licking his fingers. He remembered then their desperate need and how Genba had offered to work for food, and he decided they could stay on for a few days and make themselves useful in his newly enlarged household. Though how he was to pay for the added expenses, he had no idea.

Feeling lonely and dejected, he walked past them towards the house.

"Sir," cried Tora.

Akitada turned. Tora trotted up, brandishing a large, brightly painted umbrella.

"What do you want?" Akitada asked impatiently. "I am busy."

Tora's face fell. He stood, awkwardly opening and closing the umbrella. "I'm sorry. It's just . . . I thought I had better give you the message."

"Put that silly thing down! What message?"

Tora handed him the opened umbrella with a bow. "For you, sir."

Akitada kept his hands in his sleeves. "Don't be ridiculous! I could not use such a flamboyant piece of trumpery. Give it to your girl!" He turned away.

"In that case," said Tora, his voice stiff with hurt, "I think Mr. Hishiya was wise to leave before you got back. He was very proud of this umbrella. He stayed up all night and painted the pictures himself. Look! You can see every petal on the peonies and every feather in the phoenix's tail."

Akitada stopped and turned. "Hishiya? Oh, the dead girl's father! Let me see that again!" This time he took the umbrella, wincing a little as the rough handle scraped his barely healing palms, and studied the design and workmanship. "You are right. It is very fine. You will take Mr. Hishiya a gift in return. Seimei will have it ready in an hour. What did Mr. Hishiya say?"

"The police told him that you found Omaki's killer, and he wanted to thank you in person," Tora said accusingly. "But when he heard about the fire and the professor's death, he did not want to take up your time."

Akitada was ashamed. "He is a man of great courtesy," he said. "I am very sorry for my remarks about this umbrella." Akitada turned it dubiously in his hands. "It is indeed very . . . detailed. But it strikes me that it was you, Tora, who did all the hard work on the case. In fact, it was your case, not mine. And so the umbrella must rightfully be yours also." He returned it to Tora with a slight bow.

"Well . . ." Tora took the umbrella. "It is true that you did very little. As you say, I found all the clues." A slow smile spread over his face. "Right! This is just the thing for Michiko. I've been wracking my brains for something to give her for a present."

Akitada said, "Are you still seeing that little entertainer? Better watch your step. She may be no better than poor Hishiya's wife."

"Oh, Michiko is nothing like that one. And Hishiya got rid of his wife. Divorced her the day I told him I'd seen a customer waiting at his house." Tora added with a sly wink, "Imagine, the customer turned out to be one of Mrs. Hishiya's country cousins, and Mr. Hishiya objected to the generous way his wife was entertaining her relative!"

"You don't say!" Akitada exclaimed with a straight face. "All the more reason for you to accept the umbrella then. Mr. Hishiya is deeply in your debt."

The exchange with Tora had lifted Akitada's spirits a little. He felt able to deal with the many problems awaiting him. After giving instructions to Seimei about wrapping up a length of silk for Mr. Hishiya, he went to see his mother.

Lady Sugawara greeted him with outstretched arms. "My dear Akitada," she cried, "how are you feeling? And how are your hands?"

Akitada looked at her, surprised. "I am fine. I came to ask about Tamako, Mother."

His mother gave him a searching look. "She is calm. Seimei gave her some more of his tea to make her sleep last night and she looked much better this morning. I should have done the same with you. Come, sit down! You must have something to eat." Ignoring Akitada's protests, she clapped for Kumoi and told her to bring hot tea and some rice and vegetables.

Akitada sampled the food reluctantly, still awkward with the chopsticks, but after the first bite it tasted surprisingly good. His mother waited until he had finished before saying, "She plans to cut her hair and become a nun, you know."

Akitada stared, aghast, and stumbled to his feet. "Where is she?"

Lady Sugawara studied her fingernails. "She has your younger sister's room."

Akitada found Tamako alone, seated on the small veranda outside. She was dressed in the white robes of mourning, her hair very dark against the silk and her pale skin. He had expected dejection, violent tears, anger—he knew not what—but he found instead utter calm and composure.

"Akitada!" she said in her light voice, smiling a little. "I am so glad you came. Please sit down for a minute. I have to thank you for so many things. It was very kind of you to take care of the funeral and offer me shelter."

He remained standing. "My mother tells me you wish to renounce the world." His voice was harsh with emotion. "Is this true?"

She looked up at him calmly. "Yes, of course. It is the wisest thing to do under the circumstances. One of my father's cousins is a nun in Nara. I shall go to her."

"You are too young and beautiful to shut yourself away like that," Akitada cried angrily. "I won't permit it!" He corrected himself. "I mean, your father would not have approved."

"I think he would understand."

"No. You should marry. You could be my wife. That is what he wished."

She turned away then. Her slender hands twisted in her lap. "It is impossible."

"Why?" he cried, "Why can't you marry me, Tamako?"

She did not answer and kept her face turned from him. All the fears about his own inadequacy returned, and they were worse than before. How much she must detest him, if she could not even now accept the refuge he offered her from destitution and distress! "It is not impossible," he shouted. "It is you who are impossible!" With an incoherent cry, he turned and stormed away.

All the way to the university, he searched again for a rational explanation of Tamako's rejection of his offer. And as before, he found no answer other than that she must dislike him or his family. He set the students to reading a chapter in the *Book of Documents* and went to Hirata's room to sort through his belongings, working with feverish concentration to banish his despair.

Setting aside such personal things as his daughter might wish to have, he went on to sifting through Hirata's papers. There was much, the work of a lifetime. Not only had Hirata kept copious notes on legal matters, but he had preserved many of his students' papers. Akitada even came across one of his own efforts. Throughout the years of his teaching, Hirata had taken enormous and loving pains with his students. Often he had written appreciative comments on their papers. It seemed wrong to discard all that, but there was no point in saving any of them.

He turned to the books next, and it was here that he found the diary. It spanned the past year and contained small memos Hirata had written to himself about things he planned to do that day. Akitada turned to the final entry, made the last time Akitada had seen Hirata, the day he had decided to go with Nishioka instead of speaking to his old friend.

Hirata had written, "I think A. is still angry with me over the matter of the examination. Poor Tamako. My conscience will give me no peace until I make one more effort to set things right. An announcement that a mistake has been made and that the poor dead boy should have won would at least please his family."

Akitada laid the journal down with a shaking hand. It confirmed his dreadful suspicion. He wondered if Hirata had wanted to consult him before taking a dangerous step. What if he had, in fact, started to "set things right"?

Tucking the journal into his sleeve, Akitada went to dismiss the students early. Then he walked to the ruins of the Hirata house.

There was nothing left but charred timbers. A single fireman was raking apart the debris of the main house. Akitada picked his way to where Hirata's study had been.

"What are you looking for, sir?" the fireman asked, walking up.

"I was trying to see where the fire started."

The man pointed. "Right there. Started outside. On the veranda."

Akitada looked at a pile of ashes, then at the man. He had an intelligent face and bright, curious eyes. "How do you know that?" he asked.

"Oh, I've seen plenty of fires. You get to where you can tell. It was hottest on the veranda. See, there's nothing left of it. The room burned up later, and the supports are still there. Fire burns up, not down."

"But how could a fire start outside?"

"Oh, any number of ways. Careless maid drops a brazier full of coals or spills a lantern full of oil and is too scared to tell. This one must've been oil. You can still smell it a bit. I expect it dripped down between the boards."

Akitada could not smell anything but the acrid odor of burnt wood that hung over the whole compound, but he knew the man was right. He also knew that the oil had not been spilled accidentally.

He asked the fireman's name and walked to police headquarters.

Kobe was in and still in a friendly mood. "Come in, come in!" he cried. "I have good news." He took a closer look at Akitada's drawn face and said, "You look terrible. Have you been ill?"

"No. Are you aware that Professor Hirata died in a fire in his home five nights ago?"

Kobe's face lengthened. "Yes. I saw the report. Forgive me for not expressing my sympathy. You were close, weren't you?"

"Yes. I came to tell you that the fire was arson. The professor was murdered by the same man who killed Oe."

Kobe sighed. "Now, now," he said soothingly. "I can see that you've been under a lot of strain and are upset about this. But I read the report, you know, and there's nothing in it about arson. And Oe's killer wasn't anywhere near Hirata's place that night."

Akitada raised a distracted hand to his face and sat down. So much had been happening that he found it hard to concentrate. He felt the outline of Hirata's diary through his gown. "It is a long and complicated story," he said, pulling the diary from his sleeve and sliding it across the desk towards Kobe. "Turn to the last page and read the entry."

Kobe read and then leafed through the journal. "This is Hirata's?"

"Yes. I found it when I was clearing out his papers at the university. He and I had been investigating a report of cheating during the spring examinations, but I had thought that he had decided to leave the matter alone."

"Does this have anything to do with Ishikawa and Oe?" Kobe asked.

"Yes, indirectly. A very mediocre student was given first place, because Ishikawa, who is quite brilliant, wrote his essay, and Oe, one of the proctors, passed it to the candidate during the examination. Oe was subsequently paid, but Ishikawa got very little for his troubles. He sought to rectify the situation by blackmailing Oe. By accident the note was passed to Hirata instead."

Akitada had Kobe's full attention now. "Go on!"

"Hirata asked my help in discovering the blackmailer and his target. We were on the point of confronting Ishikawa and Oe when the murder happened. I have tried to reconstruct the sequence of events. No doubt Ishikawa continued to pressure Oe who, in turn, asked the candidate for more money to pay Ishikawa."

Kobe frowned. "He asked whom for more money?"

When Akitada told him, he protested, "His name has not come up once in this investigation."

"Because everybody looked for the suspect among Oe's colleagues. The killer had a better reason to wish Oe dead than anyone, and his personality fits the circumstances of the crime perfectly. Nishioka, who makes a study of such things, would agree. As for opportunity, he was at the contest and, if I am not mistaken, Oe recited a poem which contained a direct threat to this man. I think he left the park and followed Oe to the Temple of Confucius, perhaps to reason with him. When he saw Ishikawa come out alone, he went in and discovered a helpless Oe tied to the statue of the sage. The temptation to kill him was too great to resist."

Kobe pondered this. After a while he shook his head. "It's pure assumption. I have to have proof to make an arrest. By the way, that blackmail note Hirata got, where is it?"

"Probably lost in the fire."

Kobe threw up his hands.

"Ishikawa can confirm the examination fraud—if he is still alive. That reminds me." Akitada passed a hand over his face to wipe away perspiration. It came away streaked with soot from the Hirata ruin. "I asked at the Ninna temple. Ishikawa is not there."

"That was my good news! He's alive and we've got him. He was brought in yesterday from the Onjo temple southeast of the city. So far he hasn't said much, but believe me, we've got our killer. Do you want to talk to him?"

Akitada thought of the bamboo whips which were an inevitable concomitant of police interrogations and shuddered. But he nodded.

Kobe got up. "Come on then!"

They walked across the courtyard to the jail building. Kobe gave orders and invited Akitada to sit on the wooden floor of the staff room. A clerk took his place behind a desk, rubbed some ink and shuffled papers. Then the prisoner was brought in.

Two guards dragged his unwilling body between them. Akitada did not recognize the handsome and haughty graduate student in the miserable creature who was pushed down to his knees before them. Ishikawa wore a stained and torn monk's robe. His shaven head bore several bloody gashes, as did his bare feet and chained wrists, and his face was swollen and bruised almost past recognition. He cowered before them, shivering.

"Fought like a tiger," muttered Kobe in explanation to Akitada. Then he shouted to the prisoner, "Sit up!"

When Ishikawa did not react immediately, one of the guards kicked him in the ribs and shouted, "Pay attention, dogmeat!"

The student cried out and struggled upright. His right eye was swollen shut, and his nose had bled and stained the front of his robe. But his good eye recognized Akitada. He straightened his shoulders a little and bowed.

"Well, are you ready to talk now?" demanded Kobe in a threatening voice.

"Sir," muttered the prisoner, his good eye fixed on Akitada, "please tell them who I am and that I have done nothing."

"What are you doing in monk's garb?" asked Akitada.

"I was hiding because I was afraid."

"Hah!" cried Kobe. "Then you admit you killed the professor!"

"No! I did not kill him." Ishikawa's voice rose. "I swear I did not do it. I only tied him up. Why would I kill him? He paid me to read his papers, and he would have recommended me for a good position once I passed the examination." He looked at Akitada again. "Please tell him, sir!"

Akitada leaned forward, looking at the student intently. "Do you admit that you tied Oe to the statue of the sage?"

"Oh, yes." Ishikawa's lips twitched at the memory. "He was so drunk he kept falling down, so I arranged for some appropriate support."

"That was surprisingly kind of you," said Akitada, raising his brows, "when you had just had a violent altercation with him. You remember meeting him behind the pavilion at the contest? What was that all about?"

Ishikawa opened his eyes wide. "I have no idea what you are talking about."

"Come, come! I saw you with my own eyes. You assaulted Oe."

A sullen expression settled on Ishikawa's bloodied face. "It was nothing! He was drunk and babbled nonsense."

Kobe suddenly leaned forward and shouted, "You lie, you piece of dung! He threatened you and you struck him."

Immediately the guard belabored Ishikawa's head and shoulders with the butt of his whip. Ishikawa fell forward screaming.

Akitada winced, and Kobe gestured to the constable to stop. The man withdrew a little, but Ishikawa remained prone.

Giving Kobe a hard look, Akitada said to the student, "Sit up and answer the questions truthfully and you won't be beaten. This is a murder case. An intelligent fellow like you should be able to grasp that cooperation is a good idea."

Ishikawa struggled up. "All right," he muttered. "Can I have something to drink?"

When Akitada turned to ask for water, Ishikawa shot him a hopeful glance. He drank greedily from the wooden ladle a guard had dipped into a bucket of water. Wiping his mouth, he said, "The bastard had cheated me and I told him so. It was like this: Oe got this idea to make some money on the side by letting this wealthy fellow place first in the examination. Knowing that I didn't even have enough for a hot meal and was cleaning the kitchens and dormitories for a few coppers a day, he asked me to withdraw my name as candidate but write the paper on the examination topic and pass it to him. He offered me a large sum of gold and promised me first place and a fine position the following year. Well, my placing first was a foregone conclusion and I didn't want to hang around another year, so I refused. That's when the bastard started threatening. He'd see to it that I didn't get first place, that there was another candidate equally qualified, and that he would not recommend me even if I did place first. Well, I cooperated, but he never paid me the promised gold. Sure, he let me read his students' papers for a few coppers and kept telling me he'd not been paid himself. But I found out differently. He was building a villa for his retirement on the money that should've been mine and he was selling his position." He spat, his one good eye flashing with anger.

Akitada wished he could find some satisfaction in having his theories confirmed, but Hirata's death and the sordidness of the whole affair overwhelmed him. Ishikawa, on the other hand, seemed to have regained his old cockiness.

He met Akitada's eyes and grinned lopsidedly. "Since you had to put your nose into it, Professor, at the poetry match I was reminding Oe of what I was owed, that's all."

Anger caused Akitada to speak coldly. "Hardly all. You made a pretty good thing out of betting on Oe's candidate and won five hundred pieces of silver, I hear. How did Oe feel about that?"

Kobe grunted with surprise, and Ishikawa stared in shock at Akitada. "Whose side are you on?" he asked, glowering.

"Explain your involvement in the illegal gambling operation!" growled Kobe. "Or I'll have you beaten again."

Ishikawa cursed both of them. He shouted, "You're all alike! You'll pin the murder on a poor student who can't help himself and protect the real killer because he's one of the 'good' people!

Yes, I had a fight with Oe. He cheated me! Yes, I pushed the fat bastard and, yes, I tied his sorry figure to the mealy-mouthed saint of all you hypocritical bastards! But I did not kill him! A lot of people hated Oe, but you pick on me because I don't have anybody to speak up for me. Damn Oe! Damn all of you for that matter!" He broke off with a sob and collapsed.

The guard raised his whip and looked at Kobe for orders.

"No!" Turning to Ishikawa, Akitada said, "I believe you, but I shall see to it that you are expelled from the university. Your character is despicable."

The student spat. "I shall not forget your kindness, sir," he said with a sneer.

Kobe sighed. "We're not getting anywhere." He nodded to the guards. "Take him away and clean him up. Then lock him in one of the cells and watch him!"

When they walked back, Akitada asked Kobe, "Surely you don't still believe him guilty?"

"It does not matter what I believe," said Kobe. "There is no proof for your theory, and plenty of proof of Ishikawa's guilt."

Akitada felt very tired. He muttered, "You cannot beat a confession out of an innocent man. He might confess simply because he cannot bear the pain any longer and would rather die. I would not want that on my conscience."

"Curse you and your damned conscience!" exploded Kobe. "You tell me how to get new evidence then! You don't want it to be Ishikawa, but you can't give me any proof to make another arrest! I wish you would stay out of my business from now on!"

Some of the constables in the courtyard stopped to stare at them.

Akitada thought of the dead Hirata. "Forgive me, Captain, if I have been a nuisance," he said quite humbly. "There is only one thing I must ask for. Hirata's death weighs on my mind. I would be deeply grateful if you could talk to the firemen who put out the blaze that killed him. One of them told me it started on the veranda. If Hirata was asleep in his study, he could not have started the fire himself and he never troubles his servant after dark. I would not ask this, if I did not feel it was important to the case."

Kobe was so startled by Akitada's uncharacteristic humility that he looked hard at him for a moment. Then he relented. "Very well, I'll look into it."

TWENTY-ONE

THE WISTERIA BRANCH

*I*t was already dusk when Akitada walked away from police headquarters, still blaming himself for Hirata's death. He had distanced himself from his old friend, from the blackmail, and from Oe's death at least partially out of pique and injured pride. He had left all the questioning to Kobe and Nishioka, while he had plunged into the investigation of the Yoakira case, telling himself that the boy was in danger. Throughout he had behaved like a self-righteous fool!

The fact that he had solved the murder of the prince to his own satisfaction had not made any difference to the child's safety—at least not yet, and perhaps it never would. However, he had promised to see Sesshin. He turned towards the university, stopping first by his own office to gather the documents Seimei had copied.

Sesshin was at his devotions when Akitada arrived, but a young acolyte showed him into the bishop's study and brought him some fruit juice. Akitada waited, trying to gather his wits. Sesshin, for all his august descent and high position in the Buddhist hierarchy, was someone with surprising sensitivity for the feelings of others. This fact gave Akitada something to hope for, but having grossly misjudged the man, he had been guilty of the most shocking behavior towards him, and now he worried about this, wondering how to make amends. He finally came to the decision that nothing was to be gained by abject apologies. He would continue to speak frankly and hope for the best.

Sesshin appeared in due time, apologized for having been delayed, and accepted some juice from his young assistant. "Well," he said, when they were alone again, "what news do you bring?"

"Your Reverence will think that I have taken unpardonable liberties in meddling in your family affairs," Akitada murmured nervously.

Sesshin smiled a little. "Well, you struck me as the sort of person who pays little attention to soothsayers, omens or various taboos," he said dryly. "Under the circumstances it would be too much to assume that you would believe in a miracle."

Akitada looked down at his hands. The angry red patches where the skin had peeled off reminded him of the fatal consequences of procrastination. He sighed. "Perhaps I formed an opinion, and when your great-nephew approached me, his suspicions of Lord Sakanoue fit in with my own views. Perhaps I felt sorry for him and his young sister." He looked up at Sesshin. "It does not matter how I came to believe that your brother was murdered by Lord Sakanoue, only that I have succeeded in proving it." He cast an anxious glance at Sesshin, but the bishop's face remained calmly interested.

"Please explain."

"If I may, I shall tell you about the steps I have taken so far." The bishop nodded.

"From the beginning, I had to contend with the problem of Lord Sakanoue's dramatic rise in rank and influence. That meant I had to work as secretly as possible. I could not find many people who would take the boy's part. Even now I am not in a position to proceed against a man of such stature, and neither is Sadamu because of his age. To begin with, I had my secretary search the government archives for documents that would throw some light on a motive." Akitada passed the bundle of papers to Sesshin. "I believe these will reveal certain improprieties in Sakanoue's management of your brother's estates both before and after his death."

Sesshin took the papers and set them aside. "Never mind that now. Go on!"

Akitada plunged into the heart of his report. "I next visited your brother's mansion and talked with his driver. Then I interviewed the Lords Yanagida, Abe and Shinoda. General Soga unfortunately was not available, but his evidence can be gathered later. Finally, my servant and I visited the Ninna temple and spoke with the recorder there. Each conversation was separately suggestive, but all of them together confirmed my conviction that Sakanoue had plotted your brother's disappearance. Yet without a body I still had no proof of murder. I finally found the proof in the hall where your brother was said to have disappeared."

Sesshin sighed. "I know what you found. After your visit to him, Shinoda came to me and told me what he and Sakanoue had done. I cannot speak for Sakanoue, but Shinoda wanted to protect my brother's memory."

Akitada nodded. "To continue with the motive and execution of the murder, I believe that Lord Sakanoue is an excessively proud and ambitious man who was dissatisfied with his hereditary position as bailiff. Shortly before the murder, Prince Yoakira called him to the capital for an accounting. Whether or not Sakanoue could defend himself against the charges, his relationship with the prince became very strained. It was during this time that he must have met the prince's young granddaughter, and seen in a marriage to her his chance to secure his position and win a fortune."

Sesshin muttered, "Poor child! I blame my brother's household for permitting him access to the girl."

"Apparently the prince discovered what had happened too late, and on the very day before his customary temple visit. He was furious and confronted Sakanoue immediately. He then gave orders for the removal of the family to the country the following day. Had he not insisted on performing the customary visit to the Ninna temple first, he would be alive today."

Sesshin sighed. "That was like my brother. He never forgot to fulfill his vow."

"Yes. No doubt Sakanoue was aware of it. In any case, here is what I believe happened next." Akitada detailed the events of the night journey and the movements of Sakanoue as he had done for Tora. Sesshin listened with increasing horror, interrupting only twice.

On the first occasion he said, "If the quarrel between my brother and Sakanoue took place before the trip to the temple, my brother would hardly have invited the man to accompany him."

"Exactly. It was one of the first things that puzzled me."

Sesshin's second question concerned a possible accomplice.

Akitada said, "If there had been political reasons for removing your brother, I would have considered a conspiracy, but in this instance there was no motive other than personal gain. In a crime of that magnitude, considering the rank of the people involved, the rewards and the extraordinary method used, even a single accomplice would have been too risky. Sakanoue acted alone."

When Akitada had finished, Sesshin bowed his head. His beads passed through his fingers, making small clicking sounds in the still room. After a long time, he looked up and asked, "Why bring the head? Why did the foolish man have to dismember my brother's body? Was it not enough to kill him?"

"I am afraid not. He needed proof of death to gain immediate access to the estate. Also, he may have counted on the fact that His Majesty would bestow appointments on him out of respect for your brother."

A silence fell. Then Sesshin sighed. "Poor confused man! What he must have suffered to take such incredible risks. How he must have hungered for the empty things of this world! How desperate he must have been when my brother confronted him!"

Akitada said angrily, "Don't waste your sympathy, Your Reverence! This murder was planned carefully. Sakanoue had to have made the arrangements for the sutra reading during your brother's visit well ahead of time."

Sesshin seemed to shrink into himself. "Anger is a futile

emotion. Besides my vows forbid the sort of action that should be taken by the law," he said. "I must think what to do." He paused again, then asked, "What has become of the rest of my brother's body?"

Akitada had expected and feared this question. "I do not know, but I can suggest a possibility. Sakanoue apparently insisted on taking the last cart into the country himself. It contained several clothes chests from your brother's rooms and left long after nightfall, hours after the rest of the goods. I suspect that Sakanoue made a brief stop at Rashomon."

"Rashomon?" For the first time, Sesshin looked truly shocked. "You think my brother's body was put amongst the cadavers of the wretched to be burnt and his bones tossed into a mass grave?"

Akitada said quickly, "It is equally possible that Sakanoue stopped somewhere along the road and buried the body."

Sesshin stared past Akitada into the distance. Then he said, "It seems I must break my vows long enough to secure the future of my brother's family. Thank you for your frankness. You may leave matters in my hands now. I have already made arrangements for my great-niece to go to her cousin, who is the priestess of the Ise shrine. No men are allowed in those sacred precincts, and she will be safe there. I would be very grateful if Sadamu could remain with your family for a while longer. I hope this is not a serious imposition?"

Akitada smiled. "Of course not. We have all become very fond of the boy. Even . . ."—He was going to say "my mother," but caught himself in time—"my servant Tora."

The look of pain on Sesshin's faced eased a little. "In that case, perhaps you would allow me to call on Sadamu at your house? I must begin to make amends for my neglect."

Akitada expressed himself honored and took his departure.

Outside he turned towards the main gate and home. It was almost dark, the same hot, dry darkness of the past week. Fireflies sparked on and off in the black foliage like disembodied spirits. Just as Akitada passed the Temple of Confucius, he was hailed by a familiar voice.

"Sugawara? Is that you?" Nishioka's gown flapped about his

bony frame as he ran out of the gate. "How lucky that you were passing just as I decided to get a breath of air, though fresh it certainly is not. Something very strange has happened."

Akitada was tired and burdened with his own troubles. He looked at Nishioka's lantern-jawed face with weary distaste. "Can't it wait? I have urgent business at home."

Nishioka's long face fell. "Oh, yes. I forgot! Poor Hirata. They say you have taken in his daughter. What a great loss! The students are taking it badly, too. How is his daughter?"

"As you might expect. What is your problem?"

"I don't want to trouble you, but you might have some advice. It concerns our rats."

"Your rats?" Akitada wondered if Nishioka had gone mad.

"Perhaps it would be better if you would just come and see for yourself. It will only take a moment. I am quite distracted." He ran an agitated hand through his hair and dislodged his topknot, which slipped over his right ear.

"Very well, but I cannot stay."

Sighing inwardly, Akitada followed the man to his study. The room was in the same state of disorder as the last time Akitada had been there. Near a set of shelves holding sagging and toppling stacks of papers, assorted wine cups, empty oil lamps and unmatched rice bowls, Nishioka paused and pointed to the floor.

There, among remnants of roasted walnuts spilled from their box, lay the corpses of three rats.

Akitada moved the animals with his foot. They were quite stiff, their teeth bared in futile snarls. Poisoned! "I thought you had no walnuts left. Did you buy more?"

"That's just it. I've had no time. Anyway, those are not my walnuts."

"No? It looks like the same box."

"Oh, it's my box all right. But they are not my walnuts. I told you about the old woman who makes mine? Well, hers are almost black and shiny. These are ordinary brown ones."

Akitada eyed Nishioka thoughtfully. "When did you discover this?"

"Just a little while ago. I haven't been in my study since yesterday, because Professor Tanabe and I have been working in the library."

"Have you been discussing any more of your suspicions with people?"

Nishioka paled. "You think someone wants to kill me. But who? I thought Ishikawa was in jail." Nishioka began to look terrified.

Akitada said, "I think you should report the matter immediately to Kobe, along with all your suspicions. Then go home and keep your doors locked."

Nishioka's long jaw dropped.

Akitada left Nishioka staring at the rats with an expression of terror on his face and walked home through the dark night, devising a plan to stop the killer from making another attempt on anyone's life.

Genba opened the gate again. "All's been quiet, sir. The little lord and Tora have been catching fireflies with the young ladies in the garden."

"Thank you. I want you and Hitomaro in my study in a little while. I shall have two letters for you to deliver."

At his desk, he pulled his writing materials closer and began to rub the ink. The correct wording was crucial in the case of the first letter. The second letter also presented problems. He had to be convincing enough to make certain of cooperation, and spell out the details of the plan carefully so that no mistakes were possible. What he was about to do could easily cost his life. This fact did not trouble him particularly—he had little to lose—but he would regret leaving a killer, or perhaps two, at large.

Eventually, he completed both letters to his satisfaction, addressed and sealed them, and sent for Hitomaro and Genba. They arrived promptly, received a letter each along with detailed instructions and trotted off.

Only then did Akitada take off his formal clothes and order a bath prepared. He scrubbed himself as well as he could before slipping into the steaming tub. The hot water eased his aching muscles and gritty skin, but was too painful to his hands, and he rested them on the rim of the tub. A long soaking, accompanied by another careful analysis of his plan for flaws, left him calmer and more resolved than he had felt for days. He returned to his room, wrapped in a loose cotton gown, and found Seimei waiting with a tray of steaming food. He ate hungrily, his mind surprisingly alert.

Genba and Hitomaro returned within moments of each other. Each brought a short answer. Akitada read and nodded. He told the two men, "The danger here is past, so you may go to sleep tonight. Tomorrow I shall have another assignment for you."

They bowed, murmuring their thanks.

Left alone, Akitada unrolled his bedding and lay down. In the darkness he considered again the danger he might face the next day. His family affairs were in reasonable order, his mother was a strong woman who could look after his sisters' future, and Sesshin was going to look after the boy. That left only Tamako. Thinking about her set him to brooding again. All the past uncertainties and failures of his life passed through his mind to culminate in his loss of Tamako and his responsibility for her ruined future. He needed sleep, for tomorrow he would have to be at his best, but the thoughts chased each other in his head like a dog snapping at its own tail.

Suddenly there was a soft scratching at the door.

"Who is there?" he called irritably.

The door slid open, and his younger sister's face, illumined by the candle she carried, peered in. "It's only me. Am I disturbing you?" she asked anxiously.

Akitada smiled at her. "No. Of course not. Come in, Yoshiko!" How pretty she was getting! He had spent too little time with his sisters lately.

She slipped in, in her night clothes, and sat down decorously next to his bedding. "I came to report on our guests, but I see you were going to sleep."

"Never mind! I was still awake, and it was very kind of you. Please go ahead!"

"The young lord is very nice and polite for his age. Our mother has provided him with books, games and musical instruments. He spends much time with Tora, but Akiko and I have paid him visits and played some games with him. We also performed on the zither for him. He made very flattering speeches to us."

"I am gratified to hear that my family is so conscientious in entertaining a guest," Akitada said, suppressing a smile.

"Our other guest is also very pleasant, but sad."

Akitada's smile vanished. "That is natural under the circumstances. Tamako has lost her father and her home. Besides it cannot be a very happy prospect to become a nun at her age." He added in a tone of finality, "And now, if you are finished, I had better try to get some sleep. I have a full day tomorrow."

But his sister did not budge. "It is my belief," she said stubbornly, "that Tamako does not wish to become a nun at all."

"Neither you nor I can interfere in the matter," Akitada said curtly, "and I forbid you to speak to her about it."

"Why don't *you* speak to her? We are all so very fond of her, and even Mother hoped you two would marry. Tamako has been massaging Mother's neck when she gets those headaches and steaming herbs for her to inhale. Now Mother thinks Tamako can cure anything. If you could just bring yourself to tell her how you feel, I know she would change her mind."

"Enough!" thundered Akitada. "This is none of your business!"

Frightened by his fury, his sister jumped up and retreated to the door. There she stopped, tears welling over, and cried in a trembling voice, "I don't care if you hate me, but it seems to me that you should stop telling her that you think of her as your sister. It would confuse any girl who was hoping to marry you." She gulped and slipped out.

Akitada's anger turned to blank astonishment. Then he started to laugh. It was probably just some female foolishness. Surely Tamako would not have rejected his offer for such a childish reason, but . . . Suddenly resolute, he rose. He had to make certain.

The gallery and courtyard between his room and the women's quarters were dark and silent. He was glad he had sent Hitomaro and Genba to bed. Walking softly on bare feet to Tamako's room, he seated himself on the veranda outside her door and cleared his throat. At first there was no response. He repeated the sound, somewhat louder this time.

From inside the closed shutters came the rustling of bed-clothes. "Who is there?" a soft voice asked.

"Akitada."

Another rustling and Tamako slid open the door. "Akitada! What is it?"

Akitada looked at her in the dim light. Her long, thick hair was loose and streamed over the thin white silk of her under-robe. She looked anxious. With her face slightly flushed from sleep, she was very beautiful. He was overcome with longing, and realized that he had no idea how to broach the matter of a possible misunder-standing.

"I wanted to see you," he said lamely.

"Oh! I thought . . . what about?"

He frantically searched his mind. This surely was not the time to discuss his suspicions about her father's death. Neither could he tell her about his sister's visit. "To apologize," he finally muttered, "for this morning. I was rude. I should not have spoken to you that way."

She smiled a little sadly. "No need to apologize. I know you were upset out of concern for me. It is quite natural and I thank you for caring."

Akitada shifted uncomfortably. "I . . . I cared for myself more, I think. The thought of . . ." He took a deep breath and plunged. "It has occurred to me that you might think that I wished to marry you because we have always been very close; that is, like brother and sister, and because I owed your father a debt of grati-tude. But that was not it at all."

Her eyes were very bright in the moonlight. "No?"

Akitada gave a her a beseeching look. "You must understand that our relationship in the past has tended to obscure my true feelings." He stopped, flushing with embarrassment at his stilted language. "What I mean is that I never realized until I saw you again how much I really loved and needed you."

She gave a soft sigh. "I did not know," she whispered. Suddenly she extended her hand. "Let me see your hands, please!"

He hesitated, then held them out, palm down. She turned them over gently and peered at the scarred skin. "Oh," she sighed. "I did not know it was so very bad." Her eyes sought his. "Seimei came to me for herbs. I see they are healing. Do they still pain you very much?"

He hid his hands in his sleeves, and shook his head. Her concern had filled him with hope. "You will change your mind then? We will be married after all?"

"I don't know," she faltered. "I am so confused."

"Ah! Yoshiko was right then! It was all a silly mistake. She said that you were confused because I had been treating you like a sister. Was that it? Was that the reason you rejected my offer?"

"Yoshiko told you this?" Tamako cried, moving even farther away from him. "Oh, how embarrassing!" She hid her face in her hands.

Akitada saw her withdrawal and began to feel foolish. He had hoped in vain and now he had made her uncomfortable when she had told him plainly that she did not wish the subject to be mentioned again. He sighed.

Tamako lowered her hands. "That was not the only reason," she said softly. "Father told me that he had proposed the match to you and that you seemed surprised, but had agreed to think about it. Oh, Akitada! I could only think how Father had taken advantage of your good nature to force you into an unwanted marriage. Of course I could not agree to that. I was angry with him for a long time, but in the end I saw that he acted out of love for me. Father was not well and wanted to see me settled before his death."

"Oh!" said Akitada. "But . . ." He stopped, for he remembered how bitterly he had resented Hirata's manipulation. How to explain that he had come to want her and love her for her own sake?

At his hesitation, Tamako withdrew a little further into herself. "And now," she said in a brittle voice, "you offer again, but this time out of pity and obligation or whatever foolish notion you may have. I simply cannot accept such a sacrifice."

"Sacrifice?" he cried. "What sacrifice, when I have spent the past weeks agonizing over losing you? When I have worried about your reason for rejecting me until I could not concentrate on my work or on the murders! I thought of my poverty and of my mother's difficult temperament, of my plain face and my dull conversation, my lack of poetic talent and my undistinguished career, and, driven to the point of insanity, even of another man."

"Oh!" Tamako gasped and hid her face again.

Ashamed, he prepared to leave, saying in a choking voice, "Forgive this rude visit, please! It is late and I have disturbed your sleep."

She took her hands from her face and touched his arm. "Please, don't go!" she murmured. He saw that her cheeks were wet with tears, but in her eyes shone a deep happiness.

For a moment he was confused. Then the confusion changed to amazement and joy. He was up in an instant with an incoherent cry of endearment. Sweeping her into his arms, he carried her inside.

◆

The sun was just rising over the gabled roofs of his home when Akitada stepped down into the main courtyard. Tora was at the well, drinking water from the ladle and then sluicing off his head and arms.

"Tora," Akitada called.

"Just coming, sir. It's still early," Tora cried cheerfully, drying himself with the skirt of his cotton gown.

"I know. I want you to take this to Miss Hirata," Akitada said, extending a branch of flowering wisteria with a twist of paper attached to it.

Tora received this with a look of consternation. "Wisteria? And in bloom. Where did you find that? We don't have any."

"I walked to the Hirata garden this morning. The vine survived the fire and I found this single late blossom."

Slowly understanding dawned in Tora's eyes. "Well done, sir!" he cried. "My heartiest congratulations to both of you."

"Thank you," Akitada said stiffly, and turned to go back to his room.

There he waited anxiously for her reply. His experience with composing next-morning poems was minimal, and his skill at composition fragmentary at best, but he had left her, fast asleep in the darkness, knowing what he wished to say. All the way to her garden and back he had rehearsed the words in his head:

> Little did I think,
> Under the blooming wisteria vine,
> That its fragrance would so deeply
> Move my soul.

Tora returned quickly, still grinning broadly. He extended the wisteria branch, now without its bloom, but with a bit of paper, tinted a delicate shade of purple, tied into a bow around it.

"Thank you. You may go," Akitada said, already eagerly undoing the paper as Tora walked out the door whistling a popular love song.

She had written:

> Wisteria blossoms fade,
> Their season all too short,
> But their fragrance lingers
> In my soul forever.

He read her words several times, then tucked the slip of paper carefully inside his gown where it rested against his bare skin. A moment later Seimei stuck his head in. He entered smiling, carrying a tray.

"I have brought your morning rice," he said. "It is a great day for the house of Sugawara, sir."

Akitada felt himself flush. "Er, thank you, Seimei. I see you have spoken to Tora." He drank his tea thirstily. "I think we shall plant some wisteria in the garden," he remarked, turning to the boiled rice and pickled radish. "Remind Tora to see to it."

TWENTY-TWO

STORM WARNING

𝒯he following day passed with dreary slowness. Akitada chafed under his teaching duties, his mind distracted by thoughts of Tamako and the extraordinary way in which another human being had suddenly become his, closer than any sister ever could be, or any parent, and more necessary to him, in a way, than food, water or air. His skin warmed at the thought of holding her in his arms again.

However, he owed it to her and to her dead father to catch his murderer, and he was determined to do so this very night, before returning home. The risk, he hoped, would be negligible. He had guarded against surprises. Now that he had new responsibilities, he could not afford to play the hero.

These thoughts preoccupied him, causing him to forget to set the students a topic for their next lesson, and made him stare blankly at Ushimatsu when he asked permission to go to the latrine. Even after the students finally left, he sat looking dreamily into space.

"Sugawara? May I come in?"

Akitada blinked and saw to his astonishment the burly music master in his doorway. "Yes, of course, Sato."

"I took a chance." Sato bowed briefly and cast a glance at the papers scattered over Akitada's desk. "Am I interrupting?"

"Not at all. Please sit down. A cup of wine?"

In the slanting light of the setting sun, Sato's large eyes looked like black pools under his heavy brow. He seemed ill at ease. "I won't stay long. No, no wine, thank you. I came to see you on a personal matter." He sat.

Akitada asked, "What is it?"

"It's about Oe's murder. That police captain stopped by this afternoon to ask more questions. He sounded . . . I don't know . . . it seemed like a veiled threat. He said the case was about to be solved and that you were assisting the police. Is that true?"

Akitada felt a flash of irritation with Kobe. He had expected more discretion from the man. He said, "Kobe may have exaggerated. It is true that I have shared some of my conclusions."

Now Sato looked distinctly frightened. "I knew it. You told him about me, and now he thinks I did it! Please, you must believe me when I say that I had nothing to do with Oe's death."

Akitada raised his eyebrows. "What makes you think I suspect you?"

"Don't pretend!" cried Sato. "You saw me with Omaki, and I could tell what you thought of me. Then, as my lousy luck would have it, you walked in when my wife was visiting. When I could not explain the situation, you assumed I was entertaining another female, and that Oe was about to dismiss me with good cause. I'm the one with the perfect motive. Believe me, I often fantasized about killing the bastard, but I did not do it."

"That talented lady was your wife? In the Willow Quarter, I am told, she goes by the name Madame Sakaki."

Sato bit his lip. "Her professional name. She could hardly work there under my name."

"I see the problem. But surely you put your wife into an impossible situation? She is a true artist. Could she not have found a more respectable setting for her performances?"

A look of acute misery passed over Sato's face. "I know she deserves much better, but we are poor and have six small children and two sets of parents to support. My salary here does not begin to feed all those mouths. And I am afraid we are not in the class of those who are invited to the parties of the great."

Embarrassed by the naked shame in the other man's face, Akitada looked out at the deserted courtyard. The heat shimmered on the gravel, and there was a strange sulphurous hue to the green of the trees. A hot wind was rustling through the dry weeds outside the veranda. "I think," he said, turning back to Sato, "you should tell your story to the president of the university. I have found Bishop Sesshin a very understanding man, and he may be able to help your wife. He has many friends among the great.

"I wish I could be more reassuring about Kobe. Though I did not discuss your situation with him, he has other sources, and I am afraid he knows that Oe was not the kind of man who would have accepted your wife's occupation calmly."

Sato looked down at his clenched hands. "That was the main reason for all the subterfuge. But the more we tried to cover up, the more gossip we created. Because I went to the Willow Quarter regularly to watch over my wife, I soon had a reputation of being a drunkard and womanizer. I got Omaki as a student on one of my visits. My wife was against the private lessons, but we needed the money. Oh, that pompous devil Oe would not begin to know what it is to have a family and be poor." He gave Akitada a beseeching look. "But you, Sugawara, you have a mother and sisters to support, I'm told. You must know that I would never do anything so desperate as kill a man. If I were caught, my family would starve to death. Please speak to Kobe for me, will you?"

They looked at each other. Akitada tried to reassure the man. "I know exactly what you mean and I believe you. Do not worry about Kobe! Go home to your wife and children, and tomorrow speak to Sesshin."

Tears of gratitude welled up in Sato's eyes. Too overcome to speak, he bowed very deeply and left. His footsteps receded quickly, and silence fell over the courtyard again.

Akitada sat, thinking of the devotion of those two people to each other and their family. He had himself only just come to understand fully the sacrifice a man made to the one he loved. He, too, would gladly accept any hardship and humiliation to secure Tamako's happiness.

It was then that the sound of distant thunder startled him. He rose to walk outside. The sun, bright as molten gold, was disappearing over the tiled rooftops of the student dormitories, but the sky northward and to the east was filling rapidly with heavy, roiling black clouds. A storm was moving in, and the long heat wave was finally about to break. Akitada thought worriedly that the weather might keep his visitor away.

Thunder growled again. Sighing, Akitada returned to his classroom to pass the time till darkness fell by grading his student papers.

He had to light his oil lamp early. It spread a yellow glow over his papers, but left the corners of the room in murky shadows. There was, from time to time, a far-off rumble of thunder, but the storm seemed to hold off.

He was not sure how long he had been working when he heard the sound of footsteps crunching on the gravel of the courtyard. When he glanced outside, there was still some faint light in the east. Surely it was too early! And Kobe had not arrived.

Feeling a sudden twinge of nervousness, he forced himself to remain calm by breathing deeply and concentrating on the coming encounter. The steps ascended the wooden stairs, approached to within a few feet of the open door, and then halted outside in the murky gloom.

"Please come in!" Akitada called out.

To his stunned surprise, the tall figure of Ishikawa stepped through his doorway. The student looked positively frightening in the uncertain light and against the backdrop of dark purple clouds. His face was still dreadfully disfigured by swellings and bruises. Both his scalp and his face were covered with stubbly growth that, together with his stained and torn robe, made him look like a cutthroat. Moreover, his sneering expression and distinctly threatening manner signalled that this visit was more than just ill-timed.

"Working late all by yourself?" the student scoffed, looking about with a mocking grin. "What an admirable devotion to duty!"

Akitada rinsed out his brush and laid it on its rest. "How did you get out of jail and what do you want?" he asked curtly.

Uninvited Ishikawa sat down on the other cushion in the room. "Not very hospitable, are you? I had the same problem in our municipal jail. That's why I decided to leave. That and some unfinished business here." He gave Akitada a very unpleasant smile. "You might as well relax! I mean to take my time."

Akitada's first thought was about Kobe. Did he know the student had escaped? Was he even now out searching the town for him? For a moment he debated whether it would be possible to get rid of Ishikawa, but a glance at the other's face convinced him otherwise. He snapped, "Please be brief! I expect another visitor."

Ishikawa glanced out the door. "I doubt it. A bad storm is coming. The whole place is deserted." He gave Akitada another of his menacing smiles. "Anything can happen here without a soul being the wiser. Besides, your plans mean nothing to me. People like you are always demanding respect from others, but are nothing but shams themselves. Every day you and the other teachers urge poor fools like me to study hard, but when we have done our utmost and excel, you give the prize to the highest bidder." The wind rustled in the dry shrubs outside, and Ishikawa paused to listen intently. Branches were scraping against the supports of the veranda as lighting zigzagged against the darkening sky. The flame of the oil lamp flickered, causing Ishikawa's eyes to glitter strangely. "I am referring, of course," he continued, "to that rich simpleton Okura who bought first place honors in the last examination. *He* is a secretary in the Bureau of Ranks now and has prospects of even higher office, while I am headed back to the gutter I came from. A prime example that money will buy anything, while a poor man cannot succeed in spite of his efforts and superior intelligence."

Akitada looked at the student coldly. "If you are trying to justify yourself, it appears to me that you have demonstrated exceptionally foolish and unethical behavior throughout this affair. Get to the point!"

"The point?" Ishikawa's eyes narrowed to mere slits. "The point is that people like you and the other professors detest students like me! I was someone who wouldn't keep quiet. Oh, yes. I know all about you. Kobe let it slip out that he arrested me on your word. Tell me, have you ever been in jail?"

Akitada shook his head. No point in telling this young hothead that there were other ways in which a man might learn about such places.

"Of course not! Well, let me inform you, Sugawara, that the so-called keepers of the peace are low animals. They are ex-criminals who do their dirty work for a daily bowl of rice and what they can extort from the prisoners. They take a sadistic pleasure in inflicting pain."

"You have only yourself to thank. You are an admitted blackmailer."

Ishikawa flared up, "Oe owed me."

"You also prostituted your education by helping Okura cheat."

"So that's it!" Ishikawa smiled unpleasantly. Outside thunder cracked and rumbled away. When all was quiet again, he sneered, "And that, of course, is the unforgivable sin to you! You make me sick! I've heard all about you from Hirata. The university's perfect graduate, the exceptional student, the promising young official with his foot on the bottom rung of the ladder to greatness!" The student leaned forward, fixing Akitada with his angry eyes. "Let me tell you something: that numskull Okura, who cannot compose so much as a sentence in Chinese without making a gross error and who has neither understanding nor intellectual curiosity, has already surpassed you and will continue to do so by many ranks and degrees. In this world neither excellence nor honesty have any value. Money and influence rule everything. And when I discovered that fact, I attempted to rectify an unfair situation by trading a bit of my intelligence for his money. I consider that an act of justice in an unjust world." He resumed his position with an air of satisfaction.

Akitada did not respond immediately, watching instead the

threatening skies. The wind was picking up, he noted. In a flash of lightning, he saw that small whirlwinds of debris danced about the courtyard and the treetops tossed their branches. The breeze blew in, almost extinguishing the lamp, and cooled briefly the sweat-soaked back of his robe. "Your act of 'justice'," he said finally, "caused one of your fellow students to take his life. Another poor young man, I believe."

Ishikawa's face contorted. He jumped up. "How dare you blame me for that!" he screamed. He advanced a few steps, his fists clenched at his side. "I had nothing to do with it, do you hear? He would have lost one way or another! If Okura had not won, *I* would have." Leaning over Akitada, he shook a clenched fist in his face. "I won't take any more of your sanctimonious drivel, you damned hypocrite! You ruined me! I was the best student these old fogies have had for years. I could not fail! " His voice rose shrilly. "I could not fail until you showed up! Now your damned meddling and your cursed righteousness have cost me the place I had earned with my brains and years of drudgery."

Akitada met the angry eyes without flinching and without response. After a moment Ishikawa dropped his fist and looked away. Returning to his seat, he said tiredly, "For four years I have sat in my classes all morning, cleaned up after the rich boys in the afternoons and evenings and studied during the night. All for nothing! And what have *you* gained by ruining me? You have preserved a corrupt system which will continue to grind good people into the dust, while putting power to rule into the hands of the incompetent."

Akitada snapped, "I disagree. A system is corrupted by its members. With the exception of you and Oe, I have found the rest of the faculty and students to be decent and hardworking people. It was precisely because of your dishonest activities that my friend Hirata asked me to investigate."

Ishikawa threw back his head and laughed. "You're a fool! There isn't one of your colleagues who wouldn't gladly have taken what Oe did. And it was one of those 'decent' fellows who killed him—a cowardly crime, for the drunken sot was dangling helplessly from Master Kung's neck when his throat was cut."

"And you made that possible," Akitada pointed out grimly.

Ishikawa sneered, "Oh, yes! I had my little revenge. When the swine fell flat on his face on the road outside, I helped him into the temple hall. That's when I got the idea. I leaned him up against old Kung, untied his sash and passed it under his arms and around the statue. His trousers fell down, adding an unexpected touch to the tableau. He was babbling and snoring through the whole thing. I took away the trousers, thinking to myself that it was high time that the rest of the august institution saw their great scholar in a new light."

"You left him to die!"

Ishikawa jumped up again. "Enough!" he said through clenched jaws. "My career may be over, but you shall not enjoy your little triumph either!" Lunging for Akitada's throat, he seized his collar with one hand and pulled back his fist.

Akitada flung himself backward, grasping Ishikawa's wrist. The tall student overbalanced and went sprawling across him. For a moment they struggled together on the floor, then Akitada rolled out from underneath, twisted one of Ishikawa's arms behind his back, and knelt on him.

The room was suddenly filled with people.

"Good work!" growled Kobe. His two constables flung themselves on Ishikawa.

"Thank you," said Akitada, rising to his feet. "This visit was somewhat unexpected and I did not know whether you had had time to arrive yet." It occurred to him belatedly that perhaps he had taken too great a chance in relying so completely on Kobe.

Kobe eyed the captive Ishikawa. "Put the chains on him a bit more tightly this time," he told the constables. "This one takes advantage of good treatment." To Akitada he said, "Well, your trap caught the sly fox! And now we got him on new charges. We heard what he told you. It's as close to a confession as I had hoped. Add the jailbreak and trying to murder you and he's as good as condemned."

Ishikawa made some gurgling protest as one of the constables knelt on him and the other tightened the thin chains around his wrists and neck.

"There was no attempted murder!" cried Akitada, shocked. "He brought no weapon and had nothing more in mind than giving me a good drubbing. As it turned out, I was easily able to defend myself. And he only confessed to tying Oe up, not to slashing his throat."

Ishikawa, jerked to his feet by the constables, protested and one of the constables slapped him viciously, telling him to shut up.

Kobe watched with great satisfaction as the two constables marched the moaning and grimacing student out of the room and down the steps into the courtyard.

Akitada said angrily, "Did you hear what I said? There was no need for this violence."

Kobe grinned. "After the lashing my men got for letting him escape they are understandably put out with Ishikawa. What do you think would happen, if I were to take the prisoner's side against them?"

"But he did not kill Oe! Let him go with a warning!"

Kobe looked surprised. "I thought your note made it clear that you meant to trap the killer. Maybe you didn't expect that it would turn out to be Ishikawa, but *I* believe we got our man. He's too deeply involved to be an innocent bystander." He rubbed his hip with a grimace. "Oh yes, I heard everything the arrogant bastard said. The crawl space under this hall is not very comfortable, but you can hear every word." There was another flash of lightning. "Beastly weather," Kobe muttered, glowering at the sky. "Well, I must be off and you had better go home, too."

"But you know very well whom we expected tonight."

"Not 'we.' I never believed there was anything to that," Kobe grunted. Flexing his shoulders, he stalked out. As if to punctuate his exit, a long peal of thunder rumbled overhead.

Akitada opened his mouth to call him back, but thought better of it. Kobe had made up his mind. Shaking his head, he went back to his desk. He no longer seriously believed that the murderer would come, certainly not after all the commotion of Ishikawa's arrest. It would have to wait for another opportunity. But he wished he could get the matter over. He needed to do this as much for Tamako and her father as for himself. There would be no peace for them until Hirata's death was avenged. Perhaps there was still a chance the killer might come. Rubbing fresh ink, he bent over his student papers.

Time passed slowly. Outside the storm seemed to have stalled. For the past hour, there had been little change. The darkness was now impenetrable except when lightning played behind the clouds, followed by the rumbling sound of thunder. The wind tossed the branches of the pines from time to time, but there was no rain yet. Akitada thought again of leaving. Chances were good that he would not get a soaking if he went now. Perhaps he could have his dinner with Tamako if Seimei kept their secret. They had so much to say to each other that somehow had not been said the night before. It was strange how with the act of lovemaking a relationship became so utterly changed that one had to begin to discover the other person all over again. Akitada smiled, warmed by a joy which was as new to him as it was all-consuming.

He stared at the paper he was reading. It was dull and full of repetition, and he had a feeling he had scanned the same words for the third time. He made up his mind to leave as soon as he had finished it and had deciphered and corrected another sentence, when suddenly there was again the crunching of the gravel. He froze and listened.

Light steps, accompanied by a rustling of stiff silk, ascended the wooden stairs and crossed the veranda towards his room. Akitada looked at the open doorway and saw a patch of yellow light growing brighter.

Short and dapper, Okura stepped in and closed the door. In spite of the threatening rain, he was dressed in a court costume of heavy green silk and his formal hat was tied firmly under the weak chin. In one hand he carried a lantern.

"You should really keep that door closed against the storm," he said in his high voice, peering around the plain room. "I see you poor teaching fellows must be hard at it till all hours," he added genially, echoing Ishikawa.

Akitada nodded. "As you say." He wondered what he should

do, now that Kobe and his men were long gone. Well, something would occur to him. "Please take a seat. I am glad you decided to accept my invitation."

His guest made no move towards the cushion, but walked past Akitada and into the dark main hall. "Hmm," he said, holding up his lantern and looking about him, "It's a pleasure to visit the old classrooms again. You don't mind?" Without waiting for Akitada's answer, he walked away towards the other rooms.

Akitada got up and followed him. The small foppish figure tripped along in such a childlike manner that he could not work up any fear of the man. He had handled the much larger Ishikawa. Okura was frail by comparison and a coward to boot. The real difficulty was in getting him to confess to Kobe.

Okura's lantern bobbed along ahead of him, its yellow glow disappearing into one room after another, then shining out on dark verandas circling the outside of the hall. He was making sure they were alone.

In due time, he strolled back, saying, "Yes, it brings back memories, though it looks even shabbier than I remembered. I would have asked you to my own office instead, but I expect to move to larger quarters soon." He preened a little, brushing a finger over his tiny mustache. "Perhaps you have heard the rumors? I am marrying into one of the most powerful families in the realm. The Otomos' mansion is in Sanjo ward, and I shall reside there in the future. The adoption proceedings are almost completed and will result, naturally, in promotions and a higher rank."

"My congratulations," remarked Akitada dryly.

"Thank you. The fact is that you have caught me at a good moment. A month later and my rank would not allow us to meet on this familiar footing."

They returned to Akitada's room, where Okura blew out the light in his lantern and minced to the cushion, seating himself and arranging his figured silk robe carefully around him. "Now, what is all this nonsense about Hirata having visited me to discuss Oe's death?"

Akitada brought out the journal and opened it to the last page.

He passed it to Okura and went to sit down himself. "I have been puzzled by this entry. Perhaps you would like to explain?"

Okura read and sighed. Putting the journal into his sleeve, he rose. "My dear fellow," he said silkily. "Surely you don't think I will stand still for more blackmail? No, no! You must not even think it. I paid dearly for first place. Oe struck a very sharp bargain, but I paid off. Is it my fault that the greedy fellow would not share and could not handle that radical, Ishikawa? What a slimy bunch all of you professors are."

"I am afraid you must return the journal. It is evidence against you in Oe's murder."

Okura raised thin brows to stare down at Akitada. "Don't be silly! This is nothing. It does not mention names. To be sure, if one were curious, one might guess. But the whole thing is so easily explained away as a simple matter of rewarding one's favorite professor. And who would dare question me now on such charges?"

"You have committed two murders, and there would have been three if Nishioka's rats had not got to the poisoned walnuts first. Not even your exalted new relatives can get you out of those charges."

Okura's bland face became a closed mask. His head cocked sideways, he regarded the seated Akitada for a moment. Then he returned to his cushion and sat down. "You know," he said in an almost conversational tone, "I have always had a good deal of admiration for you. When you came here and asked questions, I confess, you made me uneasy. With good reason, as it turned out, for Oe panicked. I gather you know about the examination?"

Akitada nodded.

"Ah. That was clever of you. It is really too bad that we find ourselves on opposite sides in this matter. I could have used you."

Akitada said nothing.

"But perhaps our differences may be overcome? I dare say you have considered your position and what a man like myself can do for you? Oe practically twisted my arm to let him help me cheat. His problem was that he got greedy. He expected that I was good for a fat income for life. When I refused to pay more, he had the gall to threaten me publicly by reading that insulting poem at the contest in the Divine Spring Garden. I was outraged!"

"So you followed him and killed him?"

"That was not precisely my first intention. One does not like to dirty one's hands in person. As soon as possible after he left, I went to our usual meeting place, expecting him to be waiting for me. You can imagine my surprise when I found him tied to the statue of Confucius and too drunk to care. All I had to do was put him out of his misery." Okura's hand crept to his sash. He chuckled at the memory. "Oh, yes. It was me. No harm admitting it here just between the two of us. It was truly amusing how the police suspected all of you fellows and Ishikawa, when I was the one. And you must admit I did the university a service. Where would the country be with crooked professors like him? Think of the scandal I saved you all from."

"Did you act for the same altruistic reasons when you set fire to Hirata's study?" Akitada asked, trying to keep his anger from showing.

"What else? Oh, Hirata was not as open about it as Oe had been. He dithered on and on about his conscience bothering him and about how he wanted to make things right for the parents of the fellow who killed himself. He proposed that I resign my first place so it could be awarded posthumously to the other student. Now I ask you: what kind of a fool did he think me? What good is first place to a dead man? No money goes with it, no rank, no position. No, no! I saw right through that. He would have accepted a hefty sum from me, pretending, of course, that he would pay it to the parents. Hah! I fobbed him off, told him to wait till I had secured my rank, and then I'd resign." Okura giggled at the thought, and Akitada suddenly wondered if he was quite sane.

Suppressing his rising horror, he asked, "But you went that night and set the fire?"

"That was a really clever move. All the talk about lack of rain and the danger of fires gave me the idea. I went that very night, carrying a small flask of lamp oil with me. The gate was only latched. Hirata has always been a trusting fool. I walked in and made my way to his study. Most of us were invited to his house when we were students. And there he was, fast asleep, sitting amongst his books and papers. And not a servant in sight! I am constantly amazed at the squalid lives you professors lead in private. No wonder you sink to blackmail. Anyway, I poured the oil over the veranda just outside his door and used my candle to light it. It blazed up magnificently and almost instantly caught the straw mats on fire, and then the papers joined the merry blaze. He woke, of course. Briefly." Okura rubbed his pudgy hands together and smiled. "Houses burn down all the time. No one will ever connect me with that."

Akitada shuddered. He had no words, but his eyes never left Okura's face and he saw that the horrible smirk of satisfaction gave place to a slight frown.

"I was not so clever with Nishioka, it seems. I wondered about that when there was no news. So the nosy little weasel escaped? Tsk, tsk!" Okura grimaced. "Every one of us knew of Nishioka's weakness for walnuts. He used to munch them while he was teaching. Disgusting! Well, never mind! They'll blame it on the walnut vendor."

If only Kobe were here! Akitada asked, "And what do you plan to do about me, or Ishikawa?"

Okura chuckled. "Ishikawa is no longer a problem. I made sure he would run if he found his cell unlocked and the guard elsewhere. Money has its uses. He'll be caught again shortly, and then nothing he says to implicate anyone else will be believed. I fully expect him to be found guilty of Oe's murder. But you . . ." Okura fingered his mustache and studied Akitada with small bright eyes. "You are something of an inconvenience, I admit. Actually you really have no evidence, you know, and when it comes to your word against mine, I am very much afraid, my dear Sugawara, that you don't have a leg to stand on. However, as I mentioned before, I am presently engaged in some rather delicate negotiations. You could do some damage there. I am therefore prepared to make you an offer for your silence about this"—he tapped the journal in his sleeve—"and other matters. Shall we say two hundred pieces of gold, a manor with six farms and the guarantee of two promotions within the next two years?"

Akitada almost laughed out loud. The bribe was enormous, particularly for someone in his modest circumstances, but he had expected something more dramatic, like an attempt on his life. This meek offer of hush money was disappointingly anticlimactic.

"Certainly not," he said, getting to his feet. "I am afraid that you won't be in a position to keep such a bargain, because I shall take you to the police myself and lay murder charges against you. You will return the journal to me now." He extended his hand.

Okura looked up at him. "I did not take you for such a fool," he said. "Of course I shall not accompany you to the police. Neither shall I return the journal. And please remember whom you address!"

Akitada made a grab for Okura's sleeve, but the little man twisted aside deftly and jumped to his feet. "How dare you?" he squeaked.

Akitada was becoming irritated. "Listen, Okura, you are not leaving here except to walk to police headquarters. Don't make me tie you up!" He took a step towards his visitor.

"Don't touch me!" shrieked Okura, retreating. "I'll make you pay for that! Don't touch me, I say! I am under the protection of the emperor himself, and you will be very sorry tomorrow."

"Nonsense!" Akitada snapped. "You are a nobody. Your background does not justify your boasting and as soon as the world finds out that you bought first place honors, you are through. That is why you had to kill Oe and Hirata. I'm afraid it's all over!" Feeling rather silly, he made another lunge for Okura who dashed away, shrieking for help.

Akitada almost burst into laughter. "Stop shouting," he said. "You checked the building yourself. No one can hear you."

Okura gave him a frantic look and rushed for the door to the veranda. It was closed, and he lost precious time scrabbling at the handle. Akitada caught up with him and put a hand on his shoulder. But he had underestimated his adversary once again. Okura turned, his teeth bared like a cornered rat, and pulled a knife from

his sash. He slashed viciously at Akitada's face. Akitada jumped back and retreated a few steps.

Okura was trembling with rage or fear. For a moment it looked as though he would attack. Then he slipped away along the wall. What followed was another frustrating chase. Akitada could not get close enough to disarm Okura, who was small but surprisingly agile and dashed from corner to corner and finally out into the dark hall, with Akitada on his heels.

Okura's dimly seen form disappeared into the shadows. Akitada rushed after, a foolish mistake that almost cost him his life. He could not see Okura against the solid blackness, but Okura could see him, his figure perfectly outlined from behind by the light from his room. One moment he was groping along the wall, the next something hissed past his right ear and hit his shoulder. He flung himself forward, reaching for Okura, but caught only a piece of silk which tore noisily while he overbalanced and fell, hitting the floor with his chin so hard that he momentarily blacked out. When the pain receded enough for him to roll out of the way of his attacker, he wondered why the knife was not in his back. Crouching in the darkness, he listened. Silence. Then a soft rustle moving away from him. He rose and followed as quietly as possible. For many long minutes they both groped around in the darkness, pausing to listen, then moving again, until there was a thud and a cry of pain. Okura had collided with a pillar. He panicked and, much to Akitada's relief, ran back into the lighted room.

When he followed, Okura lost control completely. He was swinging his knife wildly and screamed, "Get away from me or I'll kill you!"

Akitada quickly moved around him to block his escape via the veranda, keeping his eye on the madly slashing blade, wishing he had some weapon to defend himself or that Okura would lose courage again and give Akitada an opening to disarm him. But this time Okura attacked, his eyes murderous. Akitada raised an arm to protect his face and crouched to go for Okura's middle.

At that moment the door behind him opened abruptly, propelling him forward. He fell to his hands and knees, someone or

something kicked him, there was a rush of footsteps, the sound of a blow, and then Okura started shrieking.

When Akitada staggered to his feet, he saw Tora. He had Okura by the scruff of the neck and shook him like a kitten until the knife fell from his fingers. Then Tora pushed him so sharply that he collapsed in a heap on the floor. Snatching up the knife and holding the blade under Okura's nose, Tora snarled, "Sit still and shut up! I'd just as soon kill you as put up with your wailing."

The dapper little man choked back a howl, opened his eyes wide, spat out a broken tooth and some blood, and burst into tears.

"What are you doing here?" asked Akitada, looking from Tora to Hitomaro and Genba who had hovered outside but now joined them, looking pleased.

Tora grinned. "Your lady sent us. She was nervous about you. When we saw you had company, we hid under the veranda, just in case."

"Tamako sent you?" asked Akitada in disbelief.

Tora nodded.

Akitada digested this. A new thought struck him. "Did you hear what we said?"

"Yes," Tora said. "Nasty little monster, isn't he?" He gave Okura a kick which produced another bout of wailing. "We figured you could handle him until we heard all the rushing about and screaming."

Akitada flushed. Not only had Tamako thought it necessary to send reinforcements, but they had witnessed how Okura had got the advantage of him. But perhaps their account of the conversation would convince Kobe to lock Okura up. And the harsh treatment meted out to prisoners might encourage Okura to admit his guilt.

It had been a long day and suddenly Akitada was bone-tired.

"Take him to police headquarters," Akitada told Tora. "Tell Kobe what happened, and that I hope he will charge Okura with the murders of Oe and Hirata."

"Right!" grinned Tora, eyeing the sobbing Okura with satisfaction.

"No!" Okura raised both hands to Tora pleadingly. "If you let me

go, I'll give you gold, lots of gold, more than you have ever dreamed of." He started fumbling in his sash, but Genba jumped forward and jerked both of his arms behind him where Hitomaro tied them with rope. Okura let himself go limp and burst into tears again.

Hitomaro had a quick whispered conversation with Tora, who asked Akitada, "How about coming along and sharing a pitcher of wine to celebrate after we get rid of him?"

Akitada stretched. He felt stiff with fatigue. They were kind to offer, but he had better things to do. Shaking his head with a smile, he said unwisely, "Thanks, but no. At the moment I am only thinking of bed."

Tora snorted, and Genba and Hitomaro turned their heads to study the sky. As if on command, a bright streak of lightning hung for a moment over the black trees and distant roofs, casting its white light over the whole room. It was followed quickly by a sharp crack of thunder.

Tora shook his head. "It's getting close. I can manage the prisoner by myself. Genba and Hitomaro will walk back with you, sir."

Akitada said quickly, "No. I don't trust Okura. All three of you go with him. And, Tora, remember to give my message to Kobe."

The men exchanged glances. Then Hitomaro said, "Genba and I cannot accompany Tora to the police."

Akitada stared at Hitomaro without comprehension. Outside the first heavy drops were striking the boards of the veranda. Then he understood and snapped, "I see your usefulness is limited to areas which are remote from the sharp eyes of the police. Go with Tora as far as possible and make certain that he and his prisoner get safely within the walls of police headquarters. Then wait for him and return home together."

Hitomaro's face had reddened. "As you wish, sir," he said dully.

"All right, let's go!" Tora urged.

But Hitomaro still hesitated. "Could I not come with you, sir? The streets are not safe at this hour."

"No!" Exhausted and irritated, Akitada made no effort to keep the anger out of his voice. "Do as you are told or you are both dismissed."

They trouped out the door, leaving him behind in the empty room, where the oil lamp still flickered on his desk, casting its uncertain light on student papers. Ashamed about his outburst, Akitada went to finish the paper Okura had interrupted. But he had lost his concentration and Tamako awaited him. Putting away his writing utensils, he used the flame from the oil lamp to light a lantern and set off for home.

The moment he stepped outside and locked the door, he became aware of a change in the atmosphere. The temperature had dropped, and a wet gust of wind tore at the skirts of his robe and knocked the lantern against the wall. Overhead the black clouds roiled as lightning flashed between and behind them. Thunder roared and grumbled almost continuously.

He ran quickly down the steps and into the courtyard. There another blast of wind threw wet sand into his face and blew off his hat. He caught it by the silk cord, winced as it bit into his barely healed skin, untied it and tucked the hat into his sleeve. Steadying his lantern with both hands, he bent forward into the wind.

He passed with long strides through the deserted university grounds, thinking of his bungled efforts at bringing three killers to justice. Although he had solved the cases and laid the ghosts of self-reproach about Hirata to rest, he could not be certain that Okura would be charged. He had even less assurance that Sakanoue would be confronted with his crime and punished. Only Kurata had been apprehended and would be convicted, and that was due more to Tora's efforts than his own.

Well, tomorrow he would return to his job at the ministry and this time he would make every effort to excel at his work. He would be taking a wife and could not afford any longer to chafe at the long, dusty hours among the documents or avoid unpleasant meetings with his superiors. Sato and his wife had made far greater sacrifices for each other and their family. Such patience was more admirable than any heroics he might have dreamed of in his younger years. It spoke of devotion more loudly than any of the love songs recited at the poetry contest. And patience was a small price to pay for the delight he had found in Tamako.

Cheered by blissful thoughts of their future together, Akitada crossed Second Avenue and headed east along the high earthen wall of the government enclosure. Lightning cast the long wall, the buildings and the wind-tossed trees into a momentary blue brilliance. He skirted a fallen branch. Because of the late hour and the storm, he walked alone on this normally busy thoroughfare. The smell of rain was heavy in the air and large drops stung his face, along with small bits of gravel and windblown leaves, but at least the clouds had not yet opened up and released their torrents of water. With any luck, he might reach home in time.

At the corner of the palace grounds he turned north onto Omiya, and a sharp gust caught his lantern, flung it up and extinguished the light. No matter. Another five blocks would bring him to his own gate. And to Tamako. He warmed to the memory of her, imagined hearing her soft voice, smelling her subtle fragrance, touching her skin. She was as soft as silk under his hands. Her hair, long, smooth silken tresses against his palm . . . her thin robe, silk warmed by her flesh, shifting and trembling under his caressing fingers . . . her skin, softer than silk . . . softer, warmer and more alive than anything he had ever touched before.

He came back to reality reluctantly.

At first he was dimly aware of a sharp hissing sound somewhere on the palace wall, then of a violent rustling in the branches above his head. Thinking of the storm, Akitada glanced up. From the darkness of the leaves and branches of the tree an even denser darkness separated and hurtled towards him. Too late he tried to twist aside. A sharp pain seared through his head and shoulder as a crushing weight pushed him forward. He struck the ground, felt gravel bite sharply into his face, and then his chest was crushed and the night turned black.

TWENTY-THREE

FRESH SHOOTS

*A*kitada regained consciousness in his own room. Dimly aware of discomfort, he opened his eyes on the familiar rafters of his ceiling, shadowy in lamplight. He easily deduced that it was nighttime and that he was stretched out on his own bedding, a fact further proven by the familiar feel of the hard headrest supporting his head.

Someone was talking softly.

He turned his head and immediately felt a sharp stab of pain run from his head to his shoulder. To his astonishment his small room seemed full of people. They sat around the oil lamp, their backs toward him, except for Seimei, who faced in his direction. It was he who was doing most of the talking while rummaging in his medicine case, holding up from time to time a jar or package to show to one of the others. Belatedly Akitada put names to the broad-shouldered backs: Genba, Hitomaro and Tora. Genba was the one who carried on the conversation with Seimei. The other two watched but said nothing.

Akitada croaked, cleared his throat, and tried again. "What are you doing?"

Immediately four anxious faces turned his way. Seimei and Tora got up to sit beside him.

"How are you feeling, sir?" Seimei asked, peering sympathetically down at him.

Akitada frowned and checked how he felt. His legs and arms seemed to behave normally. The skin on his face felt sore and tight, and his neck and shoulder still pained him at the slightest move. However, that discomfort was minor compared to the fact that his whole torso appeared to be paralyzed. He could not move his spine, and breathing was restricted and painful.

"I cannot move. What happened?" he asked, as a hazy memory joined panic. "Something fell on me, I think."

Tora answered. "You were attacked on the way home. By paid assassins, two of them, with knives."

"I have been stabbed?"

Seimei said, "No, no. Nothing like that. Hitomaro here got to you just in time. You only suffered a few cracked ribs when one of the brutes jumped on you out of the tree."

Akitada thought about his ribs and touched them gingerly. He felt absolutely nothing. "An overly optimistic diagnosis, old friend," he said grimly, panic tightening like a vise about his heart. "I'm afraid I am paralyzed."

To Akitada's hurt surprise, Seimei turned to grin at Genba who grinned back, then rose and joined them. He poked an exploratory forefinger into various places on Akitada's upper body. There was still no sensation. Akitada closed his eyes to hide his terror.

"I had to wrap your rib cage very tightly to keep the bones in place," boomed Genba's voice into his ears. "They should heal just fine, provided you avoid too much movement."

The relief was overwhelming. Akitada said weakly, "Oh!" and opened his eyes again. He thought. There had been something else he needed to ask. "But how did I get here? And what is this about Hitomaro?" He craned his neck, risking another jolt of pain, to look for the burly swordsman.

Tora told him, "It was a lucky thing Hitomaro did not trust

that snake Okura and went back to follow you. Come over here, Hito, and tell him what you did."

Hitomaro crept up reluctantly. "I'm sorry I disobeyed you, sir," he muttered, his eyes lowered, "but glad I could be of service."

"What happened?"

"I caught up with you on Omiya Avenue, between the corner and the first palace gate where the paulownia trees hang over the walls of the palace. They were lying in wait for you, one in the tree above you, the other on the wall. When the first one dropped down on you, the other jumped from the wall with a knife. Only by then I was there and made short work of them."

Tora cried, "Beautiful work, brother! Couldn't have done better myself."

"Heavens," said Akitada weakly. "You saved my life. Who were they?"

Hitomaro hung his head even lower. "I'm afraid I had to kill them, sir. There was so little time. But I'm sure Okura was behind this. It occurred to me that if a man promises such rewards, he doesn't expect to be called to account." He gave Akitada an earnest look and added, "If the dead thugs cause any problems for you, sir, I am prepared to turn myself in."

Akitada could guess what such a promise would mean to him. "Nonsense!" he said. "I won't allow it. It seems I owe you an apology. I am sorry for the way I treated you. What happened to the bodies?"

"I had to leave them there and carry you back."

"If they are known criminals, chances are we won't hear any more about it. However, I am deeply indebted to you, my friend, especially since you tried to warn me. Facing two armed assassins singlehandedly was a very brave thing to do."

Hitomaro grinned. "Not at all, sir. They were not trained fighters, and I had my sword."

Akitada said, "You seem to have a remarkable understanding of human nature, Hitomaro. You were quite right to warn me, and I was careless. It was highly unlikely that Okura would let me live, let alone pay off so handsomely. I owe you my life and must find a way to repay you. We have very little money, but perhaps there is some other service I can do for you. Feel free to ask for anything that may be of use to you."

Hitomaro shook his head, but he exchanged a glance with Genba.

"Come," said Akitada, "I see there is something. What is it?"

Hitomaro said shyly, "You owe me nothing, sir. I was in your service at the time. But if it would make you feel better, Genba and I have been very happy here. We would be grateful if you allowed us to serve you in the future."

Fleetingly Akitada thought of the family finances. Well, he must find a way somehow. "Of course. But I cannot pay either of you what you deserve."

Genba cried, "We want no pay. You see, sir, you're not getting a bargain. We have both committed crimes."

Akitada winced and closed his eyes. "Not murder?" he asked weakly.

"Murder," they said in unison.

"But they had no choice," cried Tora.

"Really, sir," remarked Seimei, "if you heard their stories, you might understand. Remember, though a man wear rags, his heart may be brocade. And even Master Confucius had his troubles."

Akitada grimaced. "I see it's a conspiracy. Very well. Tell me about it."

Genba said, "Thank you, sir," bowing deeply. "My complete name is Ishida Genba. I am a wrestling master by profession, just as my father before me. Our school was in Nagato province, and one day the governor watched one of our exhibition bouts and promptly sent his oldest son to me for instruction. The boy was a weakling and resented me bitterly. We quarreled and he tried every way to blacken my name. One day he threatened to tell his father a particularly nasty lie about me. During the subsequent lesson we engaged in a practice bout. There was an accident and he broke his neck." Genba heaved a deep sigh and shook his head.

Akitada looked at him with sympathy. "Accidents will happen

in your profession," he said. "If you give me your word that you did not intend to kill the boy, I am satisfied."

Genba looked at him bleakly. "Of course I did not intend to kill him. That would have been dishonorable and made me unfit to teach the sport. He insisted on trying out a dangerous move because he was angry. I had my arm around his neck when he suddenly flipped backwards. His neck snapped. But that is not the death I meant. I was arrested and killed two men in jail."

"What?"

"The night before my trial the governor sent two guards to my cell to strangle me. I killed them both and escaped."

Akitada was silent with shock for a moment. He did not doubt for a moment that the governor had meant to take revenge for his son's death. Genba would certainly have been cleared of the charge of murder. He said, "I am sorry for your misfortune. You have already paid a heavy price for what was apparently due to a spoiled boy's carelessness. I am inclined to give you the chance to prove your innocence by your future actions, but what if someone recognizes you?"

"Nagato is far from here, sir, and since I left, the governor has died. Besides I'm greatly changed in appearance."

"Very well then."

Tora and Seimei burst into relieved laughter and slapped Genba on the back. The wrestler bowed deeply and thanked Akitada with tears in his eyes.

Akitada looked at Hitomaro.

"I cannot claim either accident or self-defense, sir," the burly man said bluntly. "I meant to kill the man and went after him knowing that he was no match for my sword."

Akitada raised his brows. "A drunken brawl?"

"No. I was cold sober. And I would do it again." He met Akitada's astonishment with fierce determination.

"You are brutally honest," Akitada said. "Surely there were some extenuating facts. Were you very young?"

When Hitomaro shook his head, Tora urged, "Tell him the reason."

Hitomaro heaved a deep breath. "I have no intention of ever using it again," he said, "but my family name was Takahashi. My people are from Izumo province."

Akitada was startled. He had heard of the Takahashis. They were an old, respected military family who had come down in the world.

"Ten years ago my father, my grandparents, and all my brothers and sisters died in a smallpox epidemic. That left only my mother and myself. I took a wife to carry on the family name." Hitomaro lowered his head and stared down at his clenched fists. "My wife Michiko was very young," he murmured. "She was also very beautiful, and I . . ." He bit his lips. "The son of a neighbor, a powerful family with many manors and hundreds of retainers, saw Michiko and made advances. She told me about it, and I went to warn him off. He was a haughty sort of man and there were words. No, I did not lay a hand on him then. That came later."

Again he paused to stare at his hands. His face worked as if he had to force the rest of the story out by sheer willpower. "I had to leave home for a few days on business. When I came back, my mother greeted me with the news that my wife had hanged herself. She had been only seventeen and expected our first child. Michiko left me a letter explaining that our neighbor had raped her, and she could not live with the shame she had brought to our family."

The room had become very still. Hitomaro's eyes left his hands and wandered to the ceiling.

"That's when I went and killed him," he said calmly. "My mother and I had to flee after that. She died the following winter in the mountains from cold and lack of comfort." Looking at Akitada, he said bitterly, "I have nothing left to live for. A man in my position, whose only skill is in his sword, is always prone to being used for other men's violent purposes. It is for that reason that I wish to serve you rather than selling my fighting skills to the highest bidder."

Overcome with emotion, Akitada could not speak right away.

A look of disappointment settled in Hitomaro's face, and he said, "Well, never mind! I know I'm too much of a liability."

Akitada said quickly, "On the contrary. I am honored by your confidence. Forgive me for not speaking right away. Your story has touched me profoundly. I, too, have a wife now."

Hitomaro smiled and nodded his understanding.

"I do not blame you for your actions," said Akitada, "but there is the problem of your rank. It puts you above the status of a hired man. If it pleases you, I should be honored if you were to remain with us as our guest."

"No." Hitomaro got up. "I have neither rank nor family name. I shall serve you like Genba and Tora, or not at all."

Akitada met the fierce eyes and nodded. "As you wish."

Another round of backslapping ensued. Tora cried, "See, brothers! I told you my master is a fair man!"

"Thank you, Tora," said Akitada. "But now I wish to sleep. I shall see you all in the morning."

Tora and the two new retainers left quickly, but Seimei made no move to follow, busying himself instead with his medicine box.

"Leave it till morning," Akitada called out impatiently.

"But I cannot leave you alone, sir. You might need something."

"I need nothing but sleep. Go!"

Seimei looked mutinous, but seeing his master's expression, he obeyed.

As soon as his steps had receded outside, Akitada began the complicated business of getting up. It took several minutes and he was drenched in perspiration when he finally stood on his feet. Another minute was required to pick up a cotton gown to cover his bandaged nakedness and then he pushed the screen door open to the veranda.

The storm was long past, but it had left the garden rain-drenched. Above, the night skies had cleared. Stars blinked and a nearly full moon turned the garden into a glistening image of silver-inlaid black lacquer. Akitada walked softly on bare feet through the moisture-laden, rose-scented night to Tamako's room.

◆

Akitada did not leave his house for a week due to setbacks in the healing of his broken ribs. Genba expressed surprise that he had to repeat the wrapping process several times. Akitada, gritting his teeth against the pain, muttered, "I'm afraid I'm a very restless sleeper."

During his convalescence, a number of events took place. Bishop Sesshin made a brief visit to inquire into Akitada's state of health and to take young Lord Minamoto back to the family mansion. Sesshin told Akitada that he had appointed two legal scholars to fill the positions of Hirata and Akitada, and that Fujiwara had been given Oe's rank as eminent Chinese scholar. Sato had received special permission to accept private students, and his wife had already performed at two noble houses and was becoming quite popular.

Next Kobe stopped by to report that Kurata's trial was over and he had been condemned to hard labor on the island of Tsukushi. "Draining swamps," said Kobe with great satisfaction. "I doubt he'll survive the year."

"What about Okura?" asked Akitada.

Another grimace. "The bastard keeps petitioning the court. No telling when we'll get a trial."

The third event was the most private and most important. Tamako became officially Akitada's wife and the junior Lady Sugawara. This brought with it a surprise for Akitada. When he went to his mother to inform her of the event and to request the preparation of the special rice cakes, customarily presented to the newlywed couple on the morning of their third night together, she caused him a moment of acute embarrassment by pointing to an elegant footed lacquer tray which was covered with a square of precious embroidered silk.

"They have been ready since last night," she said, smiling a little at his discomfiture. "I had it on good authority that your injuries did not stop you from doing your duty. It was most gratifying news."

Lady Sugawara's approval of the marriage was not entirely un-expected. Akitada had discovered that Tamako seemed to have a special touch when it came to handling his mother. In fact, every day he spent with his new wife brought a new wonder to him, who had never been close to anyone before. Tamako was an indispen-sable companion in his convalescence, and he fell imperceptibly into the habit of sharing even his innermost feelings and thoughts with her.

But this blissful time, of course, could not last forever. Akitada had to return to his work at the ministry. The rainy season had started with the storm of the night of his attack. It was on a par-ticularly drizzly morning in a series of wet days, that Akitada told Seimei to lay out his official robe and hat. He and Tamako had spent the previous evening looking out at the lush wet growth in the garden as he told her of his intention to face the minister the following day. He had been frank about their precarious financial condition, his past difficulties with his superiors and slim chances for promotion, and of his own impatience with the dull paper-work. As always she had been supportive and reassuring. This morning he was in a much better frame of mind and approached the inevitable with resolution.

Ironically, a series of unforeseen events almost immediately began to change his plans.

First Kobe arrived, his official robe rain-spattered and his face full of barely contained excitement.

"You'll never guess what happened!" he cried, sitting down on a cushion and accepting a cup of tea from Seimei. He took a big mouthful, immediately gagged, and spit it back into the cup. "Are you trying to poison me?" he roared. "What is that nasty bitter stuff?"

"Tea," said Akitada.

"Phew! Don't you have wine?"

Seimei muttered something about tea being good for the belly in such wet weather, but went to fetch some wine.

"Well, what happened?" asked Akitada.

"Okura hanged himself. The guard found him this morning."

"I thought he had hopes of support from his powerful friends."

"Hah! He had visitors yesterday. They didn't give their names, but you could tell their rank by their cap colors. One third rank and two fourths. He knew them all right. I don't know what was said—they made me stay outside—but their faces were the grimmest I've ever seen. Okura was limp as a rag after they left. By the way, do you wish to press charges against Ishikawa?"

"Good heavens! Are you still holding him?"

Kobe grinned and emptied his cup of wine. "Of course. Jail has improved his manners greatly."

Akitada smiled also. "Good. Let him go now. He has been punished enough by losing any chance for a degree. Fortunately he is bright. He can get a living as a provincial teacher. They need good ones."

Kobe nodded. "As long as I don't have to see the insolent puppy again. Well, I'll be on my way then." They both rose. Kobe bowed, saying, "I suppose you will return to your former duties soon and trust they will be less exciting than your recent activities."

"Thank you, Captain." Akitada suppressed a sigh at the thought, though it had probably only been a hint to stay out of Kobe's business in the future.

He watched Kobe walk away through the drizzle, thinking about those hated duties in the archives of the ministry.

Then he squared his shoulders and returned to his room to set up the mirror and put on his formal hat. At that moment, Seimei stuck in his head. "Good, you are dressed. Come to the main hall. His Reverence, Bishop Sesshin, and young Lord Minamoto have called."

Seimei certainly knew his protocol for formal visits by high-ranking individuals. Wondering what had brought both of them out on such a wet day, Akitada rushed across via the covered gallery, noting with irritation that the roof had sprung more leaks. Skirting the puddles, he stepped into the main hall of his house.

Sesshin and the boy were seated on brocade cushions, somewhat faded and threadbare, but passable in the gray light of the

rainy day. His guests were quite dry and unexpectedly resplendent in their silk gowns. Akitada bowed, still painfully, though Genba had only that morning loosened the bandages for the first time.

Sesshin said immediately, "Please do not strain yourself, my dear fellow! How are you coming along?"

"Much better, thank you." Akitada seated himself gingerly on the third cushion, while Seimei poured tea and served sweet rice cakes. When his guests had helped themselves and Seimei had withdrawn again, Akitada said, "Actually, you see me in my formal robe for the first time today. It is time to return to my duties at the ministry."

"Oh," cried young Minamoto, "but surely you must take a longer rest, sir. It has only been a few days."

"Ahem!" The bishop gave the youngster an admonishing glance, then said, "My young charge is overeager to speak his mind, but I think there cannot be much harm in a brief delay. I trust you will take at least another day to consider your future." He regarded Akitada benevolently, his broadly smiling face and round shape disconcertingly reminiscent of the fat, jolly god of happiness. "In fact," he said, "one of the reasons we came today is to extend our best wishes to you and your new lady."

Akitada was touched. "Thank you both," he said, and turned to the boy. "Sadamu, I believe you have met Tamako, haven't you?"

"Oh, yes," grinned the boy. "I quite approve, you know."

Sesshin chuckled, and Akitada said, "I am deeply gratified."

The boy nodded solemnly. "She was very nice to me," he said. "We talked about death, my grandfather's and her father's. What she said made me feel much better. I think she has much wisdom for a woman."

"*Ahem!*" Sesshin cleared his throat again.

This time the boy blushed. "I beg your pardon," he murmured. Reaching for a small, beautifully decorated lacquer box which rested beside him, he pushed it across to Akitada. "It is the reward you have earned," he said and then glanced at Sesshin, who gave an encouraging nod. Sitting up a bit straighter, Sadamu looked earnestly at Akitada and announced, "Your loyalty to me and my family in our distress and your cleverness in seeing through Lord Sakanoue's plot have put me and my family deeply into your debt. I wish to make formal acknowledgment of the great service you have done. The Minamotos will be forever in your debt, and I shall see to it that the fact is recorded for posterity." He bowed with great dignity.

Akitada did not know what to say, so he also bowed deeply. "Thank you, my lord. I am deeply honored by your words, and shall treasure your gift."

The boy gave a sigh of relief and smiled. Then he reached into his sleeve and pulled out a small narrow object, wrapped lopsidedly but with great care in a square of brocade and tied with a gold cord. This he handed to Akitada, saying, "Please accept this worthless trifle on my own behalf."

Akitada was deeply touched. He said with a smile, "There was no need whatsoever for all this, Sadamu. I was merely lucky." He looked down at the small package dubiously.

"Well, open it!" the boy cried.

Akitada undid the many knots with some difficulty and unrolled the beautiful piece of fabric to reveal a flute. It was a lovely instrument, old and clearly made by a fine craftsman, though it was quite plain. He looked up in delighted astonishment. "A flute?"

The boy's face was alight with pleasure. "Do you like it? Is it the right thing? You told me once that you wished you could learn to play the flute, do you remember? Well, now you can!"

"Oh, my dear young friend, it is the most perfect present," cried Akitada, fingering the instrument and wishing he could try it out. "I had forgotten, but you are quite right. It will give me enormous pleasure. Thank you very much." He was tempted to raise it to his lips then and there, but confined himself to admiring its workmanship. Finally he put it back into its wrapping and placed it aside. "I trust you are comfortably settled by now?" he asked.

"Oh, yes." The boy exchanged a glance with the bishop, and explained, "My great-uncle is to be my guardian until I come of age. He has taken up his residence in our mansion to be near me and supervise my studies. But His Majesty has graciously confirmed me as head of my clan, so I have a great deal of work to do every day before I can get to my books."

"Ah," said Akitada, bowing deeply to him, "then I am indeed honored by your visit, my lord." This boy had suddenly become a very rich and powerful man. He recalled the youngster's sense of responsibility for his people and was glad.

Sesshin chuckled. "He is young, but he shows promise," he said, deflating the boy's pride a little. Then his face abruptly turned serious. "We have also some other news and a confidence to share with you. I followed your suggestions about Rashomon and, finding by good fortune a poor woman who had some information, was able to locate my brother's remains. They have been put to rest very quietly on his ancestral estate in the country."

Akitada glanced at the boy who met his eyes calmly. "I am very sorry for what happened to your grandfather," he told him. "It must be just about time for the forty-nine days to be up. I hope his spirit is at rest now."

The young lord nodded. "Yesterday," he said, his voice catching a little, "we held a service in the mansion. It was just for the family and a few servants. I was afraid that you were still too ill to attend. Kinsue and his wife, you know, were terribly worried about grandfather's spirit not finding a path into the next life when the waiting period was up. They seemed much relieved. Afterwards Kinsue took me to the old tree in grandfather's courtyard and showed me that it had put forth new leaves. He said it was a sign that grandfather has entered his new life."

Akitada thought that it was more likely that the rain had saved the old tree, but he felt again that slight shiver at the back of his neck, as if a cold finger had barely brushed his skin.

Sesshin cleared his throat. "We wish to take you into our confidence on the matter of the miracle," he said. "When I informed His Majesty about our suspicions, he immediately consulted with the chancellor and his closest advisers, and it was considered best not to destroy the people's faith in the Buddha or the reputation of the temple. Sadamu and I concur completely with His Majesty's decision."

Akitada bowed. "The wisdom of our august ruler is inspiring. You honor me with this confidence."

The bishop nodded. "I have also had some news of Lord Sakanoue. His Majesty has seen fit to appoint him 'Subduing Rebels Official' and has dispatched him to the northern frontier. There has been some particularly fierce fighting there lately. Lord Sakanoue has expressed his gratitude for being allowed to die for his country."

"Pah," said the boy. "He's a coward."

Sesshin frowned and moved smoothly to a discussion of general conditions in the north country. Akitada listened politely, wondering how long the bishop would dwell on the subject.

"The chancellor was mentioning to me just the other day that it is nearly impossible to keep good officials for any length in provinces like Noto, Echigo, Iwashiro and Uzen," he said, looking earnestly at Akitada. "The distance from the capital, the cold, the troubles with the local aristocracy all seem to drive the appointed governors and other officials to absent themselves from their headquarters for long periods of time."

More puzzled than ever, Akitada tried to look interested.

"Echigo, for example, has been without a resident governor for a number of years. Can you imagine? No senior official at all to represent the government?"

"None at all?" Akitada's real concern was stirred. He recalled vividly the problems which even a good governor had encountered in Kazusa, a province which was not nearly as far from the capital as Echigo. "Could not His Majesty replace inadequate administrators with more suitable persons? Echigo is a rich province. To leave such a significant source of income for the nation to the mercies of local interests seems a dangerous policy." He gulped. "I beg your pardon. I did not mean to criticize His Majesty, of course. Only there must be any number of good people who would gladly undertake such an assignment. The challenge alone must outweigh the lack of comforts, and the distance

from the capital is easily balanced by seeing new places and learning new things. I remember when I was sent to Kazusa some of my
friends thought this a punitive assignment, but I was jubilant. . . ."
Akitada broke off in some confusion. When no one commented,
he flushed with embarrassment. "I beg your pardon, Your Reverence," he murmured.

He risked a glance at Sesshin's face. The old monk was smiling
benignly and nodding his head. "I am very glad to hear you say so.
It is understandable that His Majesty's august rule should not always be understood by the people in distant places where the civ-
ilizing forces of the capital can only be transmitted by His
Majesty's appointed representatives. Sadly, unlike you, too few of
our young men are willing to accept such assignments, even if
they have a more enlightened idea of the conditions there than
their elders."

Akitada's heart had started beating more rapidly. Surely
Sesshin was speaking in a very pointed manner. He glanced at the
boy and saw that he was watching him expectantly. Looking back
at Sesshin, Akitada said, "I am certain the emperor can find many
able persons eager to exchange the stodgy routine of their duties
in one of the bureaus and ministries for the excitement of travel
and the freedom to improve conditions in one of our provinces."

"Ah," said Sesshin, smiling more widely and nodding. "Perhaps one or two. At any rate, that is what I told the chancellor
when he expressed his worries about affairs in Echigo." He
glanced out at the cloudy sky. "But the rain is letting up and we
must not keep you any longer. It was a very pleasant visit. Please
compliment your servant on the excellent tea and cakes."

His heart still pounding exultantly, Akitada expressed his gratitude for the visit, the box and the flute and, inwardly, the glorious
new hope he hardly dared to acknowledge to himself. He accompanied his illustrious visitors to their carriage and watched them
leave in a bemused trance.

Back in his room, he bent to pick up the box and flute to place
them on a shelf. The box seemed astonishingly heavy. He opened
it and saw with consternation that it was filled with gold bars. His

reward, the boy had said. There must be more than three years worth of salary here, enough to mend the roof and pay the wages and costs of his newly increased household, and still leave something in reserve.

Filled with the joy of it, he went to tell his wife. But the little maid informed him that her mistress had gone to her former home as soon as the rain had eased a little. Akitada felt a sudden concern for her safety and peace of mind and decided to follow her.

The sky was clearing partially, and he risked going without his straw raincoat. Walking as quickly as the many steaming puddles permitted, he crossed the town, worried how he would find her on this, her first visit to the place of the tragedy which had taken both her father and her childhood home from her.

Although he had sent workers to clear away the large debris, the grounds looked dismal after the rain. There was bare black mud where the house had once stood, and charred trees clawed with naked, twisted fingers towards the skies. All the lush flowers and shrubs had shrivelled into sodden clumps of brown decay. Tamako's garden had died as surely as had her father and her past life.

She stood, huddled in a straw cloak, near the wisteria vine, looking up at its bare twisted remnants clinging to the old trellis. It was leafless now, but miraculously he had found there that single bloom he had sent her after their first night together. That she should have come to this spot cheered him. He called out to her.

She turned, hiding muddy hands under the rain cape, and he saw that the dark silk gown she still wore in mourning for her father was streaked with dirt along the hem and there was a smudge of mud near her nose where she had brushed back an errant tress of hair. But she smiled at him, and his heart melted with tenderness.

"What brought you here?" she asked, coming quickly to him.

"I was worried about you." He gestured at the desolate garden. "It still looks very sad, but in time it will be better."

"Oh? Will you keep it then?" she asked, her eyes growing wide with excitement.

"Of course. It is your home and your garden. I thought we might just rebuild a small summer house to start with, and perhaps quarters for a gardener to take care of the place."

"Oh, not a gardener," she cried. "I'll do that. Oh, thank you, Akitada!" Her face fell. "But the money? Can we afford it?"

He was secretly pleased about that "we." "Of course," he said. "Let me tell you my news. I had several visitors this morning. Captain Kobe stopped by first, and then we were honored by the bishop and young Lord Minamoto—who is now head of his clan so I must learn to address him as 'my lord' again."

She smiled. "He is a very nice boy. What news did the captain bring?"

"Okura hanged himself."

She looked down at her hands, which had crept from the folds of her gown and were now tightly clenched. "I am glad he killed himself," she said slowly. "Father would not have wished to be responsible for another human being's execution." Then she looked back up with a smile. "I suppose Bishop Sesshin and the young lord came to thank you for your help?"

"Yes, most generously. I had really not taken the boy seriously." He told her about the gold, happy in her delight in the sudden wealth. "Of course, they also expressed their best wishes on our marriage," he continued. Pausing, he added, more diffidently, "There was some other, rather puzzling talk about the lack of able administrators in the far north. It made me wonder."

Tamako's eyes widened. "What did the bishop say?"

Akitada told her what he could recall, watching her face as he spoke. She was still smiling, but with a certain fixity that dismayed him.

"Oh," she cried, "so much good news! I think you will receive a very grand assignment. Perhaps even a governorship!" She clapped her hands. "Heavens, what a signal honor at your age!" Biting her lip, she added quickly, "It is, of course, a well-deserved honor and a fine and wise choice. How very pleased your mother will be!"

Akitada asked softly, "And you? Are you pleased?"

She blushed and lowered her eyes. "Of course. It is a very great thing for you, for all of us." Then she asked breathlessly, with a slight catch in her voice, "How soon would you be leaving? There are so many things to be got ready. If you receive the appointment, you will be gone a long time . . . four years at least." She hung her head.

"There is no point in worrying about the preparations. It may all just be so much wishful thinking on my part. No doubt I was reading too much into a chance remark. And it is hoping for too much! I am only a clerk, a mere eighth grade in rank." He stretched out his hand to raise her face to his. Her eyes were filled with tears, but she smiled bravely. "Tamako," he asked, "I really wanted to know how you would feel about accompanying me to such an outpost of civilization."

"Oh!" Her whole face lit up. "You would take me with you then?" As he nodded, the tears spilled over and coursed down her cheeks, mingling with the streaks of dirt. She fell to her knees on the muddy ground and bowed. "Thank you, my husband. You have made this insignificant person very happy."

"Tamako!" he scolded, reaching for her. "Get up! There is no one about and no need at all for this cursed formality. And you have spoiled your gown."

She rose, chuckling tearfully and brushing at the black stains on her skirt. He took a tissue from his sleeve and wiped away the traces of muddy tears.

"I was so afraid you would not come," he confessed. "Most of the ladies I know would consider such an assignment one of the more agonizing torments of hell. There are none of the refinements of city life there, and I am told the winters last for eight long months."

"But look at me!" she said with a laugh, showing her dirty hands and her ruined gown. "I am nothing like those ladies and shall be far more comfortable in the uncivilized north than here, for I am a stranger both to proper behavior and to such fine clothes." She turned to glance around at the blackened landscape, and sighed blissfully. "I came to tell Father's spirit about our marriage. And now I am glad that he could share this good news and my happiness."

"And mine."

Taking his hand, Tamako took Akitada through the ruined garden to the wisteria.

"Look!" she said, bending to point to the twisted old trunk where it rose from the barren ground. Four or five bright green shoots had emerged from the roots and were already reaching eagerly upward. "And there, and over there!" She pointed to shrubs and young trees, and Akitada saw that they were all putting forth new leaves.

And then a nightingale began to sing in the old willow by the gate.

HISTORICAL NOTE

In the eleventh century, *Heian Kyo* (Kyoto) was the capital of Japan and its largest city. Like the Chinese capital Ch'ang-an, it was a perfect rectangle with a grid pattern of broad avenues and smaller streets, measuring about one third of the great Chinese metropolis, or two and a half by three and a half miles, with a population of about 250,000. The Imperial Palace, a separate city of over one hundred buildings housing the ministries and bureaus of the central administration and including the imperial residence, occupied the northernmost center of Heian Kyo. Both the capital and the Imperial Palace were walled or fenced and accessible by numerous gates. Rashomon (properly Rashoo-mon or Rajoo-mon, the "Rampart Gate") was the most famous gate to the capital but had fallen into neglect and disrepair. By the middle of the century it may well have ceased to exist altogether. A famous tale about this gate, later a part of Ryunosuke Akutagawa's "Rashoomon" and an award-winning film, is in the eleventh-century collection *Konjaku Monogatari* (no. 29/18). Heian Kyo is said to have been quite beautiful, with its wide willow-lined avenues, its palaces and aristocratic mansions in their tranquil gardens, its temples and government buildings with their blue-tiled roofs and red-lacquered columns and eaves, its rustic Shinto shrines, its parks filled with lakes and pavilions, its many waterways and rivers crossed by arched bridges, and its surrounding landscape of mountains and lakes dotted with secluded temples and summer villas. For some of the details of the description and the maps of Heian Kyo I am indebted to R.A.B. Ponsonby-Fane's work, *Kyoto: The Old Capital of Japan*.

The imperial university, located just southeast of the Imperial Palace, was founded in the eighth century and patterned after the Chinese system. It was, like the government, soon weakened by the self-interest of the aristocracy and catered only to the sons of the so-called "good people." In later years, its professors seem to have enjoyed neither decent pay nor respect, as we know from the role they play in 1004 in Lady Murasaki's *Tale of Genji* and from other sources. There were also private colleges, established by several great families like the Fujiwaras and Tachibanas and one institution for the lower classes, founded by the monk Kobo Daishi in one of the temples. The university followed Confucian teachings with emphasis on Chinese language and classics, to prepare the future civil servants for their professions. Students were drawn primarily from families of rank or from civil servants both in the capital and the provinces. They were males who ranged in age from the early teens to middle-age due to the tough qualifying examinations for admission and for intermediate and advanced degrees. Success in these examinations was the only path to a lucrative career for many lower-ranking individuals. By the eleventh century most contact with China had stopped and the authenticity of written and spoken Chinese had declined. Also, interest had shifted away from dry subjects like history, law and ritual to the much more entertaining practice of poetry. Nevertheless, the departments of this early institution of higher learning offered, in addition to Chinese language and literature and Confucian studies, also law, mathematics, fine arts and probably medicine.

Law enforcement in ancient Japan followed the Chinese pattern to some extent in that each city quarter had its own warden who was responsible for keeping the peace. The Imperial Palace was protected by several divisions of the imperial guard. Eventually a separate police force, the *kebiishi*, was added both in the capital and in the provinces. The *kebiishi* gradually took over all duties of law enforcement, including trial and punishment. There were several prisons in the capital, but imperial pardons were common and sweeping. Confessions were necessary for convictions and could be encouraged with beatings. The death penalty was extremely rare because of Buddhist teachings, and exile was usually substituted for the most heinous offenses such as treason or murder. Apparently this often was a fate equivalent to a slow death.

Transportation was cumbersome and slow. In the city, one mostly walked from place to place, unless one's rank entitled one to an ox-drawn carriage. In addition, both men and women used horses or litters for travel.

Relations between the sexes in early Japan strike westerners as liberal to the point of immorality. A young man's clandestine visits to the room of a young woman of his class were acknowledged between the lovers by an exchange of poetry the next morning, but need not be continued. If they were continued for three consecutive nights, a marriage had taken place and the groom was accepted into the bride's family by an offering of special rice cakes. He usually took up residence in his wife's home. The status of his new wife depended on his own status, his whim, or her parents' rank, for he might have several wives in addition to more casual alliances with concubines. He could also divorce his wives by simply informing them of such a decision. However, a young woman's family usually guarded her well, often arranging for a desirable visitation through a go-between after negotiating the bride's future status and her personal property. Occasionally, as in the case of the merchant Kurata, a family without sons might adopt the husband of a daughter.

The two state *religions*, Shinto and Buddhism, coexisted amicably. Shinto is the native religion, tied to Japanese gods and agricultural observances. Buddhism, which entered Japan from China through Korea, exerted a powerful influence on the aristocracy and the government. Certain important observances, such as the

Kamo festival described in this novel, and agricultural rituals performed by the emperor and attended by the court, were Shinto, while the daily life from birth to death was governed by the worship of the buddhas, particularly Amida.

Many *superstitions* were common among all classes and well documented. One could not start the day without consulting the calendar for auspicious or inauspicious signs or directions. Puzzling events were immediately ascribed to the machinations of spirits or demons, or to human malevolence in the form of witchcraft or curses. Shinto is responsible for many taboos, including directional ones, and for the belief in shamanistic practices of divination and exorcism. Buddhism brought faith in relics and miracles along with the concepts of heaven and hell. Monsters, ghosts and demons abounded in the popular superstition, and contemporary literature is full of frightful occurrences. The story of Prince Yoakira's disappearance in this novel is based on two such tales from *Konjaku Monogatari* (nos. 15/20 and 27/9).

The *calendar* in ancient Japan was extremely complicated, being based on the Chinese hexagenary cycle and on named eras designated periodically by the government. Greatly simplified, there were roughly twelve months and four seasons as in the West, but the first month began a month later, in February. The work week lasted six days, began at dawn, and was followed by a day of leisure. By the Chinese system, the day was divided into twelve two-hour segments. Time was kept by water clocks, and the hours were announced by guards, watchmen and temple bells. The changing seasons brought many festivities. In this novel, the return of the Kamo virgin, an imperial princess, to her temple on the shore of the Kamo River is celebrated toward the end of spring. On this occasion people and houses were decorated with the leaves of the aoi plant (a member of the ginger family) which was sacred to the Kamo observance. (The modern meaning of *aoi* is hollyhock, a different plant but one which is more familiar to modern readers.)

It is not clear whether Heian Kyo had a separate *pleasure quarter* in the eleventh century, but within a few centuries there were two of these in the city. Female entertainers were certainly known at the time. They earned a living by dancing, singing and playing instruments and were held in slightly higher esteem than the later *geisha*.

The *eating and drinking* habits of the eleventh century differed little from later times. Tea drinking had not yet become common. Most people drank rice wine. Meat, with the exception of wild fowl, was rarely consumed. The diet of the poor consisted of vegetables, beans and millet. The well-to-do added rice, fish and fruit.

Many customs, superstitions, and taboos surrounded *death*. Although interment was known, cremation was preferred after the arrival of Buddhism. For forty-nine days after death the spirit of the deceased was thought to linger in his home (hence Akitada's irrational sensations in the prince's rooms). The dead could also haunt the living if they had suffered unjustly, a fact which accounts for much of Tora's aversion to ghosts. In general, contact with the dead was a form of defilement according to Shinto beliefs, and all funeral arrangements were therefore in the hands of Buddhist monks.

FOR THE BEST IN PAPERBACKS, LOOK FOR THE

In every corner of the world, on every subject under the sun, Penguin represents quality and variety—the very best in publishing today.

For complete information about books available from Penguin—including Penguin Classics, Penguin Compass, and Puffins—and how to order them, write to us at the appropriate address below. Please note that for copyright reasons the selection of books varies from country to country.

In the United States: Please write to *Penguin Group (USA), P.O. Box 12289 Dept. B, Newark, New Jersey 07101-5289* or call 1-800-788-6262.

In the United Kingdom: Please write to *Dept. EP, Penguin Books Ltd, Bath Road, Harmondsworth, West Drayton, Middlesex UB7 0DA.*

In Canada: Please write to *Penguin Books Canada Ltd, 90 Eglinton Avenue East, Suite 700, Toronto, Ontario M4P 2Y3.*

In Australia: Please write to *Penguin Books Australia Ltd, P.O. Box 257, Ringwood, Victoria 3134.*

In New Zealand: Please write to *Penguin Books (NZ) Ltd, Private Bag 102902, North Shore Mail Centre, Auckland 10.*

In India: Please write to *Penguin Books India Pvt Ltd, 11 Panchsheel Shopping Centre, Panchsheel Park, New Delhi 110 017.*

In the Netherlands: Please write to *Penguin Books Netherlands bv, Postbus 3507, NL-1001 AH Amsterdam.*

In Germany: Please write to *Penguin Books Deutschland GmbH, Metzlerstrasse 26, 60594 Frankfurt am Main.*

In Spain: Please write to *Penguin Books S. A., Bravo Murillo 19, 1° B, 28015 Madrid.*

In Italy: Please write to *Penguin Italia s.r.l., Via Benedetto Croce 2, 20094 Corsico, Milano.*

In France: Please write to *Penguin France, Le Carré Wilson, 62 rue Benjamin Baillaud, 31500 Toulouse.*

In Japan: Please write to *Penguin Books Japan Ltd, Kaneko Building, 2-3-25 Koraku, Bunkyo-Ku, Tokyo 112.*

In South Africa: Please write to *Penguin Books South Africa (Pty) Ltd, Private Bag X14, Parkview, 2122 Johannesburg.*